The House

FANTAGRAPHICS BOOKS

The House

Paco Roca

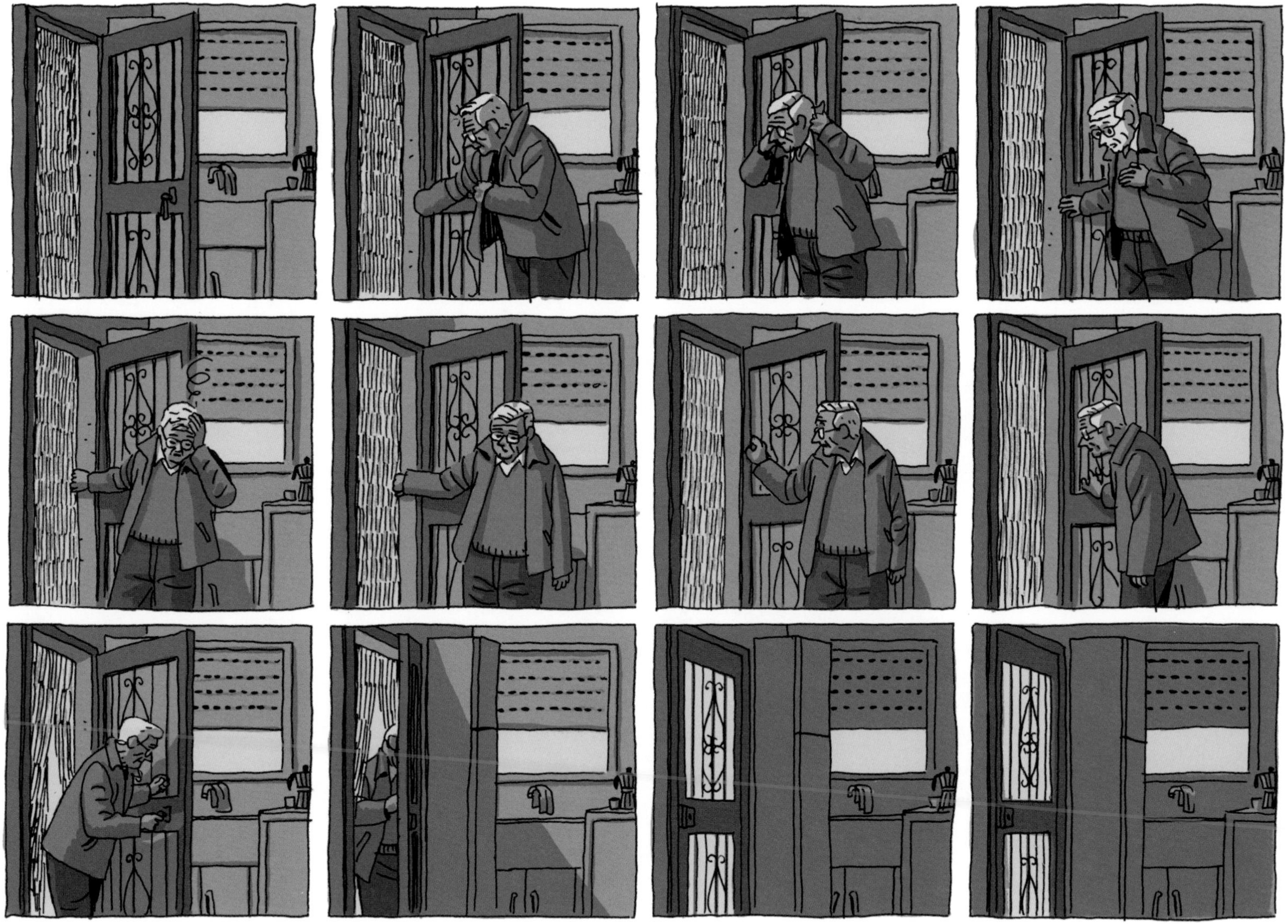

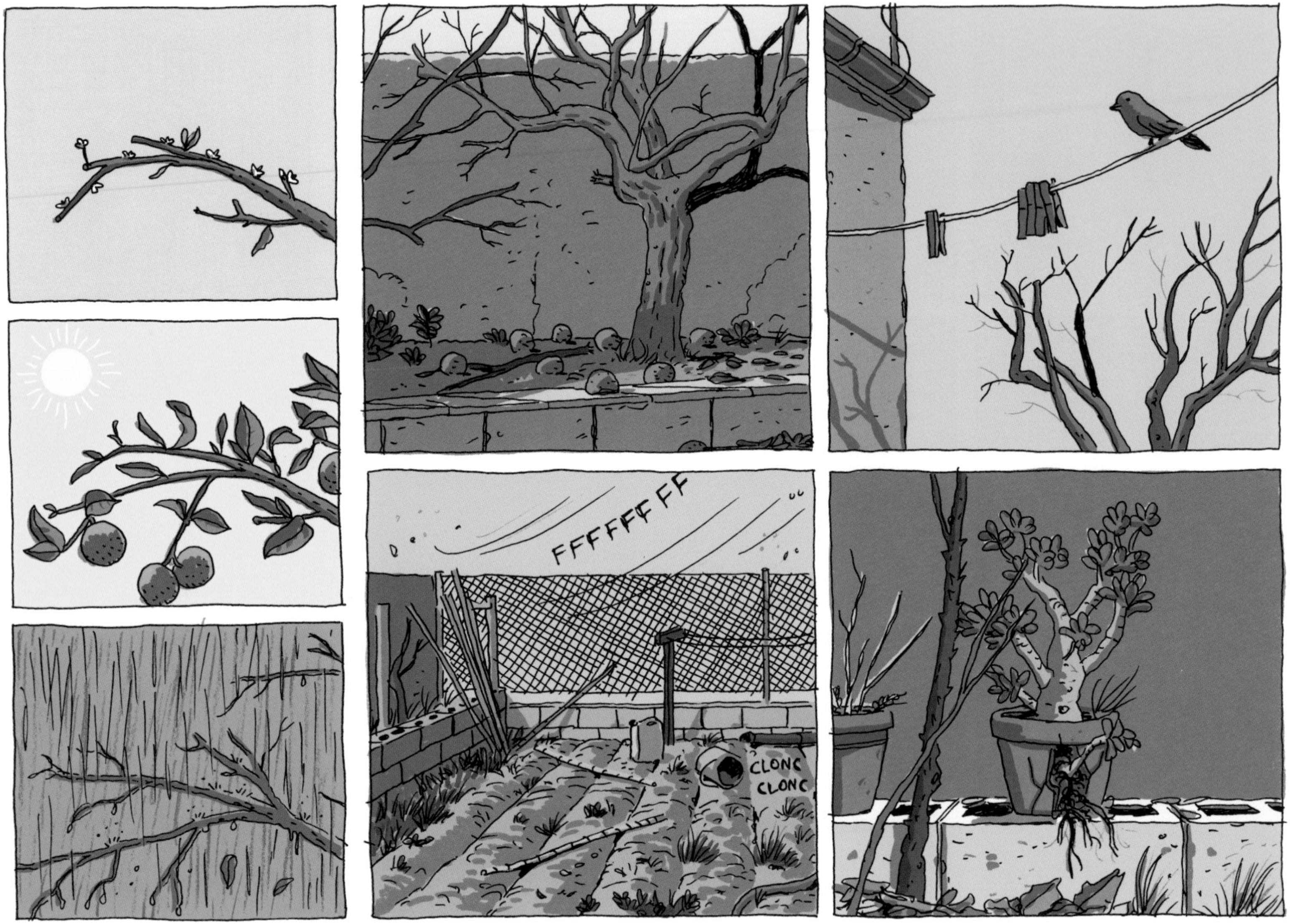
FFFFFFFF
CLONC
CLONC

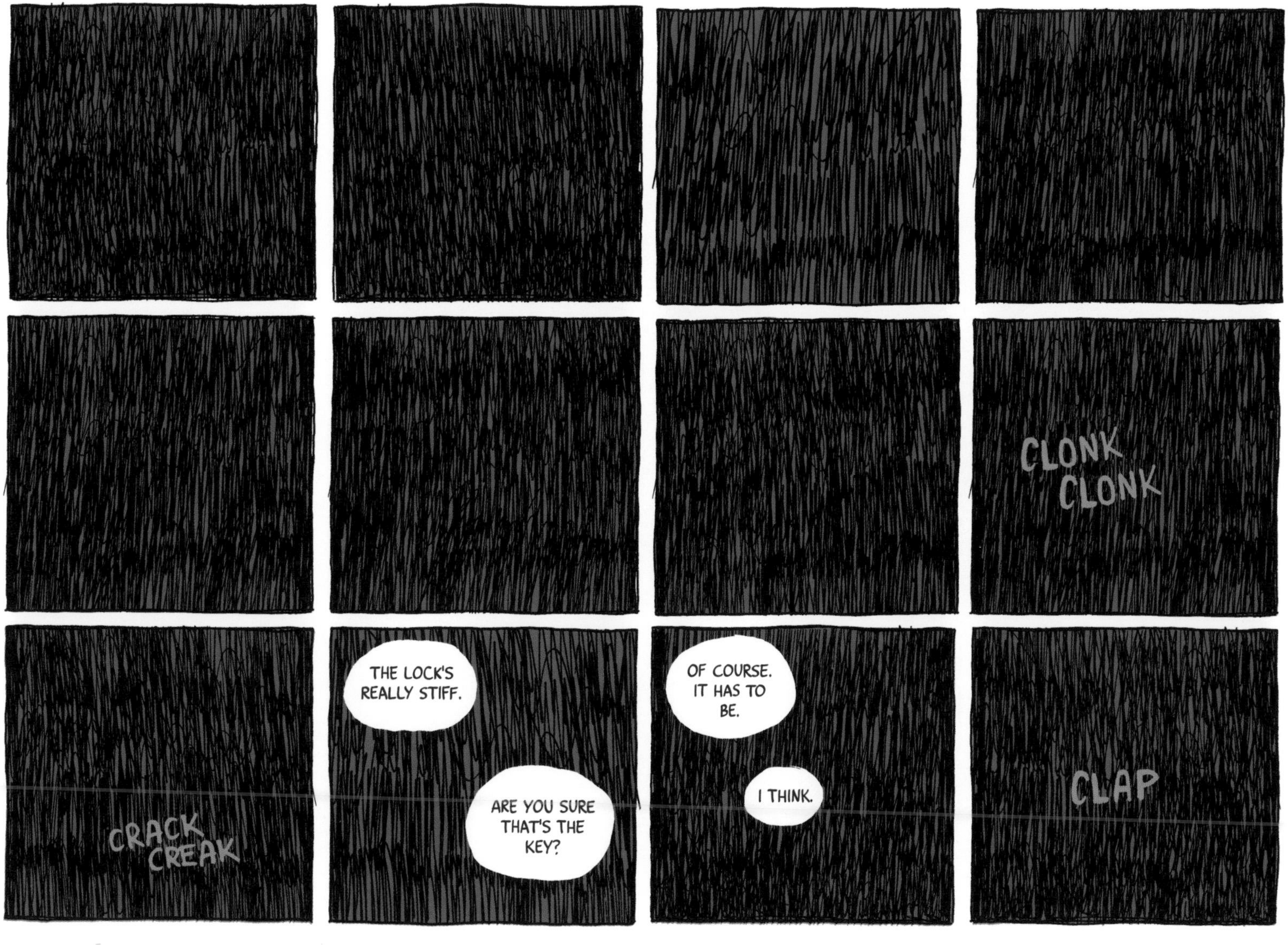
CLONK
CLONK
CRACK
CREAK
THE LOCK'S REALLY STIFF.
ARE YOU SURE THAT'S THE KEY?
OF COURSE. IT HAS TO BE.
I THINK.
CLAP

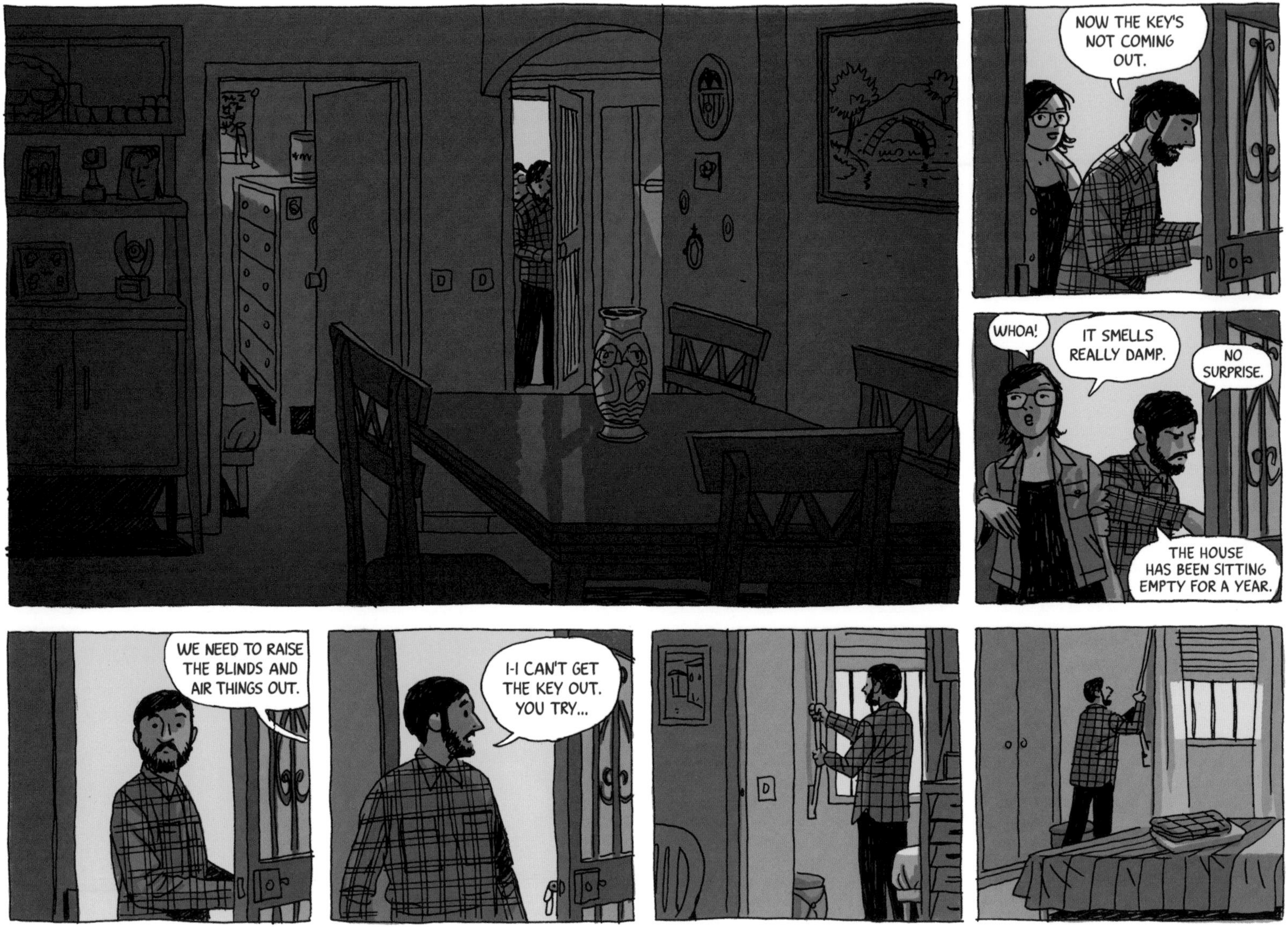
NOW THE KEY'S NOT COMING OUT.
WHOA!
IT SMELLS REALLY DAMP.
NO SURPRISE.
THE HOUSE HAS BEEN SITTING EMPTY FOR A YEAR.
WE NEED TO RAISE THE BLINDS AND AIR THINGS OUT.
I-I CAN'T GET THE KEY OUT. YOU TRY...

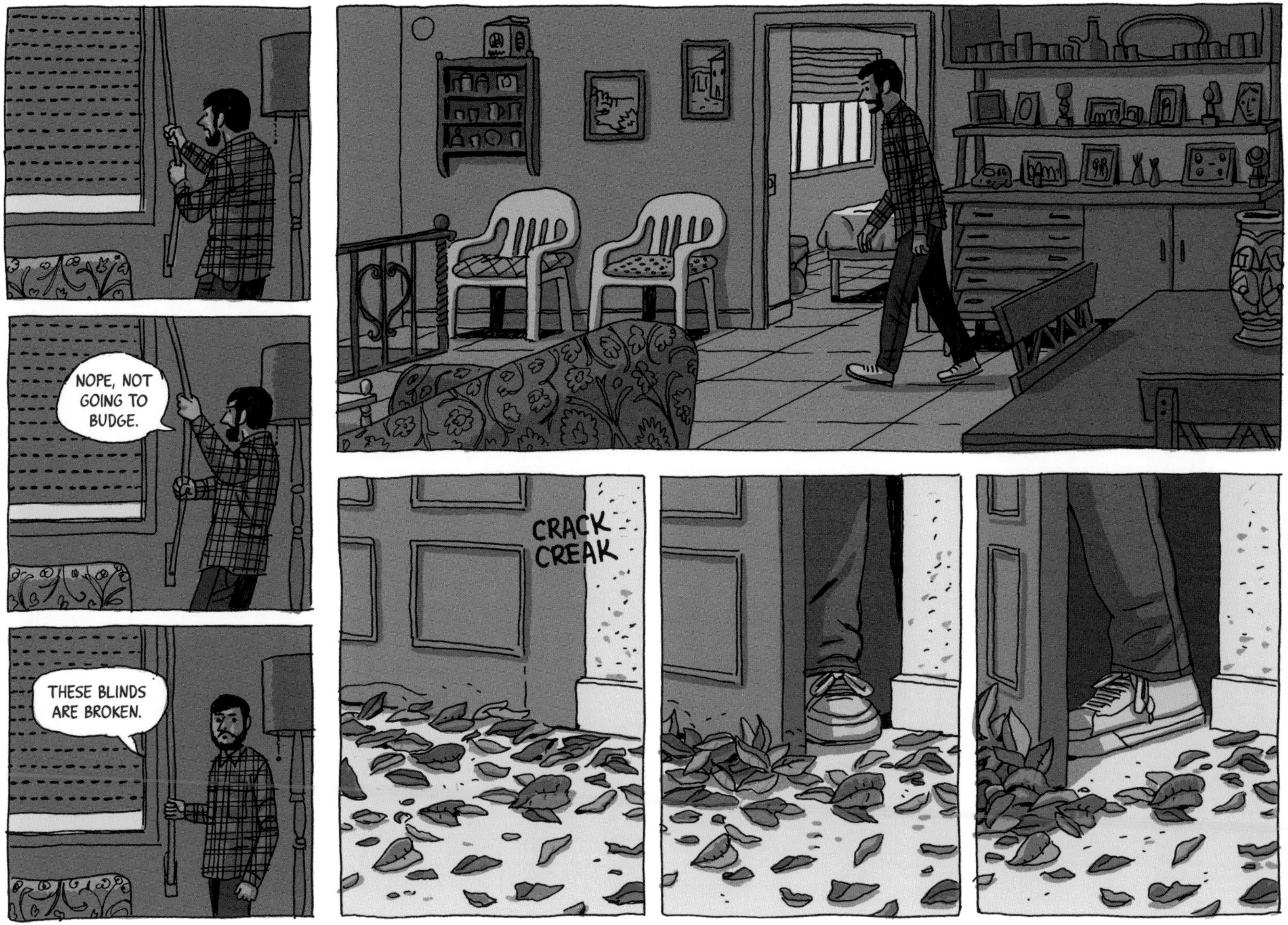
NOPE, NOT GOING TO BUDGE.
THESE BLINDS ARE BROKEN.
CRACK
CREAK

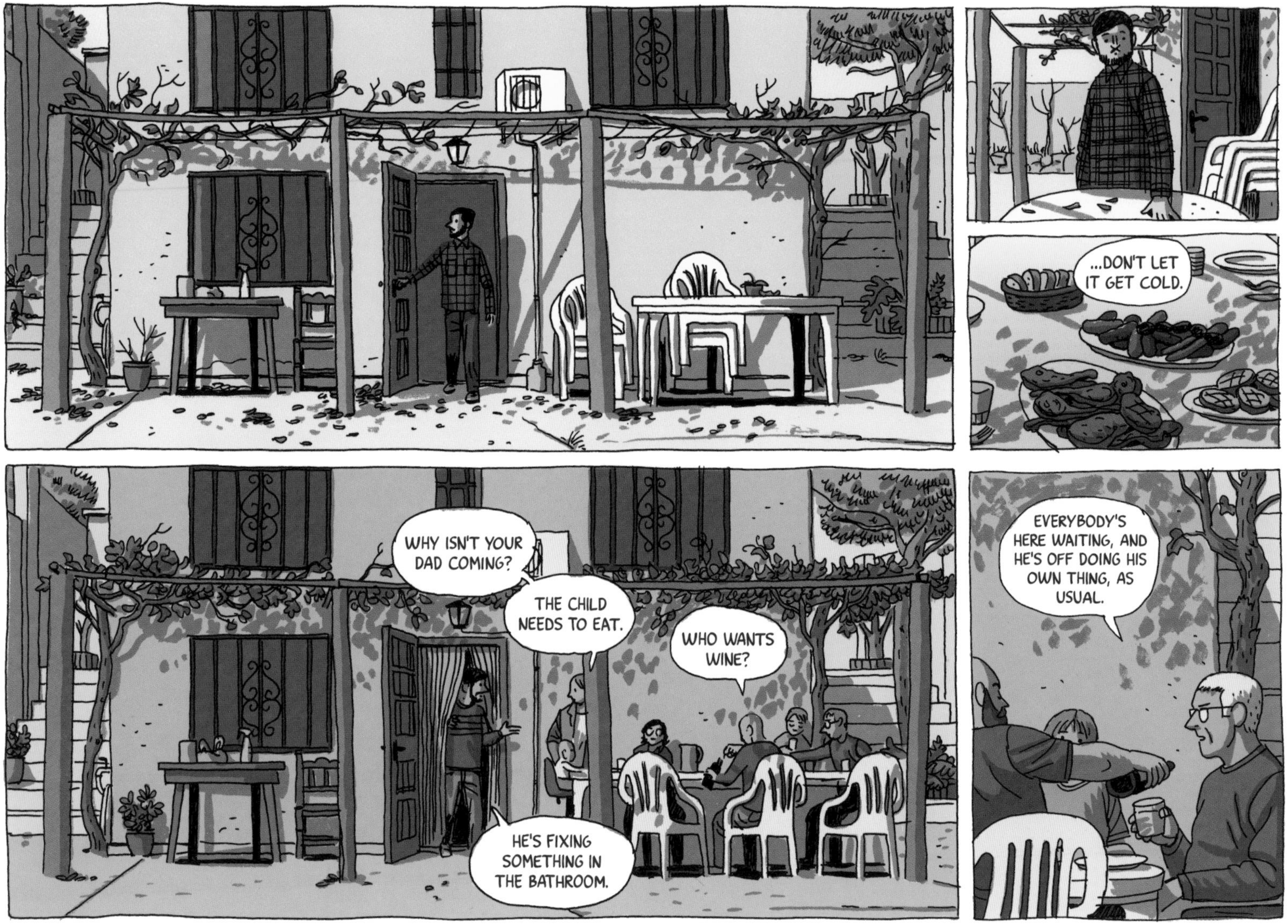
...DON'T LET IT GET COLD.
WHY ISN'T YOUR DAD COMING?
THE CHILD NEEDS TO EAT.
WHO WANTS WINE?
HE'S FIXING SOMETHING IN THE BATHROOM.
EVERYBODY'S HERE WAITING, AND HE'S OFF DOING HIS OWN THING, AS USUAL.

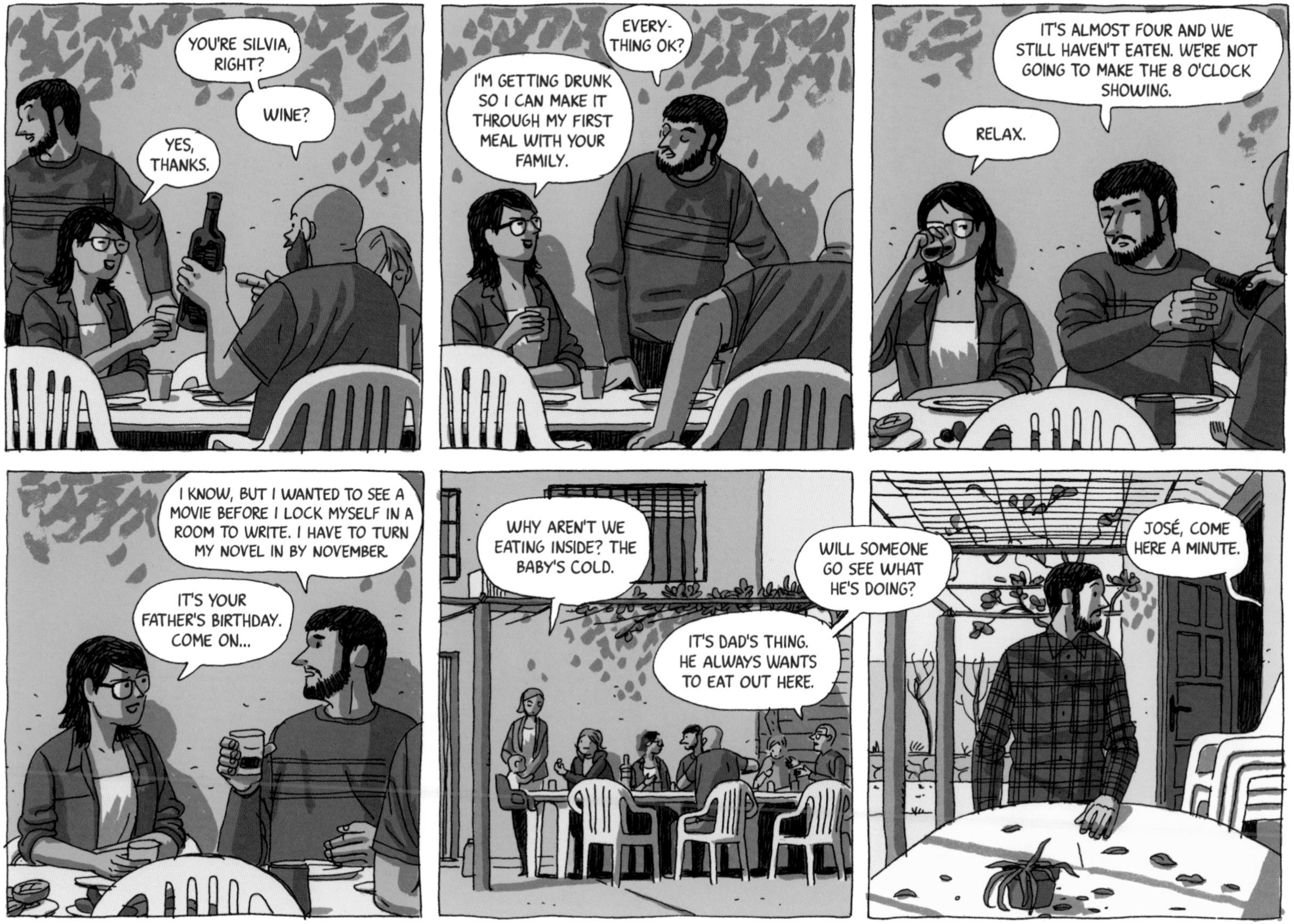
YOU'RE SILVIA, RIGHT?
WINE?
YES, THANKS.
EVERY-THING OK?
I'M GETTING DRUNK SO I CAN MAKE IT THROUGH MY FIRST MEAL WITH YOUR FAMILY.
IT'S ALMOST FOUR AND WE STILL HAVEN'T EATEN. WE'RE NOT GOING TO MAKE THE 8 O'CLOCK SHOWING.
RELAX.
I KNOW, BUT I WANTED TO SEE A MOVIE BEFORE I LOCK MYSELF IN A ROOM TO WRITE. I HAVE TO TURN MY NOVEL IN BY NOVEMBER.
IT'S YOUR FATHER'S BIRTHDAY. COME ON...
WHY AREN'T WE EATING INSIDE? THE BABY'S COLD.
IT'S DAD'S THING. HE ALWAYS WANTS TO EAT OUT HERE.
WILL SOMEONE GO SEE WHAT HE'S DOING?
JOSÉ, COME HERE A MINUTE.

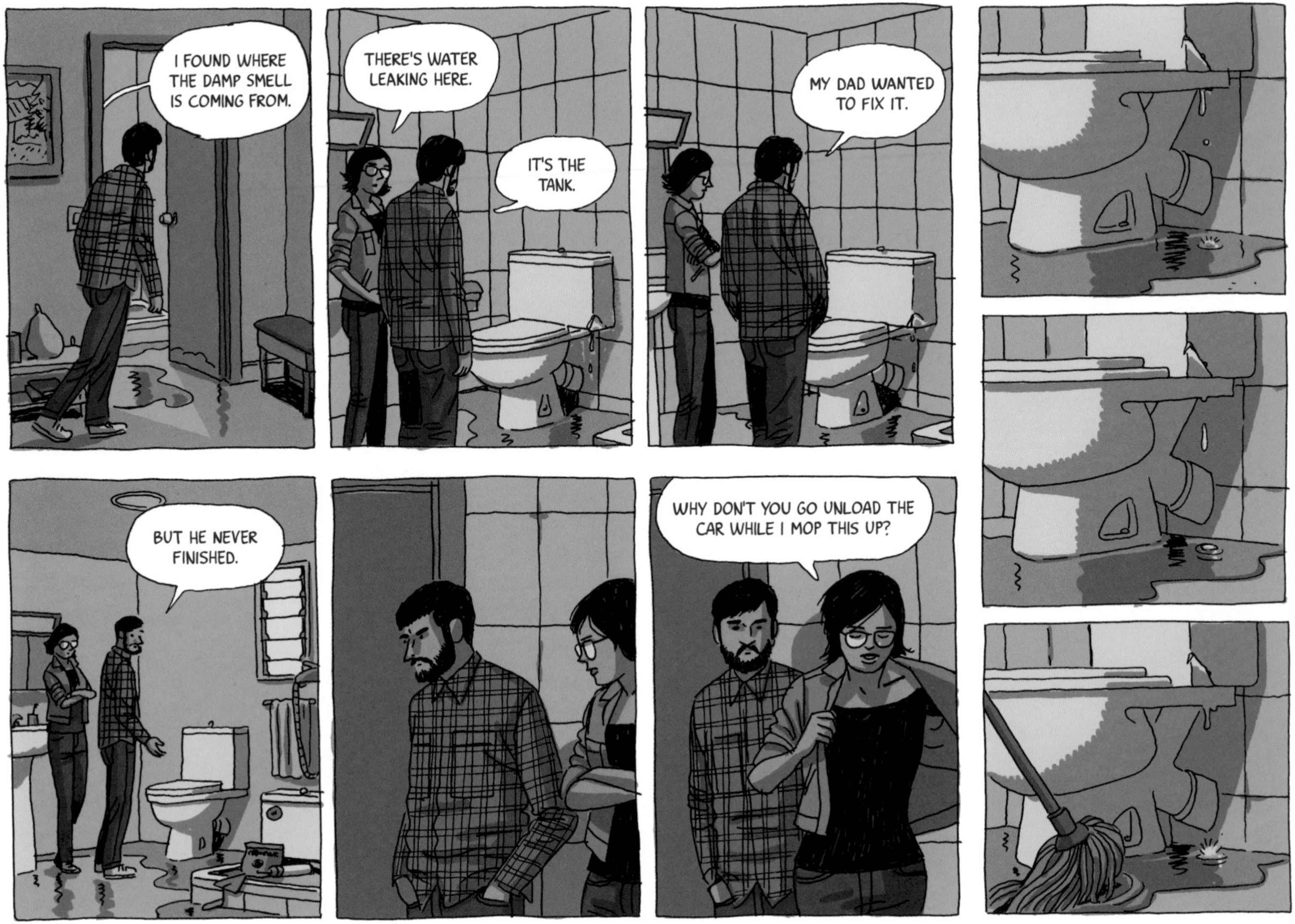

I FOUND WHERE THE DAMP SMELL IS COMING FROM.
THERE'S WATER LEAKING HERE.
IT'S THE TANK.
MY DAD WANTED TO FIX IT.
BUT HE NEVER FINISHED.
WHY DON'T YOU GO UNLOAD THE CAR WHILE I MOP THIS UP?

WHAT HAVE YOU GOT IN HERE, SILVIA? BRICKS?

ALL THIS FOR A WEEKEND VISIT?

THUNK

THUNK

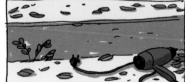

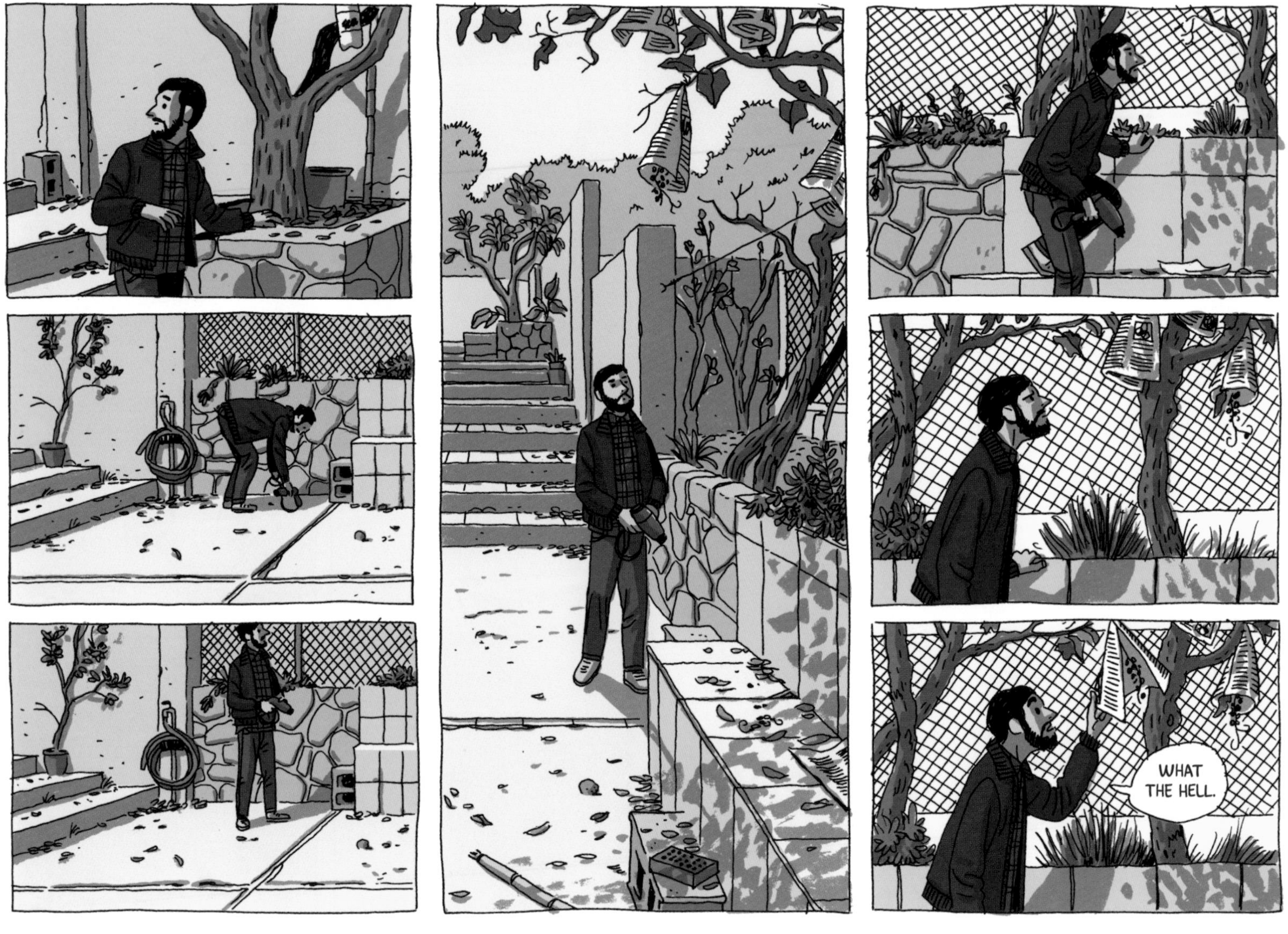
WHAT THE HELL.

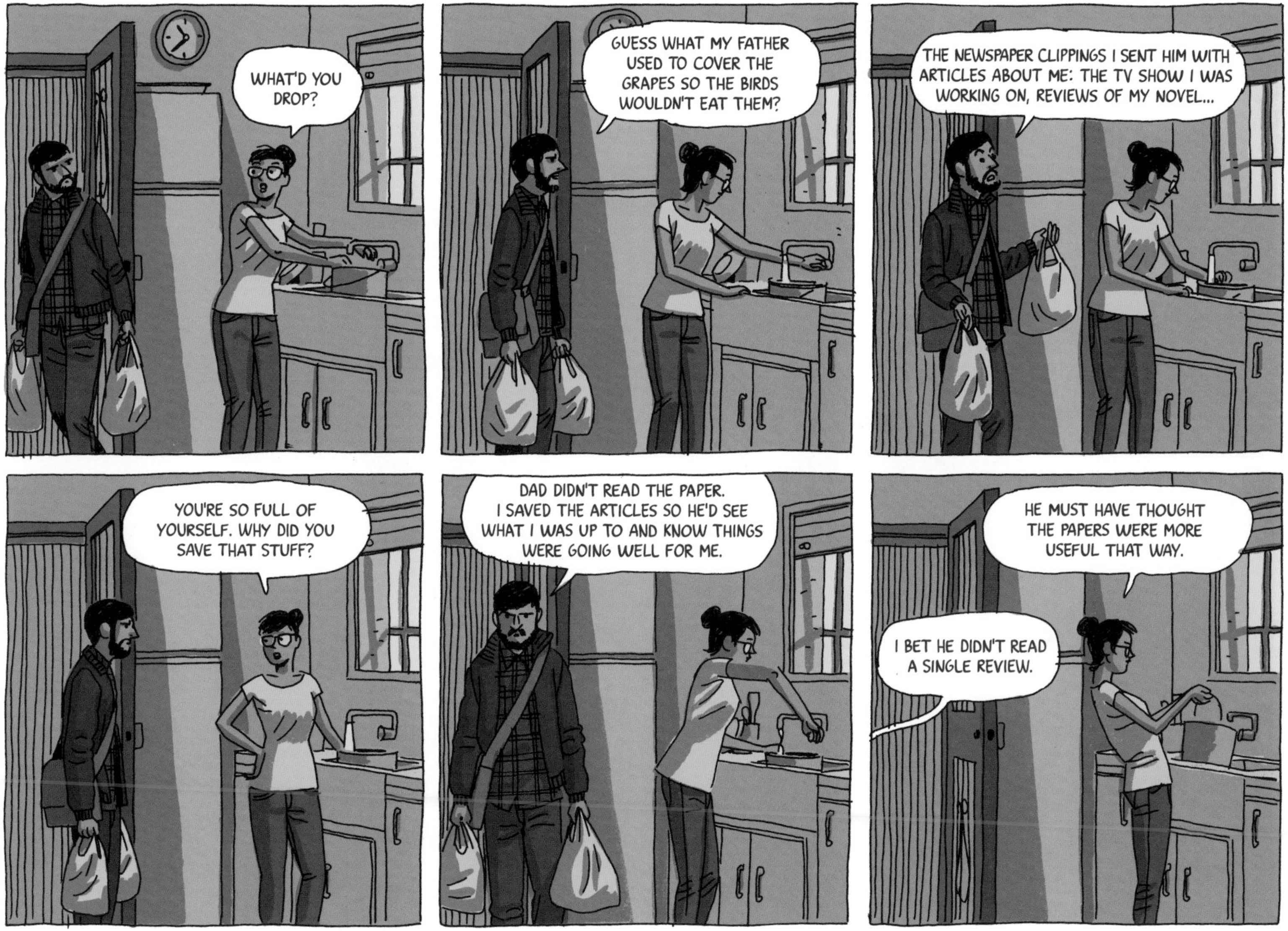
WHAT'D YOU DROP?
GUESS WHAT MY FATHER USED TO COVER THE GRAPES SO THE BIRDS WOULDN'T EAT THEM?
THE NEWSPAPER CLIPPINGS I SENT HIM WITH ARTICLES ABOUT ME: THE TV SHOW I WAS WORKING ON, REVIEWS OF MY NOVEL...
YOU'RE SO FULL OF YOURSELF. WHY DID YOU SAVE THAT STUFF?
DAD DIDN'T READ THE PAPER. I SAVED THE ARTICLES SO HE'D SEE WHAT I WAS UP TO AND KNOW THINGS WERE GOING WELL FOR ME.
HE MUST HAVE THOUGHT THE PAPERS WERE MORE USEFUL THAT WAY.
I BET HE DIDN'T READ A SINGLE REVIEW.

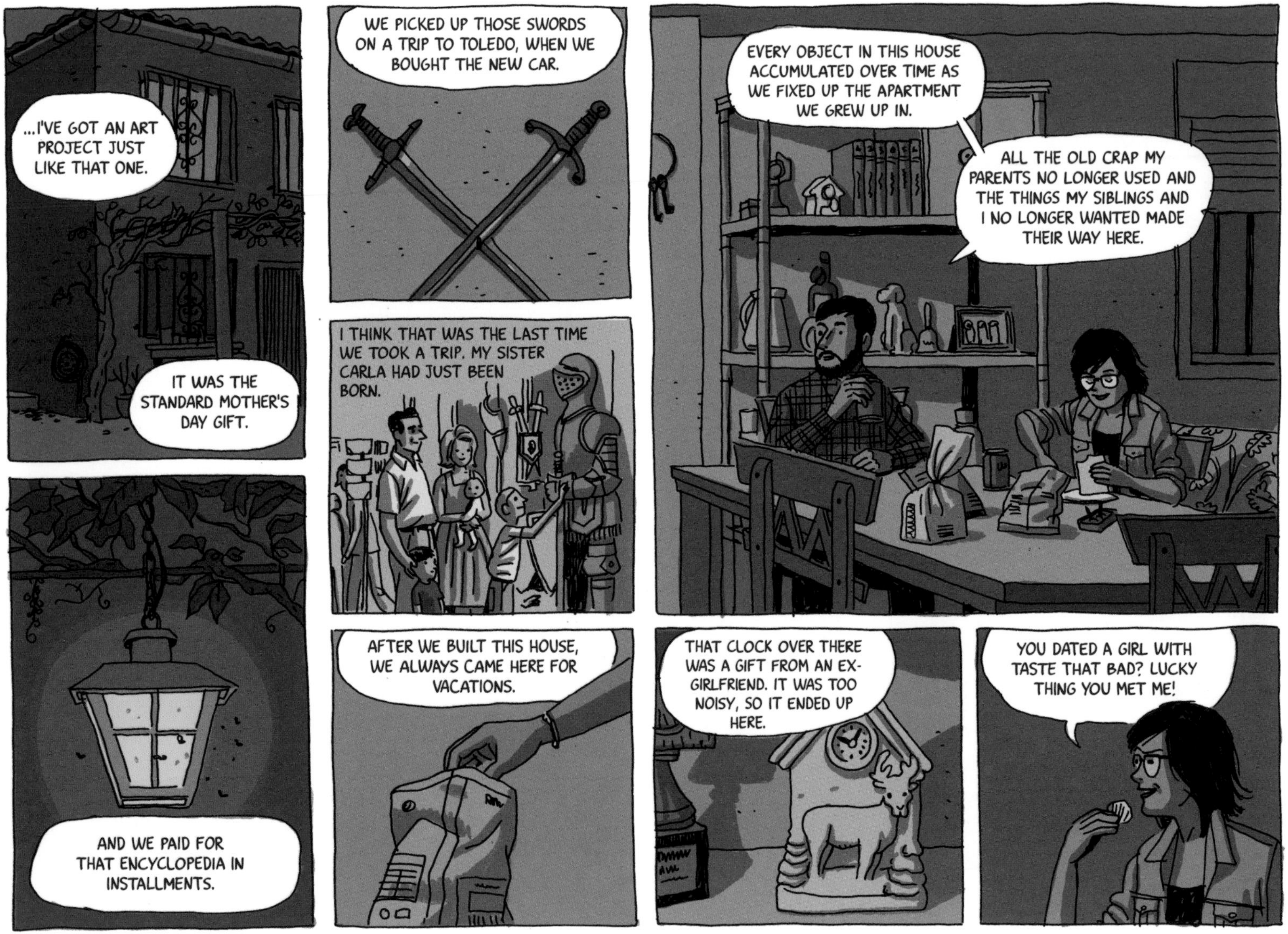
...I'VE GOT AN ART PROJECT JUST LIKE THAT ONE.
IT WAS THE STANDARD MOTHER'S DAY GIFT.
WE PICKED UP THOSE SWORDS ON A TRIP TO TOLEDO, WHEN WE BOUGHT THE NEW CAR.
I THINK THAT WAS THE LAST TIME WE TOOK A TRIP. MY SISTER CARLA HAD JUST BEEN BORN.
EVERY OBJECT IN THIS HOUSE ACCUMULATED OVER TIME AS WE FIXED UP THE APARTMENT WE GREW UP IN.
ALL THE OLD CRAP MY PARENTS NO LONGER USED AND THE THINGS MY SIBLINGS AND I NO LONGER WANTED MADE THEIR WAY HERE.
AND WE PAID FOR THAT ENCYCLOPEDIA IN INSTALLMENTS.
AFTER WE BUILT THIS HOUSE, WE ALWAYS CAME HERE FOR VACATIONS.
THAT CLOCK OVER THERE WAS A GIFT FROM AN EX-GIRLFRIEND. IT WAS TOO NOISY, SO IT ENDED UP HERE.
YOU DATED A GIRL WITH TASTE THAT BAD? LUCKY THING YOU MET ME!

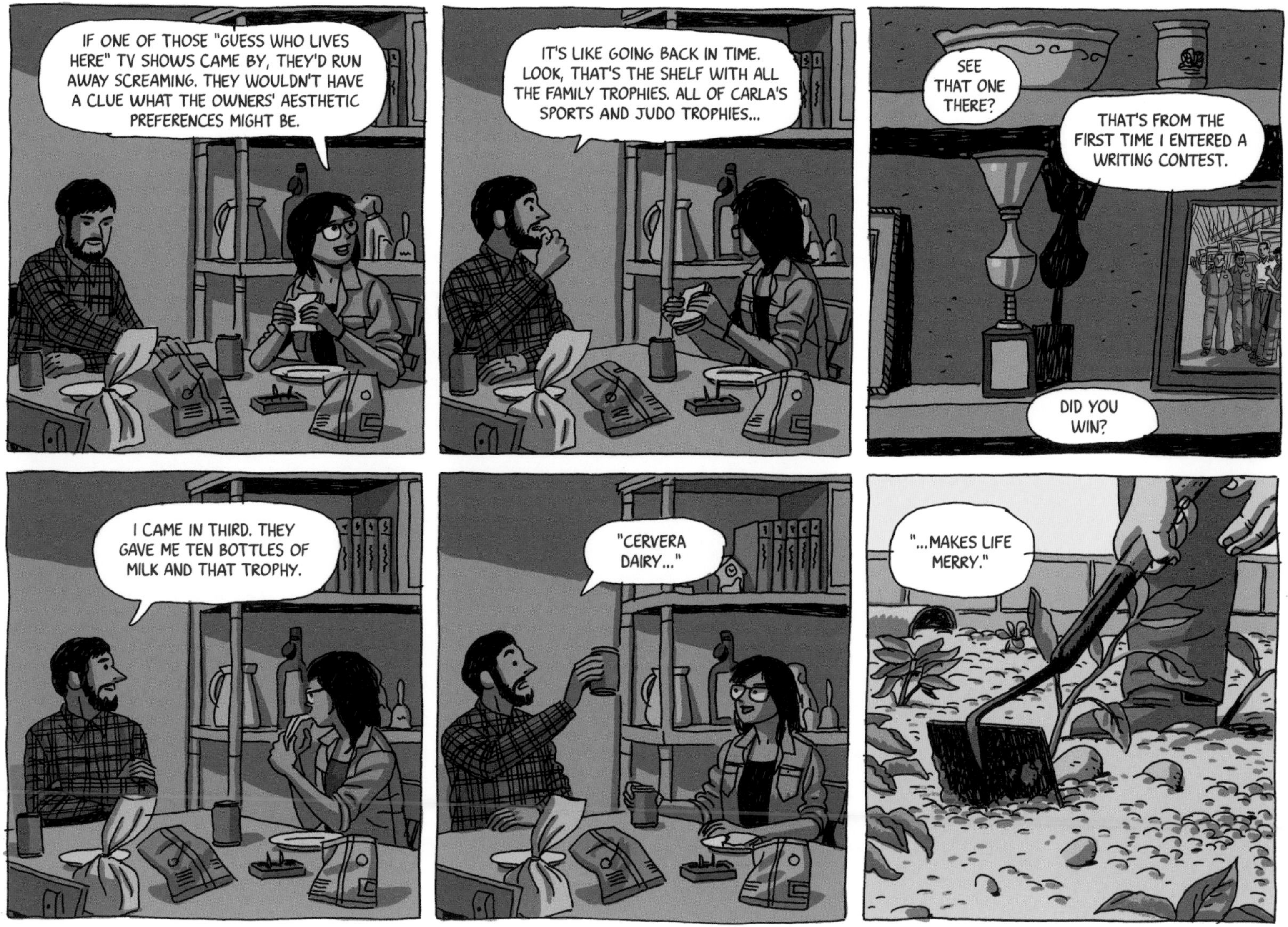
IF ONE OF THOSE "GUESS WHO LIVES HERE" TV SHOWS CAME BY, THEY'D RUN AWAY SCREAMING. THEY WOULDN'T HAVE A CLUE WHAT THE OWNERS' AESTHETIC PREFERENCES MIGHT BE.
IT'S LIKE GOING BACK IN TIME. LOOK, THAT'S THE SHELF WITH ALL THE FAMILY TROPHIES. ALL OF CARLA'S SPORTS AND JUDO TROPHIES...
SEE THAT ONE THERE?
THAT'S FROM THE FIRST TIME I ENTERED A WRITING CONTEST.
DID YOU WIN?
I CAME IN THIRD. THEY GAVE ME TEN BOTTLES OF MILK AND THAT TROPHY.
"CERVERA DAIRY..."
"...MAKES LIFE MERRY."

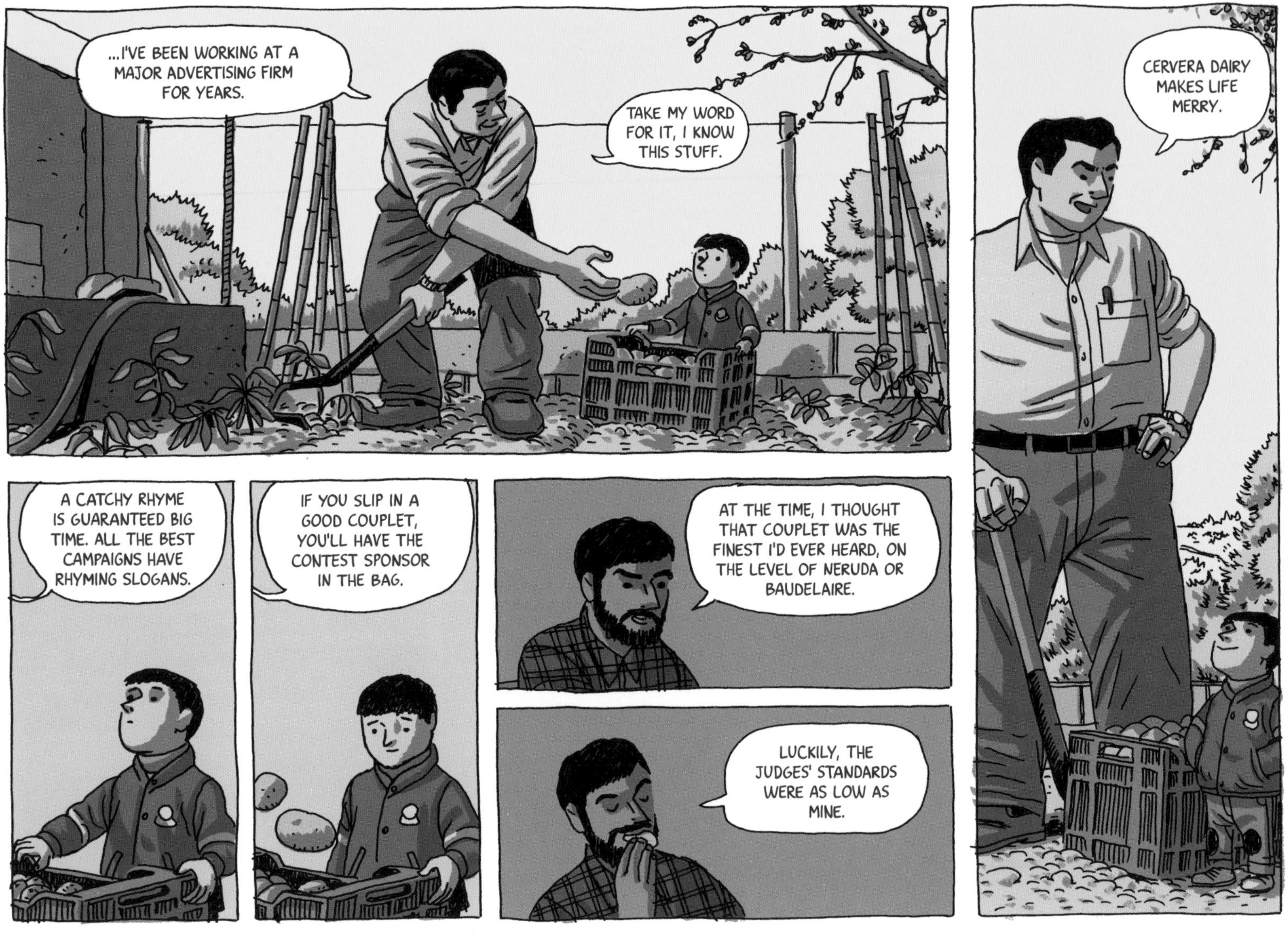
...I'VE BEEN WORKING AT A MAJOR ADVERTISING FIRM FOR YEARS.
TAKE MY WORD FOR IT, I KNOW THIS STUFF.
CERVERA DAIRY MAKES LIFE MERRY.
A CATCHY RHYME IS GUARANTEED BIG TIME. ALL THE BEST CAMPAIGNS HAVE RHYMING SLOGANS.
IF YOU SLIP IN A GOOD COUPLET, YOU'LL HAVE THE CONTEST SPONSOR IN THE BAG.
AT THE TIME, I THOUGHT THAT COUPLET WAS THE FINEST I'D EVER HEARD, ON THE LEVEL OF NERUDA OR BAUDELAIRE.
LUCKILY, THE JUDGES' STANDARDS WERE AS LOW AS MINE.

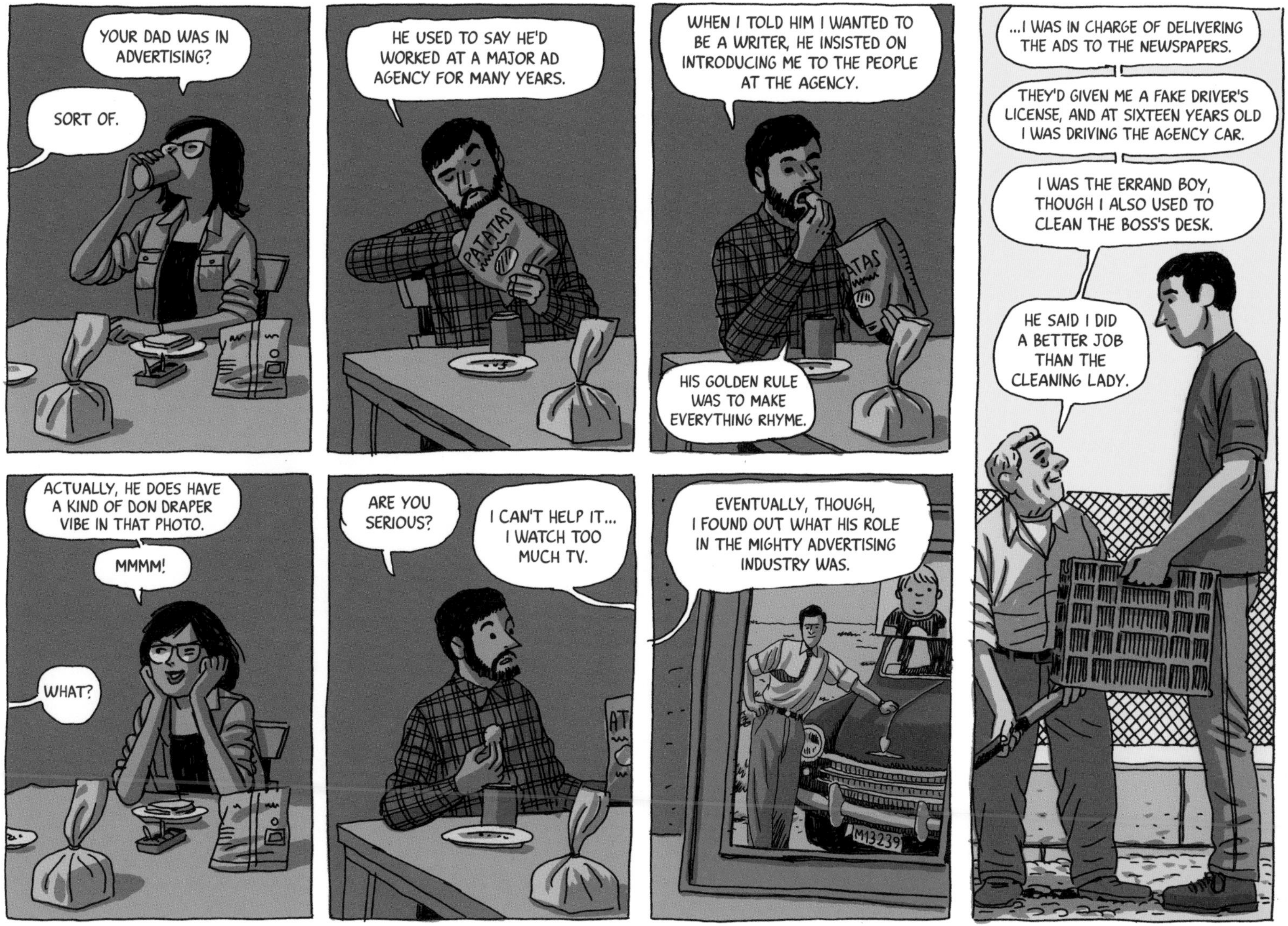
YOUR DAD WAS IN ADVERTISING?
SORT OF.
HE USED TO SAY HE'D WORKED AT A MAJOR AD AGENCY FOR MANY YEARS.
PATATAS
WHEN I TOLD HIM I WANTED TO BE A WRITER, HE INSISTED ON INTRODUCING ME TO THE PEOPLE AT THE AGENCY.
HIS GOLDEN RULE WAS TO MAKE EVERYTHING RHYME.
...I WAS IN CHARGE OF DELIVERING THE ADS TO THE NEWSPAPERS.
THEY'D GIVEN ME A FAKE DRIVER'S LICENSE, AND AT SIXTEEN YEARS OLD I WAS DRIVING THE AGENCY CAR.
I WAS THE ERRAND BOY, THOUGH I ALSO USED TO CLEAN THE BOSS'S DESK.
HE SAID I DID A BETTER JOB THAN THE CLEANING LADY.
ACTUALLY, HE DOES HAVE A KIND OF DON DRAPER VIBE IN THAT PHOTO.
MMMM!
WHAT?
ARE YOU SERIOUS?
I CAN'T HELP IT... I WATCH TOO MUCH TV.
EVENTUALLY, THOUGH, I FOUND OUT WHAT HIS ROLE IN THE MIGHTY ADVERTISING INDUSTRY WAS.
M13239

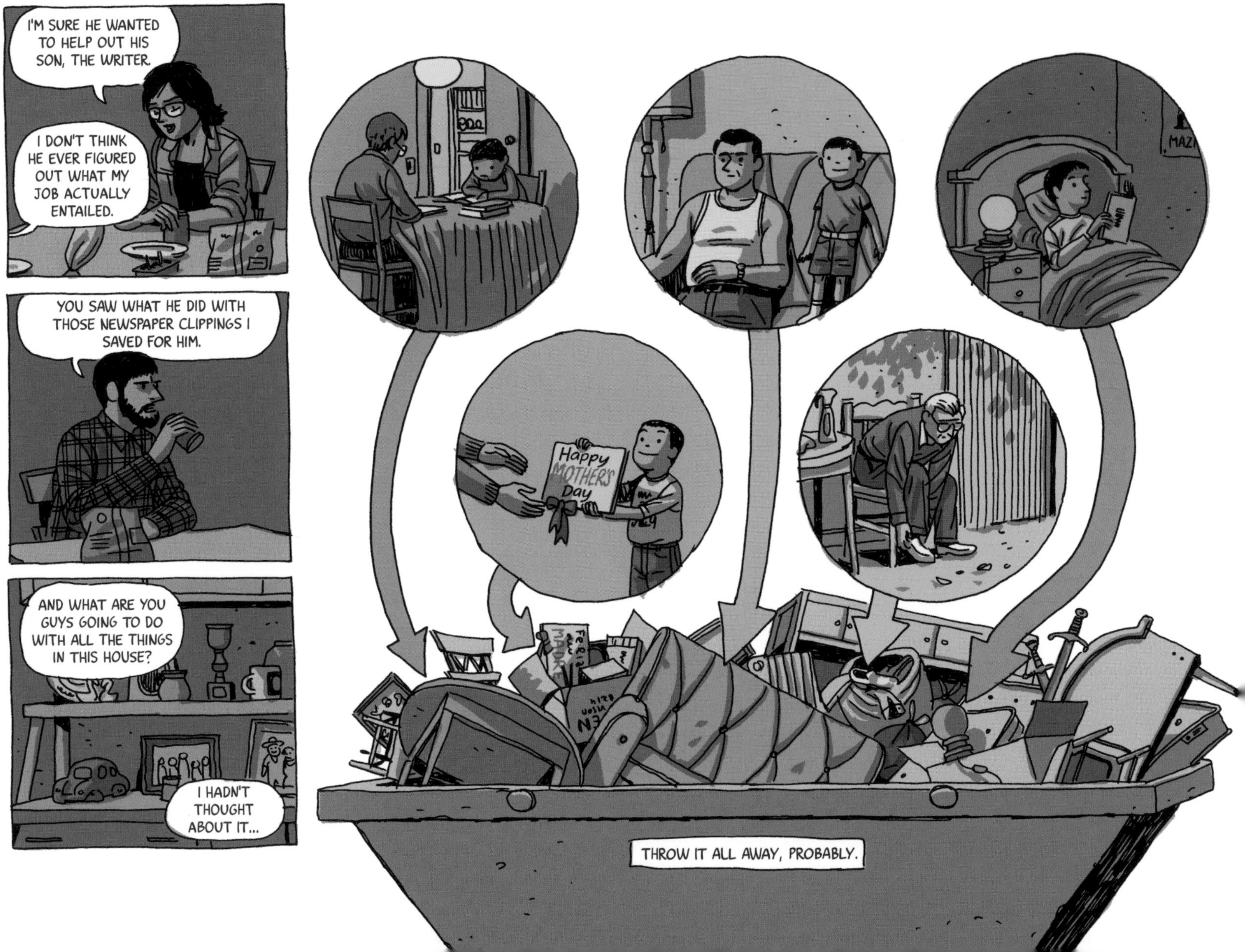
I'M SURE HE WANTED TO HELP OUT HIS SON, THE WRITER.
I DON'T THINK HE EVER FIGURED OUT WHAT MY JOB ACTUALLY ENTAILED.
YOU SAW WHAT HE DID WITH THOSE NEWSPAPER CLIPPINGS I SAVED FOR HIM.
AND WHAT ARE YOU GUYS GOING TO DO WITH ALL THE THINGS IN THIS HOUSE?
I HADN'T THOUGHT ABOUT IT...
Happy MOTHER'S Day
THROW IT ALL AWAY, PROBABLY.

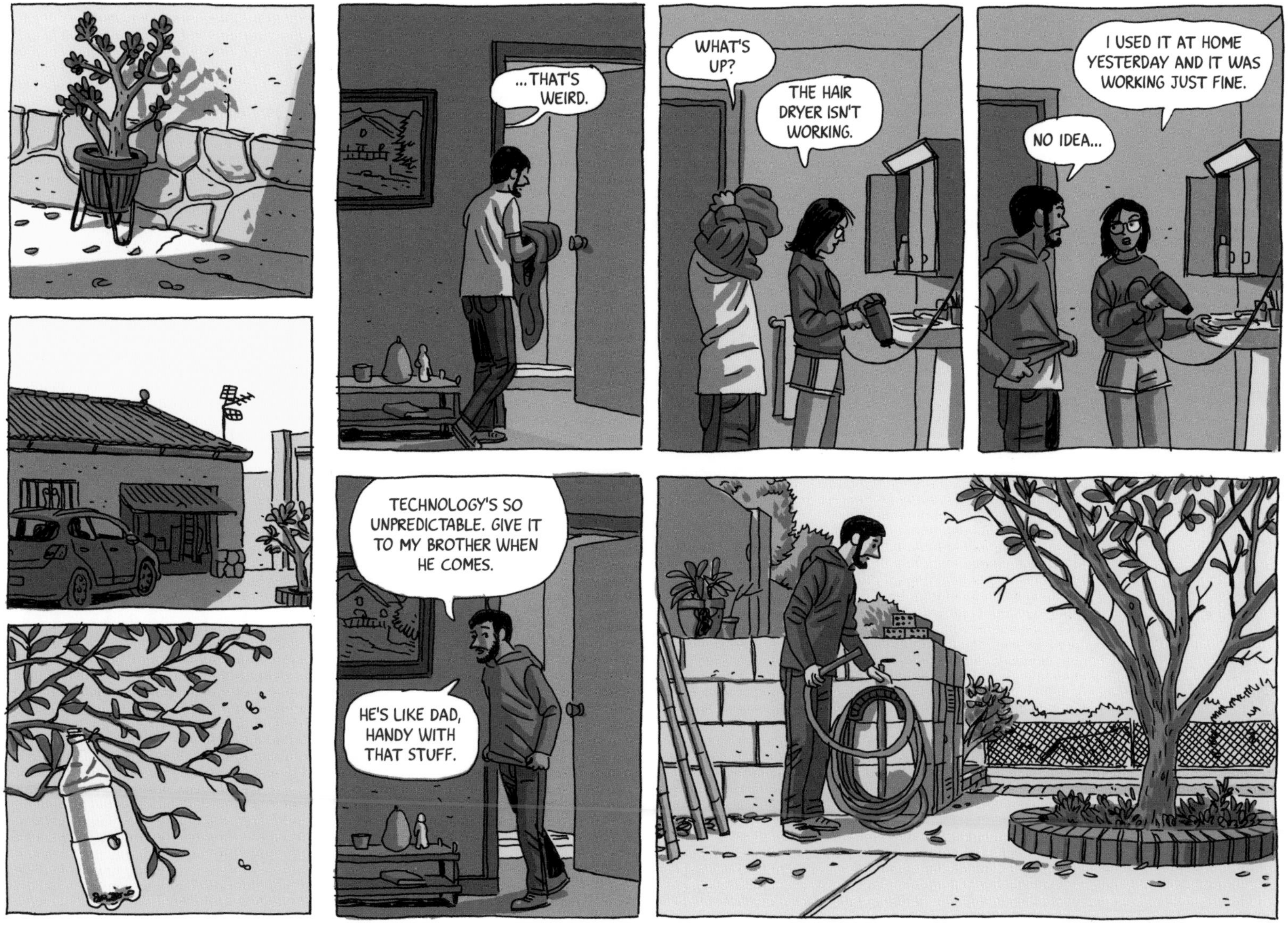
...THAT'S WEIRD.
WHAT'S UP?
THE HAIR DRYER ISN'T WORKING.
I USED IT AT HOME YESTERDAY AND IT WAS WORKING JUST FINE.
NO IDEA...
TECHNOLOGY'S SO UNPREDICTABLE. GIVE IT TO MY BROTHER WHEN HE COMES.
HE'S LIKE DAD, HANDY WITH THAT STUFF.

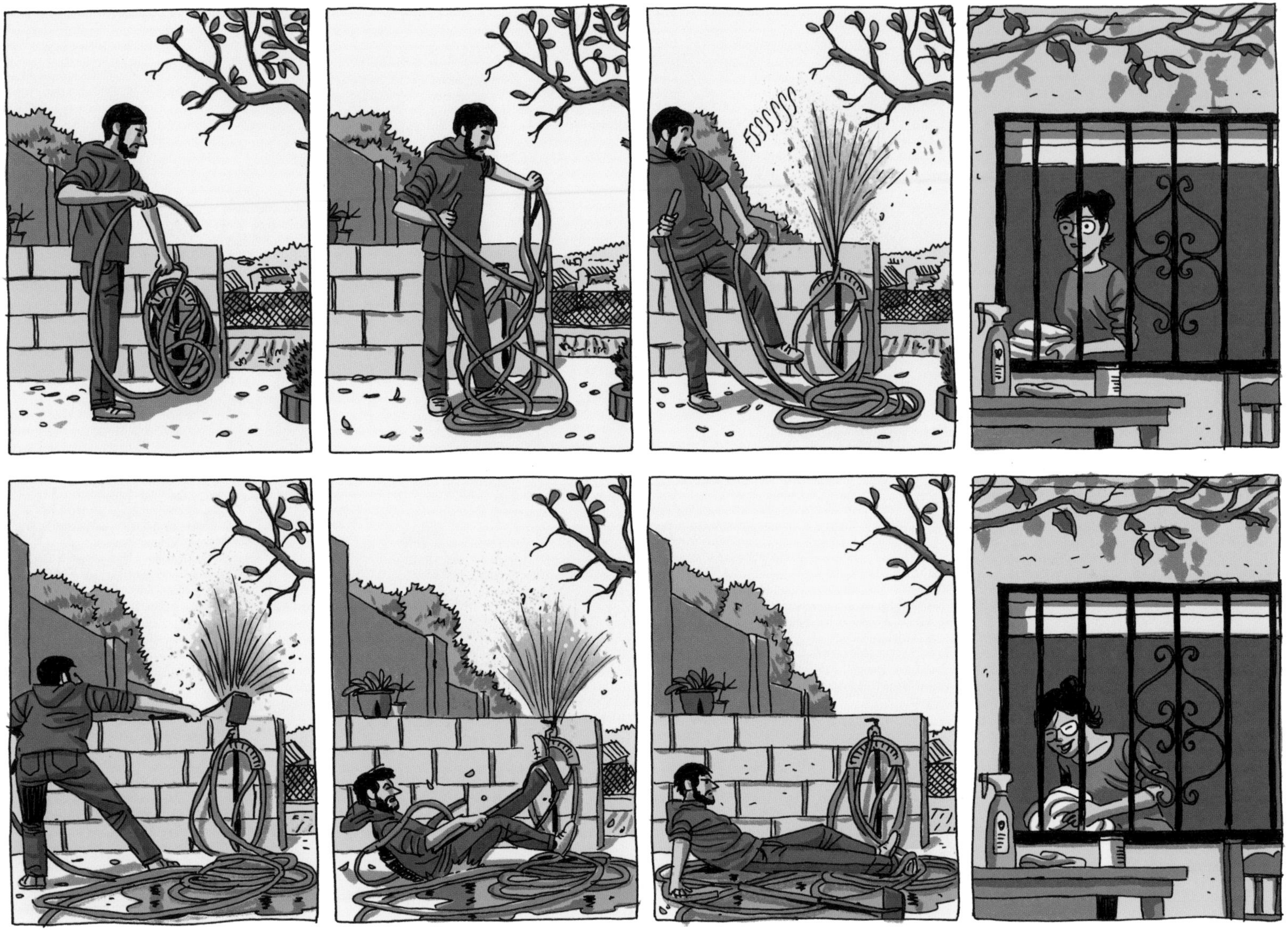
FSSSSSS

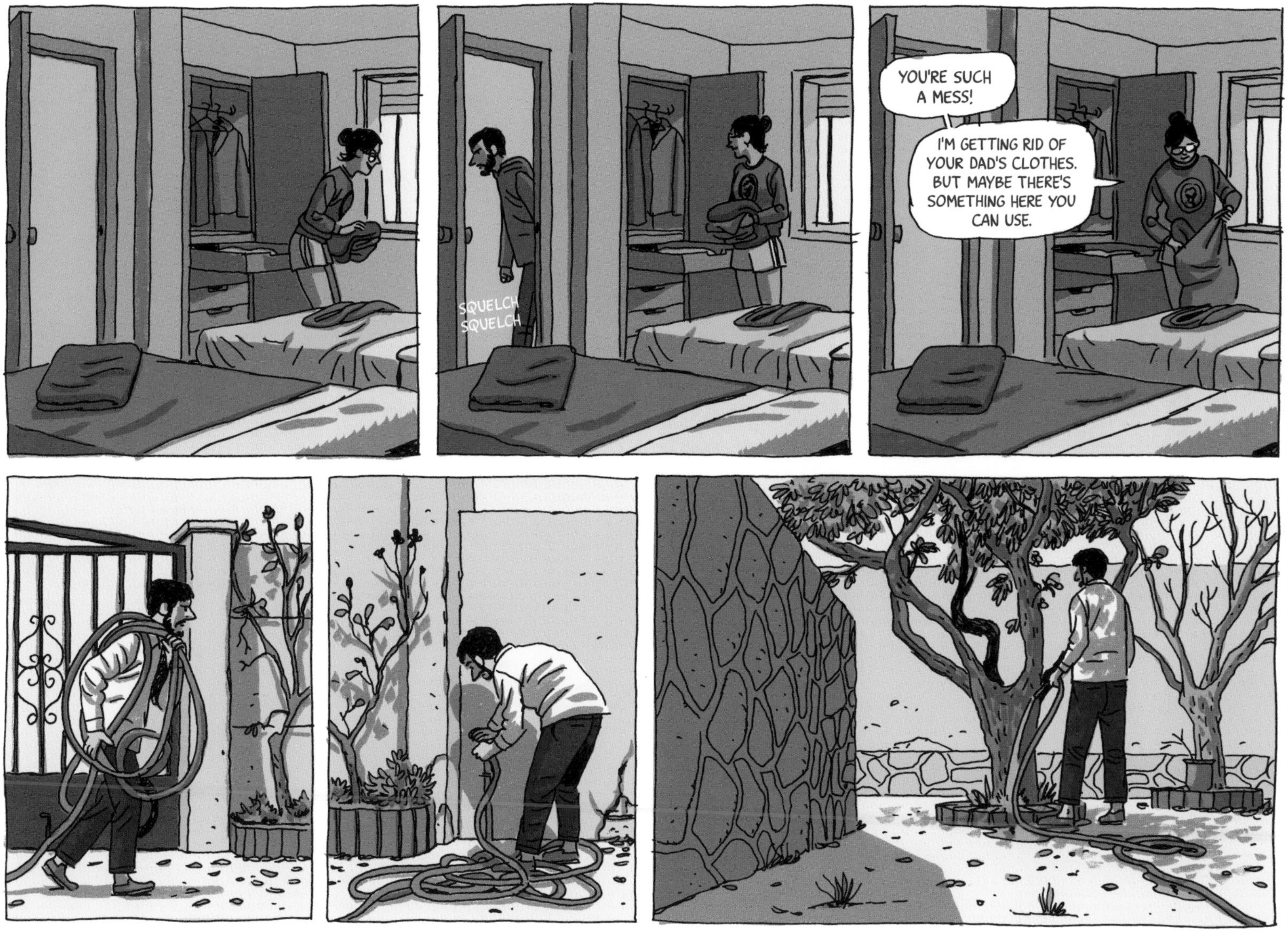
SQUELCH
SQUELCH
YOU'RE SUCH A MESS!
I'M GETTING RID OF YOUR DAD'S CLOTHES. BUT MAYBE THERE'S SOMETHING HERE YOU CAN USE.

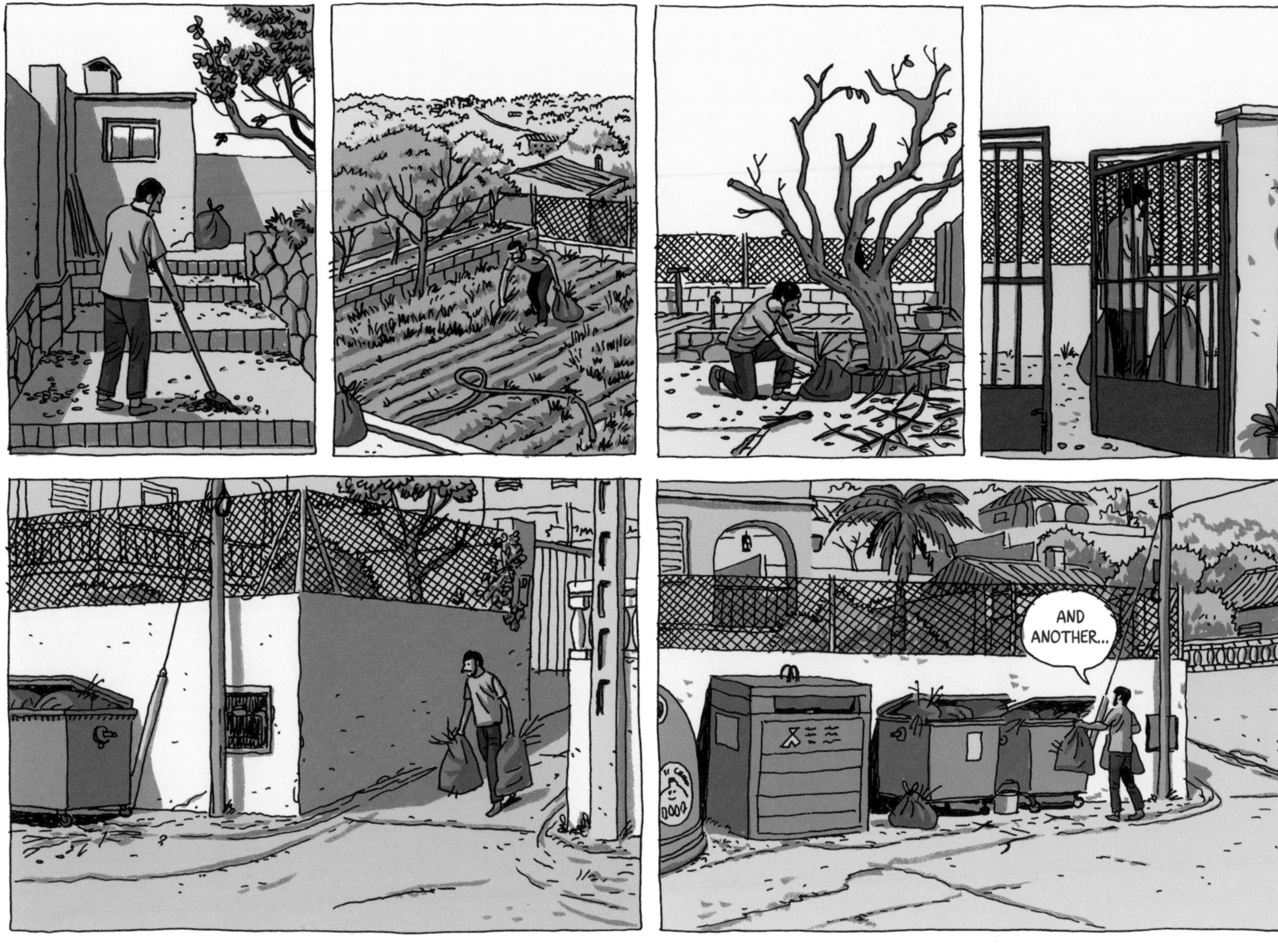
AND ANOTHER...

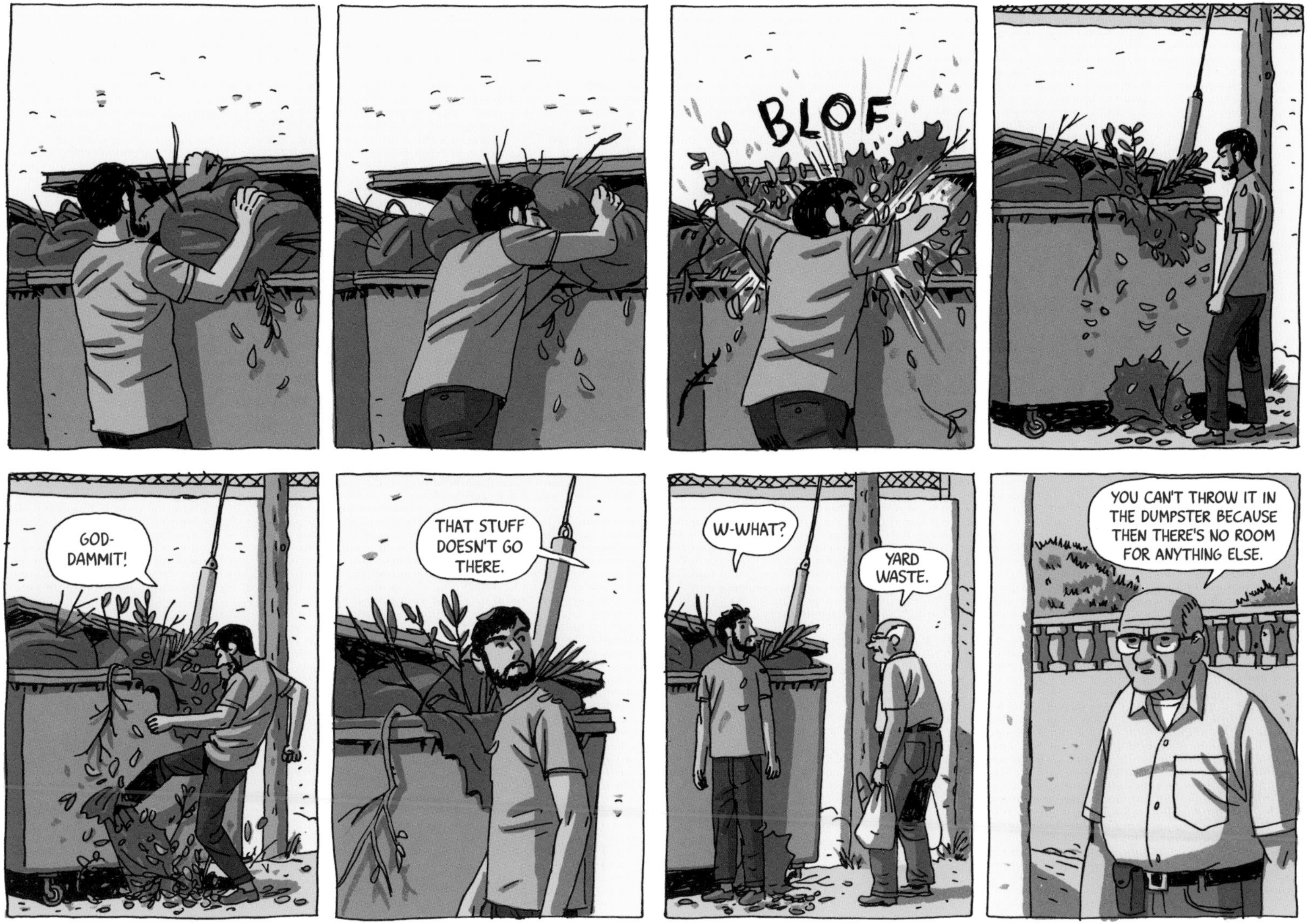
BLOF
GOD-DAMMIT!
THAT STUFF DOESN'T GO THERE.
W-WHAT?
YARD WASTE.
YOU CAN'T THROW IT IN THE DUMPSTER BECAUSE THEN THERE'S NO ROOM FOR ANYTHING ELSE.

I DIDN'T KNOW. WHERE DOES IT GO?

ARE YOU ANTONIO'S SON?

I'M JOSÉ, HIS MIDDLE CHILD.

YOU'RE MANOLO, RIGHT?

I HEARD ABOUT YOUR FATHER.

I'M REALLY SORRY.

THANKS.

I CALLED HIM ONE DAY, AFTER THE OPERATION. HE STILL SOUNDED WEAK, BUT SEEMED CHEERFUL.

THE OPERATION WENT REALLY WELL. IT DIDN'T TAKE LONG FOR HIM TO START TRYING TO GET AROUND WITHOUT CRUTCHES.

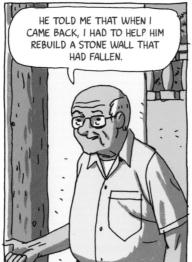

HE TOLD ME THAT WHEN I CAME BACK, I HAD TO HELP HIM REBUILD A STONE WALL THAT HAD FALLEN.

BUT HE SUDDENLY WENT INTO SOME KIND OF DEPRESSION AND RELAPSED, AND EVERYTHING HAPPENED REALLY FAST.

I WAS VERY FOND OF HIM.

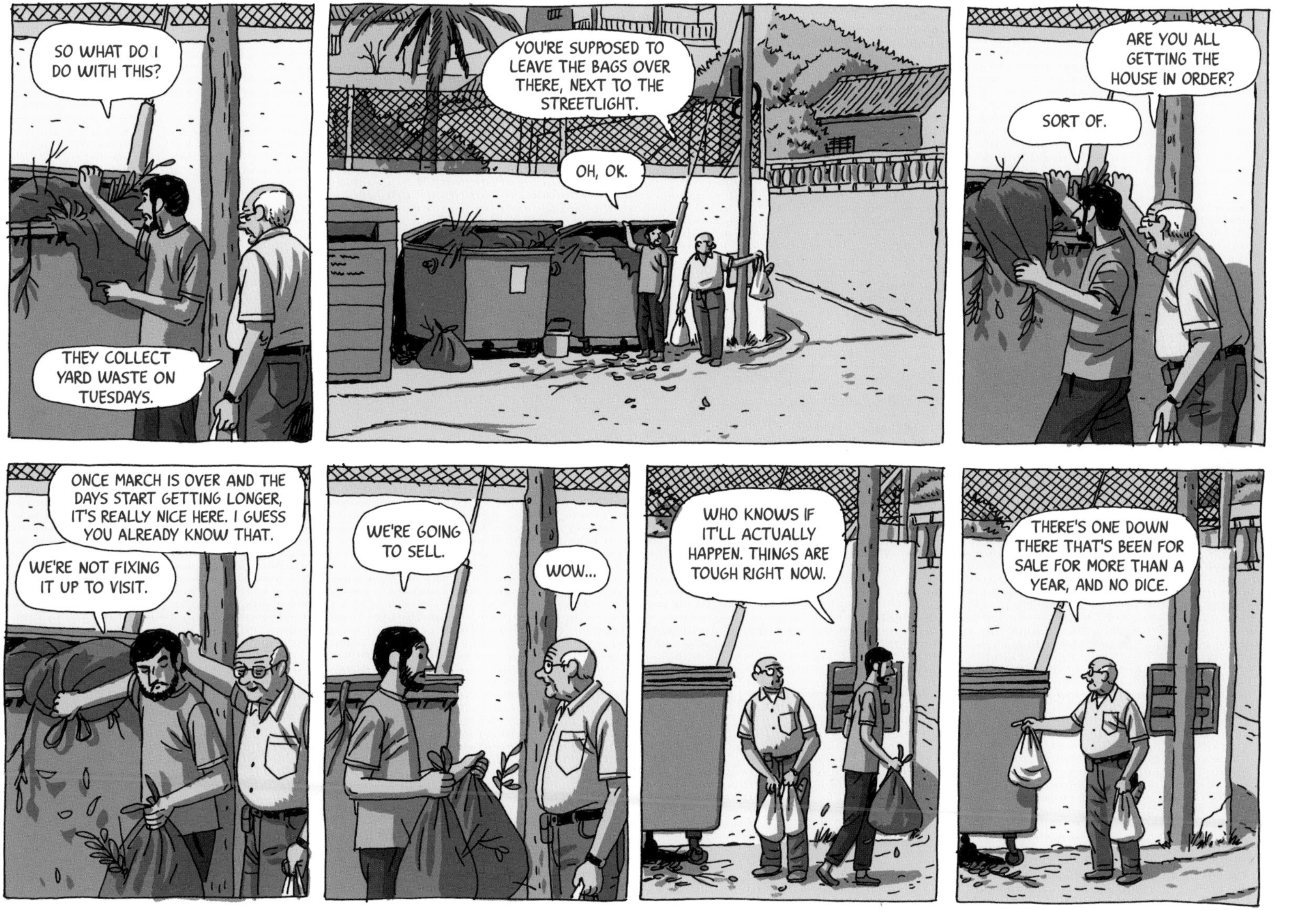
SO WHAT DO I DO WITH THIS?
THEY COLLECT YARD WASTE ON TUESDAYS.
YOU'RE SUPPOSED TO LEAVE THE BAGS OVER THERE, NEXT TO THE STREETLIGHT.
OH, OK.
ARE YOU ALL GETTING THE HOUSE IN ORDER?
SORT OF.
ONCE MARCH IS OVER AND THE DAYS START GETTING LONGER, IT'S REALLY NICE HERE. I GUESS YOU ALREADY KNOW THAT.
WE'RE NOT FIXING IT UP TO VISIT.
WE'RE GOING TO SELL.
WOW...
WHO KNOWS IF IT'LL ACTUALLY HAPPEN. THINGS ARE TOUGH RIGHT NOW.
THERE'S ONE DOWN THERE THAT'S BEEN FOR SALE FOR MORE THAN A YEAR, AND NO DICE.

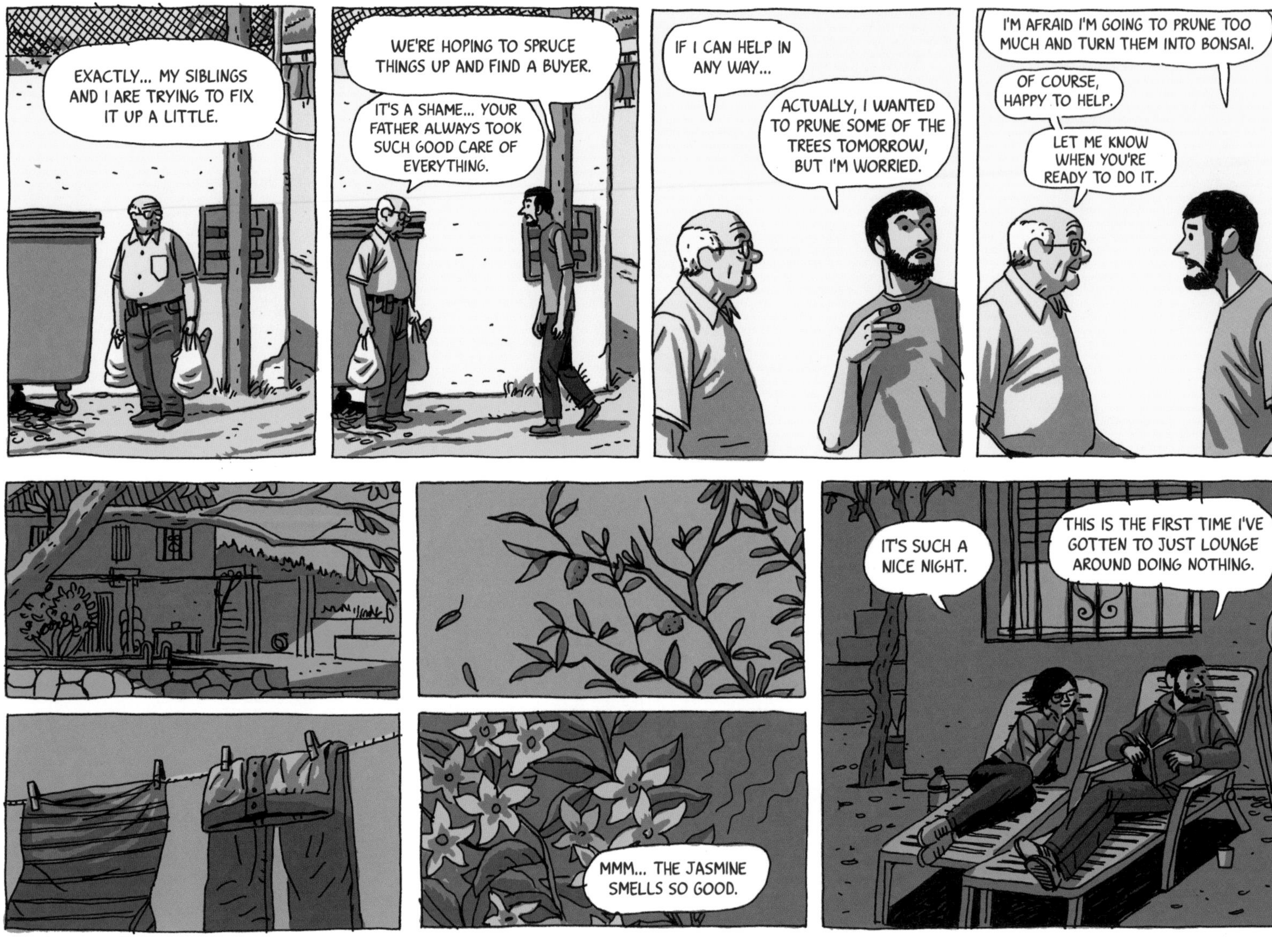
EXACTLY... MY SIBLINGS AND I ARE TRYING TO FIX IT UP A LITTLE.
WE'RE HOPING TO SPRUCE THINGS UP AND FIND A BUYER.
IT'S A SHAME... YOUR FATHER ALWAYS TOOK SUCH GOOD CARE OF EVERYTHING.
IF I CAN HELP IN ANY WAY...
ACTUALLY, I WANTED TO PRUNE SOME OF THE TREES TOMORROW, BUT I'M WORRIED.
I'M AFRAID I'M GOING TO PRUNE TOO MUCH AND TURN THEM INTO BONSAI.
OF COURSE, HAPPY TO HELP.
LET ME KNOW WHEN YOU'RE READY TO DO IT.
MMM... THE JASMINE SMELLS SO GOOD.
IT'S SUCH A NICE NIGHT.
THIS IS THE FIRST TIME I'VE GOTTEN TO JUST LOUNGE AROUND DOING NOTHING.

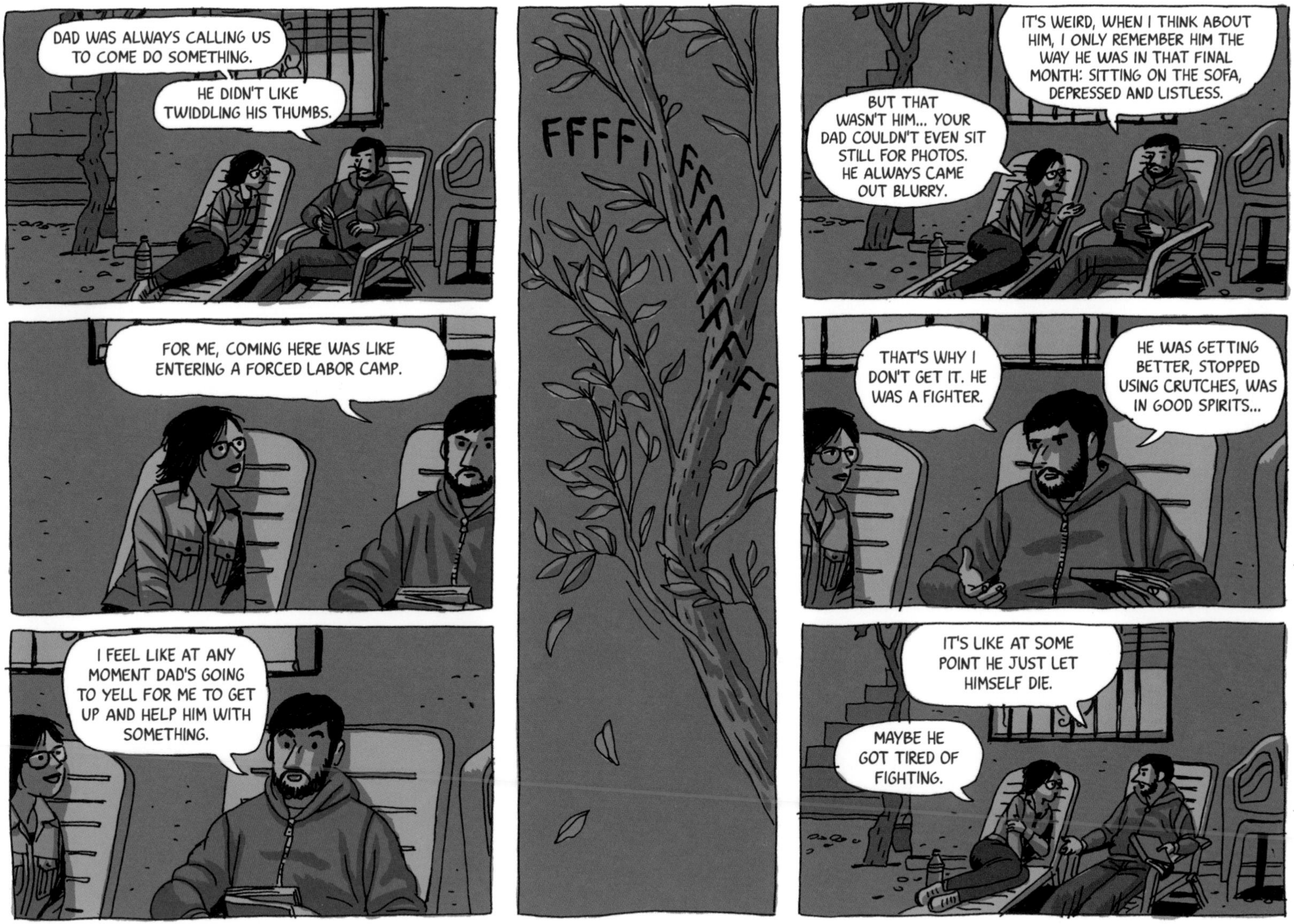
DAD WAS ALWAYS CALLING US TO COME DO SOMETHING.
HE DIDN'T LIKE TWIDDLING HIS THUMBS.
FOR ME, COMING HERE WAS LIKE ENTERING A FORCED LABOR CAMP.
I FEEL LIKE AT ANY MOMENT DAD'S GOING TO YELL FOR ME TO GET UP AND HELP HIM WITH SOMETHING.
FFFFFFFFFFFFFF
IT'S WEIRD, WHEN I THINK ABOUT HIM, I ONLY REMEMBER HIM THE WAY HE WAS IN THAT FINAL MONTH: SITTING ON THE SOFA, DEPRESSED AND LISTLESS.
BUT THAT WASN'T HIM... YOUR DAD COULDN'T EVEN SIT STILL FOR PHOTOS. HE ALWAYS CAME OUT BLURRY.
THAT'S WHY I DON'T GET IT. HE WAS A FIGHTER.
HE WAS GETTING BETTER, STOPPED USING CRUTCHES, WAS IN GOOD SPIRITS...
IT'S LIKE AT SOME POINT HE JUST LET HIMSELF DIE.
MAYBE HE GOT TIRED OF FIGHTING.

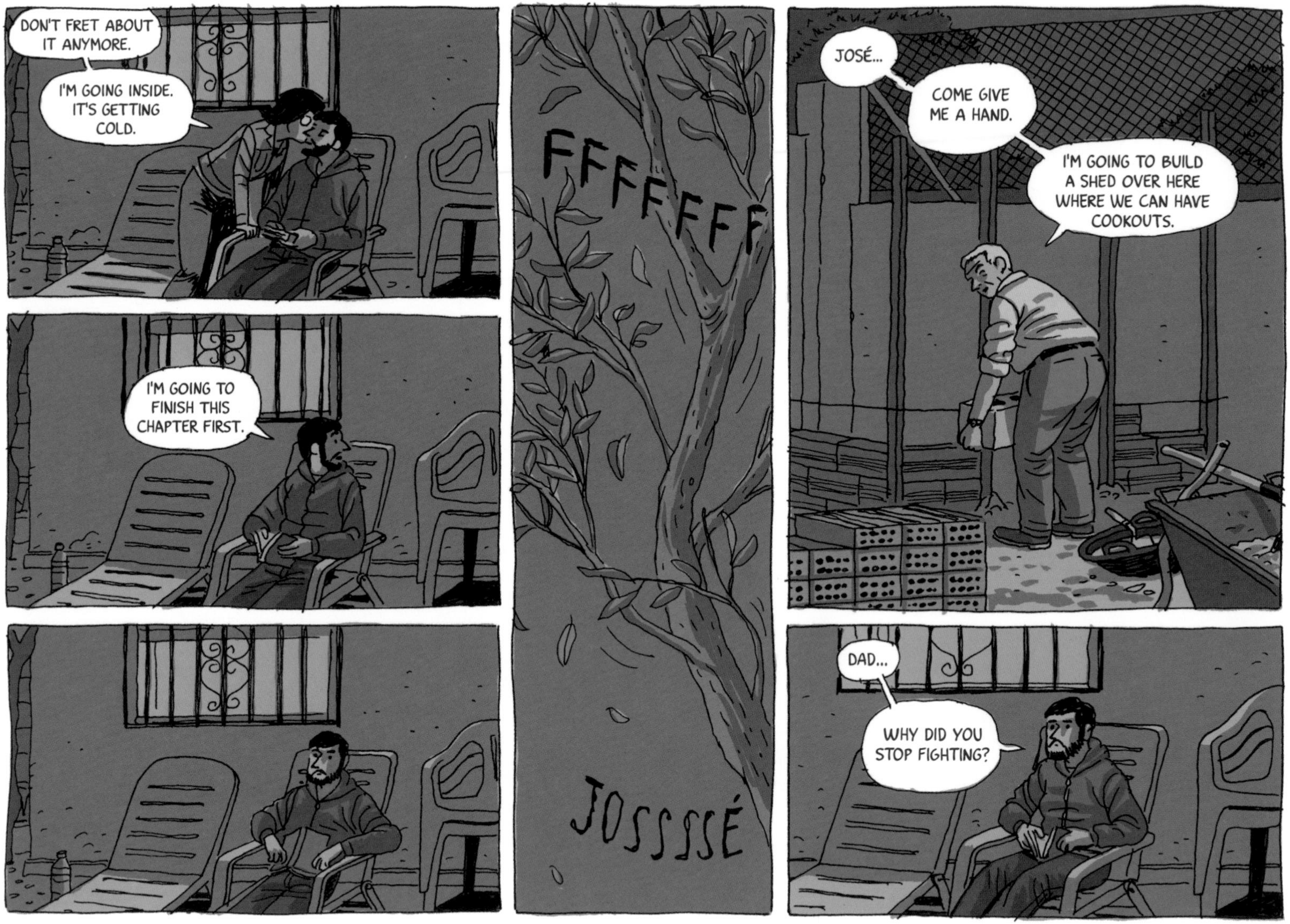
DON'T FRET ABOUT IT ANYMORE.
I'M GOING INSIDE. IT'S GETTING COLD.
I'M GOING TO FINISH THIS CHAPTER FIRST.
FFFFFFF
JOSSSSÉ
JOSÉ...
COME GIVE ME A HAND.
I'M GOING TO BUILD A SHED OVER HERE WHERE WE CAN HAVE COOKOUTS.
DAD...
WHY DID YOU STOP FIGHTING?

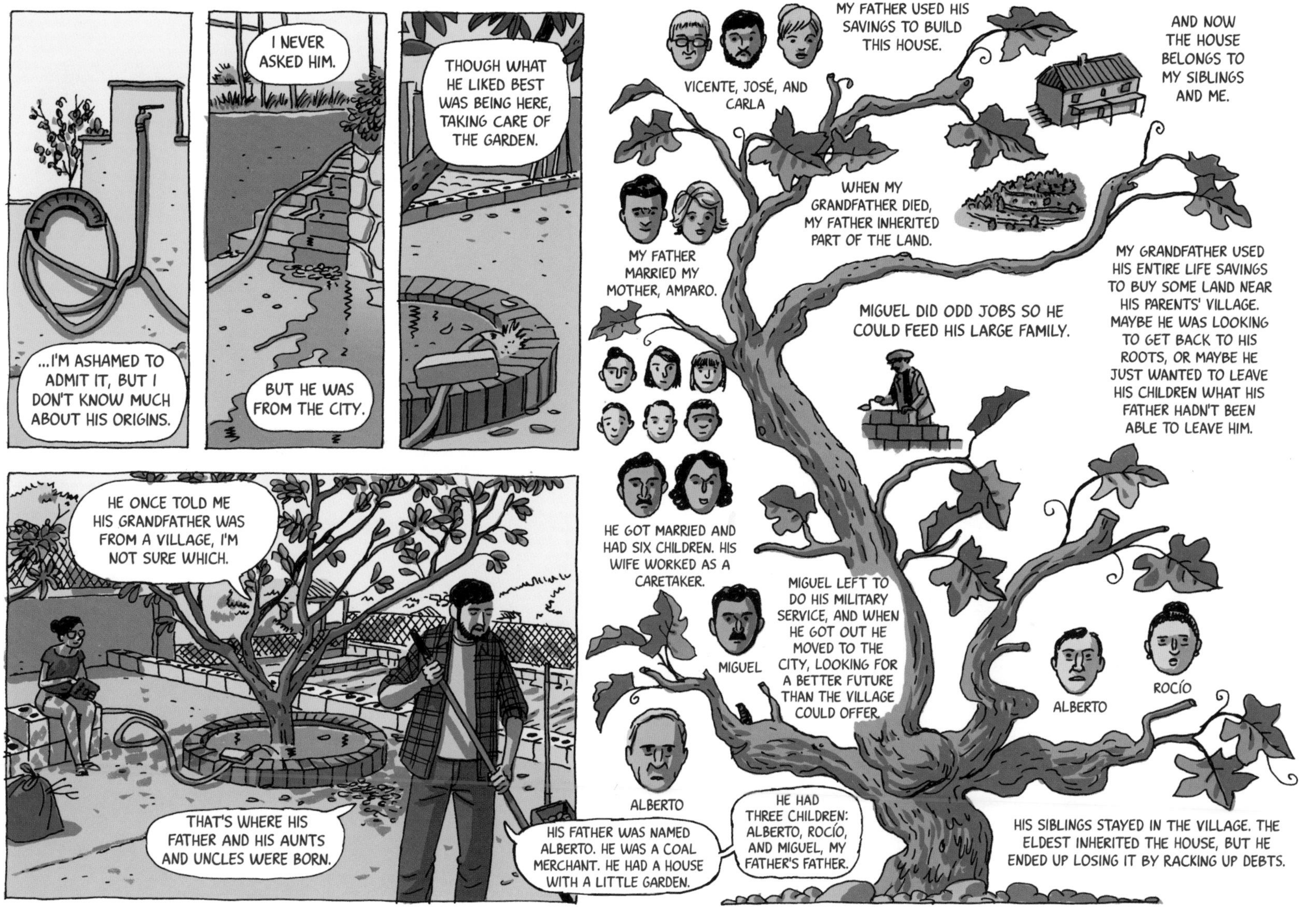
...I'M ASHAMED TO ADMIT IT, BUT I DON'T KNOW MUCH ABOUT HIS ORIGINS.
I NEVER ASKED HIM.
BUT HE WAS FROM THE CITY.
THOUGH WHAT HE LIKED BEST WAS BEING HERE, TAKING CARE OF THE GARDEN.
HE ONCE TOLD ME HIS GRANDFATHER WAS FROM A VILLAGE, I'M NOT SURE WHICH.
THAT'S WHERE HIS FATHER AND HIS AUNTS AND UNCLES WERE BORN.
HIS FATHER WAS NAMED ALBERTO. HE WAS A COAL MERCHANT. HE HAD A HOUSE WITH A LITTLE GARDEN.
HE HAD THREE CHILDREN: ALBERTO, ROCÍO, AND MIGUEL, MY FATHER'S FATHER.
ALBERTO
ALBERTO
ROCÍO
HIS SIBLINGS STAYED IN THE VILLAGE. THE ELDEST INHERITED THE HOUSE, BUT HE ENDED UP LOSING IT BY RACKING UP DEBTS.
MIGUEL
MIGUEL LEFT TO DO HIS MILITARY SERVICE, AND WHEN HE GOT OUT HE MOVED TO THE CITY, LOOKING FOR A BETTER FUTURE THAN THE VILLAGE COULD OFFER.
HE GOT MARRIED AND HAD SIX CHILDREN. HIS WIFE WORKED AS A CARETAKER.
MIGUEL DID ODD JOBS SO HE COULD FEED HIS LARGE FAMILY.
MY GRANDFATHER USED HIS ENTIRE LIFE SAVINGS TO BUY SOME LAND NEAR HIS PARENTS' VILLAGE. MAYBE HE WAS LOOKING TO GET BACK TO HIS ROOTS, OR MAYBE HE JUST WANTED TO LEAVE HIS CHILDREN WHAT HIS FATHER HADN'T BEEN ABLE TO LEAVE HIM.
WHEN MY GRANDFATHER DIED, MY FATHER INHERITED PART OF THE LAND.
MY FATHER MARRIED MY MOTHER, AMPARO.
MY FATHER USED HIS SAVINGS TO BUILD THIS HOUSE.
VICENTE, JOSÉ, AND CARLA
AND NOW THE HOUSE BELONGS TO MY SIBLINGS AND ME.

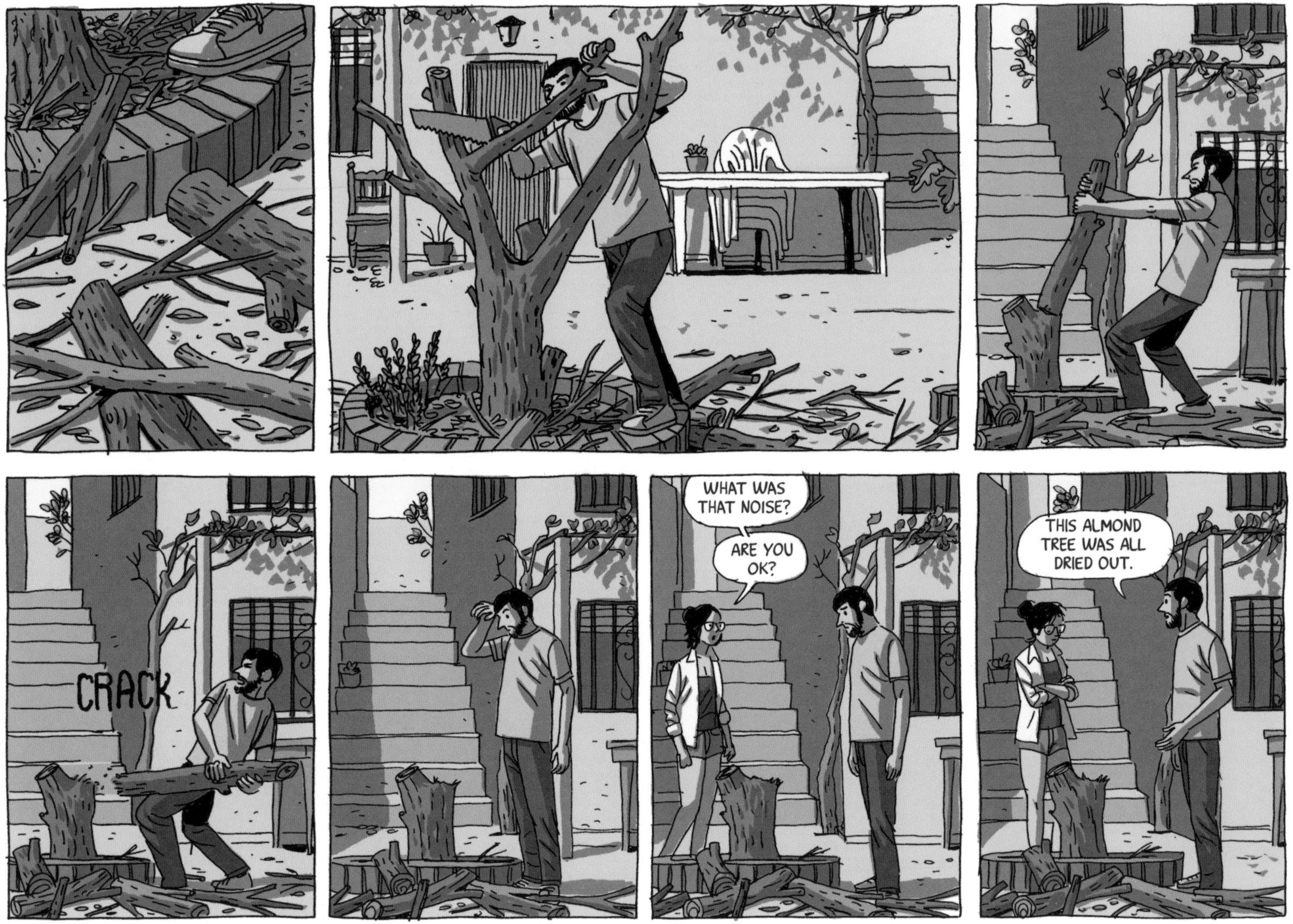
CRACK
WHAT WAS THAT NOISE?
ARE YOU OK?
THIS ALMOND TREE WAS ALL DRIED OUT.

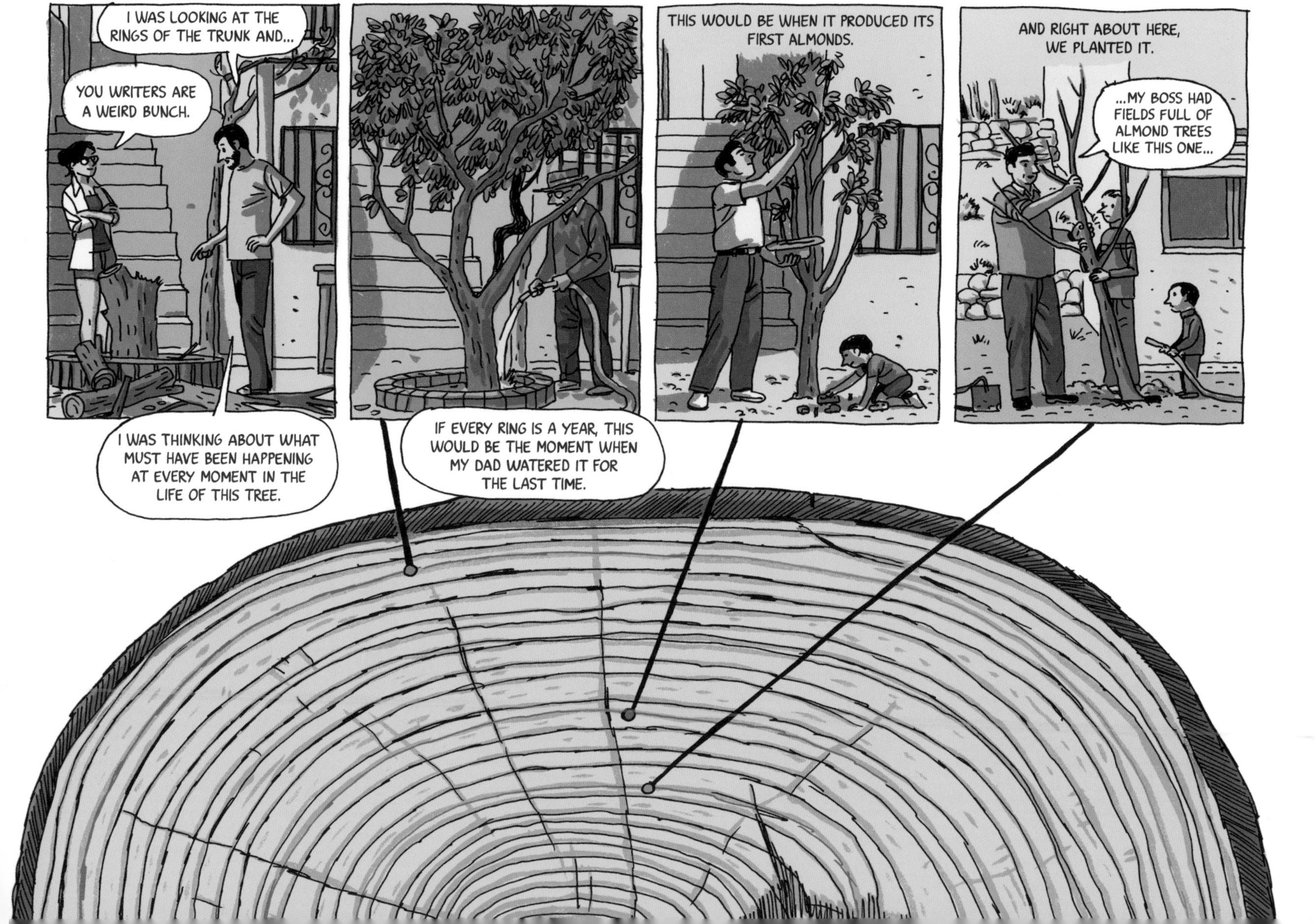
I WAS LOOKING AT THE RINGS OF THE TRUNK AND...
YOU WRITERS ARE A WEIRD BUNCH.
I WAS THINKING ABOUT WHAT MUST HAVE BEEN HAPPENING AT EVERY MOMENT IN THE LIFE OF THIS TREE.
IF EVERY RING IS A YEAR, THIS WOULD BE THE MOMENT WHEN MY DAD WATERED IT FOR THE LAST TIME.
THIS WOULD BE WHEN IT PRODUCED ITS FIRST ALMONDS.
AND RIGHT ABOUT HERE, WE PLANTED IT.
...MY BOSS HAD FIELDS FULL OF ALMOND TREES LIKE THIS ONE...

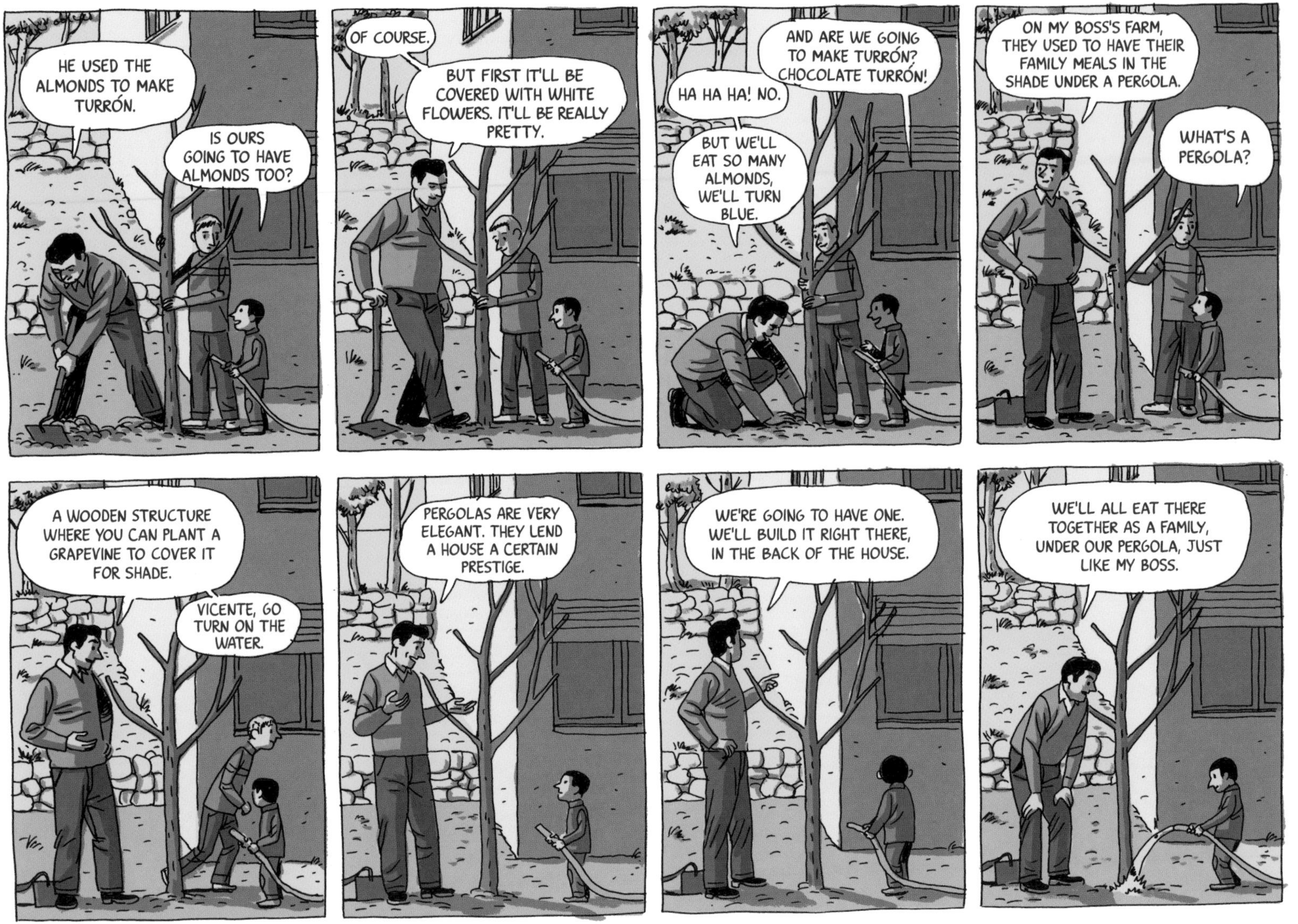
HE USED THE ALMONDS TO MAKE TURRÓN.
IS OURS GOING TO HAVE ALMONDS TOO?
OF COURSE.
BUT FIRST IT'LL BE COVERED WITH WHITE FLOWERS. IT'LL BE REALLY PRETTY.
AND ARE WE GOING TO MAKE TURRÓN? CHOCOLATE TURRÓN!
HA HA HA! NO.
BUT WE'LL EAT SO MANY ALMONDS, WE'LL TURN BLUE.
ON MY BOSS'S FARM, THEY USED TO HAVE THEIR FAMILY MEALS IN THE SHADE UNDER A PERGOLA.
WHAT'S A PERGOLA?
A WOODEN STRUCTURE WHERE YOU CAN PLANT A GRAPEVINE TO COVER IT FOR SHADE.
VICENTE, GO TURN ON THE WATER.
PERGOLAS ARE VERY ELEGANT. THEY LEND A HOUSE A CERTAIN PRESTIGE.
WE'RE GOING TO HAVE ONE. WE'LL BUILD IT RIGHT THERE, IN THE BACK OF THE HOUSE.
WE'LL ALL EAT THERE TOGETHER AS A FAMILY, UNDER OUR PERGOLA, JUST LIKE MY BOSS.

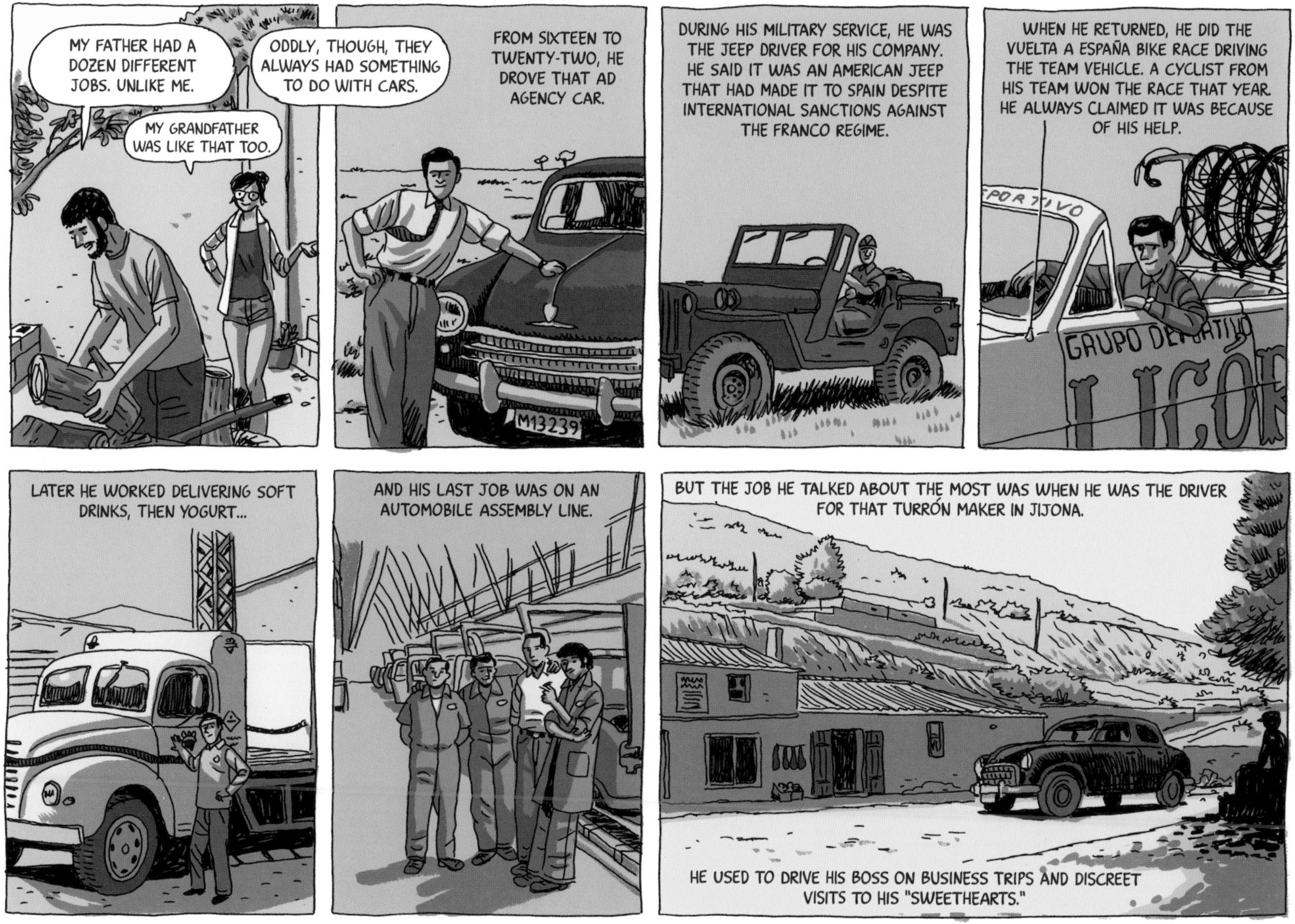
MY FATHER HAD A DOZEN DIFFERENT JOBS. UNLIKE ME.
ODDLY, THOUGH, THEY ALWAYS HAD SOMETHING TO DO WITH CARS.
MY GRANDFATHER WAS LIKE THAT TOO.
FROM SIXTEEN TO TWENTY-TWO, HE DROVE THAT AD AGENCY CAR.
M13239
DURING HIS MILITARY SERVICE, HE WAS THE JEEP DRIVER FOR HIS COMPANY. HE SAID IT WAS AN AMERICAN JEEP THAT HAD MADE IT TO SPAIN DESPITE INTERNATIONAL SANCTIONS AGAINST THE FRANCO REGIME.
WHEN HE RETURNED, HE DID THE VUELTA A ESPAÑA BIKE RACE DRIVING THE TEAM VEHICLE. A CYCLIST FROM HIS TEAM WON THE RACE THAT YEAR. HE ALWAYS CLAIMED IT WAS BECAUSE OF HIS HELP.
LATER HE WORKED DELIVERING SOFT DRINKS, THEN YOGURT...
AND HIS LAST JOB WAS ON AN AUTOMOBILE ASSEMBLY LINE.
BUT THE JOB HE TALKED ABOUT THE MOST WAS WHEN HE WAS THE DRIVER FOR THAT TURRÓN MAKER IN JIJONA.
HE USED TO DRIVE HIS BOSS ON BUSINESS TRIPS AND DISCREET VISITS TO HIS "SWEETHEARTS."

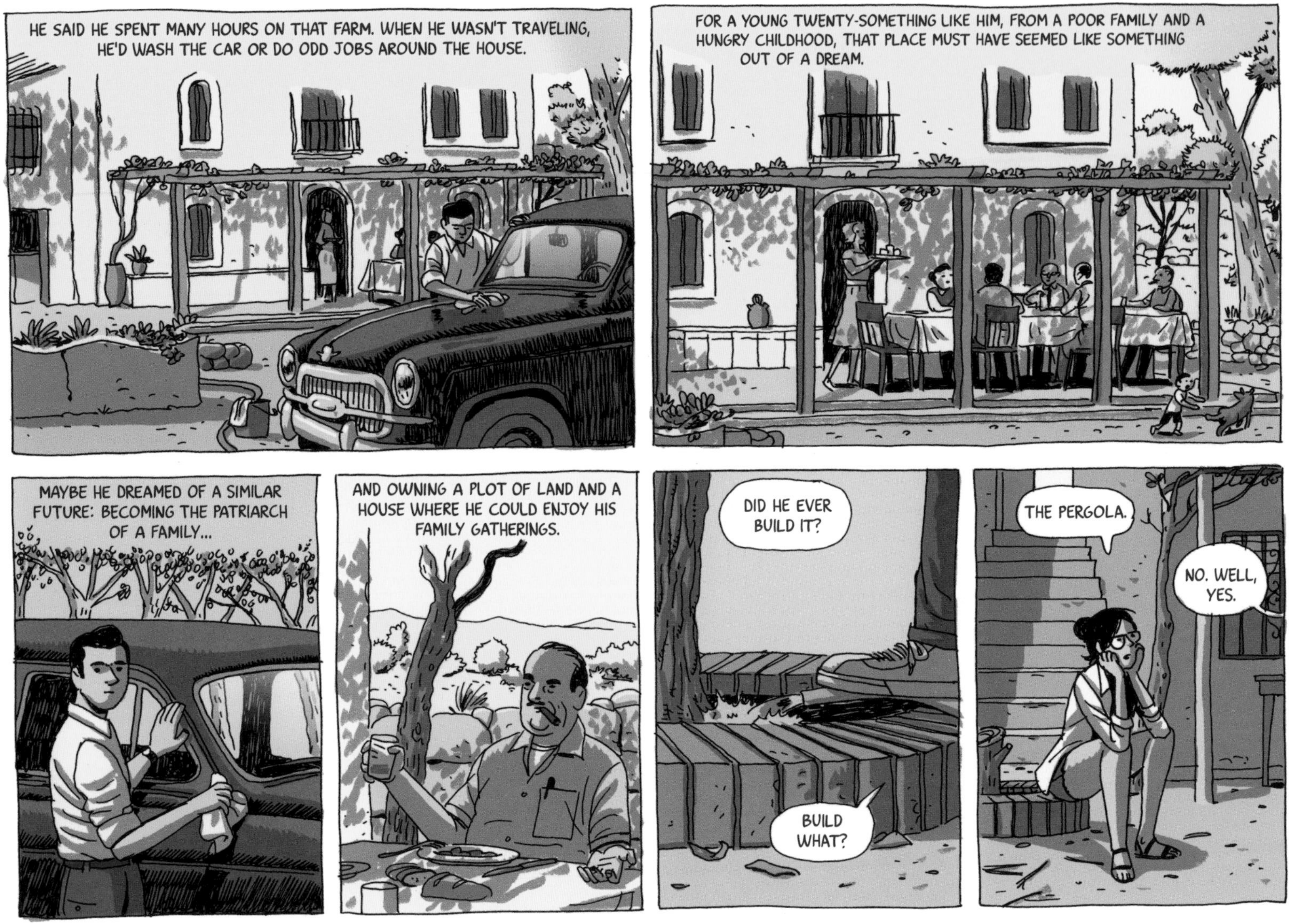
HE SAID HE SPENT MANY HOURS ON THAT FARM. WHEN HE WASN'T TRAVELING, HE'D WASH THE CAR OR DO ODD JOBS AROUND THE HOUSE.
FOR A YOUNG TWENTY-SOMETHING LIKE HIM, FROM A POOR FAMILY AND A HUNGRY CHILDHOOD, THAT PLACE MUST HAVE SEEMED LIKE SOMETHING OUT OF A DREAM.
MAYBE HE DREAMED OF A SIMILAR FUTURE: BECOMING THE PATRIARCH OF A FAMILY...
AND OWNING A PLOT OF LAND AND A HOUSE WHERE HE COULD ENJOY HIS FAMILY GATHERINGS.
DID HE EVER BUILD IT?
BUILD WHAT?
THE PERGOLA.
NO. WELL, YES.

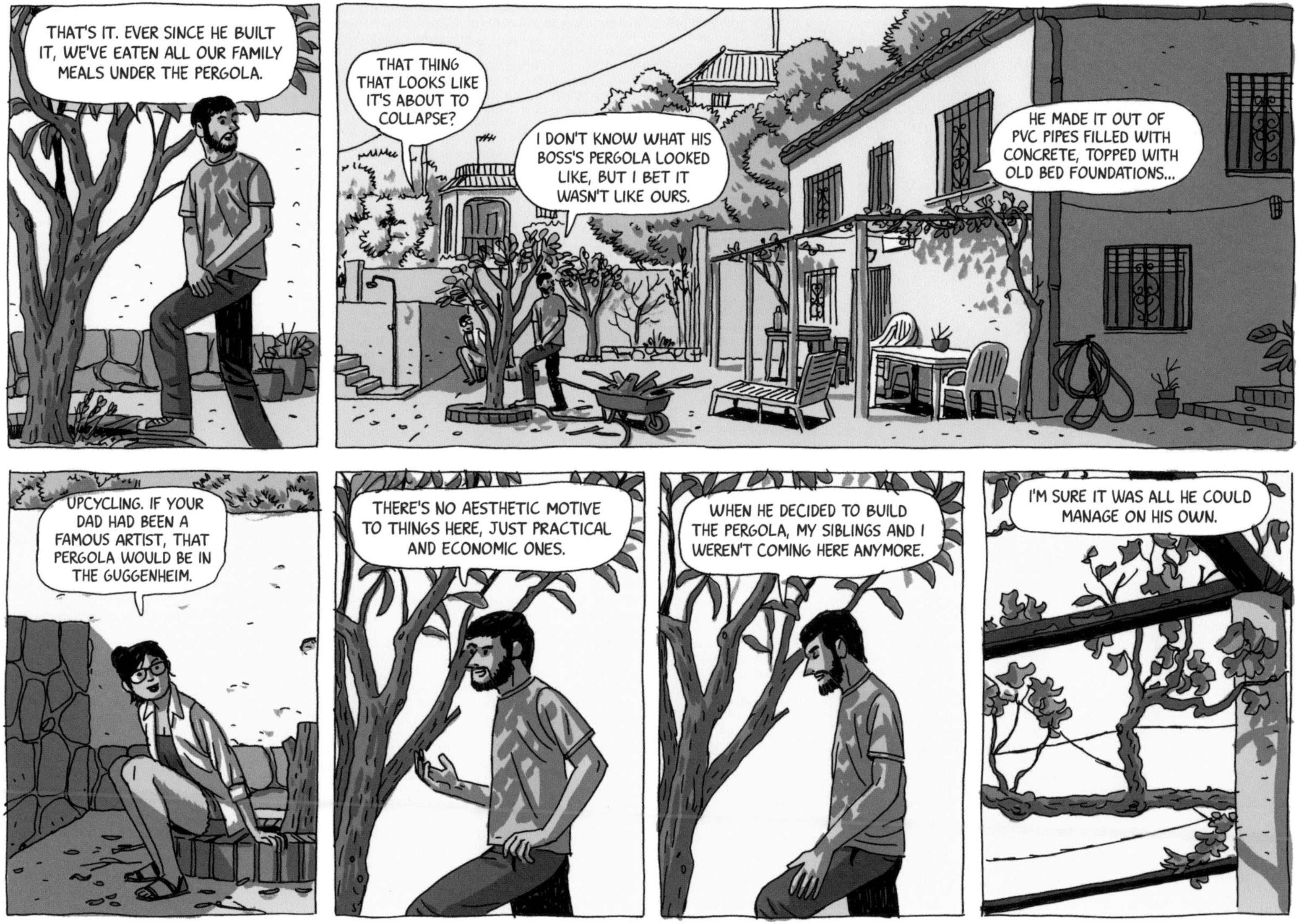
THAT'S IT. EVER SINCE HE BUILT IT, WE'VE EATEN ALL OUR FAMILY MEALS UNDER THE PERGOLA.
THAT THING THAT LOOKS LIKE IT'S ABOUT TO COLLAPSE?
I DON'T KNOW WHAT HIS BOSS'S PERGOLA LOOKED LIKE, BUT I BET IT WASN'T LIKE OURS.
HE MADE IT OUT OF PVC PIPES FILLED WITH CONCRETE, TOPPED WITH OLD BED FOUNDATIONS...
UPCYCLING. IF YOUR DAD HAD BEEN A FAMOUS ARTIST, THAT PERGOLA WOULD BE IN THE GUGGENHEIM.
THERE'S NO AESTHETIC MOTIVE TO THINGS HERE, JUST PRACTICAL AND ECONOMIC ONES.
WHEN HE DECIDED TO BUILD THE PERGOLA, MY SIBLINGS AND I WEREN'T COMING HERE ANYMORE.
I'M SURE IT WAS ALL HE COULD MANAGE ON HIS OWN.

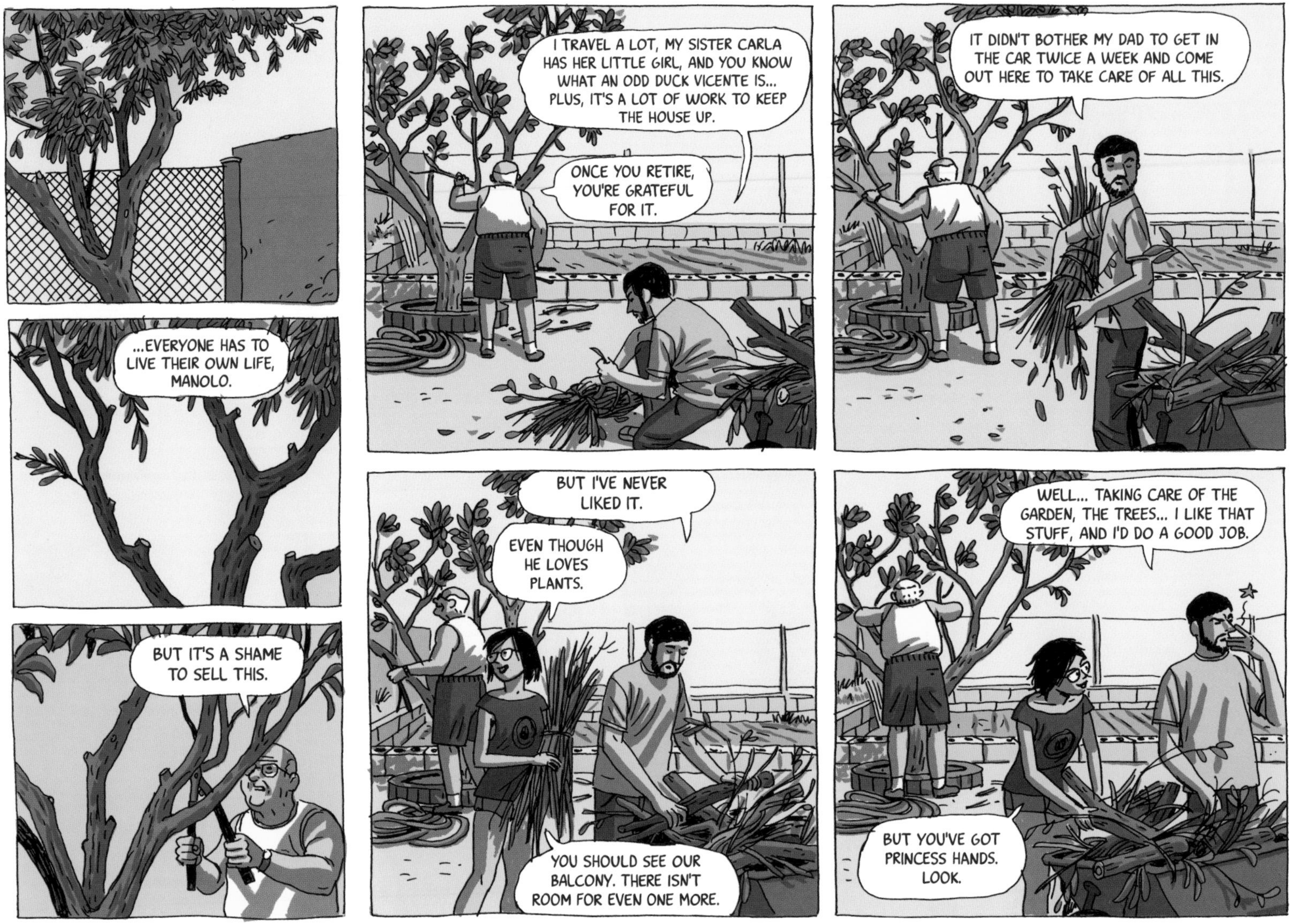
...EVERYONE HAS TO LIVE THEIR OWN LIFE, MANOLO.
BUT IT'S A SHAME TO SELL THIS.
I TRAVEL A LOT, MY SISTER CARLA HAS HER LITTLE GIRL, AND YOU KNOW WHAT AN ODD DUCK VICENTE IS... PLUS, IT'S A LOT OF WORK TO KEEP THE HOUSE UP.
ONCE YOU RETIRE, YOU'RE GRATEFUL FOR IT.
IT DIDN'T BOTHER MY DAD TO GET IN THE CAR TWICE A WEEK AND COME OUT HERE TO TAKE CARE OF ALL THIS.
BUT I'VE NEVER LIKED IT.
EVEN THOUGH HE LOVES PLANTS.
YOU SHOULD SEE OUR BALCONY. THERE ISN'T ROOM FOR EVEN ONE MORE.
WELL... TAKING CARE OF THE GARDEN, THE TREES... I LIKE THAT STUFF, AND I'D DO A GOOD JOB.
BUT YOU'VE GOT PRINCESS HANDS. LOOK.

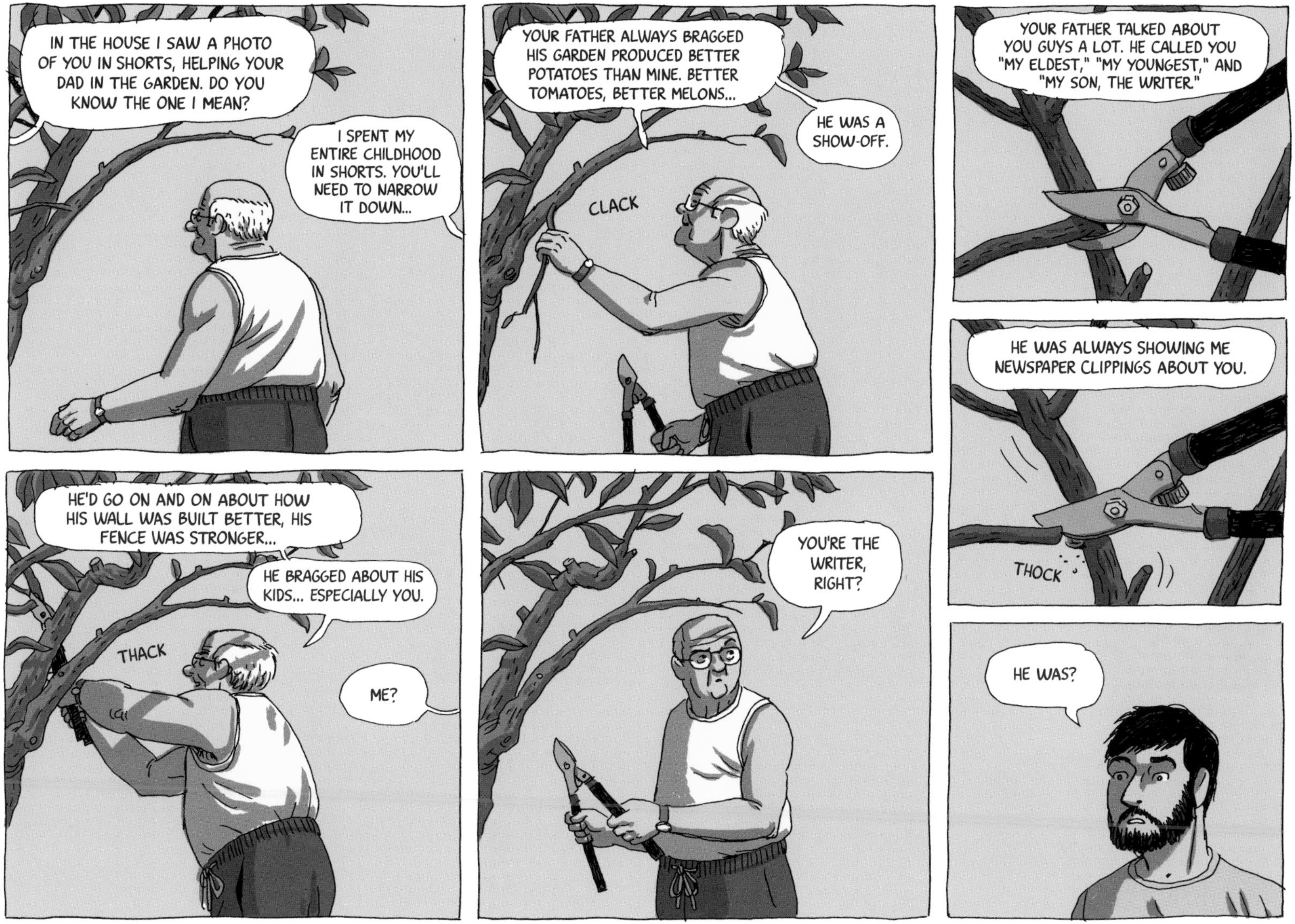
IN THE HOUSE I SAW A PHOTO OF YOU IN SHORTS, HELPING YOUR DAD IN THE GARDEN. DO YOU KNOW THE ONE I MEAN?
I SPENT MY ENTIRE CHILDHOOD IN SHORTS. YOU'LL NEED TO NARROW IT DOWN...
YOUR FATHER ALWAYS BRAGGED HIS GARDEN PRODUCED BETTER POTATOES THAN MINE. BETTER TOMATOES, BETTER MELONS...
HE WAS A SHOW-OFF.
CLACK
YOUR FATHER TALKED ABOUT YOU GUYS A LOT. HE CALLED YOU "MY ELDEST," "MY YOUNGEST," AND "MY SON, THE WRITER."
HE WAS ALWAYS SHOWING ME NEWSPAPER CLIPPINGS ABOUT YOU.
THOCK
HE'D GO ON AND ON ABOUT HOW HIS WALL WAS BUILT BETTER, HIS FENCE WAS STRONGER...
HE BRAGGED ABOUT HIS KIDS... ESPECIALLY YOU.
THACK
ME?
YOU'RE THE WRITER, RIGHT?
HE WAS?

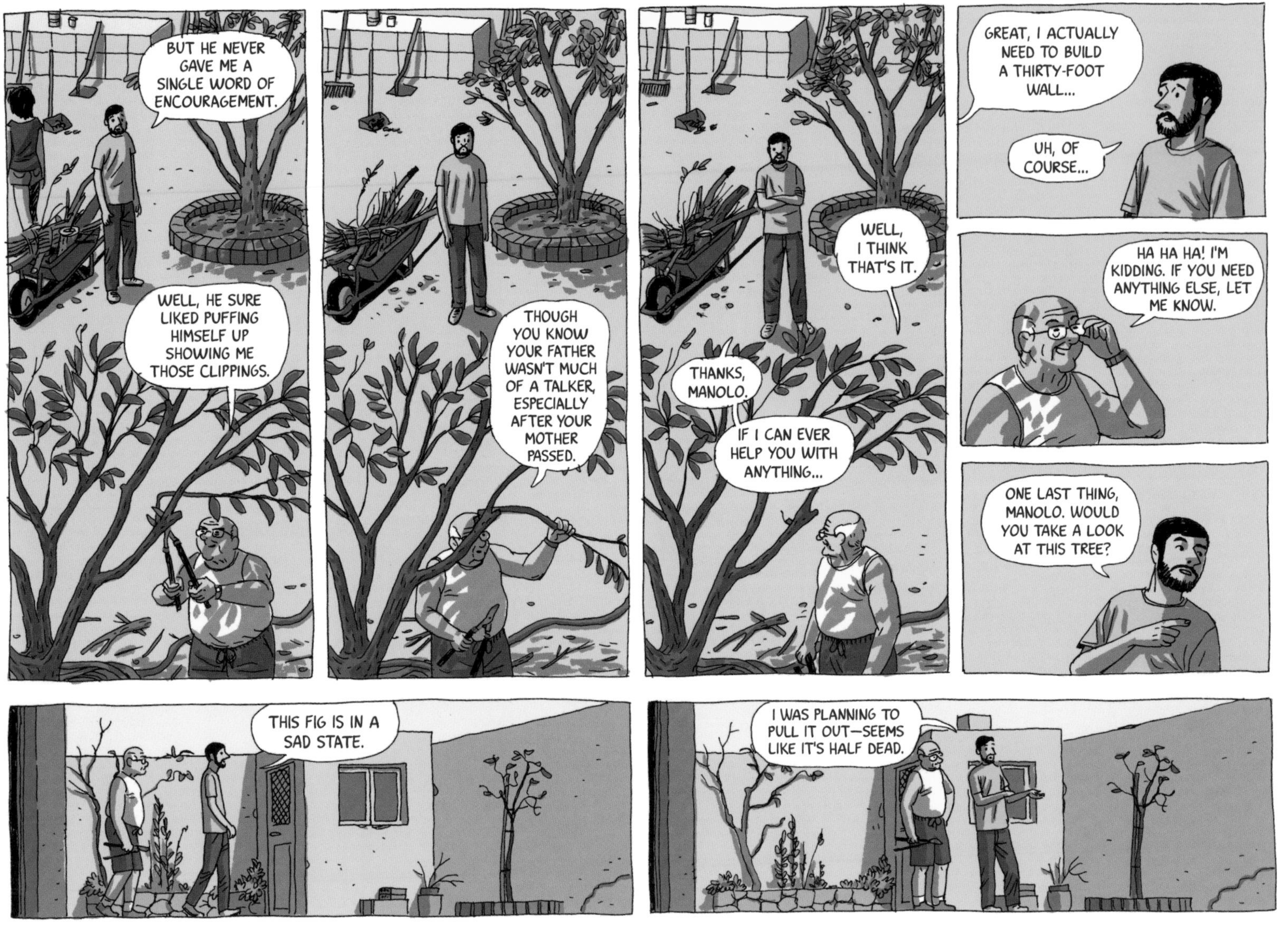
BUT HE NEVER GAVE ME A SINGLE WORD OF ENCOURAGEMENT.
WELL, HE SURE LIKED PUFFING HIMSELF UP SHOWING ME THOSE CLIPPINGS.
THOUGH YOU KNOW YOUR FATHER WASN'T MUCH OF A TALKER, ESPECIALLY AFTER YOUR MOTHER PASSED.
WELL, I THINK THAT'S IT.
THANKS, MANOLO.
IF I CAN EVER HELP YOU WITH ANYTHING...
GREAT, I ACTUALLY NEED TO BUILD A THIRTY-FOOT WALL...
UH, OF COURSE...
HA HA HA! I'M KIDDING. IF YOU NEED ANYTHING ELSE, LET ME KNOW.
ONE LAST THING, MANOLO. WOULD YOU TAKE A LOOK AT THIS TREE?
THIS FIG IS IN A SAD STATE.
I WAS PLANNING TO PULL IT OUT—SEEMS LIKE IT'S HALF DEAD.

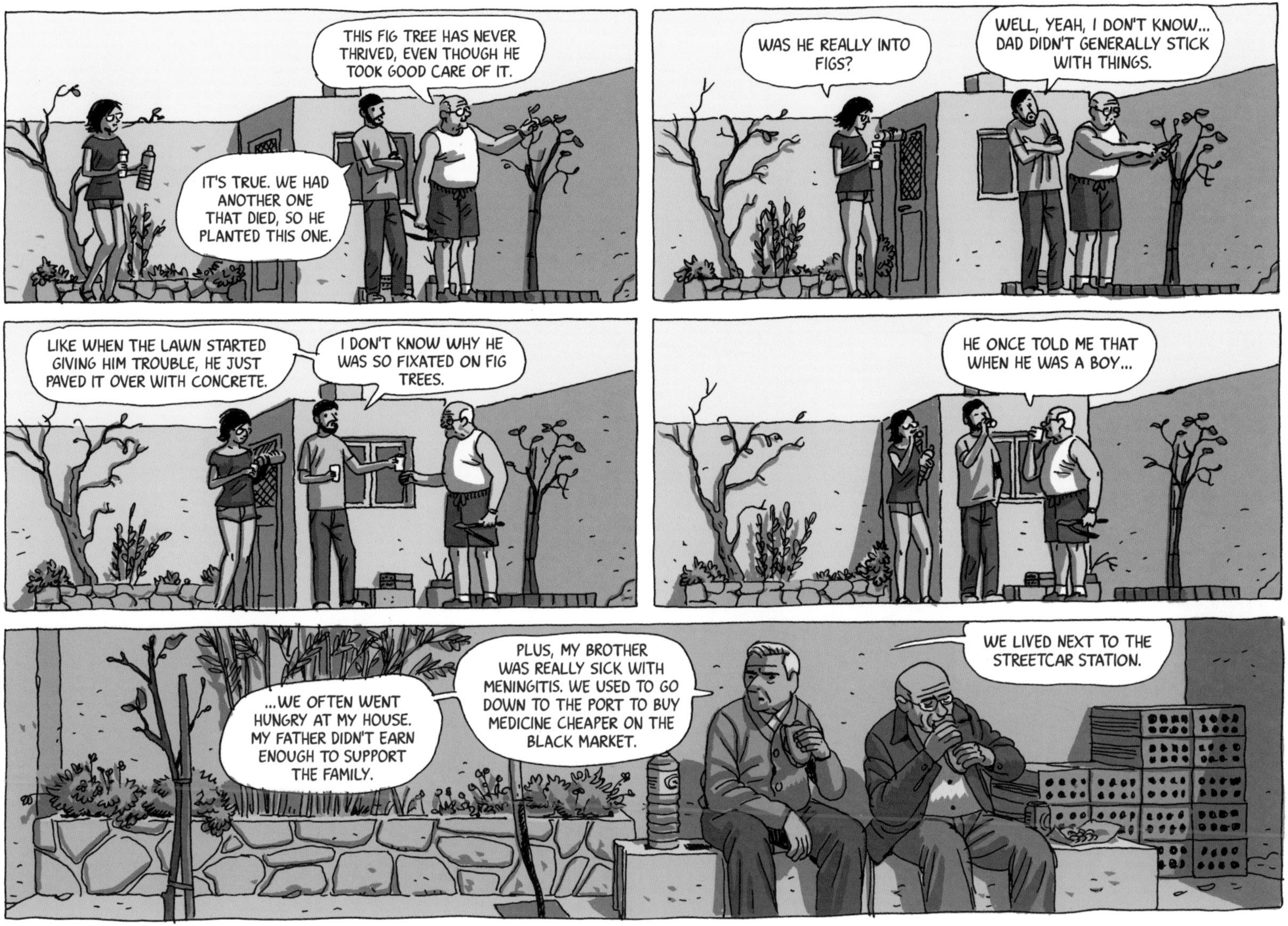
THIS FIG TREE HAS NEVER THRIVED, EVEN THOUGH HE TOOK GOOD CARE OF IT.
IT'S TRUE. WE HAD ANOTHER ONE THAT DIED, SO HE PLANTED THIS ONE.
WAS HE REALLY INTO FIGS?
WELL, YEAH, I DON'T KNOW... DAD DIDN'T GENERALLY STICK WITH THINGS.
LIKE WHEN THE LAWN STARTED GIVING HIM TROUBLE, HE JUST PAVED IT OVER WITH CONCRETE.
I DON'T KNOW WHY HE WAS SO FIXATED ON FIG TREES.
HE ONCE TOLD ME THAT WHEN HE WAS A BOY...
...WE OFTEN WENT HUNGRY AT MY HOUSE. MY FATHER DIDN'T EARN ENOUGH TO SUPPORT THE FAMILY.
PLUS, MY BROTHER WAS REALLY SICK WITH MENINGITIS. WE USED TO GO DOWN TO THE PORT TO BUY MEDICINE CHEAPER ON THE BLACK MARKET.
WE LIVED NEXT TO THE STREETCAR STATION.

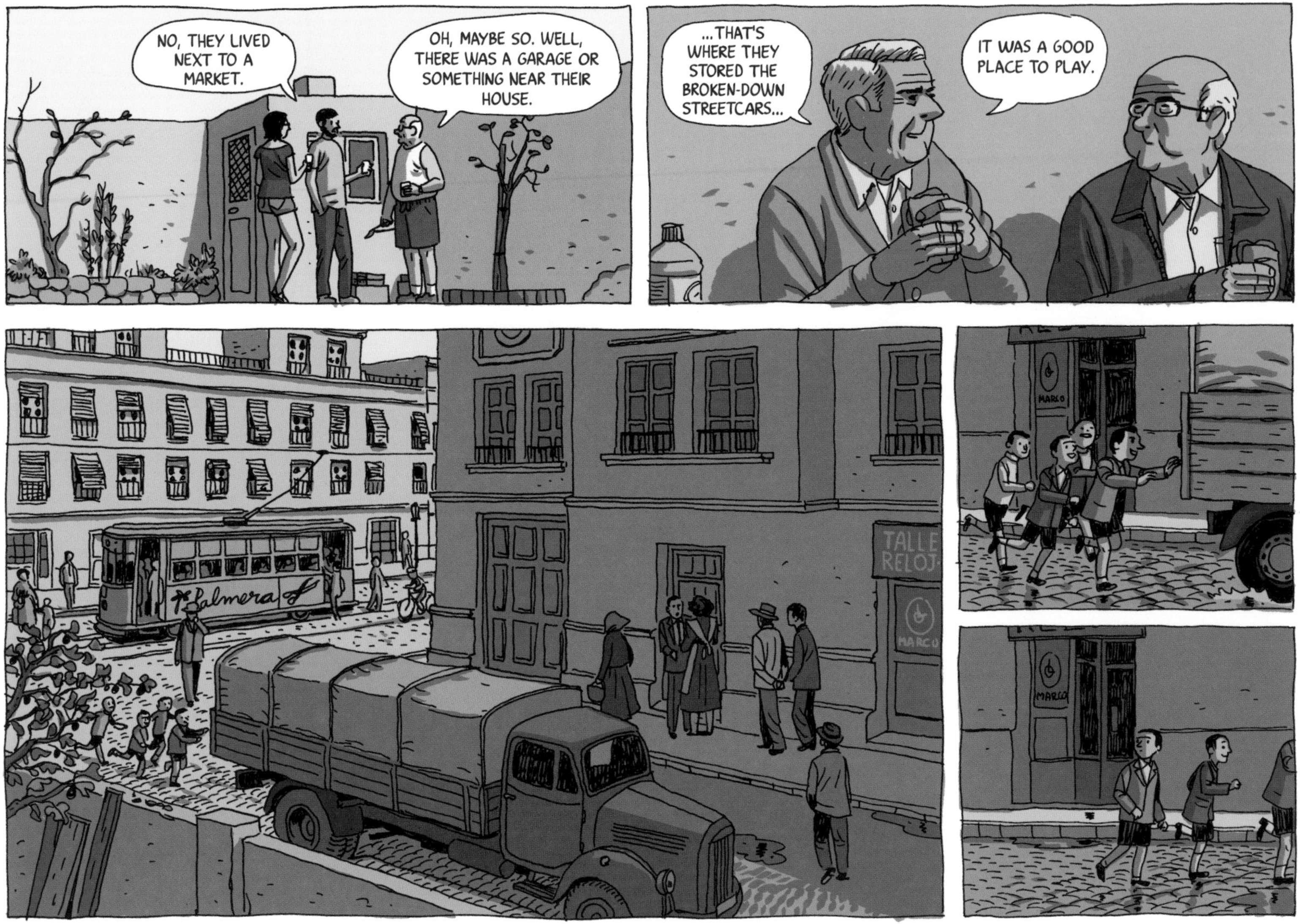
NO, THEY LIVED NEXT TO A MARKET.
OH, MAYBE SO. WELL, THERE WAS A GARAGE OR SOMETHING NEAR THEIR HOUSE.
...THAT'S WHERE THEY STORED THE BROKEN-DOWN STREETCARS...
IT WAS A GOOD PLACE TO PLAY.
Palmera
TALLE
RELOJ
MARCO

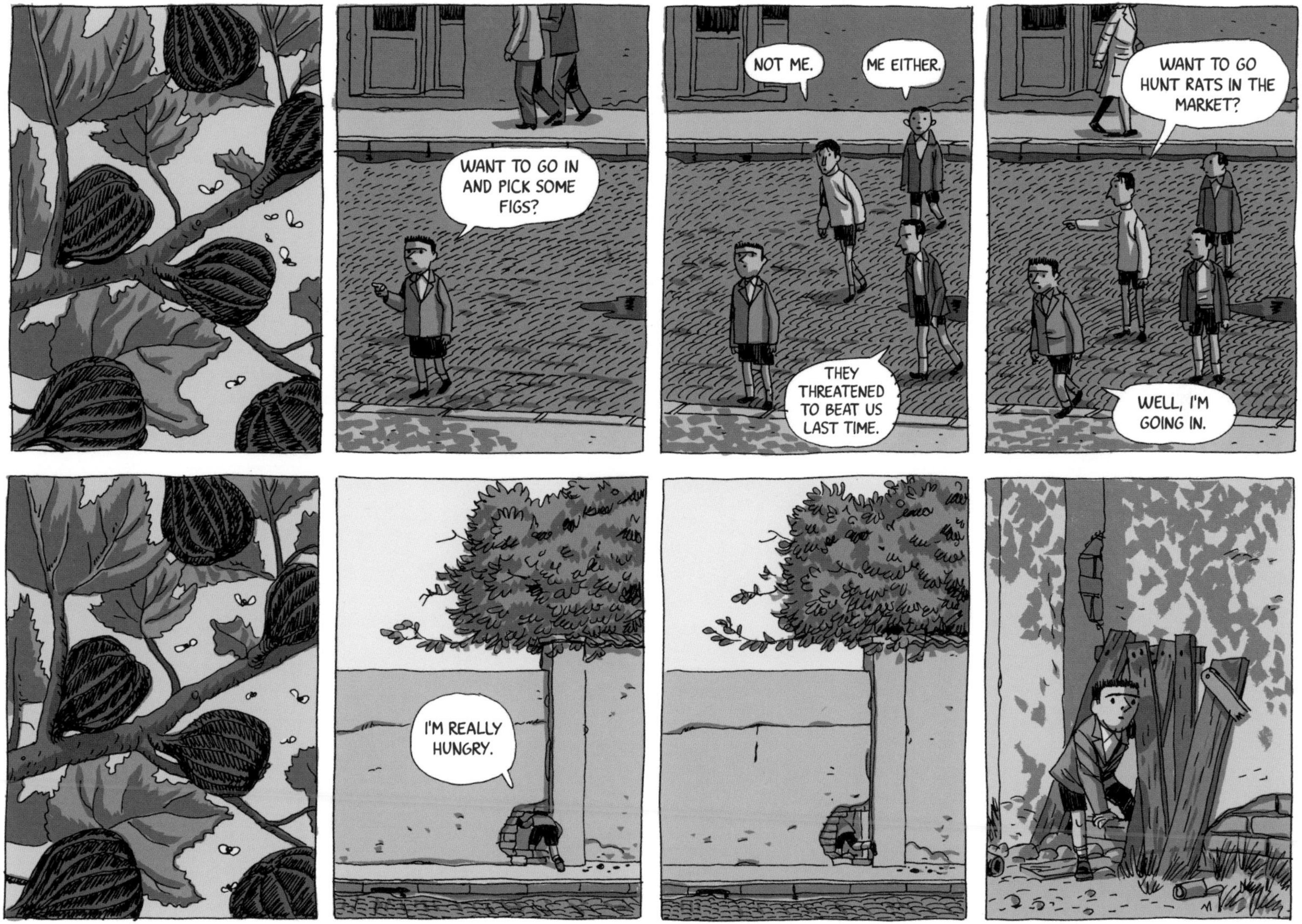
WANT TO GO IN AND PICK SOME FIGS?
NOT ME.
ME EITHER.
THEY THREATENED TO BEAT US LAST TIME.
WANT TO GO HUNT RATS IN THE MARKET?
WELL, I'M GOING IN.
I'M REALLY HUNGRY.

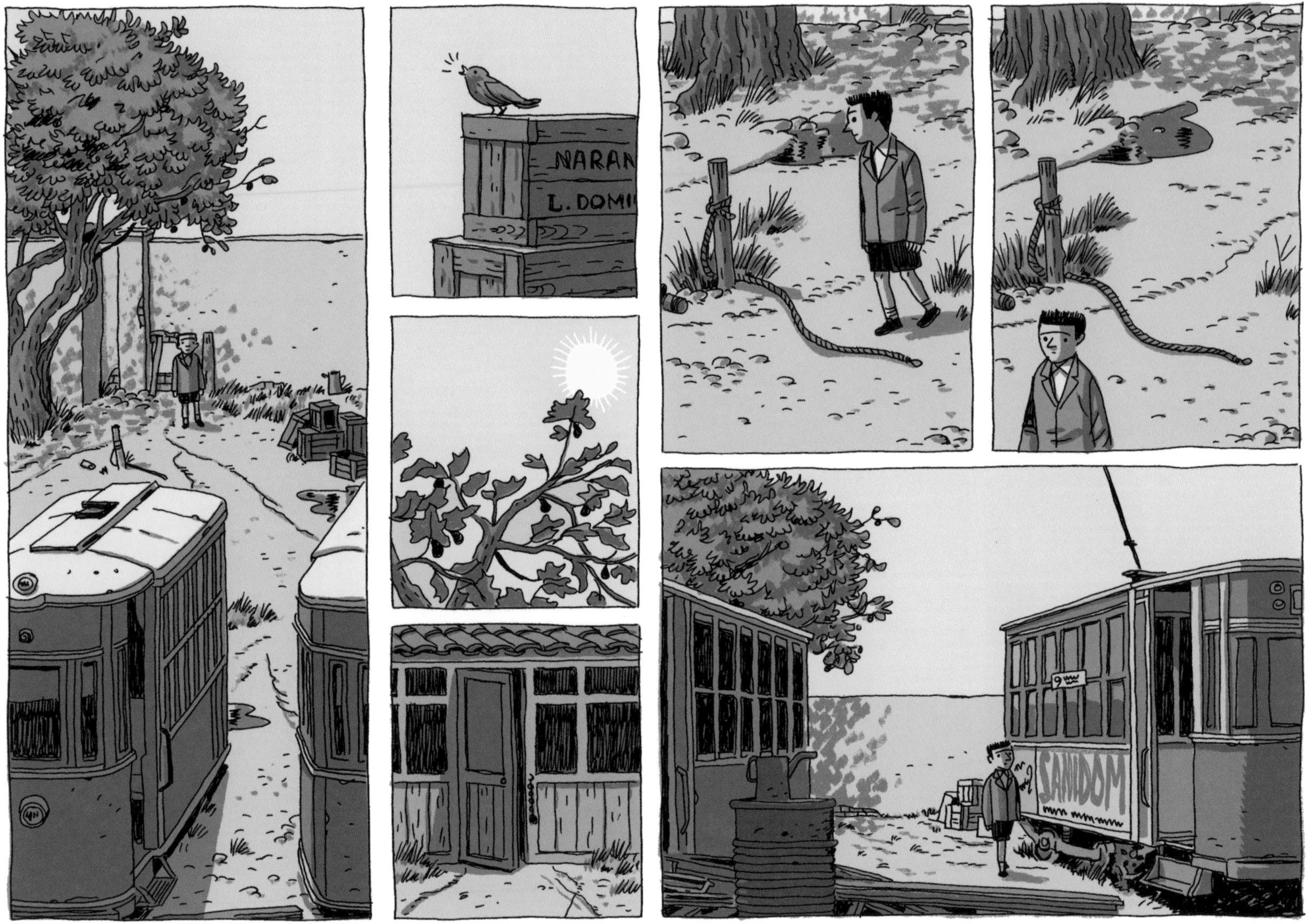
NARAN
L. DOMI
9
SANIDOM

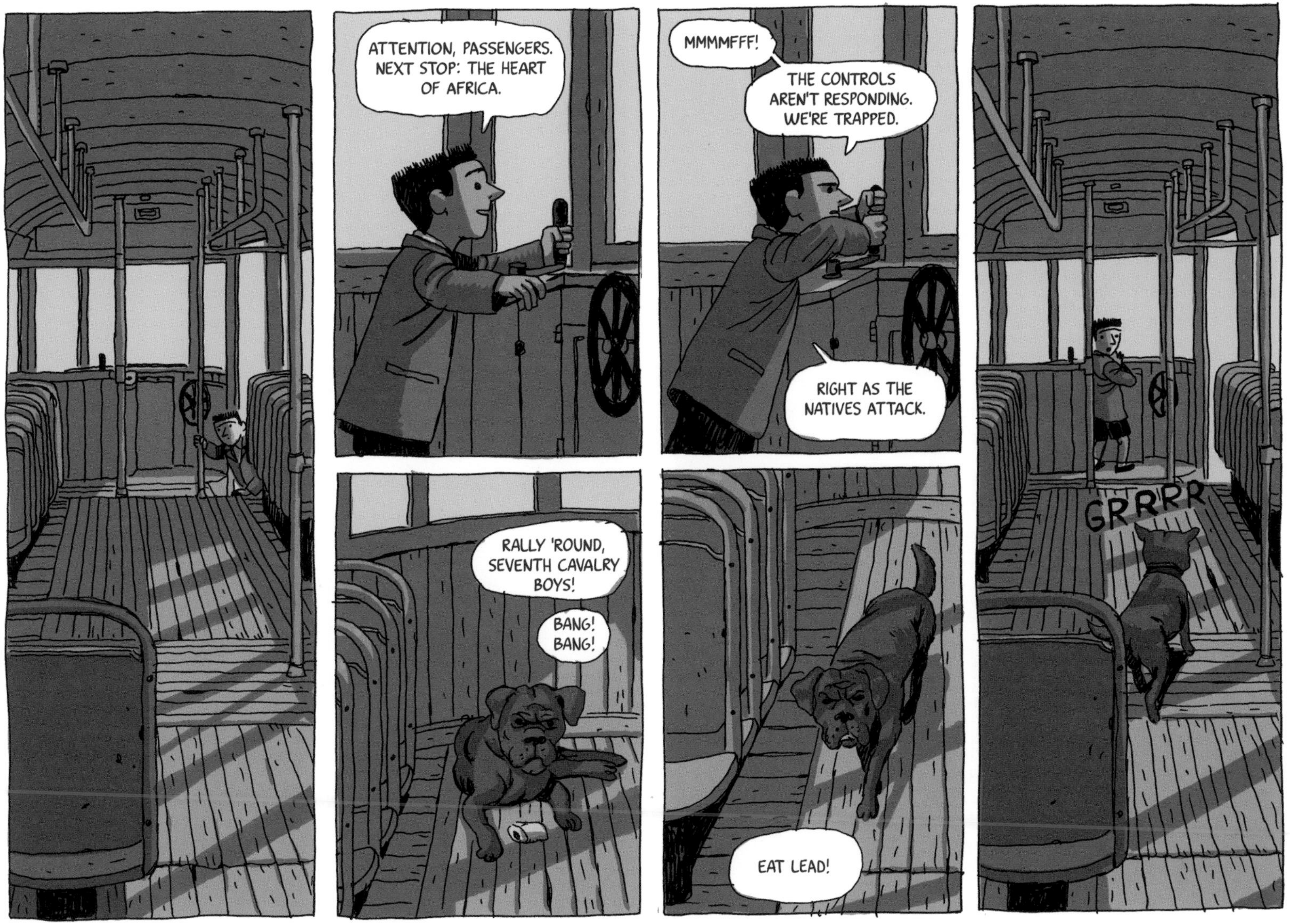
ATTENTION, PASSENGERS. NEXT STOP: THE HEART OF AFRICA.
MMMMFFF!
THE CONTROLS AREN'T RESPONDING. WE'RE TRAPPED.
RIGHT AS THE NATIVES ATTACK.
RALLY 'ROUND, SEVENTH CAVALRY BOYS!
BANG! BANG!
EAT LEAD!
GRRRR

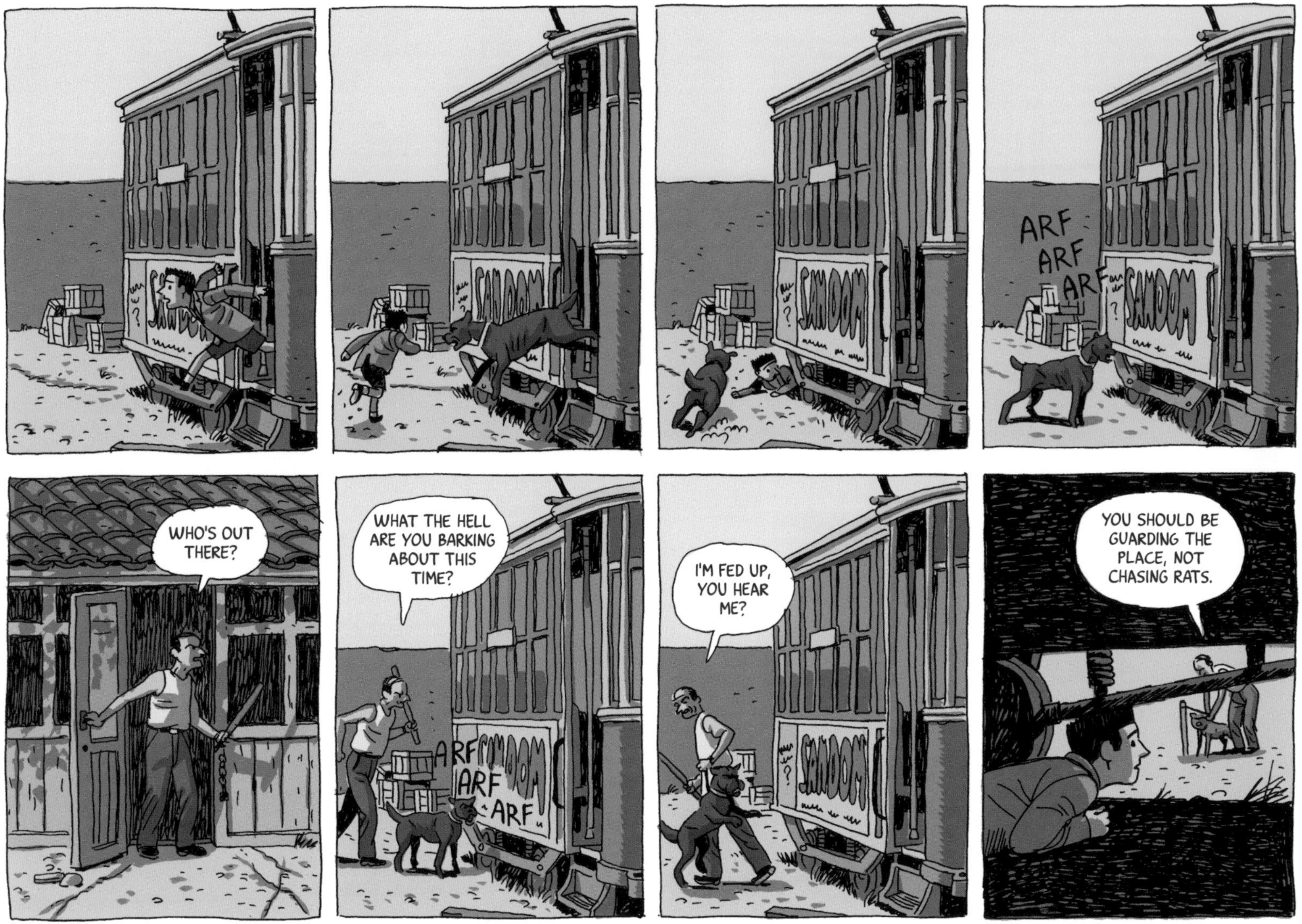
ARF
ARF
ARF
WHO'S OUT THERE?
WHAT THE HELL ARE YOU BARKING ABOUT THIS TIME?
ARF
ARF
ARF
I'M FED UP, YOU HEAR ME?
YOU SHOULD BE GUARDING THE PLACE, NOT CHASING RATS.

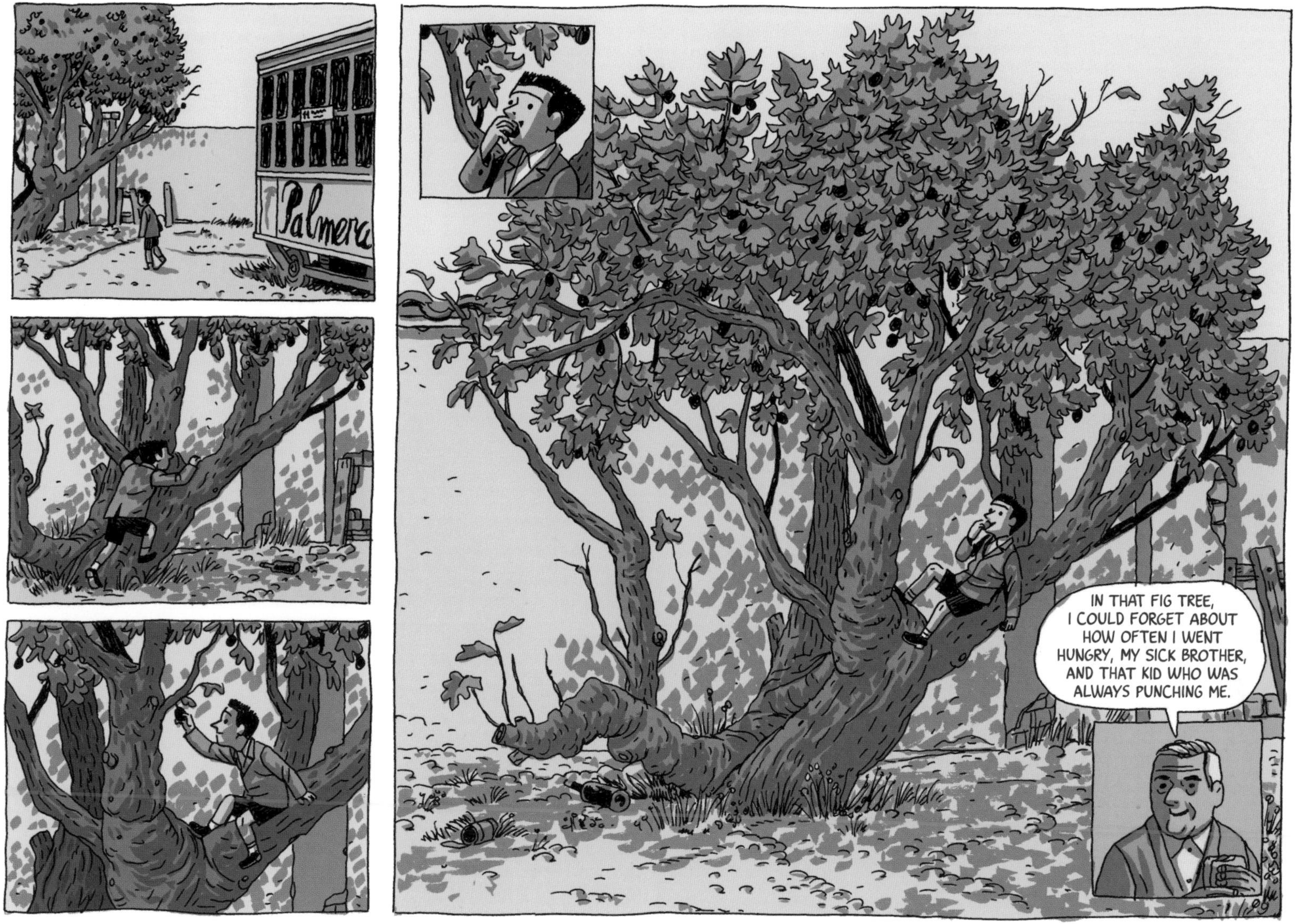
Palmera
IN THAT FIG TREE, I COULD FORGET ABOUT HOW OFTEN I WENT HUNGRY, MY SICK BROTHER, AND THAT KID WHO WAS ALWAYS PUNCHING ME.

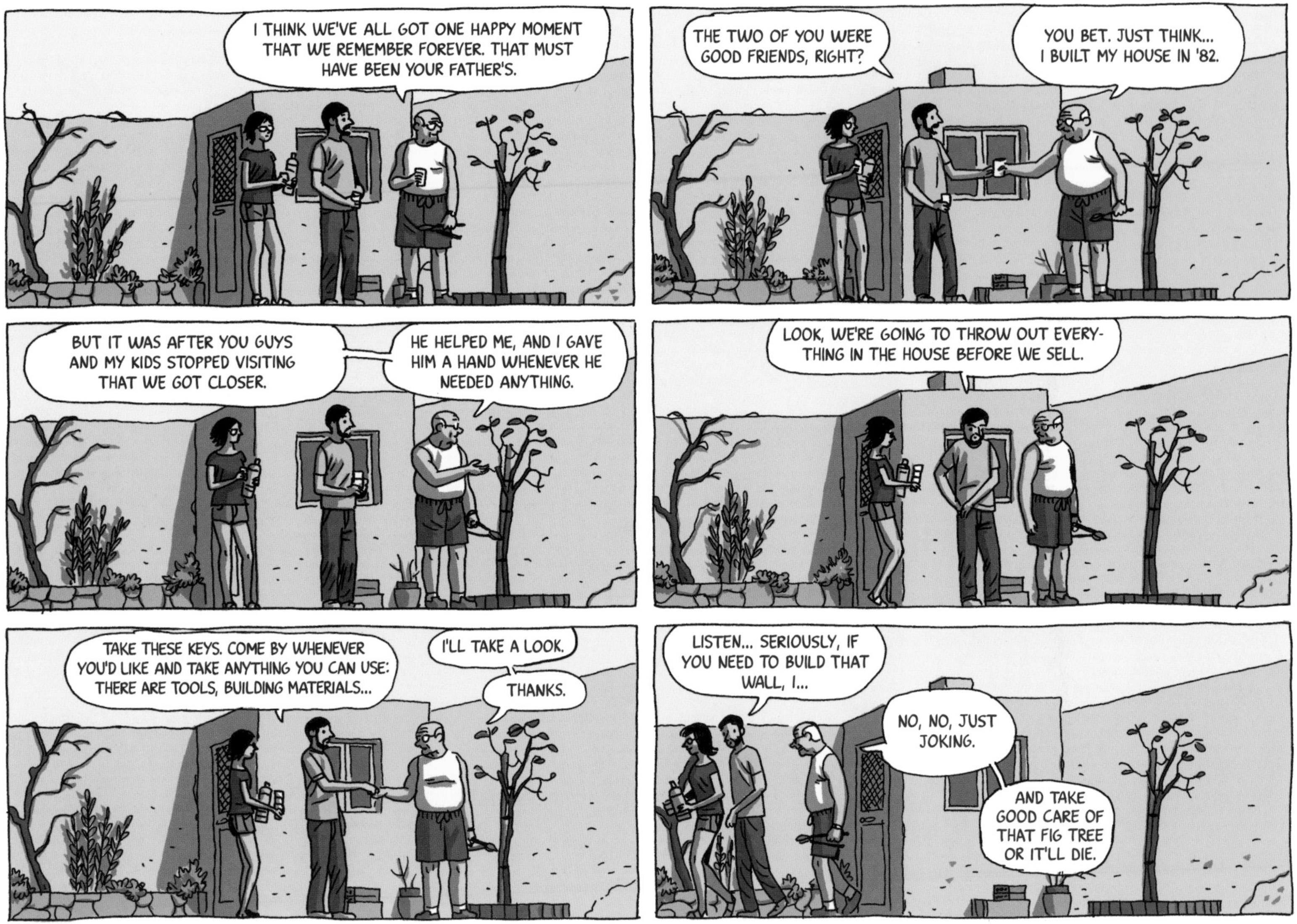
I THINK WE'VE ALL GOT ONE HAPPY MOMENT THAT WE REMEMBER FOREVER. THAT MUST HAVE BEEN YOUR FATHER'S.
THE TWO OF YOU WERE GOOD FRIENDS, RIGHT?
YOU BET. JUST THINK... I BUILT MY HOUSE IN '82.
BUT IT WAS AFTER YOU GUYS AND MY KIDS STOPPED VISITING THAT WE GOT CLOSER.
HE HELPED ME, AND I GAVE HIM A HAND WHENEVER HE NEEDED ANYTHING.
LOOK, WE'RE GOING TO THROW OUT EVERY-THING IN THE HOUSE BEFORE WE SELL.
TAKE THESE KEYS. COME BY WHENEVER YOU'D LIKE AND TAKE ANYTHING YOU CAN USE: THERE ARE TOOLS, BUILDING MATERIALS...
I'LL TAKE A LOOK.
THANKS.
LISTEN... SERIOUSLY, IF YOU NEED TO BUILD THAT WALL, I...
NO, NO, JUST JOKING.
AND TAKE GOOD CARE OF THAT FIG TREE OR IT'LL DIE.

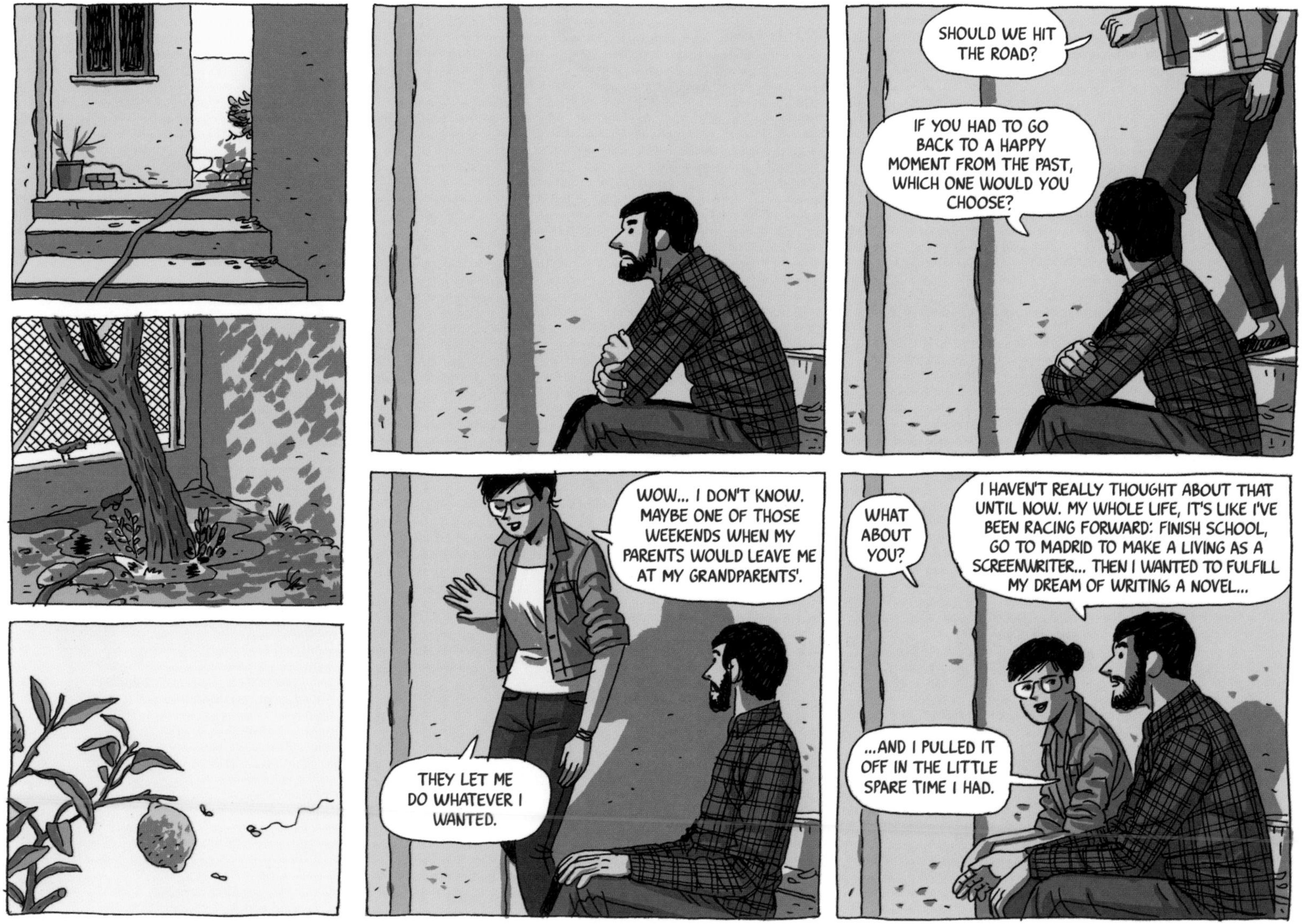
SHOULD WE HIT THE ROAD?
IF YOU HAD TO GO BACK TO A HAPPY MOMENT FROM THE PAST, WHICH ONE WOULD YOU CHOOSE?
WOW... I DON'T KNOW. MAYBE ONE OF THOSE WEEKENDS WHEN MY PARENTS WOULD LEAVE ME AT MY GRANDPARENTS'.
THEY LET ME DO WHATEVER I WANTED.
WHAT ABOUT YOU?
I HAVEN'T REALLY THOUGHT ABOUT THAT UNTIL NOW. MY WHOLE LIFE, IT'S LIKE I'VE BEEN RACING FORWARD: FINISH SCHOOL, GO TO MADRID TO MAKE A LIVING AS A SCREENWRITER... THEN I WANTED TO FULFILL MY DREAM OF WRITING A NOVEL...
...AND I PULLED IT OFF IN THE LITTLE SPARE TIME I HAD.

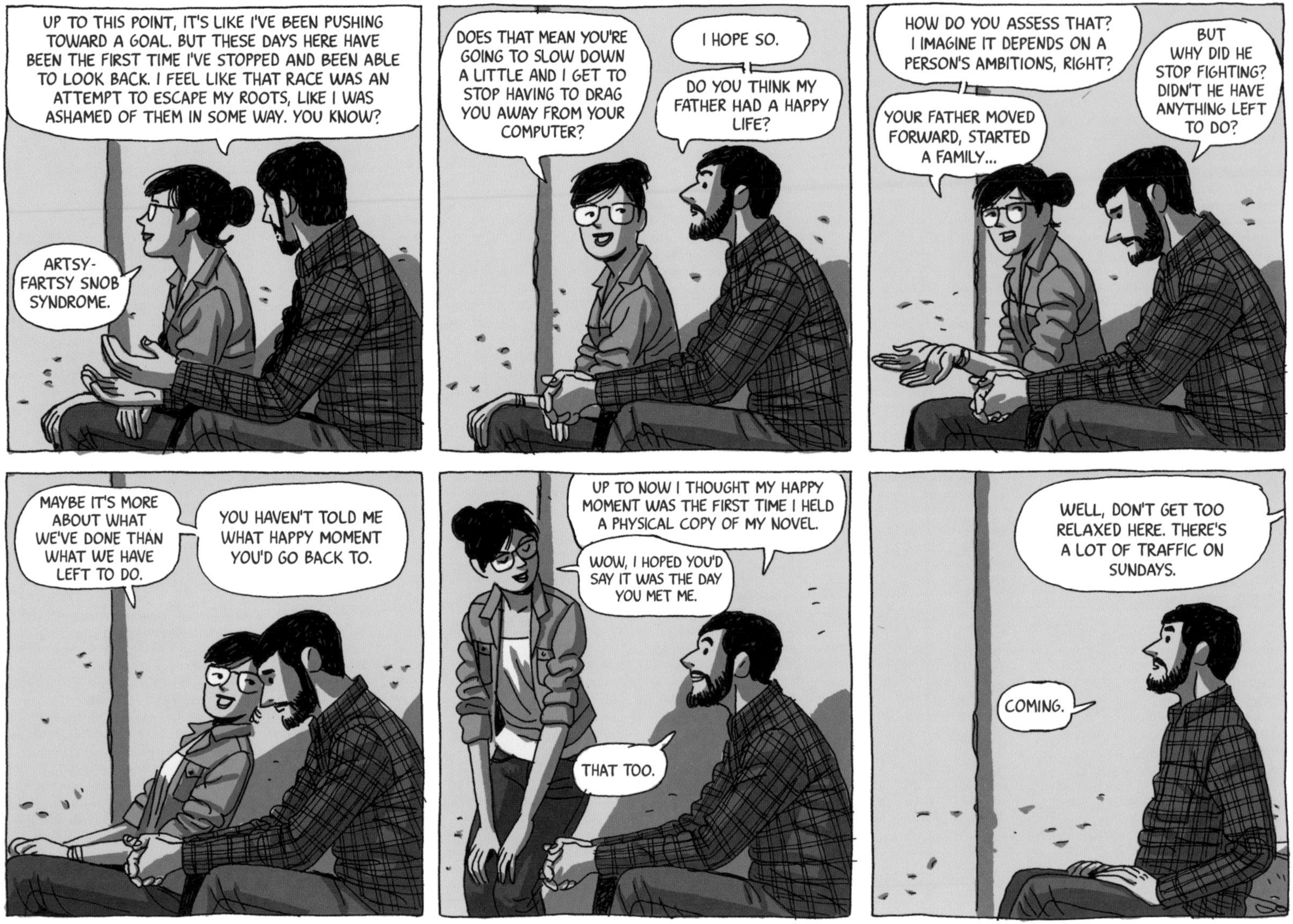
UP TO THIS POINT, IT'S LIKE I'VE BEEN PUSHING TOWARD A GOAL. BUT THESE DAYS HERE HAVE BEEN THE FIRST TIME I'VE STOPPED AND BEEN ABLE TO LOOK BACK. I FEEL LIKE THAT RACE WAS AN ATTEMPT TO ESCAPE MY ROOTS, LIKE I WAS ASHAMED OF THEM IN SOME WAY. YOU KNOW?
ARTSY-FARTSY SNOB SYNDROME.
DOES THAT MEAN YOU'RE GOING TO SLOW DOWN A LITTLE AND I GET TO STOP HAVING TO DRAG YOU AWAY FROM YOUR COMPUTER?
I HOPE SO.
DO YOU THINK MY FATHER HAD A HAPPY LIFE?
HOW DO YOU ASSESS THAT? I IMAGINE IT DEPENDS ON A PERSON'S AMBITIONS, RIGHT?
YOUR FATHER MOVED FORWARD, STARTED A FAMILY...
BUT WHY DID HE STOP FIGHTING? DIDN'T HE HAVE ANYTHING LEFT TO DO?
MAYBE IT'S MORE ABOUT WHAT WE'VE DONE THAN WHAT WE HAVE LEFT TO DO.
YOU HAVEN'T TOLD ME WHAT HAPPY MOMENT YOU'D GO BACK TO.
UP TO NOW I THOUGHT MY HAPPY MOMENT WAS THE FIRST TIME I HELD A PHYSICAL COPY OF MY NOVEL.
WOW, I HOPED YOU'D SAY IT WAS THE DAY YOU MET ME.
THAT TOO.
WELL, DON'T GET TOO RELAXED HERE. THERE'S A LOT OF TRAFFIC ON SUNDAYS.
COMING.

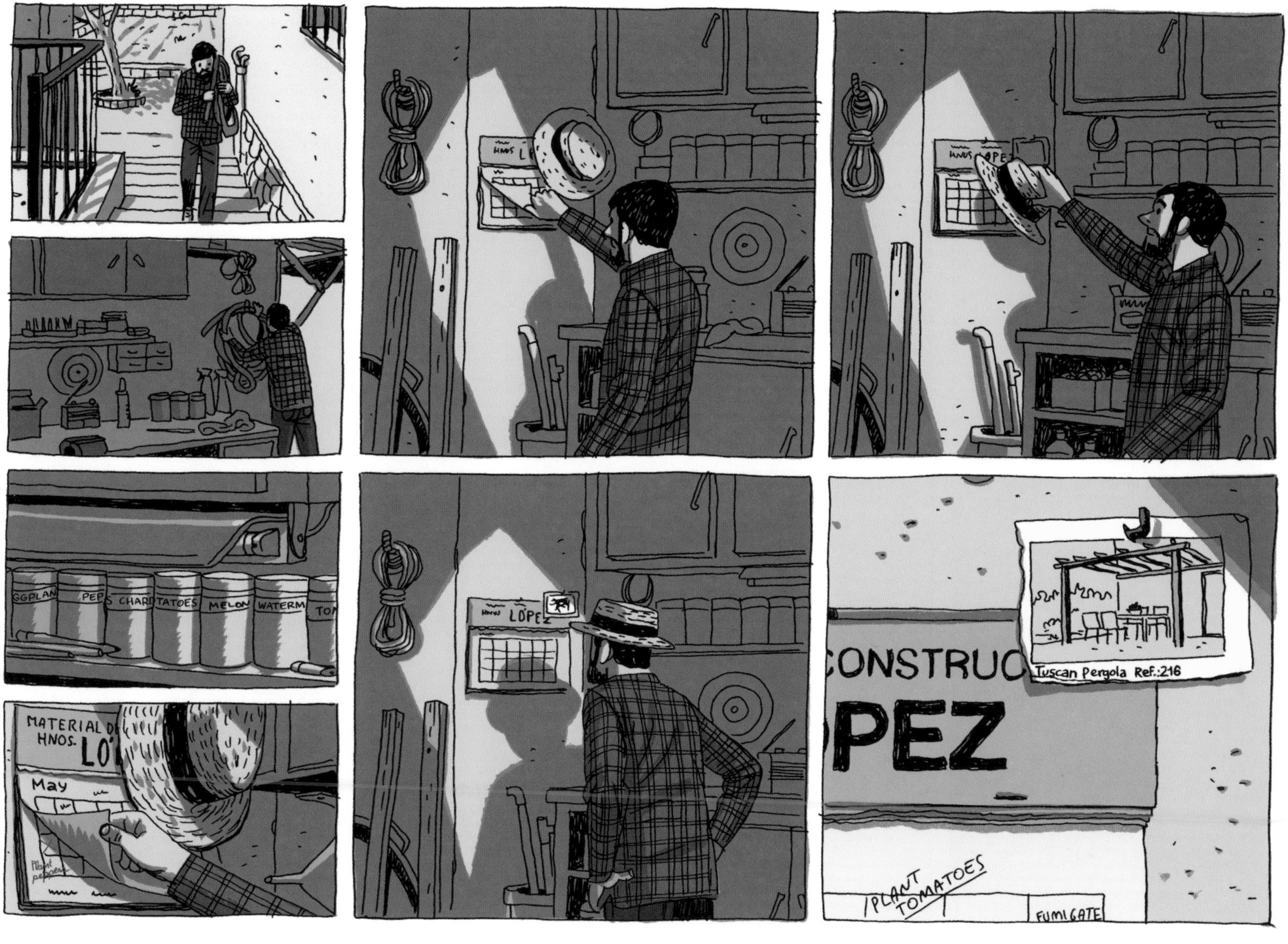
HNOS LÓPEZ
GGPLAN
PEP
S CHARD
TATOES
MELON
WATERM
TO
MATERIAL DE
HNOS. LÓ
May
Plant peppers
CONSTRUC
PEZ
Tuscan Pergola Ref.:216
PLANT TOMATOES
FUMIGATE

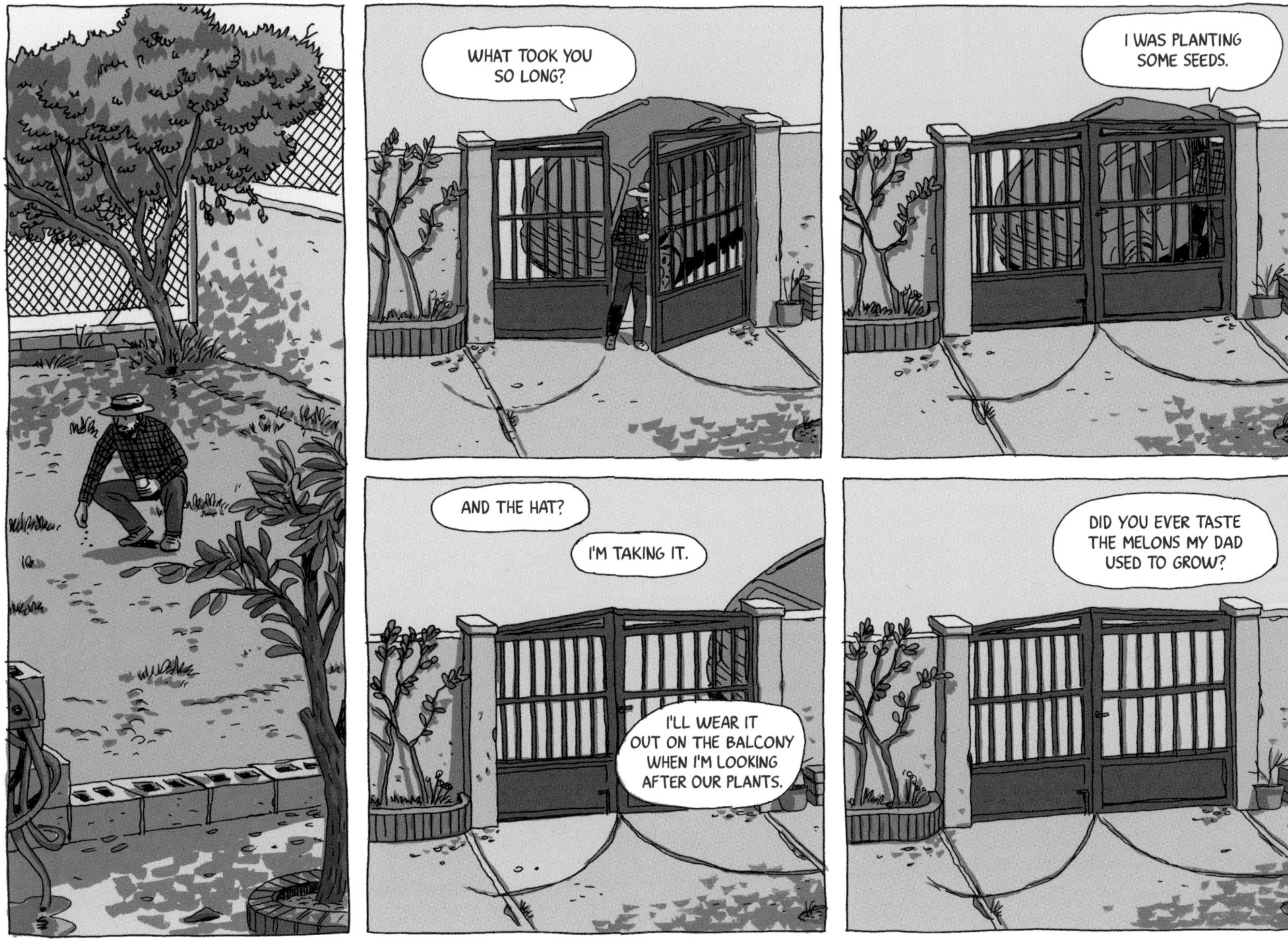
WHAT TOOK YOU SO LONG?
I WAS PLANTING SOME SEEDS.
AND THE HAT?
I'M TAKING IT.
I'LL WEAR IT OUT ON THE BALCONY WHEN I'M LOOKING AFTER OUR PLANTS.
DID YOU EVER TASTE THE MELONS MY DAD USED TO GROW?

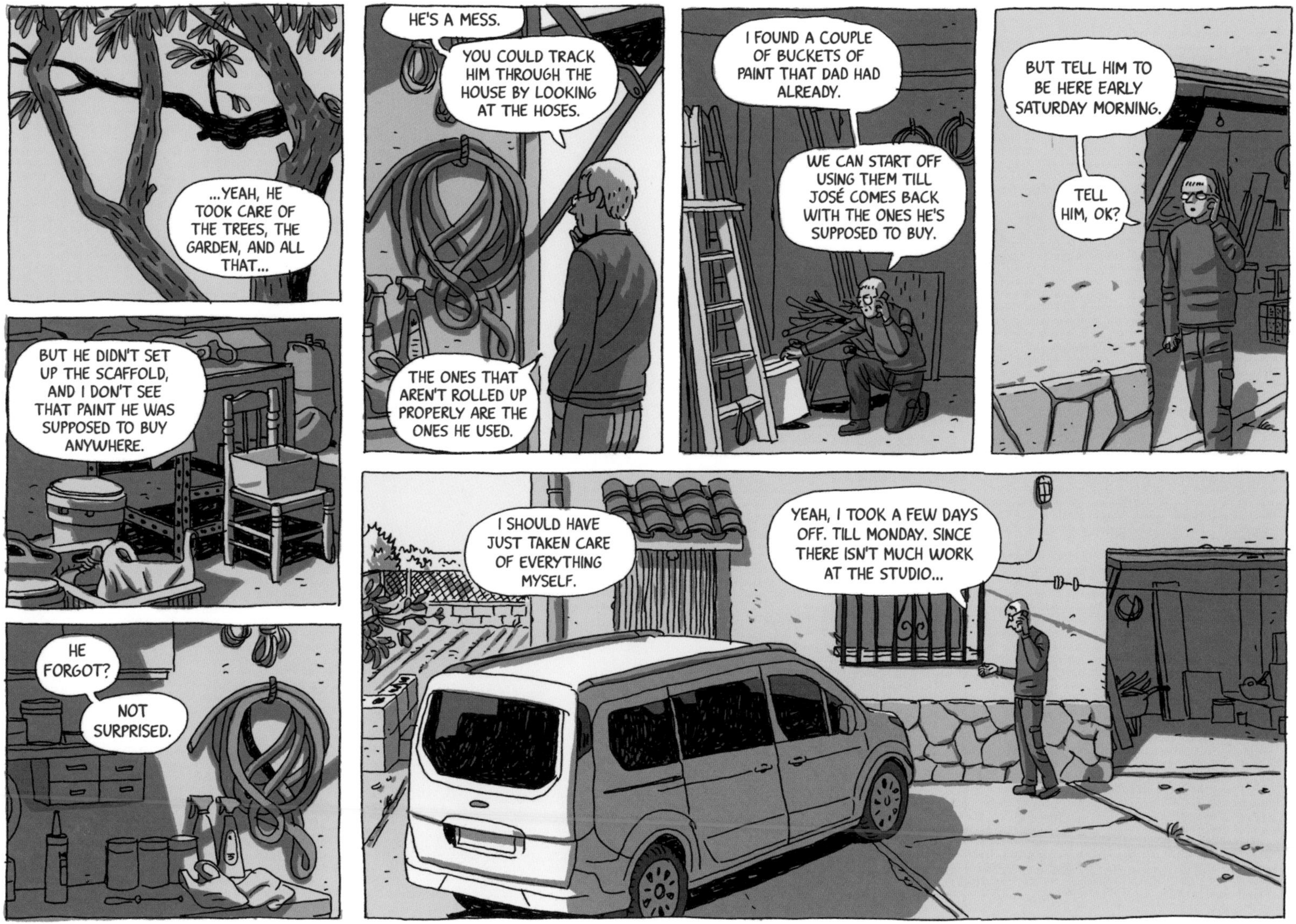
...YEAH, HE TOOK CARE OF THE TREES, THE GARDEN, AND ALL THAT...
BUT HE DIDN'T SET UP THE SCAFFOLD, AND I DON'T SEE THAT PAINT HE WAS SUPPOSED TO BUY ANYWHERE.
HE FORGOT?
NOT SURPRISED.
HE'S A MESS.
YOU COULD TRACK HIM THROUGH THE HOUSE BY LOOKING AT THE HOSES.
THE ONES THAT AREN'T ROLLED UP PROPERLY ARE THE ONES HE USED.
I FOUND A COUPLE OF BUCKETS OF PAINT THAT DAD HAD ALREADY.
WE CAN START OFF USING THEM TILL JOSÉ COMES BACK WITH THE ONES HE'S SUPPOSED TO BUY.
BUT TELL HIM TO BE HERE EARLY SATURDAY MORNING.
TELL HIM, OK?
I SHOULD HAVE JUST TAKEN CARE OF EVERYTHING MYSELF.
YEAH, I TOOK A FEW DAYS OFF. TILL MONDAY. SINCE THERE ISN'T MUCH WORK AT THE STUDIO...

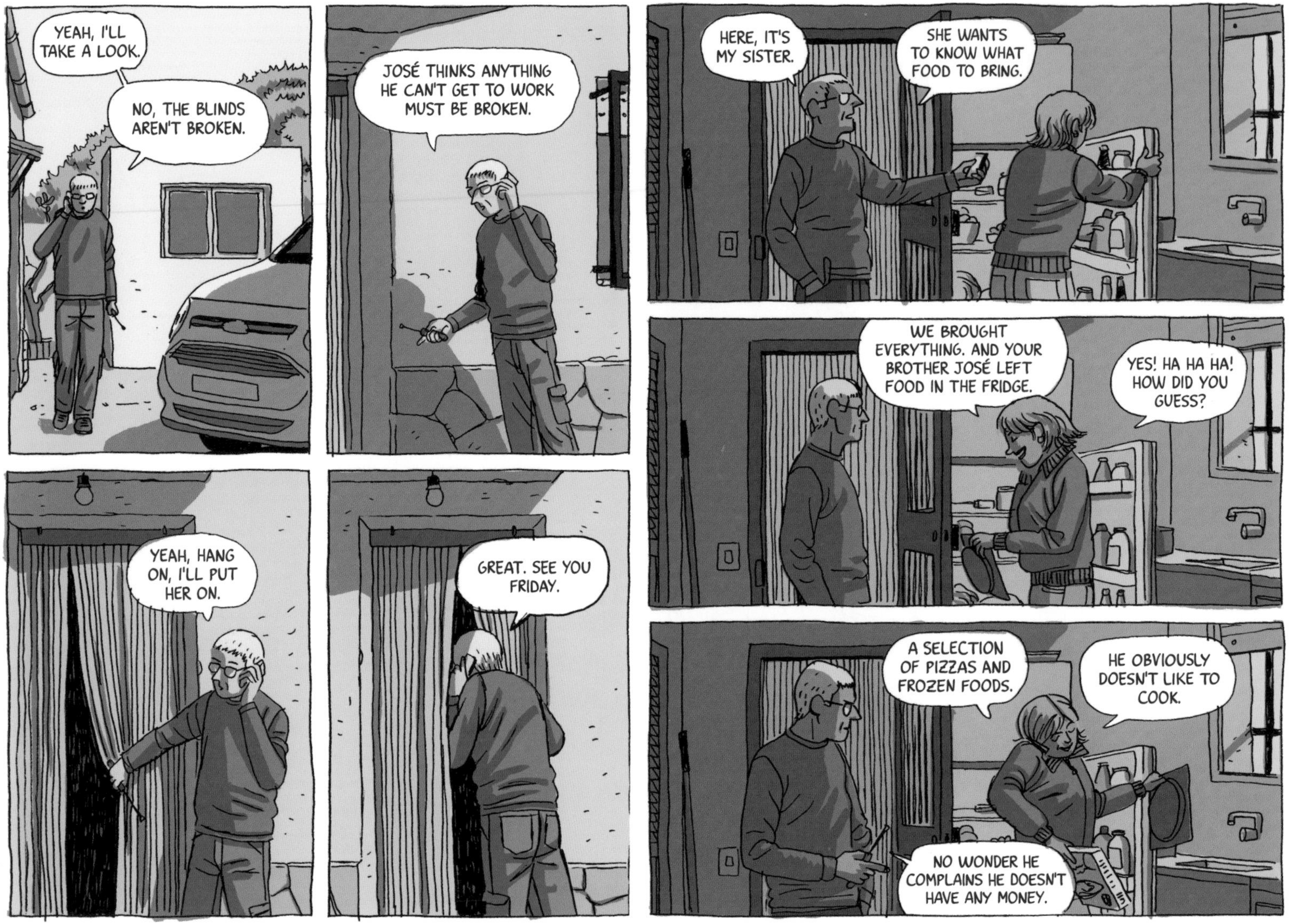
YEAH, I'LL TAKE A LOOK.
NO, THE BLINDS AREN'T BROKEN.
JOSÉ THINKS ANYTHING HE CAN'T GET TO WORK MUST BE BROKEN.
YEAH, HANG ON, I'LL PUT HER ON.
GREAT. SEE YOU FRIDAY.
HERE, IT'S MY SISTER.
SHE WANTS TO KNOW WHAT FOOD TO BRING.
WE BROUGHT EVERYTHING. AND YOUR BROTHER JOSÉ LEFT FOOD IN THE FRIDGE.
YES! HA HA HA! HOW DID YOU GUESS?
A SELECTION OF PIZZAS AND FROZEN FOODS.
HE OBVIOUSLY DOESN'T LIKE TO COOK.
NO WONDER HE COMPLAINS HE DOESN'T HAVE ANY MONEY.

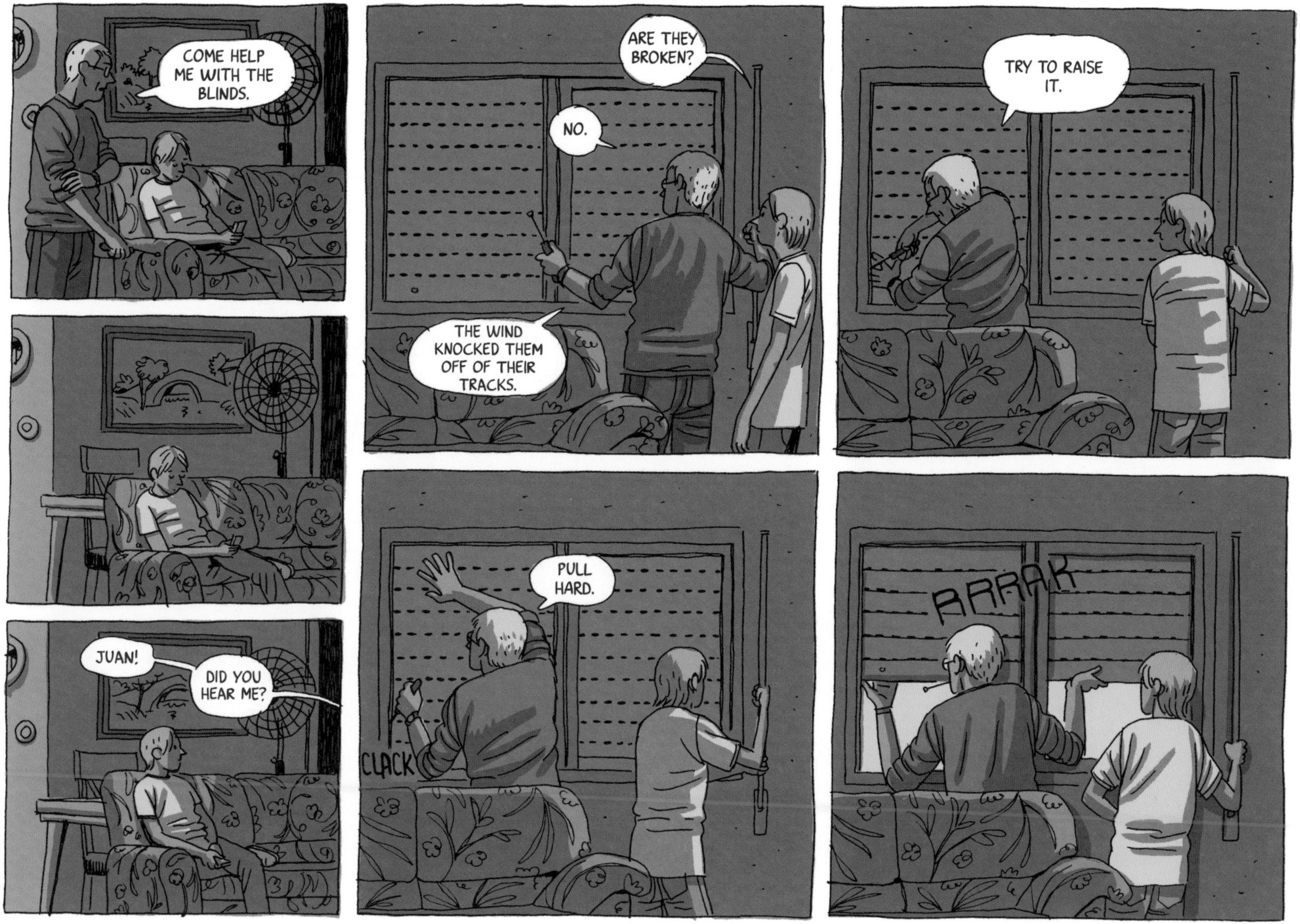
COME HELP ME WITH THE BLINDS.
JUAN!
DID YOU HEAR ME?
ARE THEY BROKEN?
NO.
THE WIND KNOCKED THEM OFF OF THEIR TRACKS.
TRY TO RAISE IT.
PULL HARD.
CLACK
RRRAK

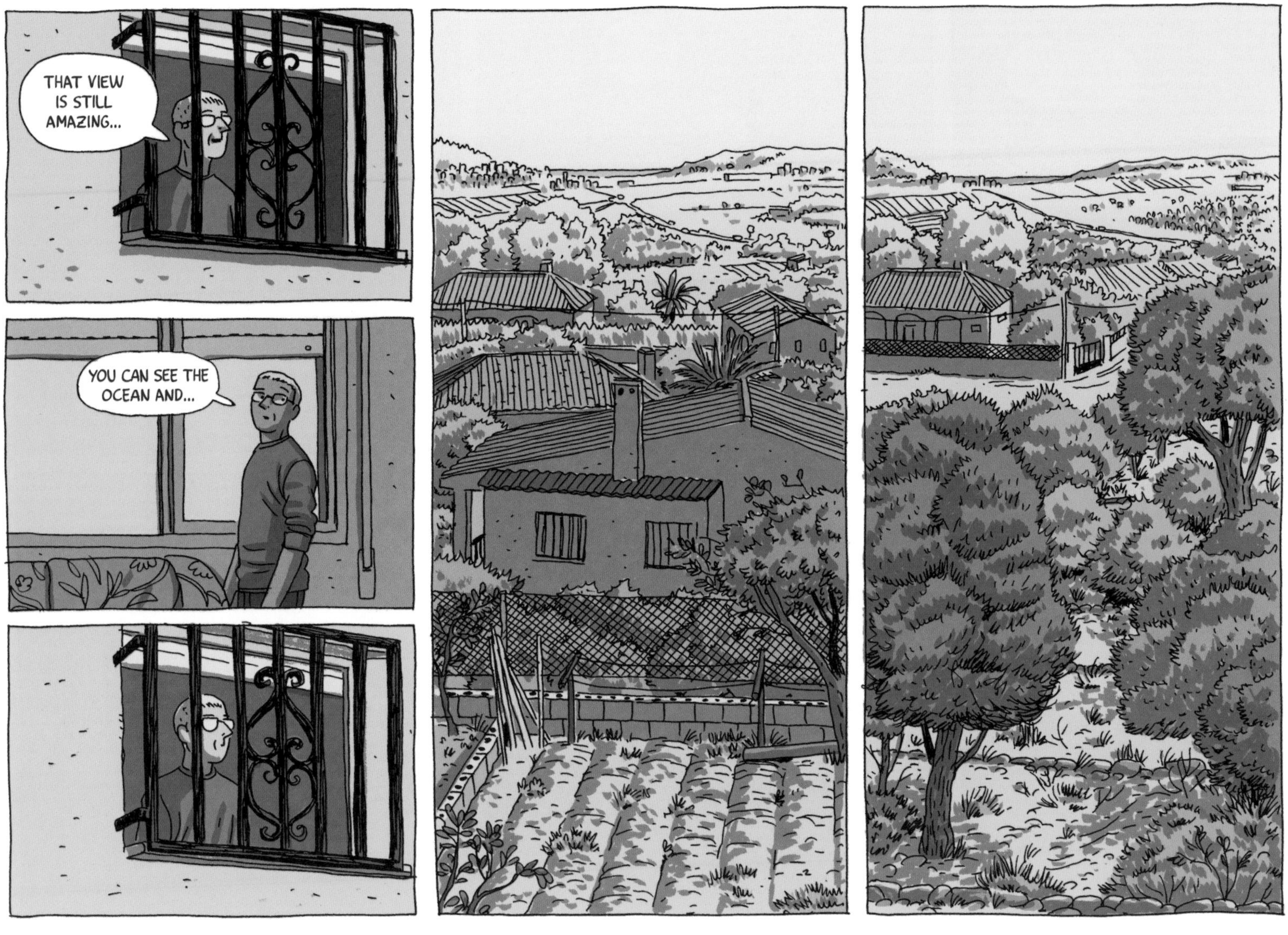
THAT VIEW IS STILL AMAZING...
YOU CAN SEE THE OCEAN AND...

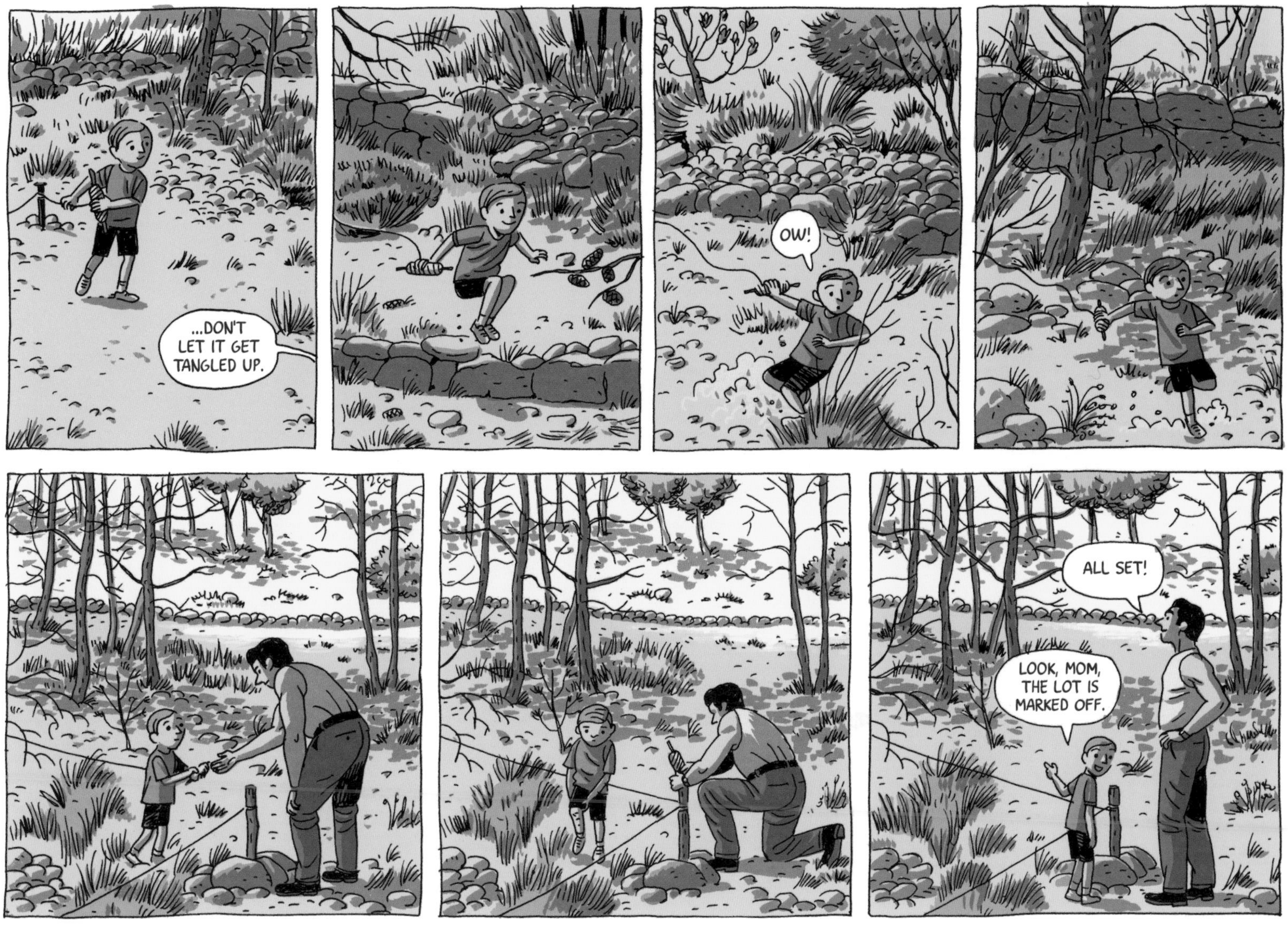
...DON'T LET IT GET TANGLED UP.
OW!
ALL SET!
LOOK, MOM, THE LOT IS MARKED OFF.

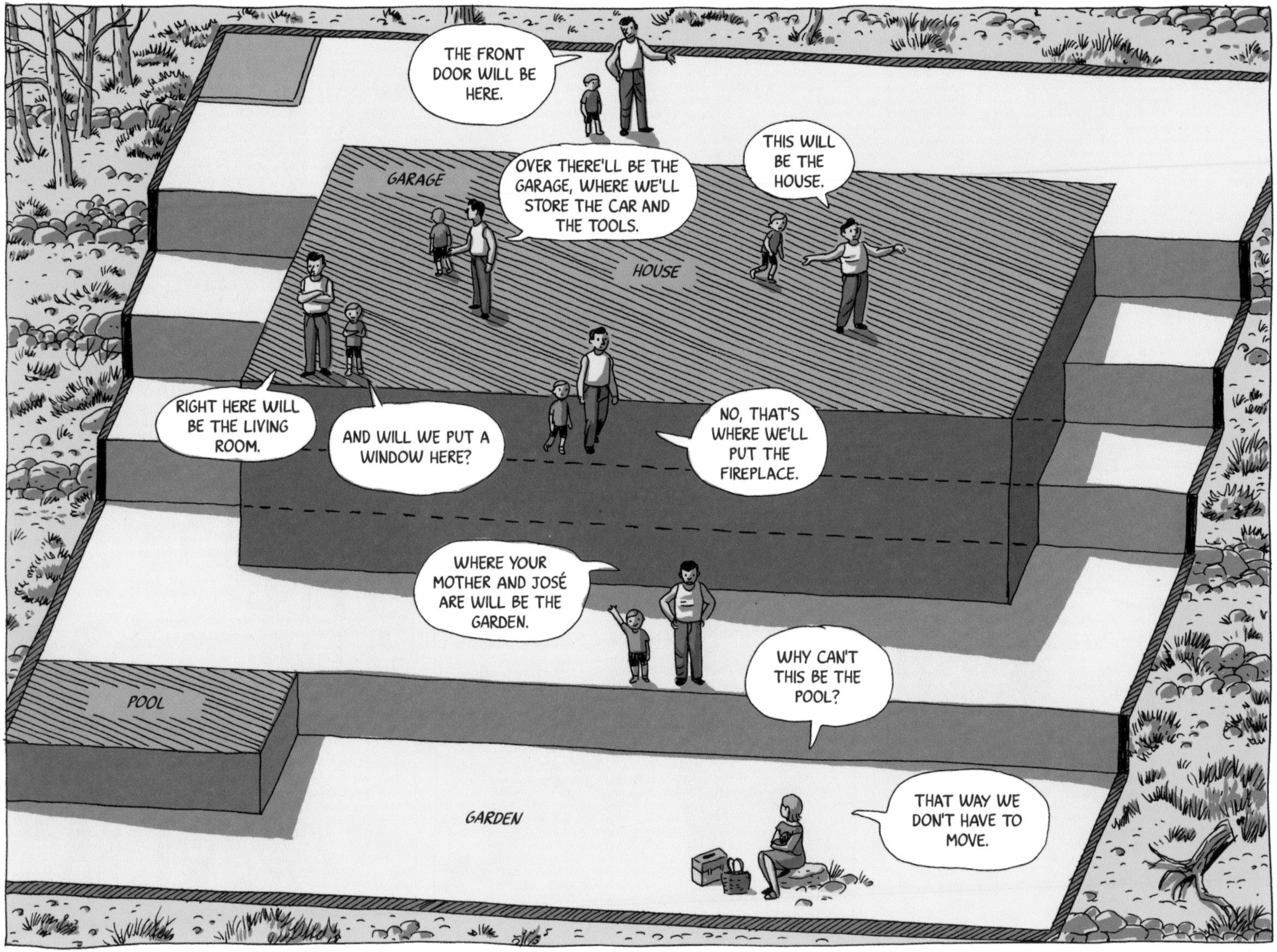
THE FRONT DOOR WILL BE HERE.
GARAGE
OVER THERE'LL BE THE GARAGE, WHERE WE'LL STORE THE CAR AND THE TOOLS.
THIS WILL BE THE HOUSE.
HOUSE
RIGHT HERE WILL BE THE LIVING ROOM.
AND WILL WE PUT A WINDOW HERE?
NO, THAT'S WHERE WE'LL PUT THE FIREPLACE.
WHERE YOUR MOTHER AND JOSÉ ARE WILL BE THE GARDEN.
POOL
WHY CAN'T THIS BE THE POOL?
GARDEN
THAT WAY WE DON'T HAVE TO MOVE.

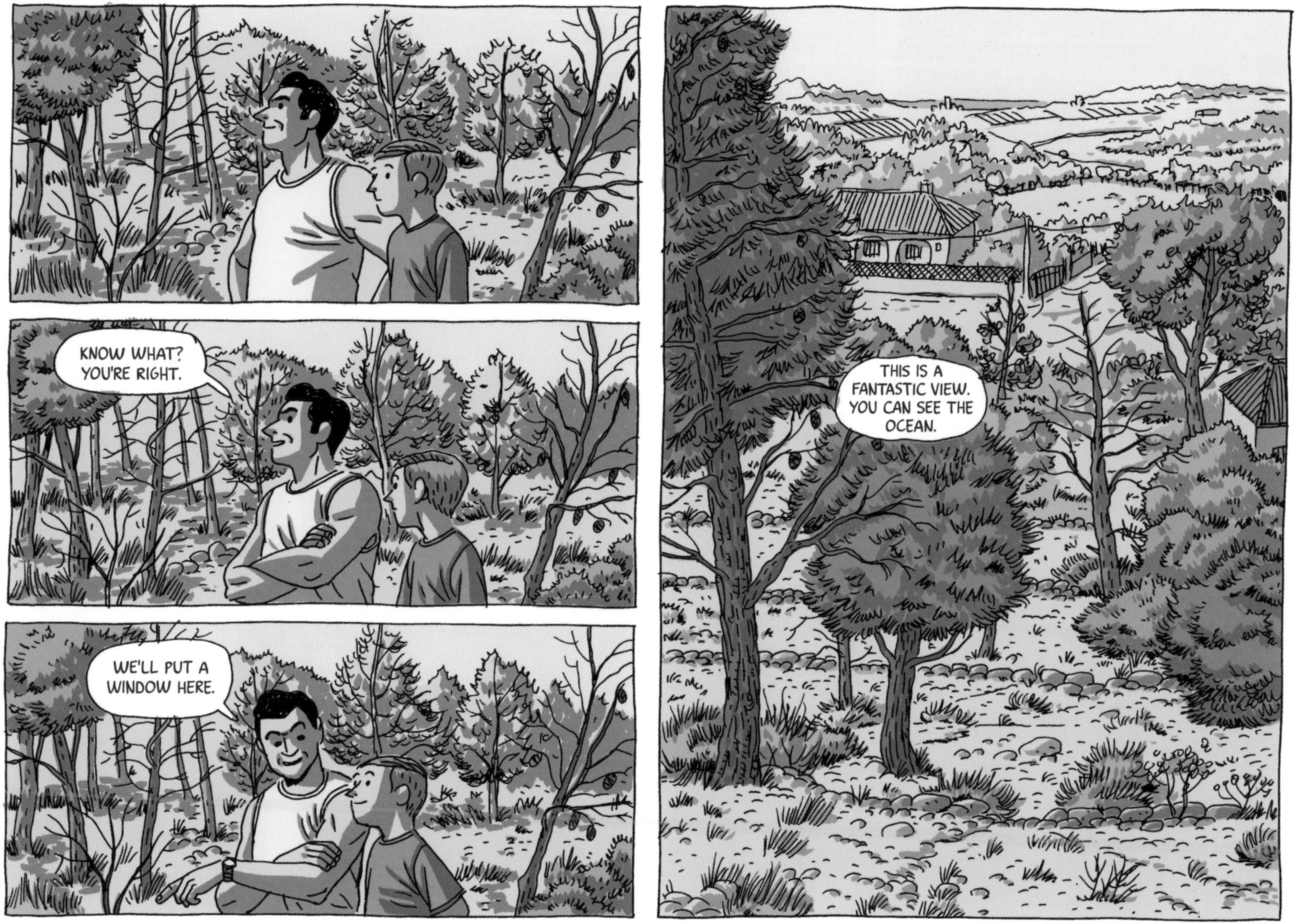
KNOW WHAT? YOU'RE RIGHT.
WE'LL PUT A WINDOW HERE.
THIS IS A FANTASTIC VIEW. YOU CAN SEE THE OCEAN.

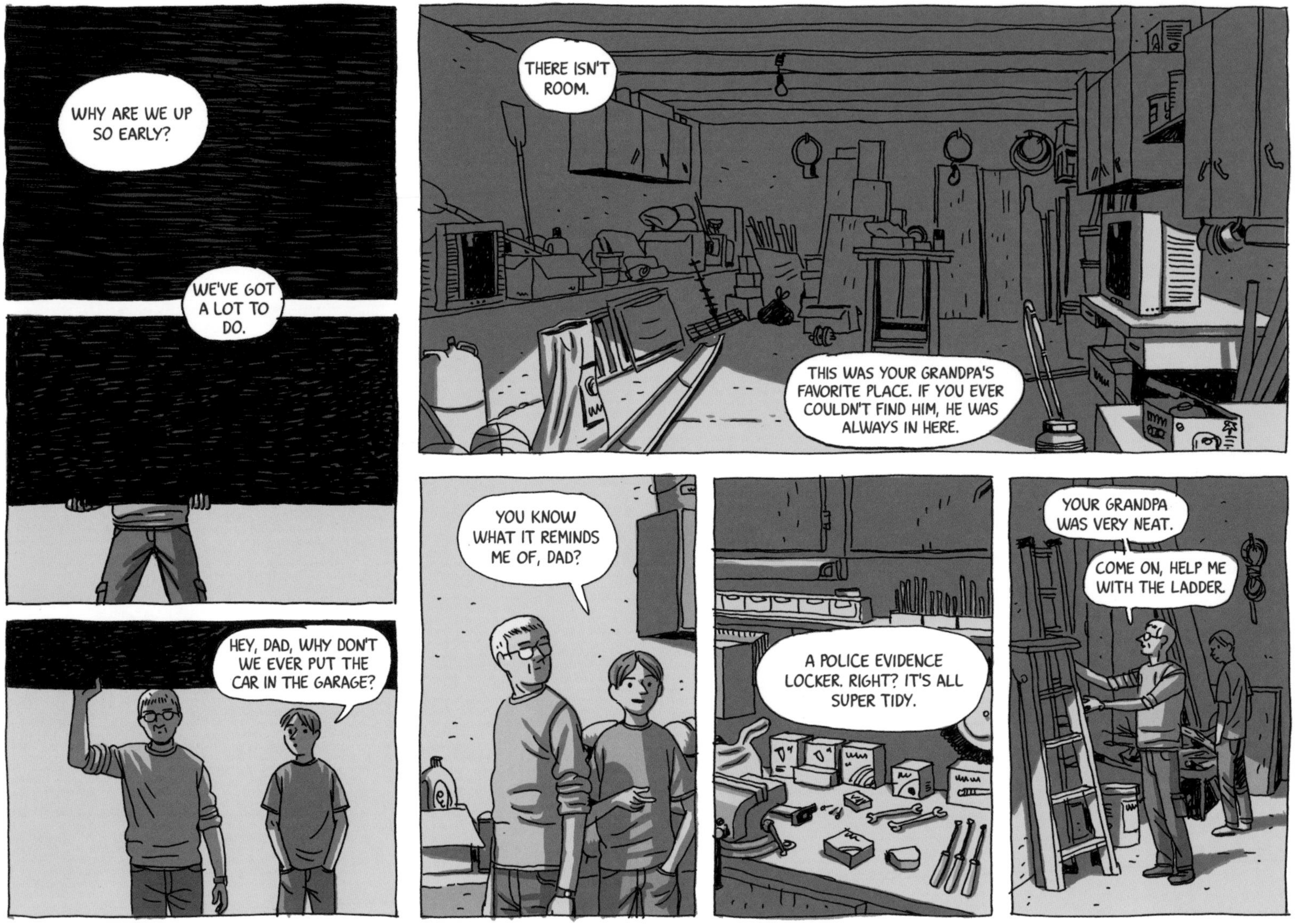
WHY ARE WE UP SO EARLY?
WE'VE GOT A LOT TO DO.
HEY, DAD, WHY DON'T WE EVER PUT THE CAR IN THE GARAGE?
THERE ISN'T ROOM.
THIS WAS YOUR GRANDPA'S FAVORITE PLACE. IF YOU EVER COULDN'T FIND HIM, HE WAS ALWAYS IN HERE.
YOU KNOW WHAT IT REMINDS ME OF, DAD?
A POLICE EVIDENCE LOCKER. RIGHT? IT'S ALL SUPER TIDY.
YOUR GRANDPA WAS VERY NEAT.
COME ON, HELP ME WITH THE LADDER.

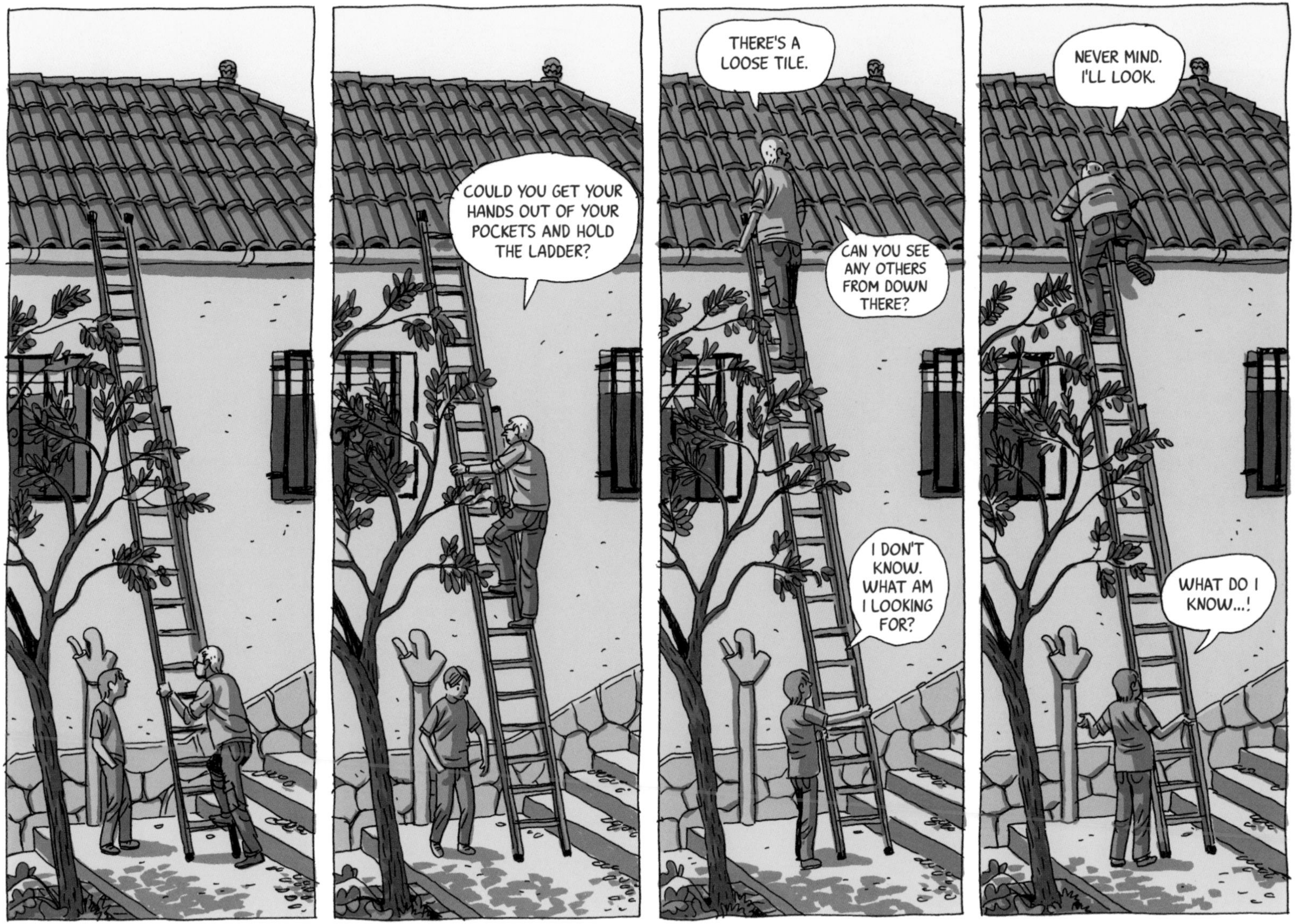
COULD YOU GET YOUR HANDS OUT OF YOUR POCKETS AND HOLD THE LADDER?
THERE'S A LOOSE TILE.
CAN YOU SEE ANY OTHERS FROM DOWN THERE?
I DON'T KNOW. WHAT AM I LOOKING FOR?
NEVER MIND. I'LL LOOK.
WHAT DO I KNOW...!

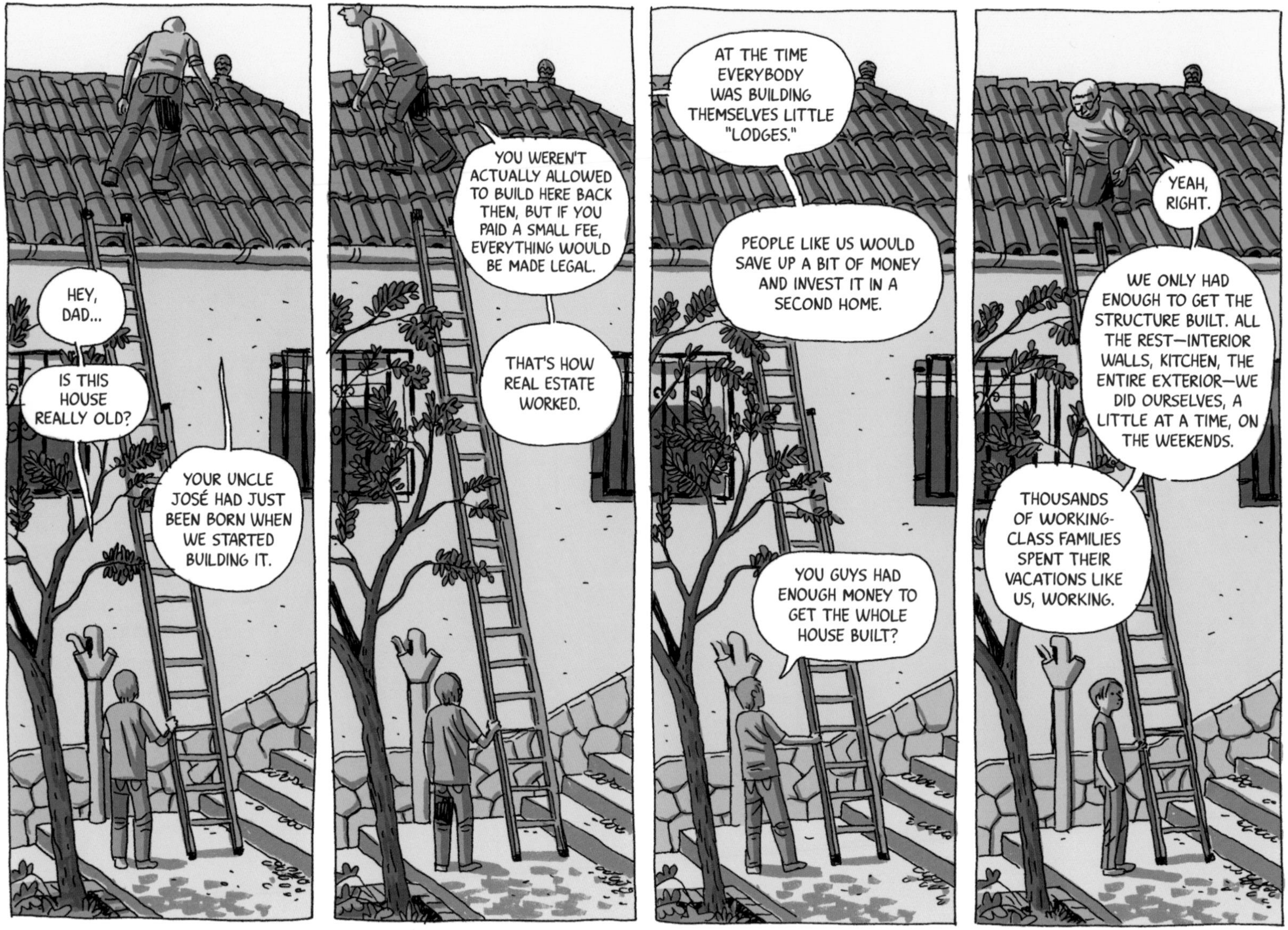
HEY, DAD...
IS THIS HOUSE REALLY OLD?
YOUR UNCLE JOSÉ HAD JUST BEEN BORN WHEN WE STARTED BUILDING IT.
YOU WEREN'T ACTUALLY ALLOWED TO BUILD HERE BACK THEN, BUT IF YOU PAID A SMALL FEE, EVERYTHING WOULD BE MADE LEGAL.
THAT'S HOW REAL ESTATE WORKED.
AT THE TIME EVERYBODY WAS BUILDING THEMSELVES LITTLE "LODGES."
PEOPLE LIKE US WOULD SAVE UP A BIT OF MONEY AND INVEST IT IN A SECOND HOME.
YOU GUYS HAD ENOUGH MONEY TO GET THE WHOLE HOUSE BUILT?
YEAH, RIGHT.
WE ONLY HAD ENOUGH TO GET THE STRUCTURE BUILT. ALL THE REST—INTERIOR WALLS, KITCHEN, THE ENTIRE EXTERIOR—WE DID OURSELVES, A LITTLE AT A TIME, ON THE WEEKENDS.
THOUSANDS OF WORKING-CLASS FAMILIES SPENT THEIR VACATIONS LIKE US, WORKING.

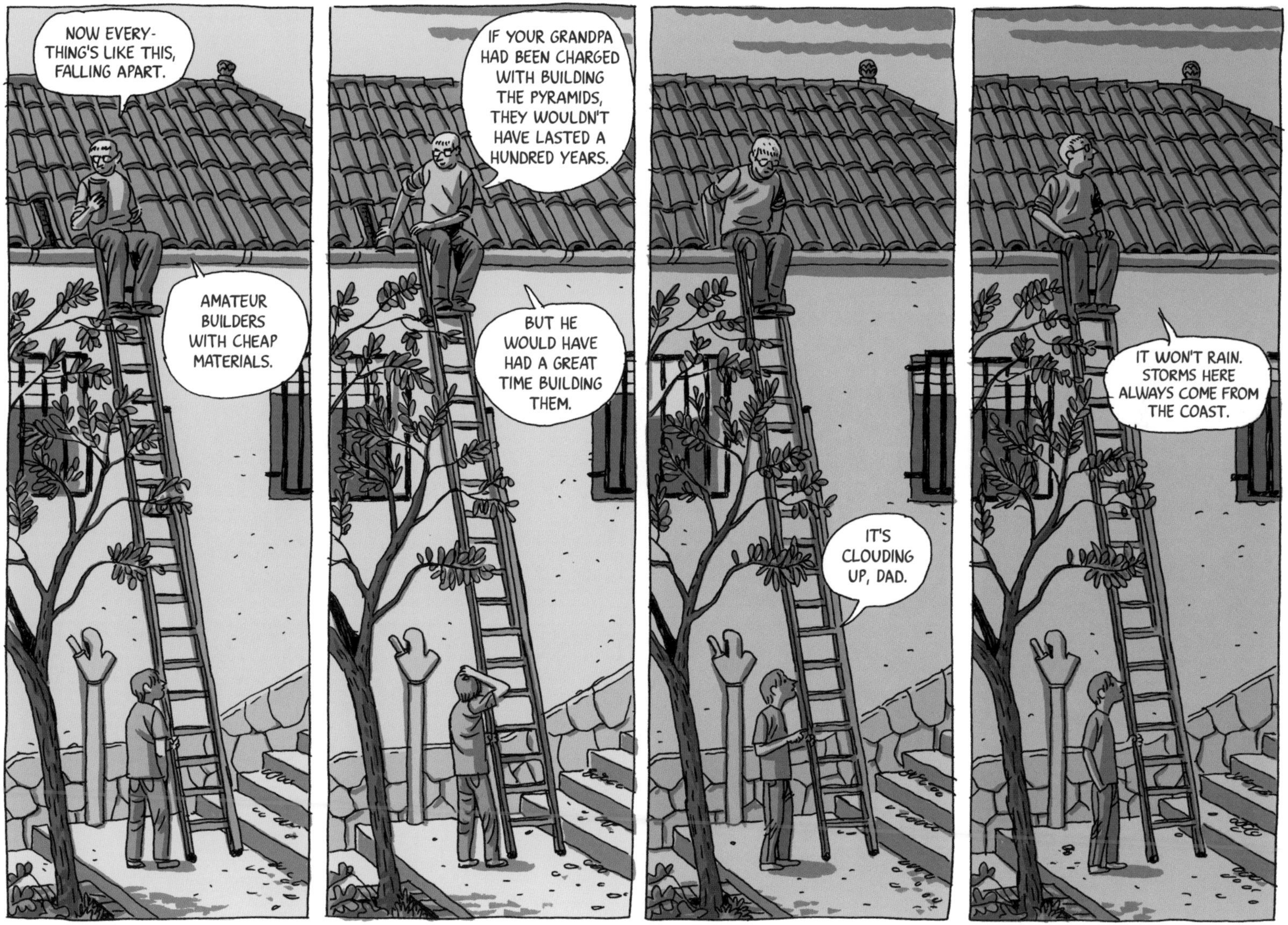
NOW EVERY-THING'S LIKE THIS, FALLING APART.
AMATEUR BUILDERS WITH CHEAP MATERIALS.
IF YOUR GRANDPA HAD BEEN CHARGED WITH BUILDING THE PYRAMIDS, THEY WOULDN'T HAVE LASTED A HUNDRED YEARS.
BUT HE WOULD HAVE HAD A GREAT TIME BUILDING THEM.
IT'S CLOUDING UP, DAD.
IT WON'T RAIN. STORMS HERE ALWAYS COME FROM THE COAST.

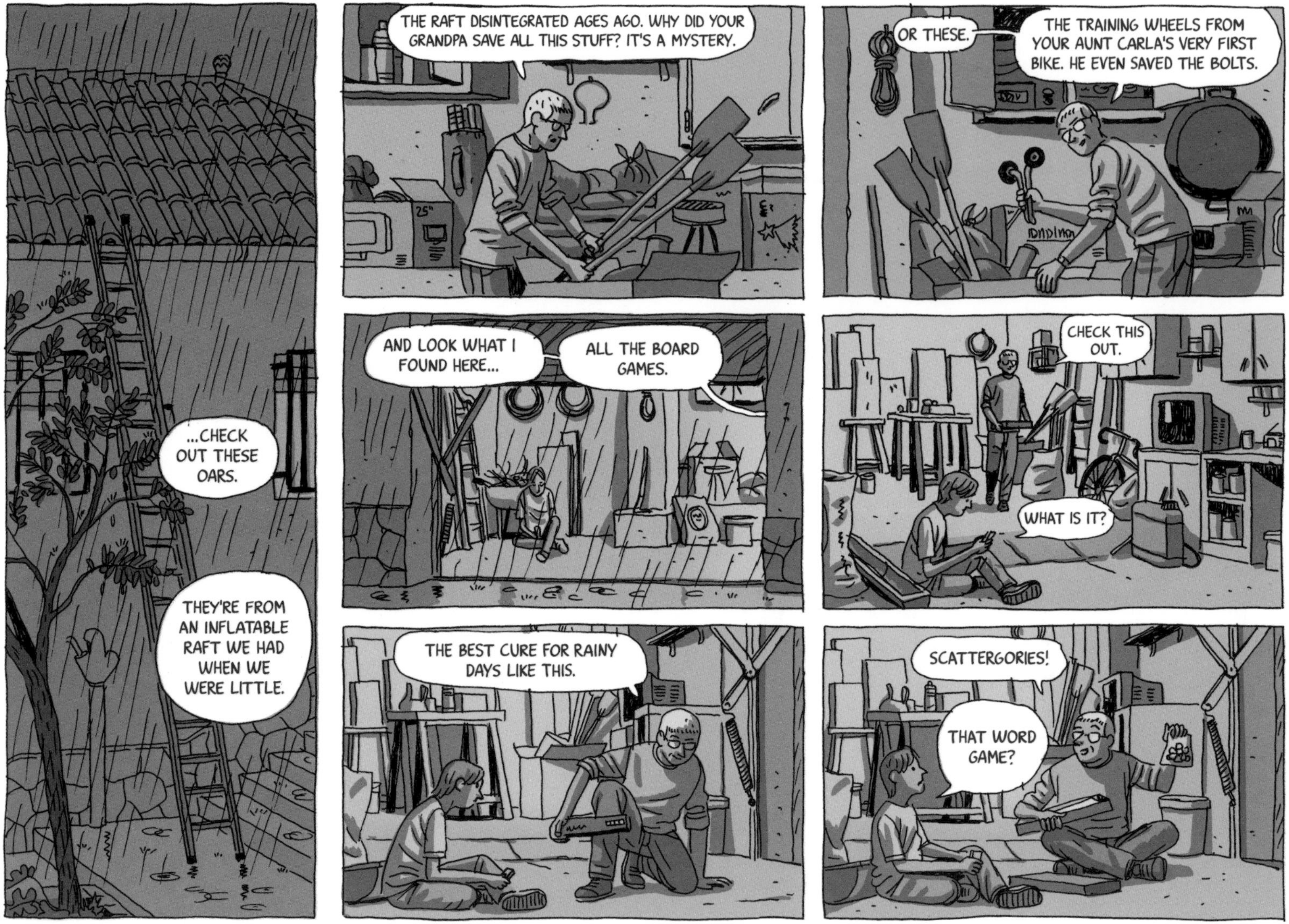
...CHECK OUT THESE OARS.
THEY'RE FROM AN INFLATABLE RAFT WE HAD WHEN WE WERE LITTLE.
THE RAFT DISINTEGRATED AGES AGO. WHY DID YOUR GRANDPA SAVE ALL THIS STUFF? IT'S A MYSTERY.
OR THESE.
THE TRAINING WHEELS FROM YOUR AUNT CARLA'S VERY FIRST BIKE. HE EVEN SAVED THE BOLTS.
AND LOOK WHAT I FOUND HERE...
ALL THE BOARD GAMES.
CHECK THIS OUT.
WHAT IS IT?
THE BEST CURE FOR RAINY DAYS LIKE THIS.
SCATTERGORIES!
THAT WORD GAME?

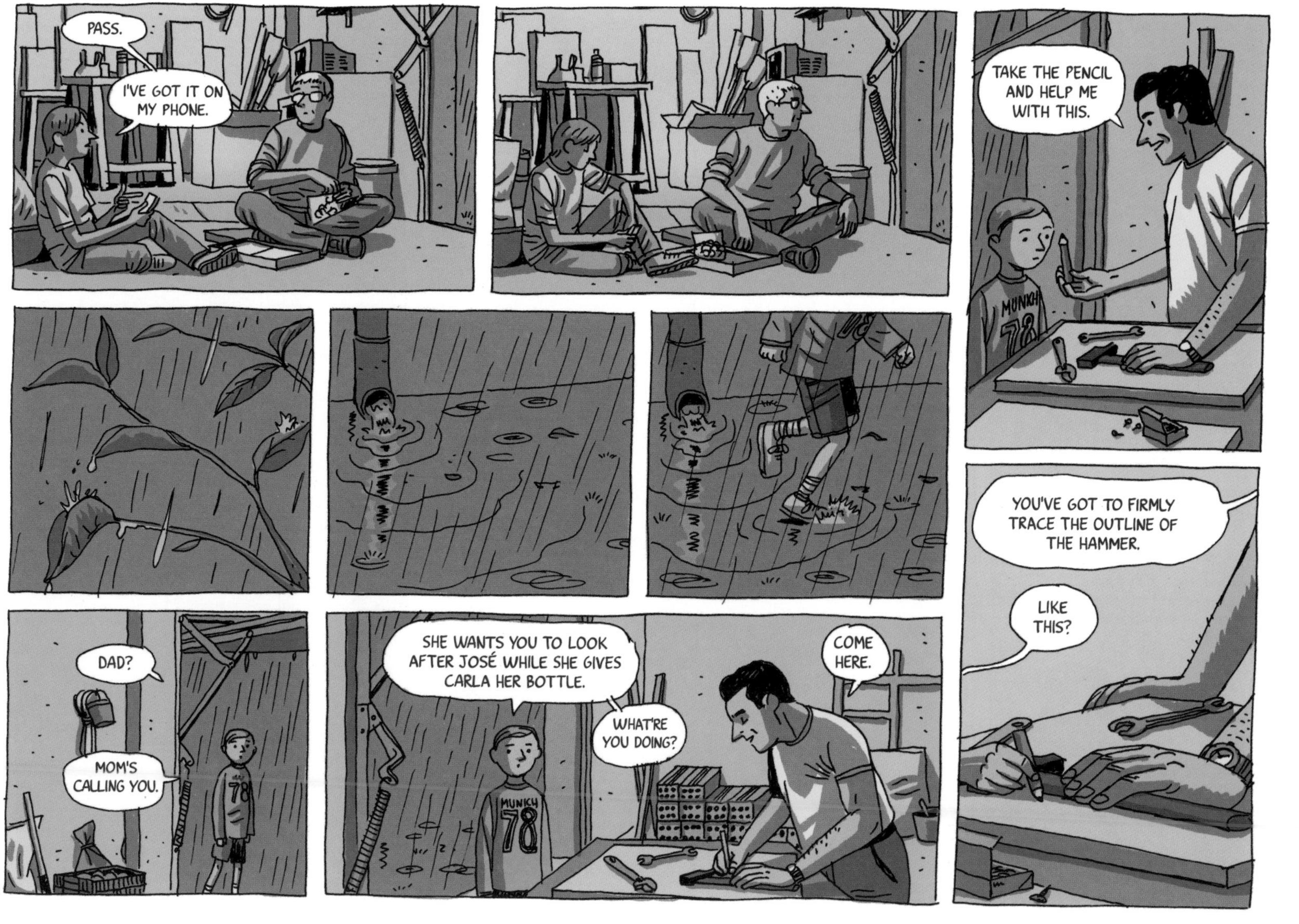
PASS.
I'VE GOT IT ON MY PHONE.
TAKE THE PENCIL AND HELP ME WITH THIS.
MUNICH 78
DAD?
MOM'S CALLING YOU.
SHE WANTS YOU TO LOOK AFTER JOSÉ WHILE SHE GIVES CARLA HER BOTTLE.
COME HERE.
WHAT'RE YOU DOING?
MUNICH 78
YOU'VE GOT TO FIRMLY TRACE THE OUTLINE OF THE HAMMER.
LIKE THIS?

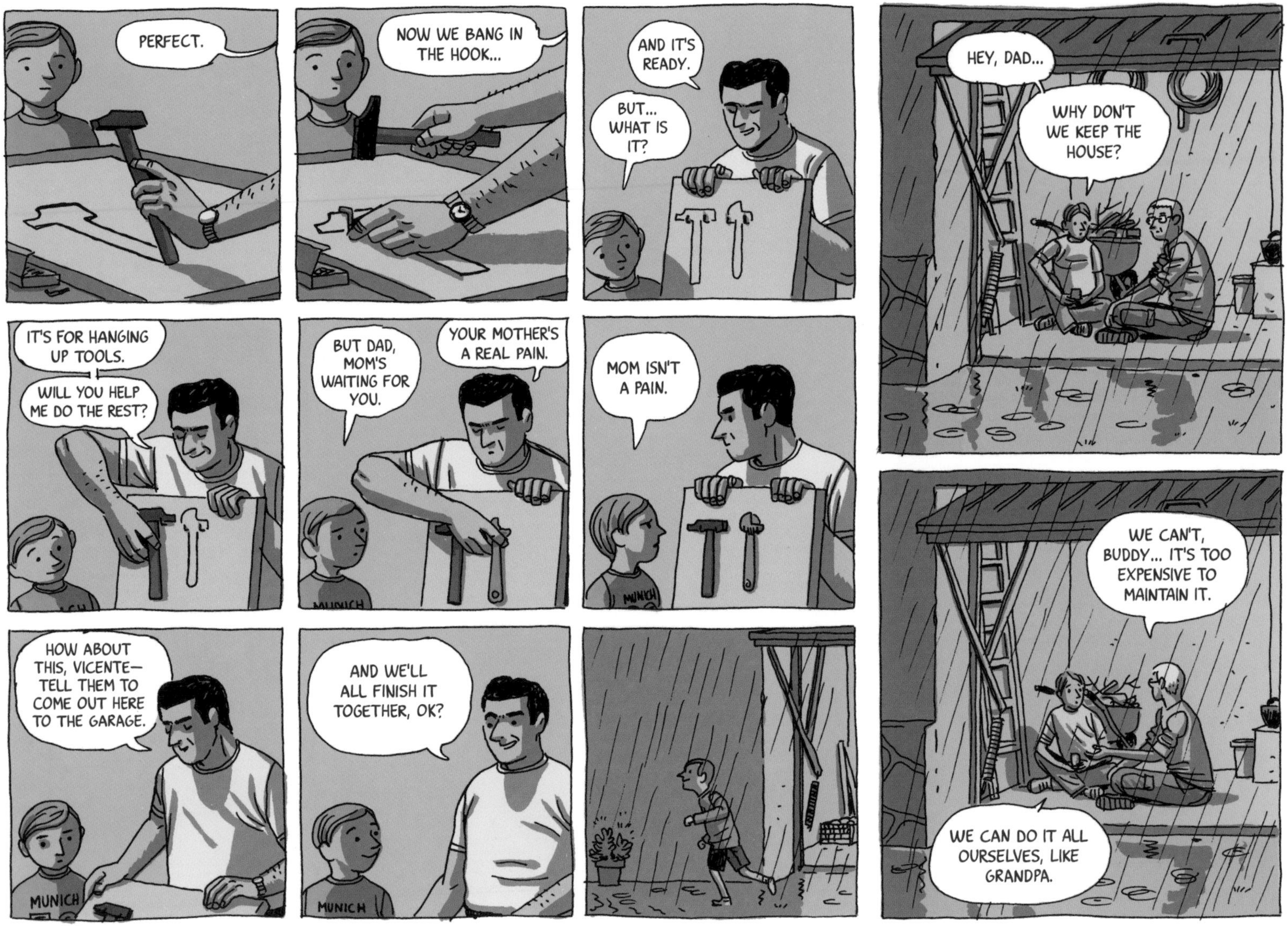
PERFECT.
NOW WE BANG IN THE HOOK...
AND IT'S READY.
BUT... WHAT IS IT?
IT'S FOR HANGING UP TOOLS.
WILL YOU HELP ME DO THE REST?
BUT DAD, MOM'S WAITING FOR YOU.
YOUR MOTHER'S A REAL PAIN.
MOM ISN'T A PAIN.
HOW ABOUT THIS, VICENTE—TELL THEM TO COME OUT HERE TO THE GARAGE.
MUNICH
AND WE'LL ALL FINISH IT TOGETHER, OK?
MUNICH
HEY, DAD...
WHY DON'T WE KEEP THE HOUSE?
WE CAN'T, BUDDY... IT'S TOO EXPENSIVE TO MAINTAIN IT.
WE CAN DO IT ALL OURSELVES, LIKE GRANDPA.

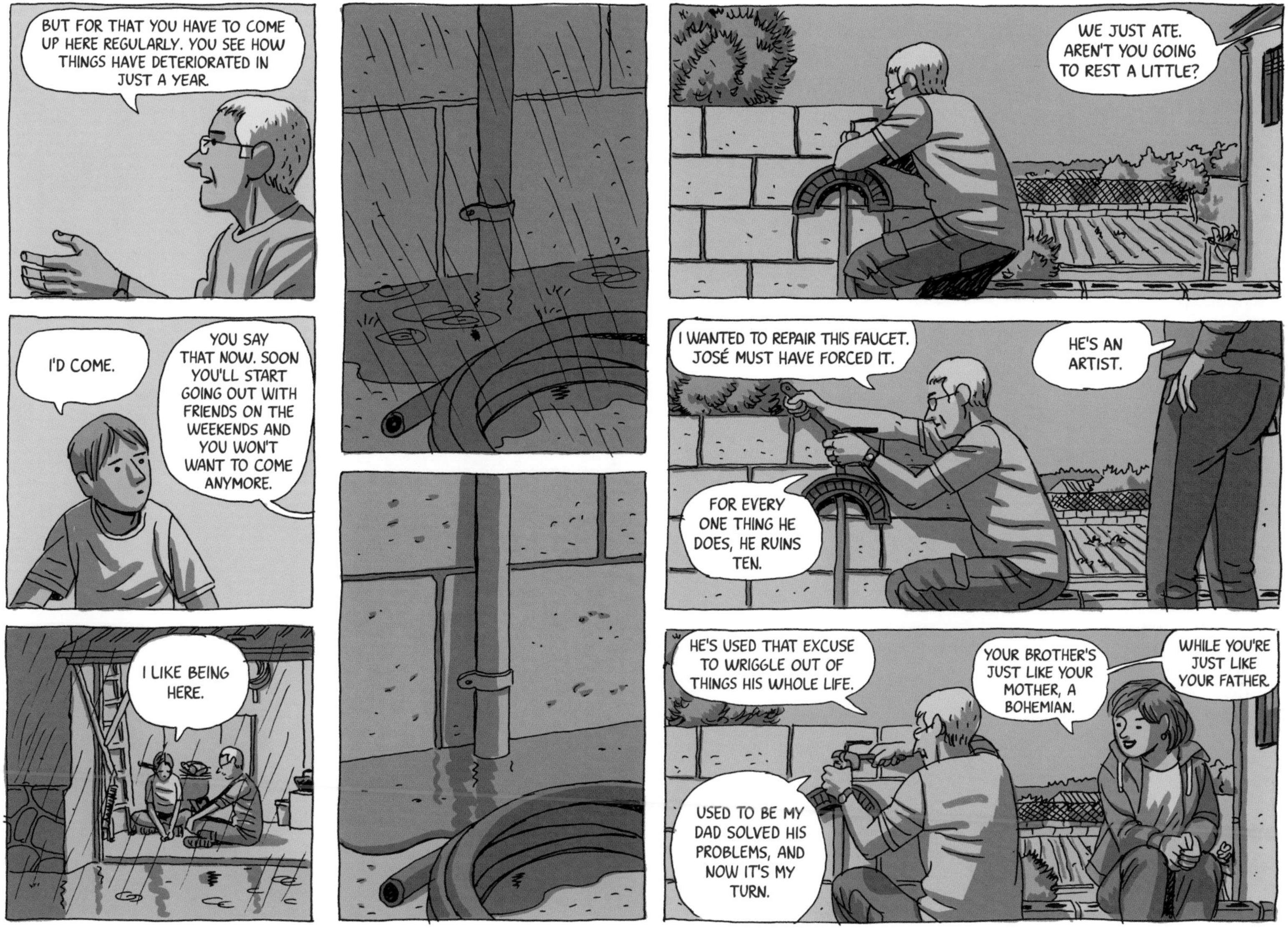
BUT FOR THAT YOU HAVE TO COME UP HERE REGULARLY. YOU SEE HOW THINGS HAVE DETERIORATED IN JUST A YEAR.
I'D COME.
YOU SAY THAT NOW. SOON YOU'LL START GOING OUT WITH FRIENDS ON THE WEEKENDS AND YOU WON'T WANT TO COME ANYMORE.
I LIKE BEING HERE.
WE JUST ATE. AREN'T YOU GOING TO REST A LITTLE?
I WANTED TO REPAIR THIS FAUCET. JOSÉ MUST HAVE FORCED IT.
HE'S AN ARTIST.
FOR EVERY ONE THING HE DOES, HE RUINS TEN.
HE'S USED THAT EXCUSE TO WRIGGLE OUT OF THINGS HIS WHOLE LIFE.
YOUR BROTHER'S JUST LIKE YOUR MOTHER, A BOHEMIAN.
WHILE YOU'RE JUST LIKE YOUR FATHER.
USED TO BE MY DAD SOLVED HIS PROBLEMS, AND NOW IT'S MY TURN.

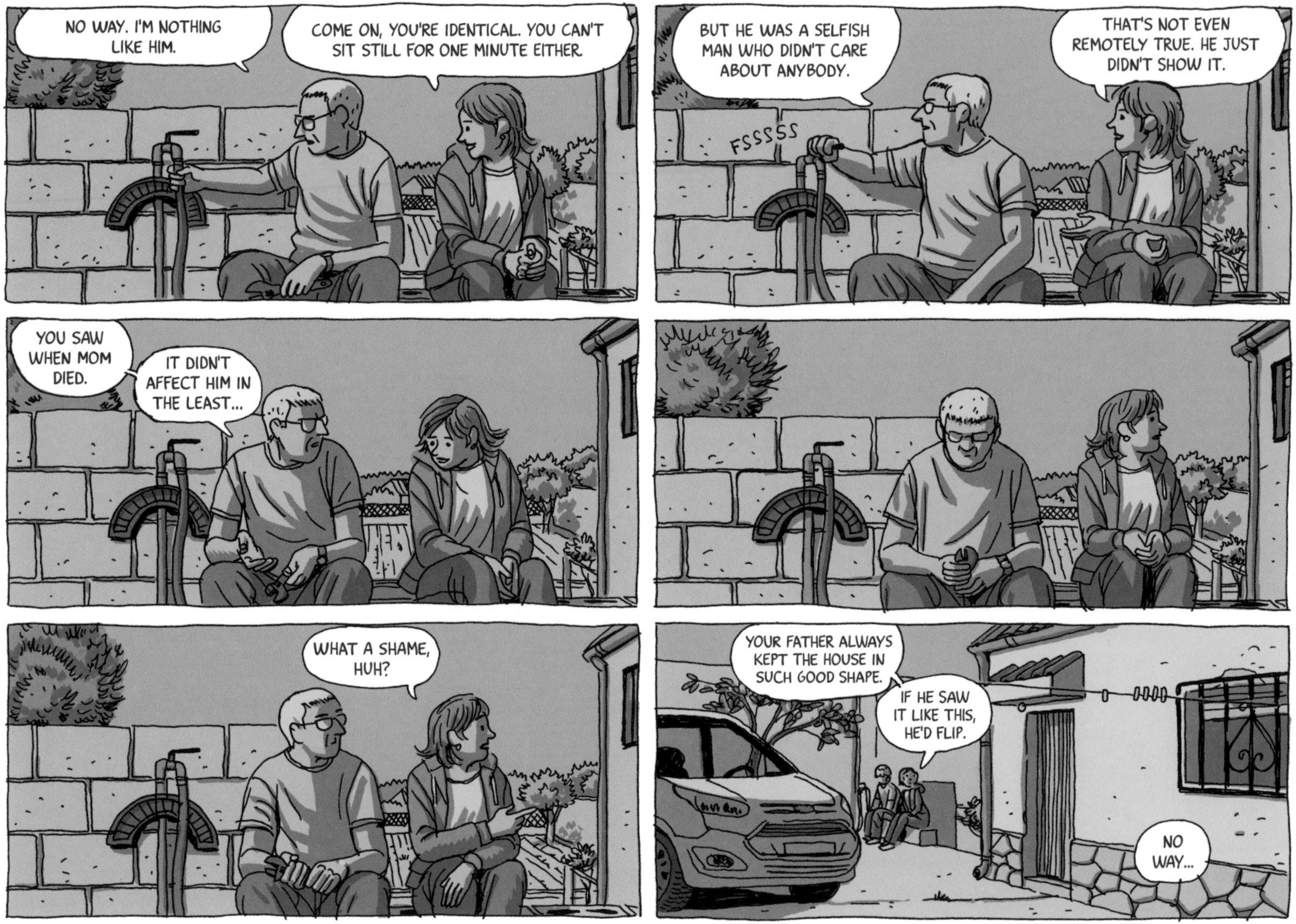
NO WAY. I'M NOTHING LIKE HIM.
COME ON, YOU'RE IDENTICAL. YOU CAN'T SIT STILL FOR ONE MINUTE EITHER.
FSSSSS
BUT HE WAS A SELFISH MAN WHO DIDN'T CARE ABOUT ANYBODY.
THAT'S NOT EVEN REMOTELY TRUE. HE JUST DIDN'T SHOW IT.
YOU SAW WHEN MOM DIED.
IT DIDN'T AFFECT HIM IN THE LEAST...
WHAT A SHAME, HUH?
YOUR FATHER ALWAYS KEPT THE HOUSE IN SUCH GOOD SHAPE.
IF HE SAW IT LIKE THIS, HE'D FLIP.
NO WAY...

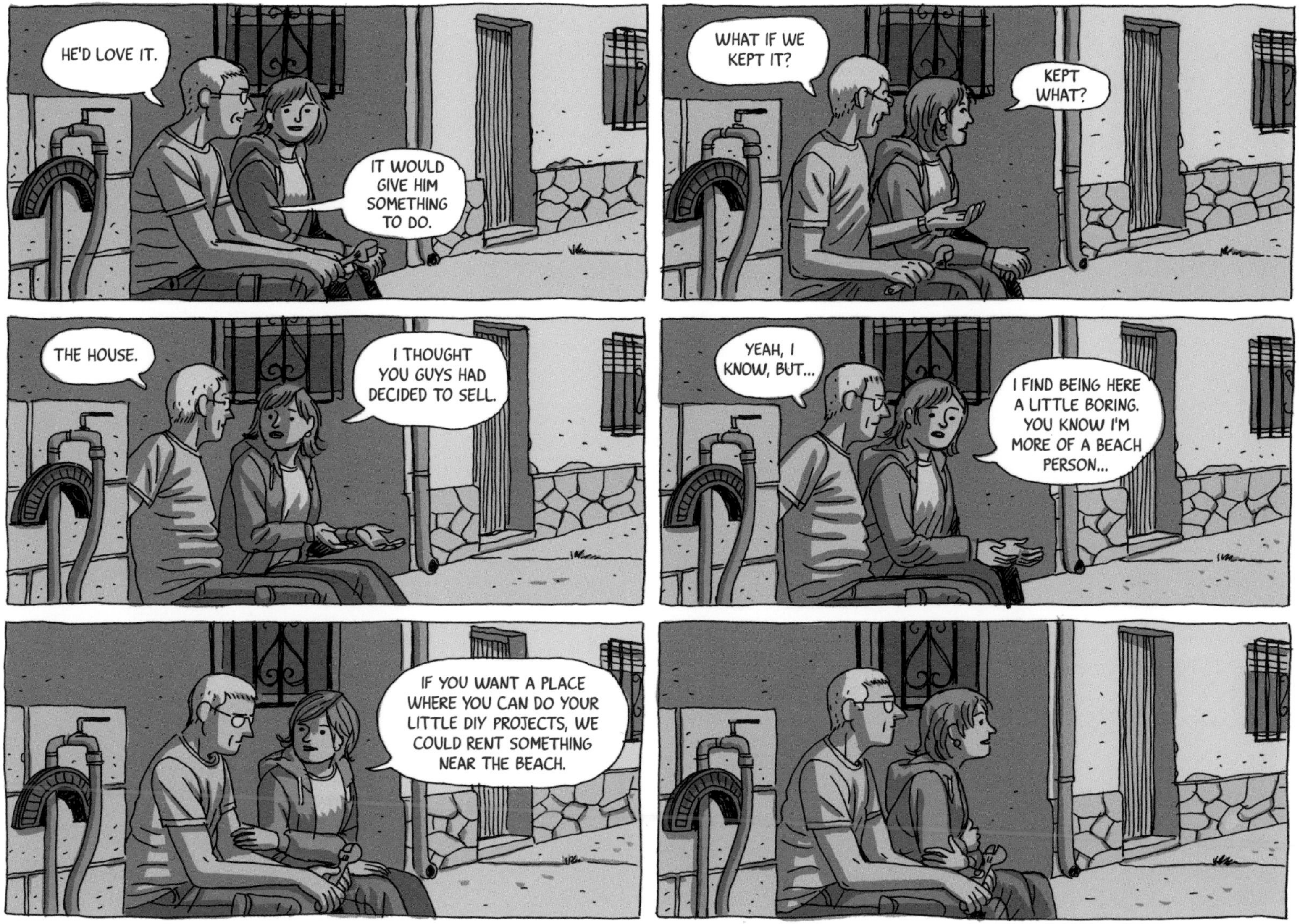
HE'D LOVE IT.
IT WOULD GIVE HIM SOMETHING TO DO.
WHAT IF WE KEPT IT?
KEPT WHAT?
THE HOUSE.
I THOUGHT YOU GUYS HAD DECIDED TO SELL.
YEAH, I KNOW, BUT...
I FIND BEING HERE A LITTLE BORING. YOU KNOW I'M MORE OF A BEACH PERSON...
IF YOU WANT A PLACE WHERE YOU CAN DO YOUR LITTLE DIY PROJECTS, WE COULD RENT SOMETHING NEAR THE BEACH.

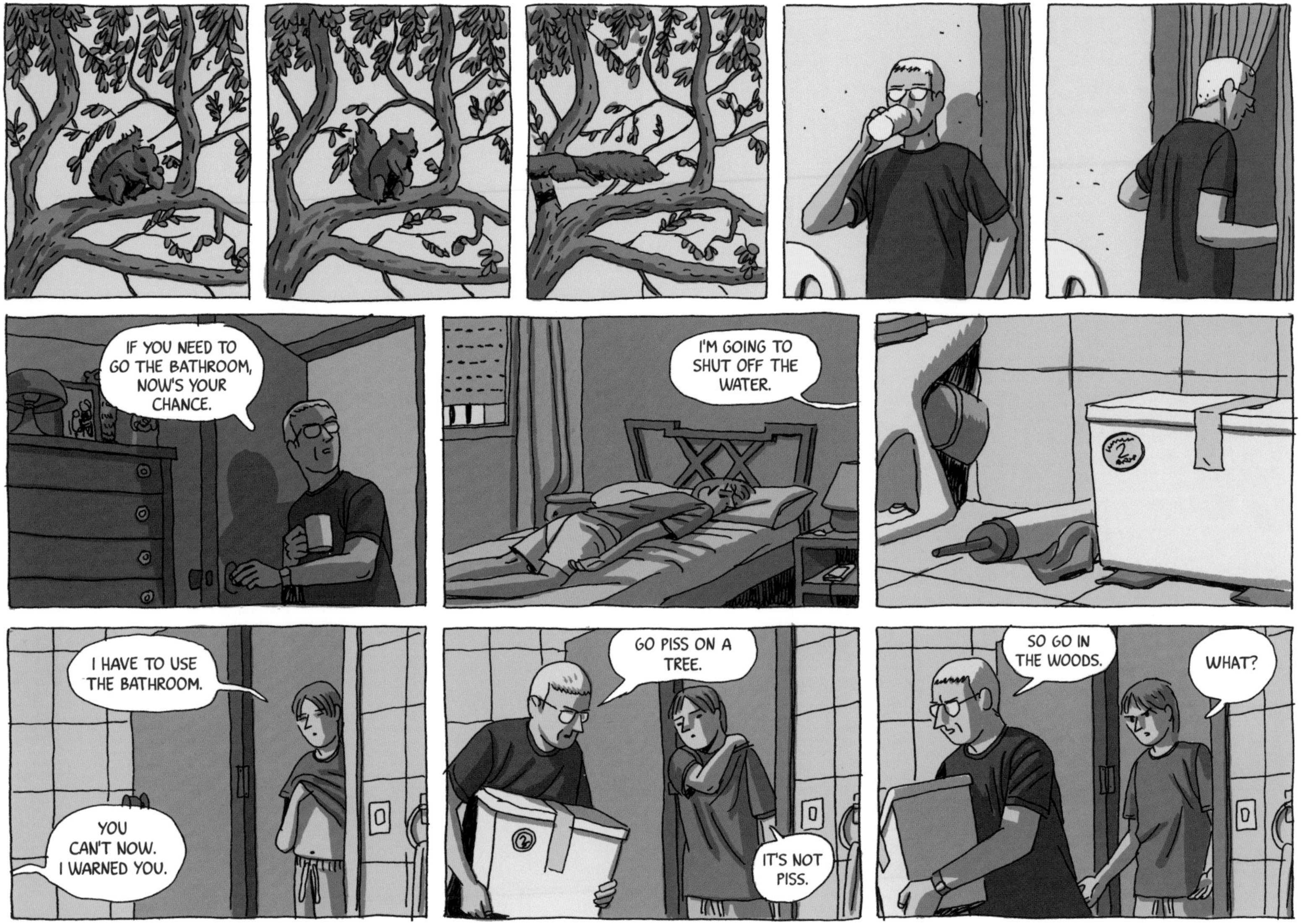
IF YOU NEED TO GO THE BATHROOM, NOW'S YOUR CHANCE.
I'M GOING TO SHUT OFF THE WATER.
I HAVE TO USE THE BATHROOM.
YOU CAN'T NOW. I WARNED YOU.
GO PISS ON A TREE.
IT'S NOT PISS.
SO GO IN THE WOODS.
WHAT?

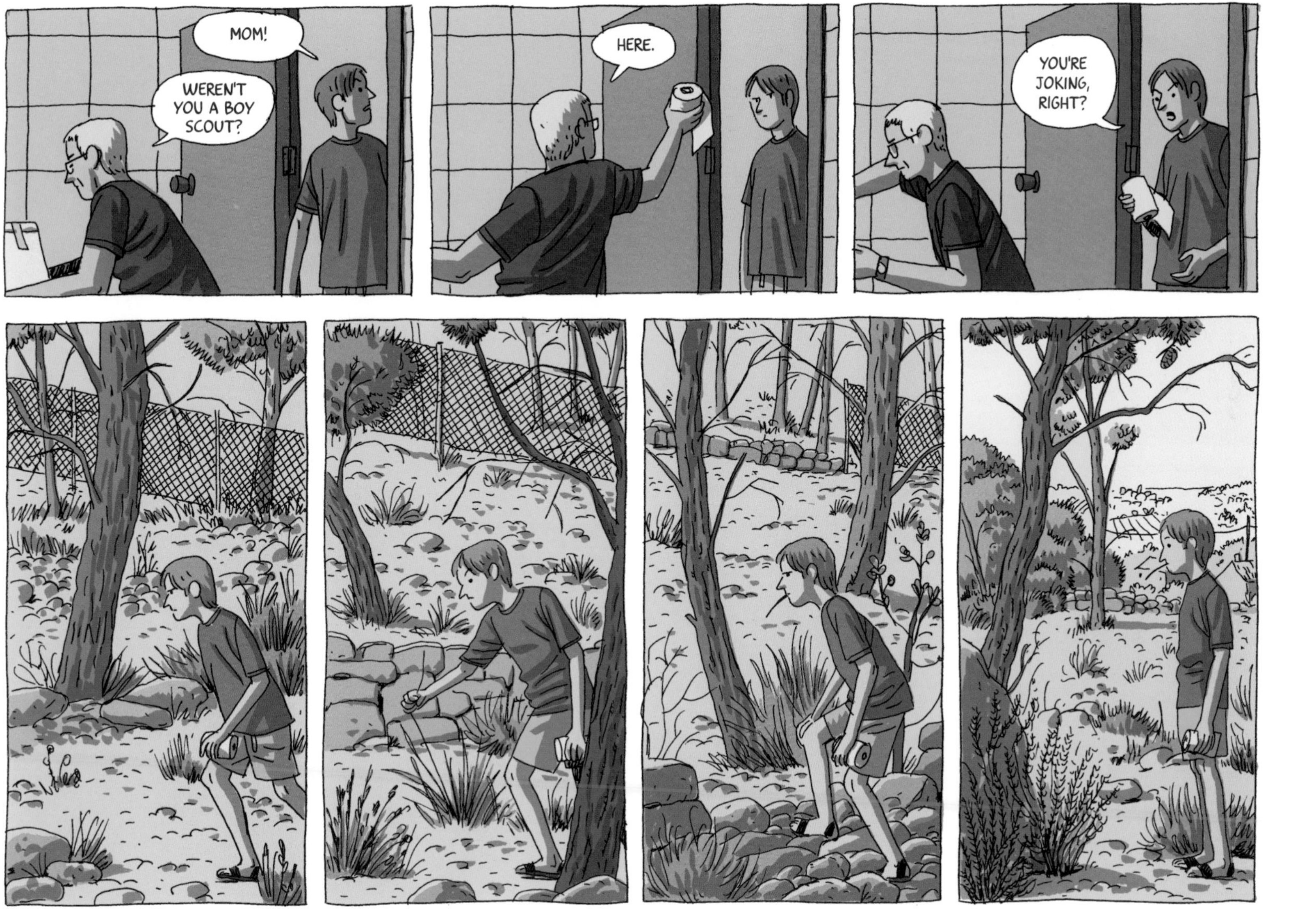
MOM!
WEREN'T YOU A BOY SCOUT?
HERE.
YOU'RE JOKING, RIGHT?

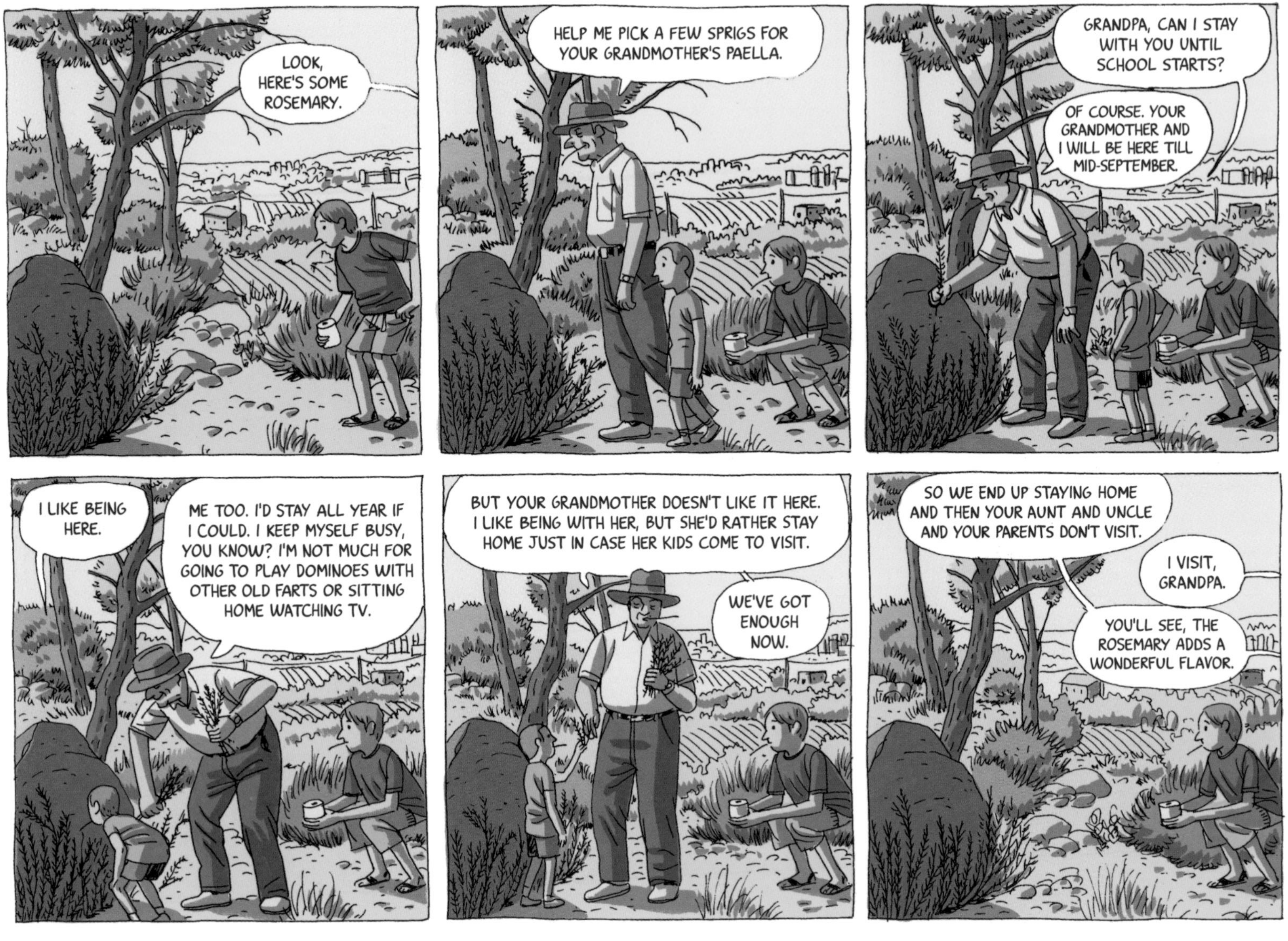
LOOK, HERE'S SOME ROSEMARY.
HELP ME PICK A FEW SPRIGS FOR YOUR GRANDMOTHER'S PAELLA.
GRANDPA, CAN I STAY WITH YOU UNTIL SCHOOL STARTS?
OF COURSE. YOUR GRANDMOTHER AND I WILL BE HERE TILL MID-SEPTEMBER.
I LIKE BEING HERE.
ME TOO. I'D STAY ALL YEAR IF I COULD. I KEEP MYSELF BUSY, YOU KNOW? I'M NOT MUCH FOR GOING TO PLAY DOMINOES WITH OTHER OLD FARTS OR SITTING HOME WATCHING TV.
BUT YOUR GRANDMOTHER DOESN'T LIKE IT HERE. I LIKE BEING WITH HER, BUT SHE'D RATHER STAY HOME JUST IN CASE HER KIDS COME TO VISIT.
WE'VE GOT ENOUGH NOW.
SO WE END UP STAYING HOME AND THEN YOUR AUNT AND UNCLE AND YOUR PARENTS DON'T VISIT.
I VISIT, GRANDPA.
YOU'LL SEE, THE ROSEMARY ADDS A WONDERFUL FLAVOR.

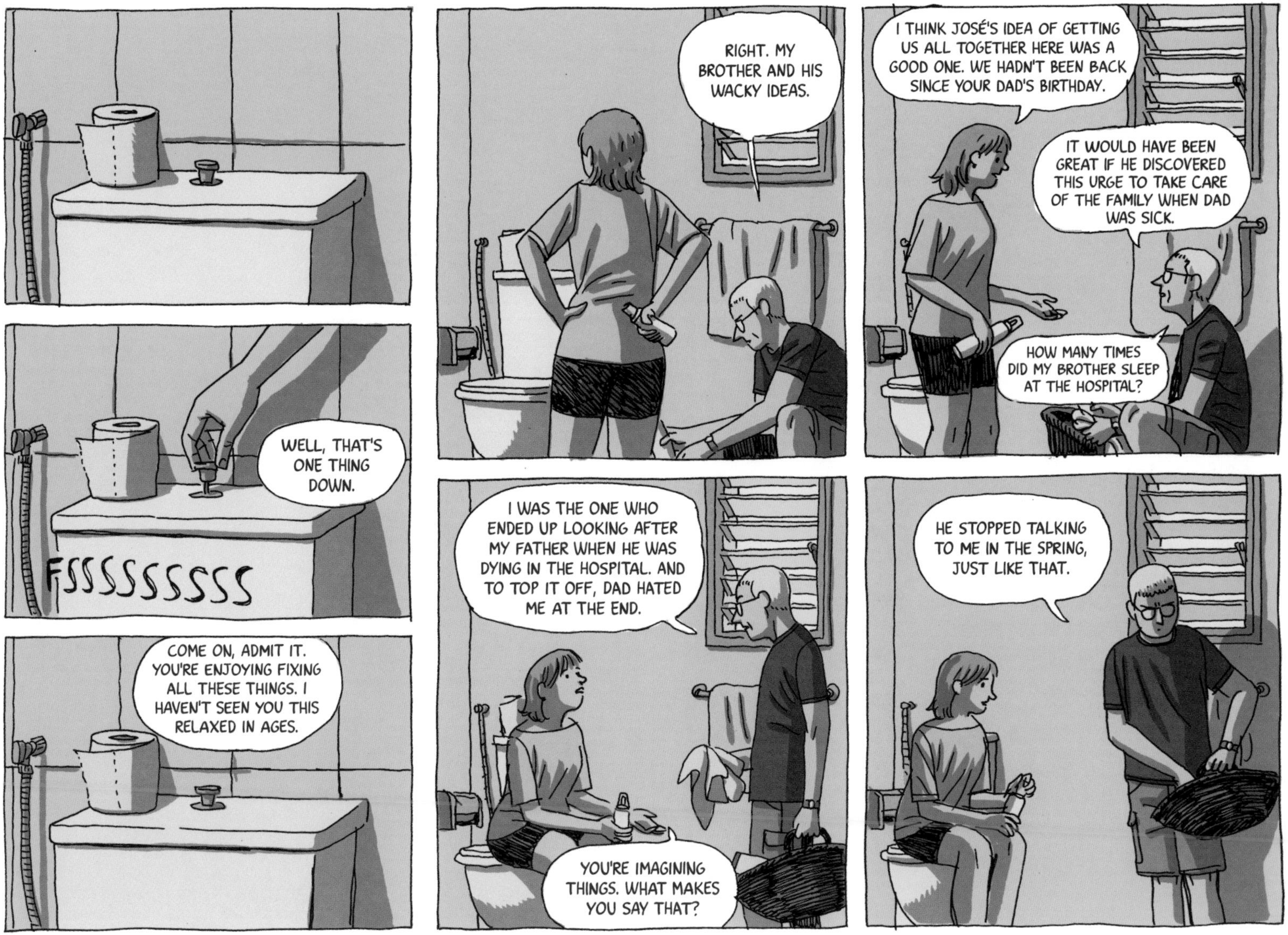
WELL, THAT'S ONE THING DOWN.
FSSSSSSSSS
COME ON, ADMIT IT. YOU'RE ENJOYING FIXING ALL THESE THINGS. I HAVEN'T SEEN YOU THIS RELAXED IN AGES.
RIGHT. MY BROTHER AND HIS WACKY IDEAS.
I THINK JOSÉ'S IDEA OF GETTING US ALL TOGETHER HERE WAS A GOOD ONE. WE HADN'T BEEN BACK SINCE YOUR DAD'S BIRTHDAY.
IT WOULD HAVE BEEN GREAT IF HE DISCOVERED THIS URGE TO TAKE CARE OF THE FAMILY WHEN DAD WAS SICK.
HOW MANY TIMES DID MY BROTHER SLEEP AT THE HOSPITAL?
I WAS THE ONE WHO ENDED UP LOOKING AFTER MY FATHER WHEN HE WAS DYING IN THE HOSPITAL. AND TO TOP IT OFF, DAD HATED ME AT THE END.
YOU'RE IMAGINING THINGS. WHAT MAKES YOU SAY THAT?
HE STOPPED TALKING TO ME IN THE SPRING, JUST LIKE THAT.

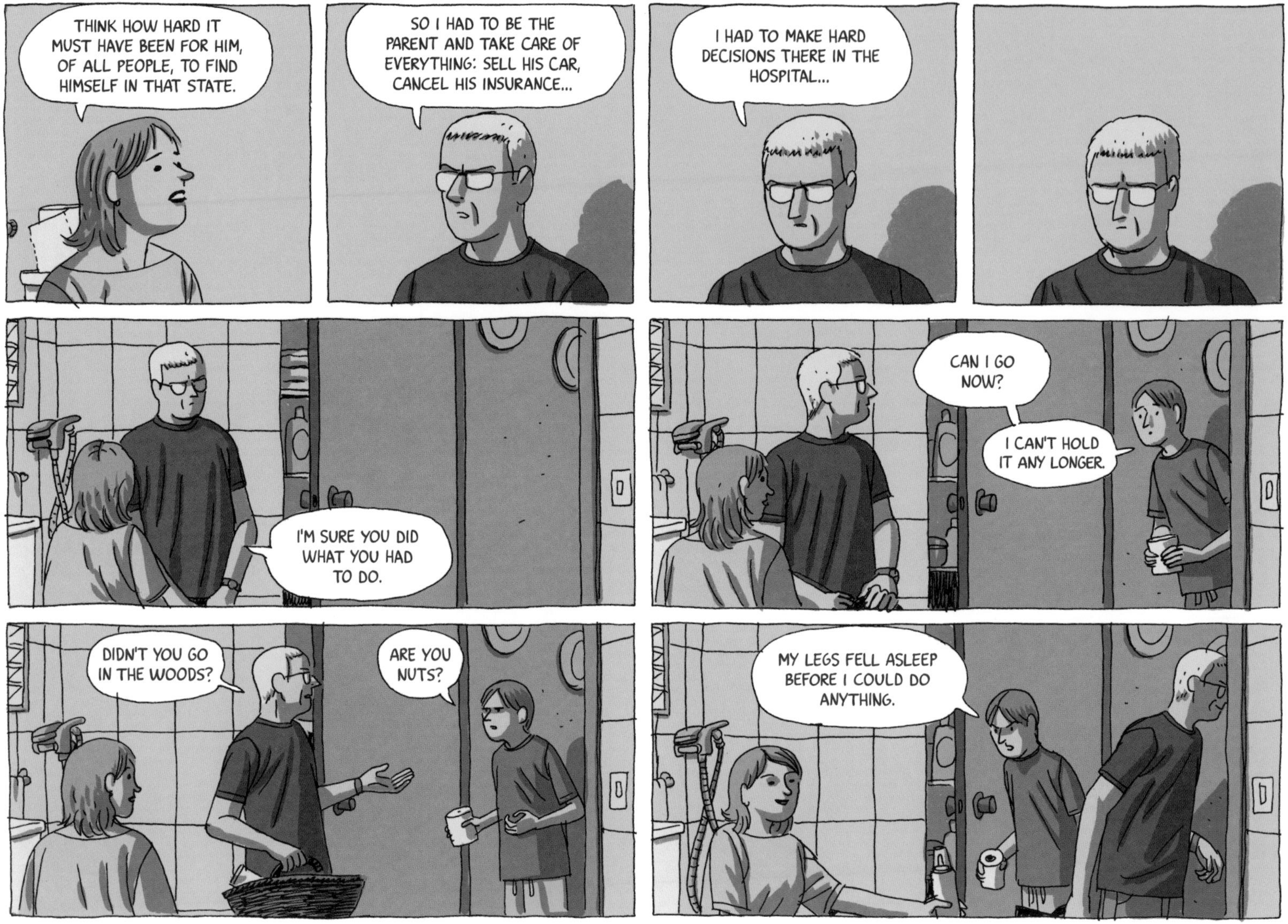
THINK HOW HARD IT MUST HAVE BEEN FOR HIM, OF ALL PEOPLE, TO FIND HIMSELF IN THAT STATE.
SO I HAD TO BE THE PARENT AND TAKE CARE OF EVERYTHING: SELL HIS CAR, CANCEL HIS INSURANCE...
I HAD TO MAKE HARD DECISIONS THERE IN THE HOSPITAL...
I'M SURE YOU DID WHAT YOU HAD TO DO.
CAN I GO NOW?
I CAN'T HOLD IT ANY LONGER.
DIDN'T YOU GO IN THE WOODS?
ARE YOU NUTS?
MY LEGS FELL ASLEEP BEFORE I COULD DO ANYTHING.

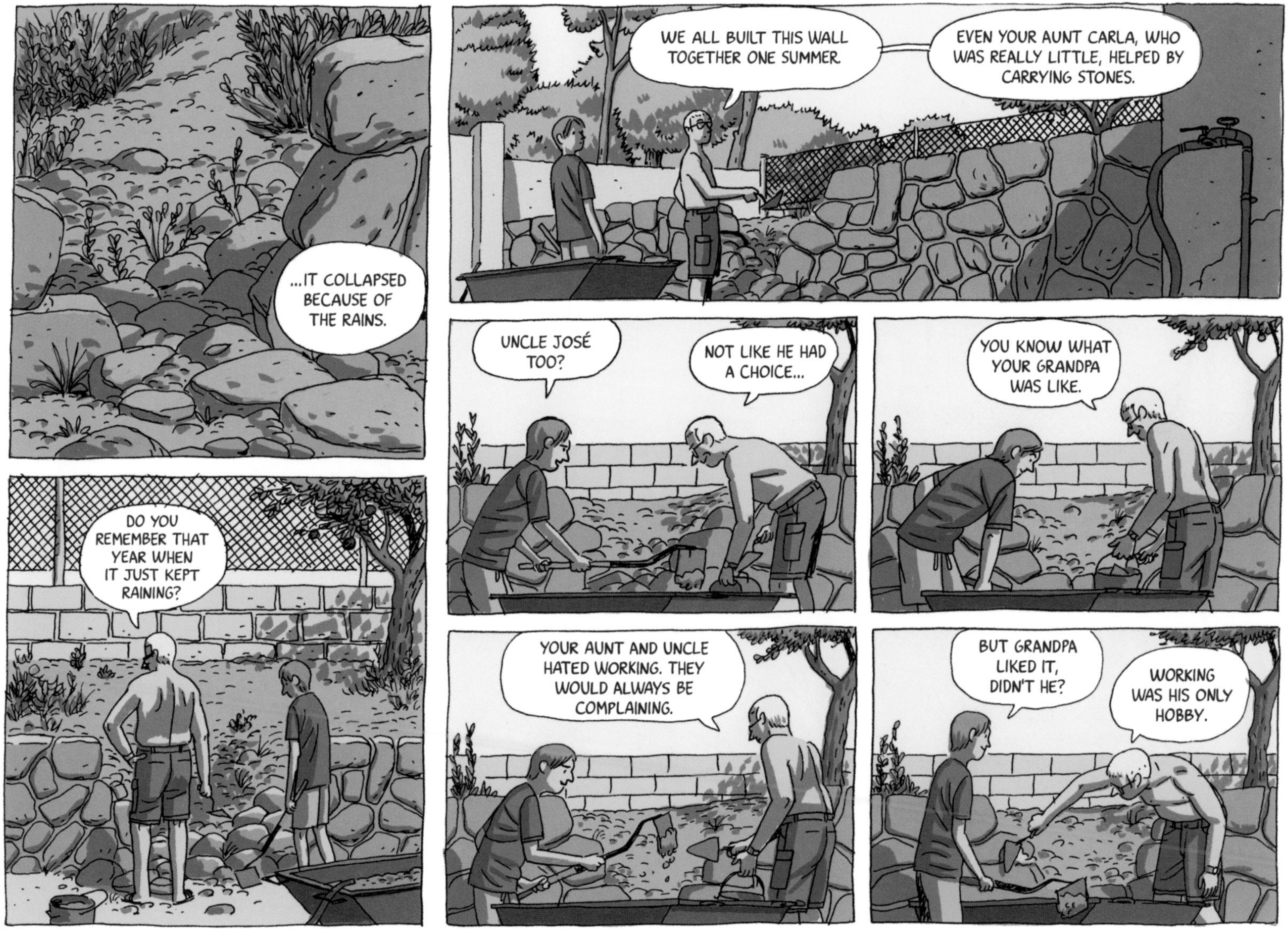
...IT COLLAPSED BECAUSE OF THE RAINS.
DO YOU REMEMBER THAT YEAR WHEN IT JUST KEPT RAINING?
WE ALL BUILT THIS WALL TOGETHER ONE SUMMER.
EVEN YOUR AUNT CARLA, WHO WAS REALLY LITTLE, HELPED BY CARRYING STONES.
UNCLE JOSÉ TOO?
NOT LIKE HE HAD A CHOICE...
YOU KNOW WHAT YOUR GRANDPA WAS LIKE.
YOUR AUNT AND UNCLE HATED WORKING. THEY WOULD ALWAYS BE COMPLAINING.
BUT GRANDPA LIKED IT, DIDN'T HE?
WORKING WAS HIS ONLY HOBBY.

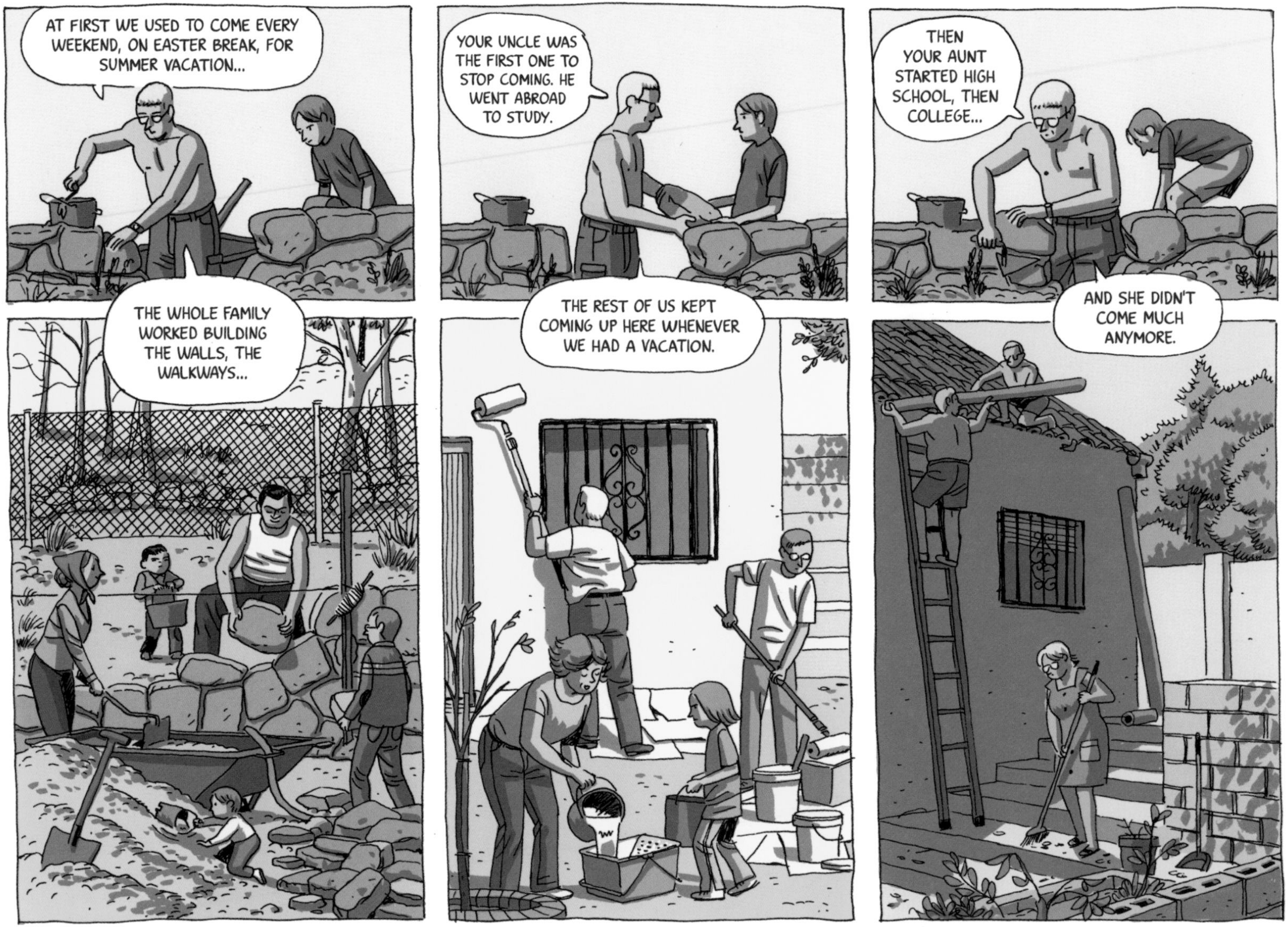
AT FIRST WE USED TO COME EVERY WEEKEND, ON EASTER BREAK, FOR SUMMER VACATION...
YOUR UNCLE WAS THE FIRST ONE TO STOP COMING. HE WENT ABROAD TO STUDY.
THEN YOUR AUNT STARTED HIGH SCHOOL, THEN COLLEGE...
THE WHOLE FAMILY WORKED BUILDING THE WALLS, THE WALKWAYS...
THE REST OF US KEPT COMING UP HERE WHENEVER WE HAD A VACATION.
AND SHE DIDN'T COME MUCH ANYMORE.

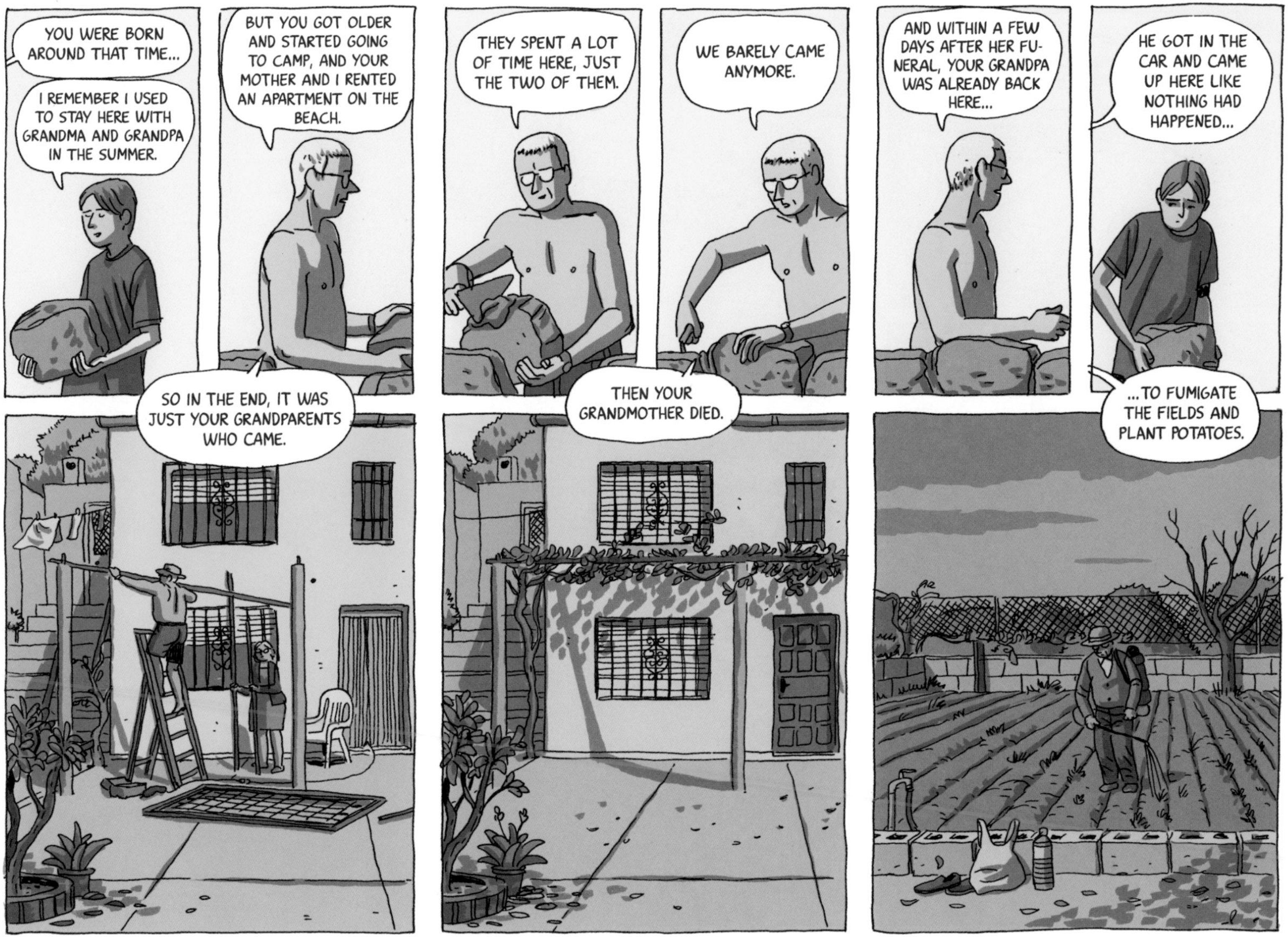
YOU WERE BORN AROUND THAT TIME...
I REMEMBER I USED TO STAY HERE WITH GRANDMA AND GRANDPA IN THE SUMMER.
BUT YOU GOT OLDER AND STARTED GOING TO CAMP, AND YOUR MOTHER AND I RENTED AN APARTMENT ON THE BEACH.
SO IN THE END, IT WAS JUST YOUR GRANDPARENTS WHO CAME.
THEY SPENT A LOT OF TIME HERE, JUST THE TWO OF THEM.
WE BARELY CAME ANYMORE.
THEN YOUR GRANDMOTHER DIED.
AND WITHIN A FEW DAYS AFTER HER FU-NERAL, YOUR GRANDPA WAS ALREADY BACK HERE...
HE GOT IN THE CAR AND CAME UP HERE LIKE NOTHING HAD HAPPENED...
...TO FUMIGATE THE FIELDS AND PLANT POTATOES.

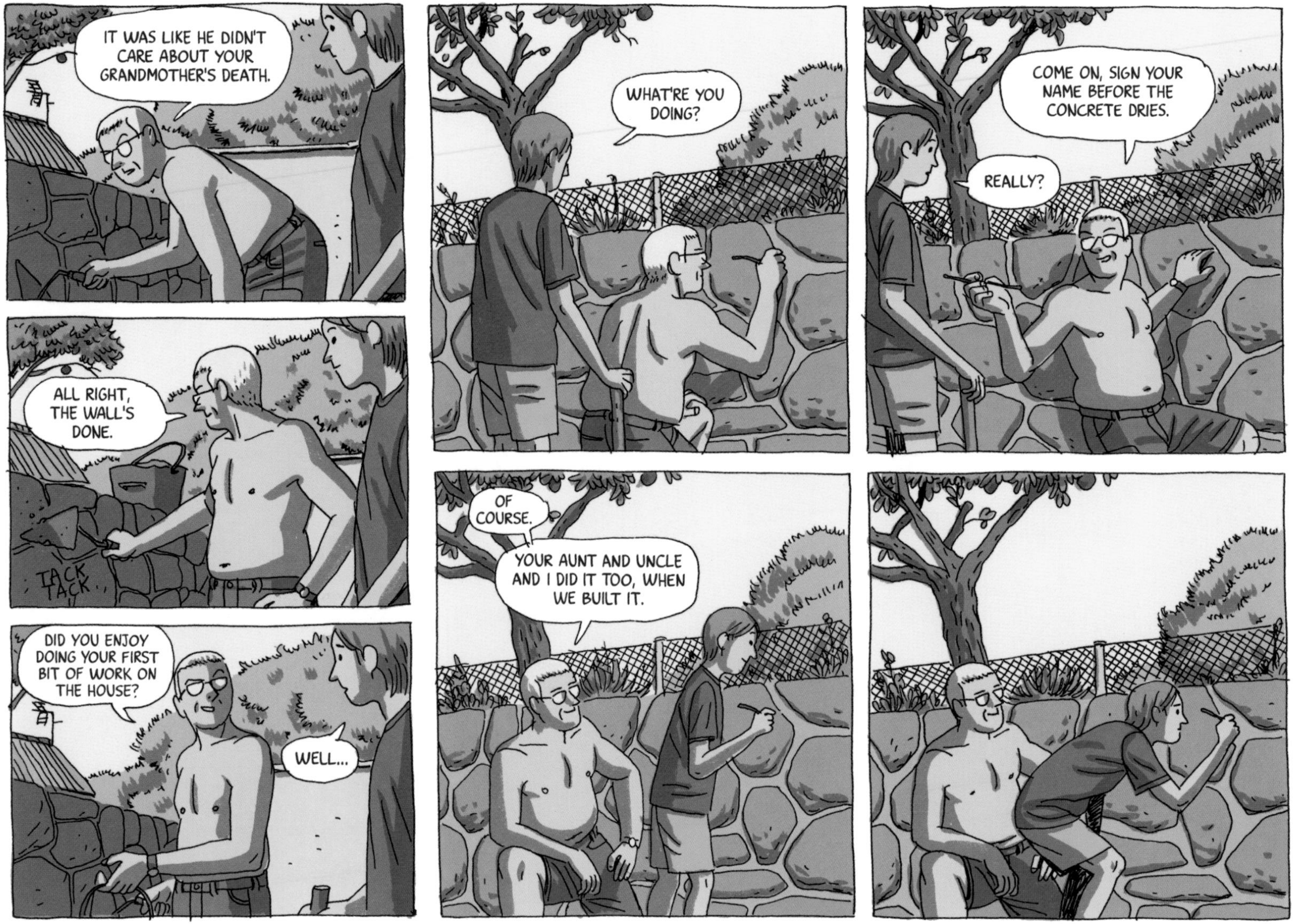
IT WAS LIKE HE DIDN'T CARE ABOUT YOUR GRANDMOTHER'S DEATH.
ALL RIGHT, THE WALL'S DONE.
TACK TACK
DID YOU ENJOY DOING YOUR FIRST BIT OF WORK ON THE HOUSE?
WELL...
WHAT'RE YOU DOING?
COME ON, SIGN YOUR NAME BEFORE THE CONCRETE DRIES.
REALLY?
OF COURSE.
YOUR AUNT AND UNCLE AND I DID IT TOO, WHEN WE BUILT IT.

ARE THERE MORE THINGS TO DO?

THERE'S ALWAYS SOMETHING TO DO HERE.

YOU WANT TO KEEP GOING?

WE'VE STILL GOT TIME TO SET UP THE SCAFFOLD BEFORE YOUR AUNT GETS HERE.

OK.

HEY, DAD...

MAYBE HE WAS LONELY.

WHO?

GRANDPA. MAYBE YOU'RE WRONG AND IT'S NOT THAT HE DIDN'T LOVE GRANDMA...

MAYBE HE FELT LESS LONELY HERE THAN AT THE APARTMENT, YOU KNOW?

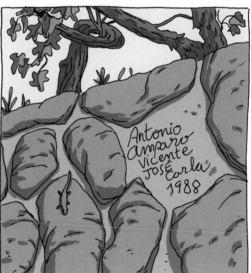

Antonio Amparo Vicente José Carla 1988

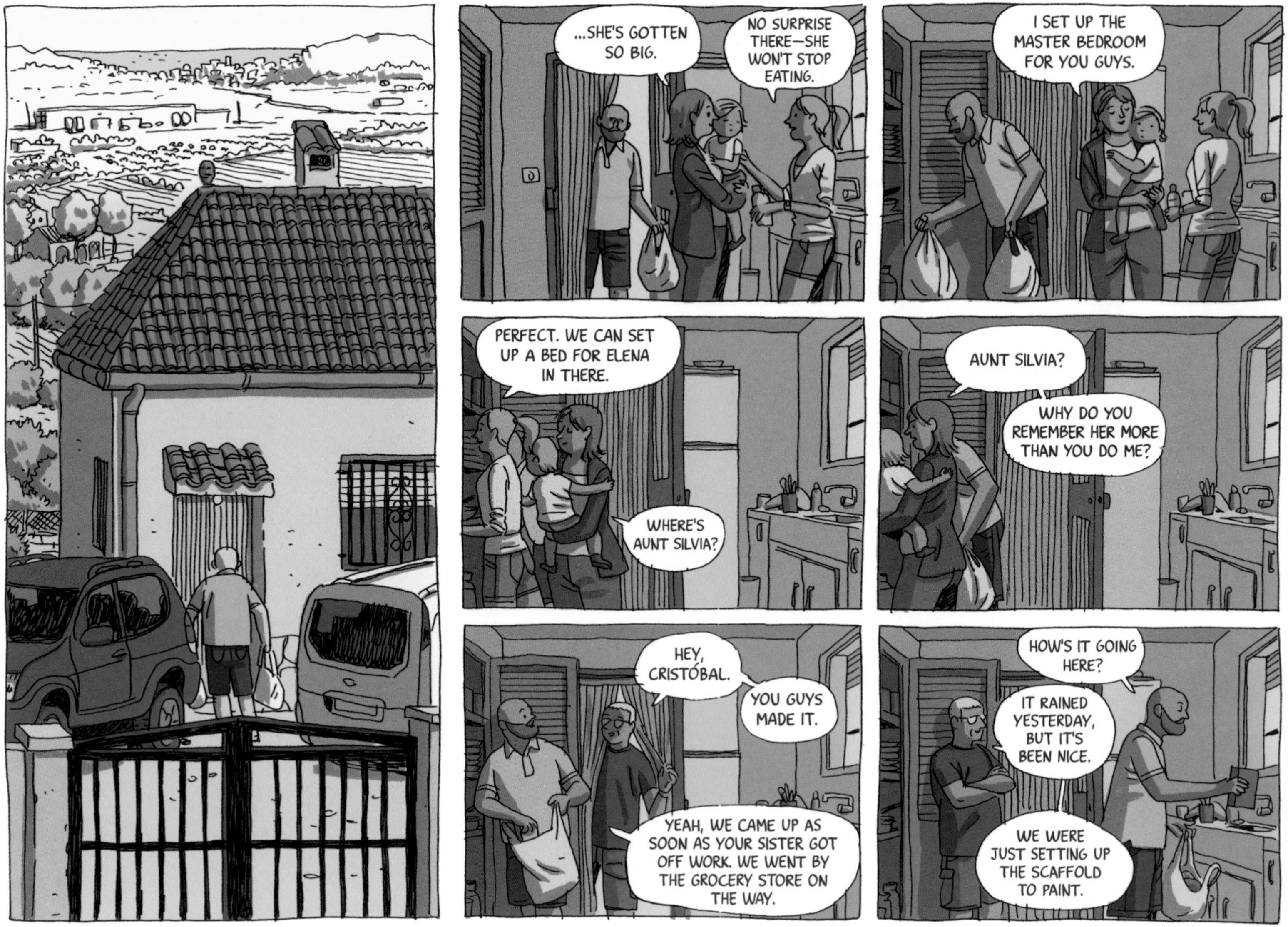
...SHE'S GOTTEN SO BIG.
NO SURPRISE THERE—SHE WON'T STOP EATING.
I SET UP THE MASTER BEDROOM FOR YOU GUYS.
PERFECT. WE CAN SET UP A BED FOR ELENA IN THERE.
WHERE'S AUNT SILVIA?
AUNT SILVIA?
WHY DO YOU REMEMBER HER MORE THAN YOU DO ME?
HEY, CRISTÓBAL.
YOU GUYS MADE IT.
YEAH, WE CAME UP AS SOON AS YOUR SISTER GOT OFF WORK. WE WENT BY THE GROCERY STORE ON THE WAY.
HOW'S IT GOING HERE?
IT RAINED YESTERDAY, BUT IT'S BEEN NICE.
WE WERE JUST SETTING UP THE SCAFFOLD TO PAINT.

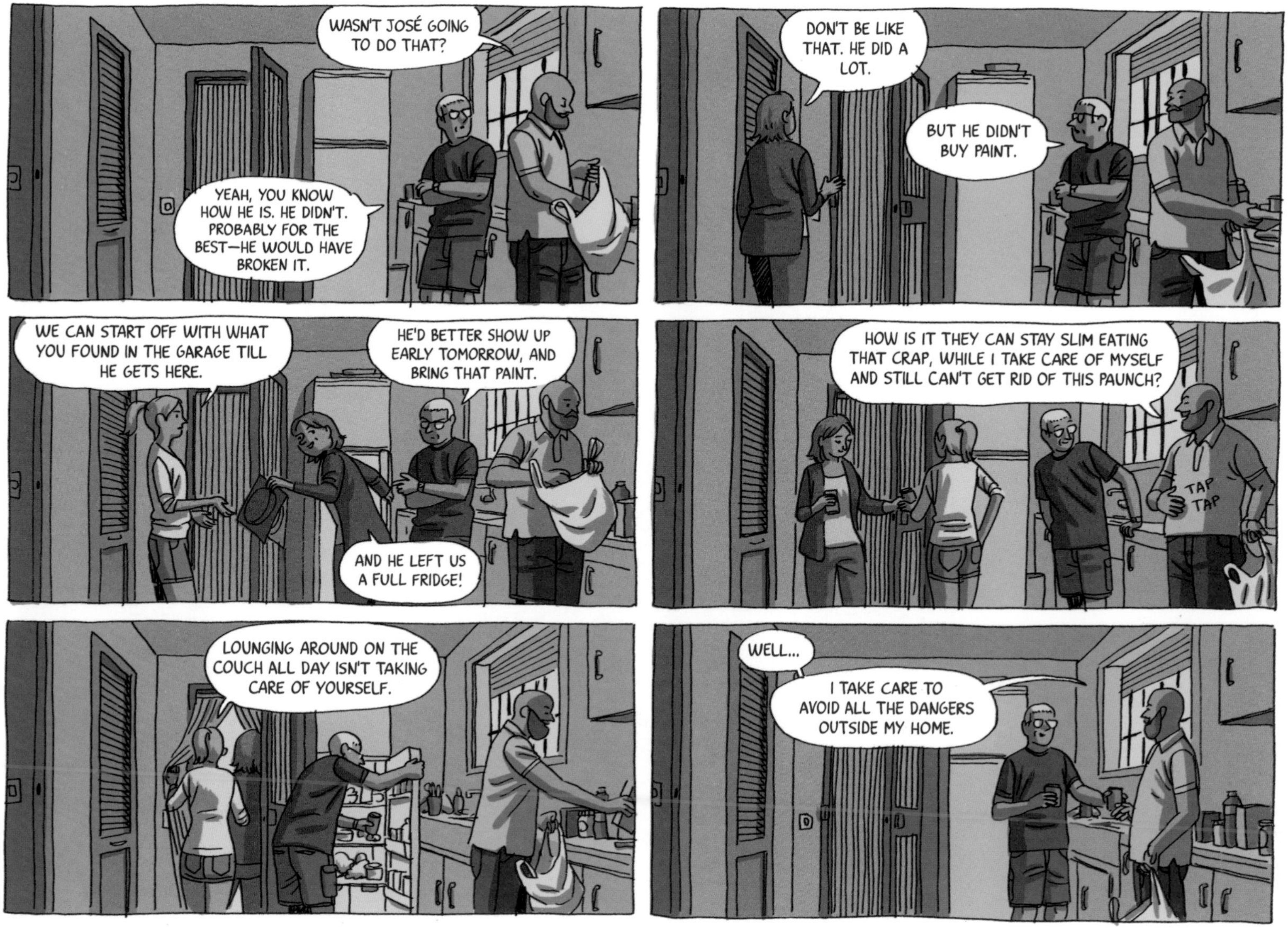
WASN'T JOSÉ GOING TO DO THAT?
YEAH, YOU KNOW HOW HE IS. HE DIDN'T. PROBABLY FOR THE BEST—HE WOULD HAVE BROKEN IT.
DON'T BE LIKE THAT. HE DID A LOT.
BUT HE DIDN'T BUY PAINT.
WE CAN START OFF WITH WHAT YOU FOUND IN THE GARAGE TILL HE GETS HERE.
HE'D BETTER SHOW UP EARLY TOMORROW, AND BRING THAT PAINT.
AND HE LEFT US A FULL FRIDGE!
HOW IS IT THEY CAN STAY SLIM EATING THAT CRAP, WHILE I TAKE CARE OF MYSELF AND STILL CAN'T GET RID OF THIS PAUNCH?
TAP TAP
LOUNGING AROUND ON THE COUCH ALL DAY ISN'T TAKING CARE OF YOURSELF.
WELL...
I TAKE CARE TO AVOID ALL THE DANGERS OUTSIDE MY HOME.

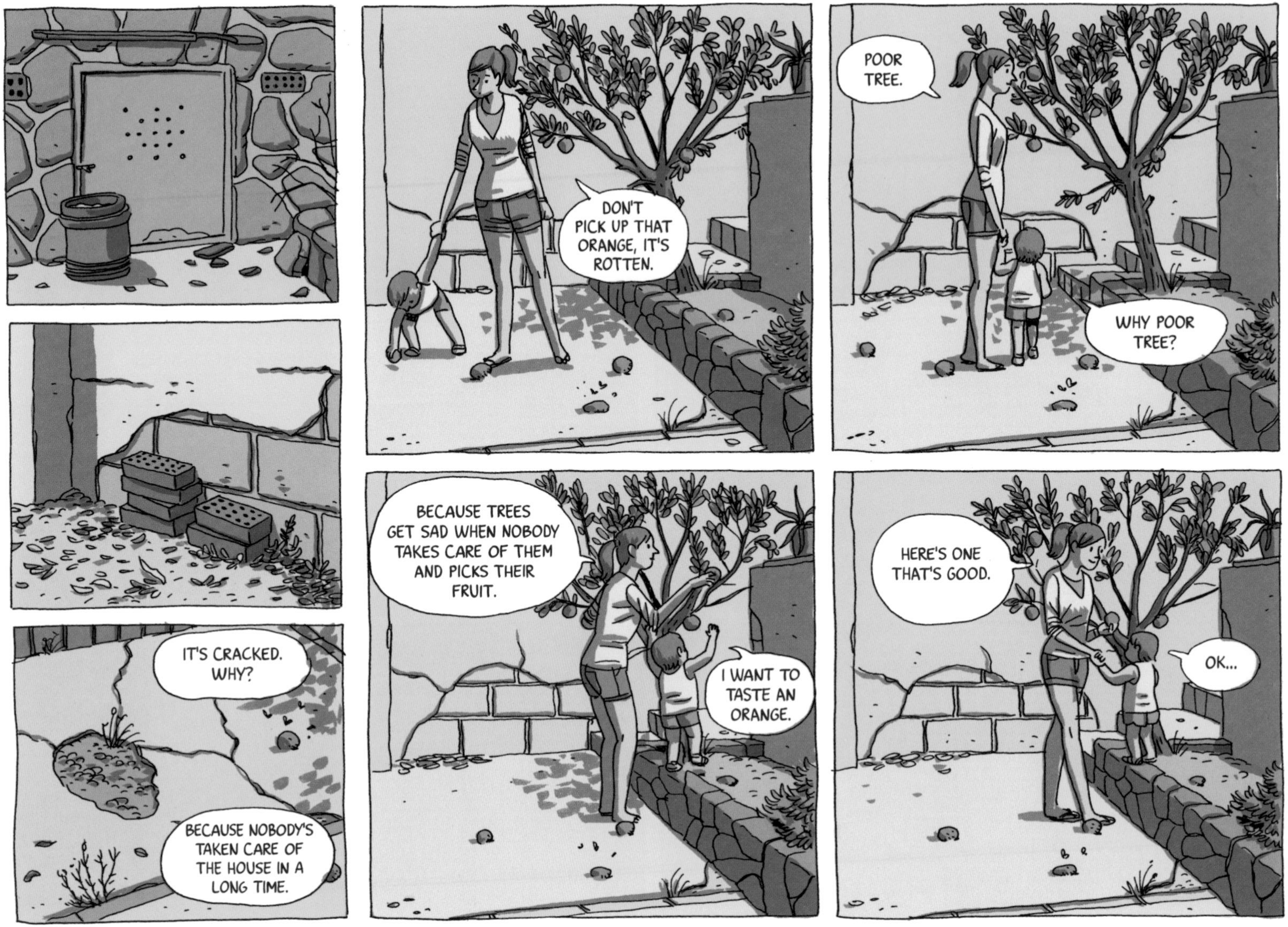
IT'S CRACKED. WHY?
BECAUSE NOBODY'S TAKEN CARE OF THE HOUSE IN A LONG TIME.
DON'T PICK UP THAT ORANGE, IT'S ROTTEN.
POOR TREE.
WHY POOR TREE?
BECAUSE TREES GET SAD WHEN NOBODY TAKES CARE OF THEM AND PICKS THEIR FRUIT.
I WANT TO TASTE AN ORANGE.
HERE'S ONE THAT'S GOOD.
OK...

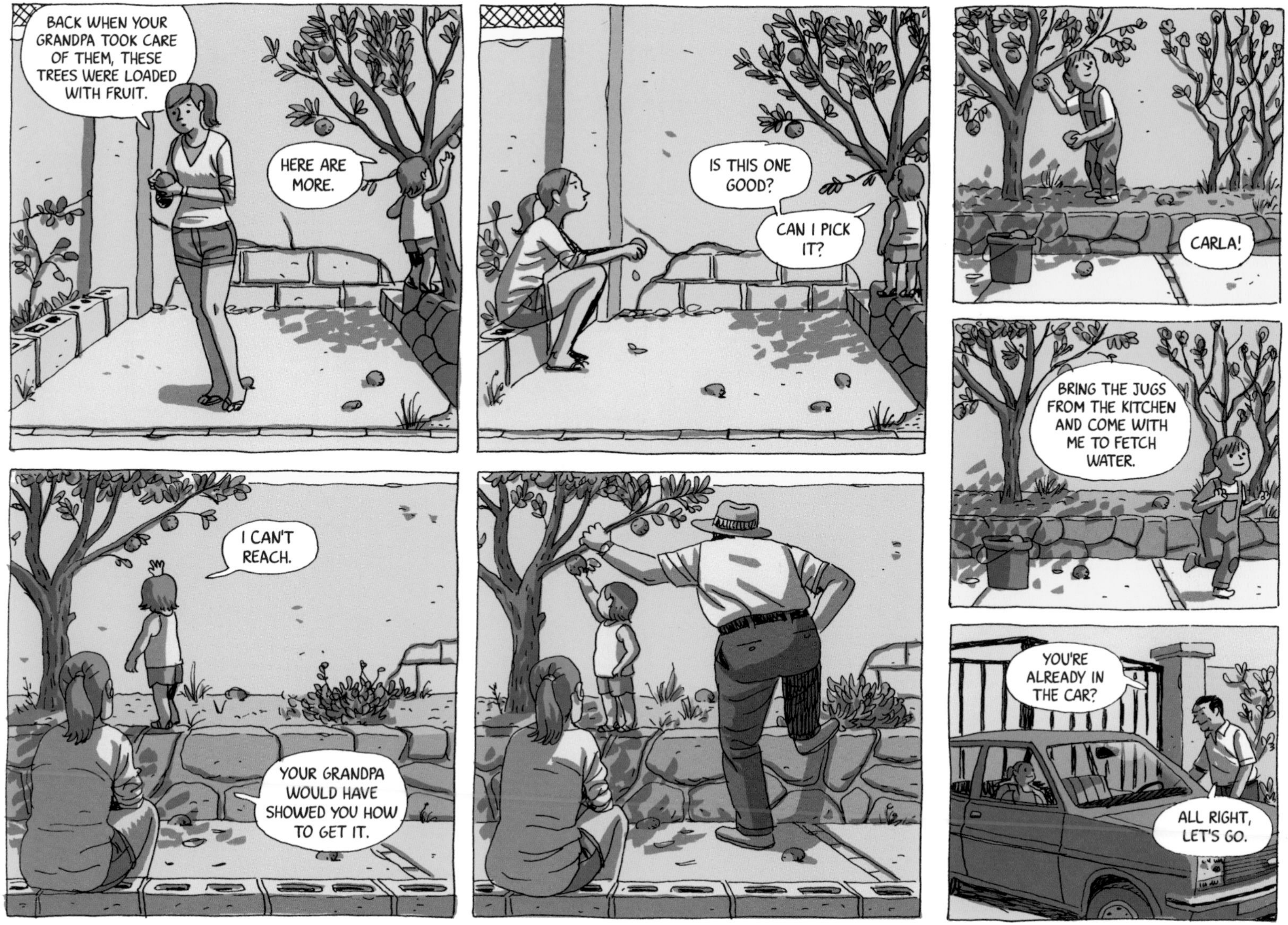
BACK WHEN YOUR GRANDPA TOOK CARE OF THEM, THESE TREES WERE LOADED WITH FRUIT.
HERE ARE MORE.
IS THIS ONE GOOD?
CAN I PICK IT?
CARLA!
BRING THE JUGS FROM THE KITCHEN AND COME WITH ME TO FETCH WATER.
I CAN'T REACH.
YOUR GRANDPA WOULD HAVE SHOWED YOU HOW TO GET IT.
YOU'RE ALREADY IN THE CAR?
ALL RIGHT, LET'S GO.

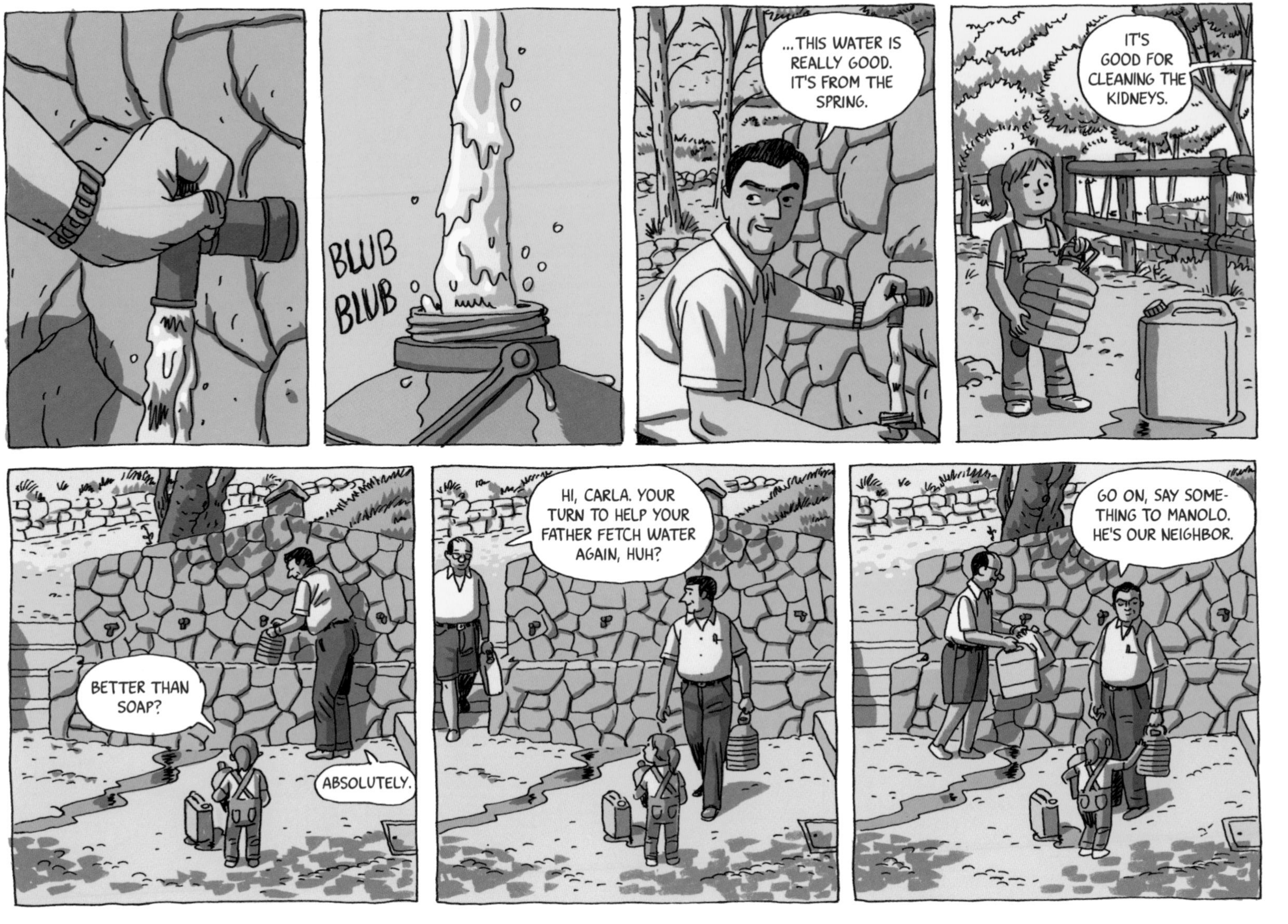
BLUB
BLUB
...THIS WATER IS REALLY GOOD. IT'S FROM THE SPRING.
IT'S GOOD FOR CLEANING THE KIDNEYS.
BETTER THAN SOAP?
ABSOLUTELY.
HI, CARLA. YOUR TURN TO HELP YOUR FATHER FETCH WATER AGAIN, HUH?
GO ON, SAY SOMETHING TO MANOLO. HE'S OUR NEIGHBOR.

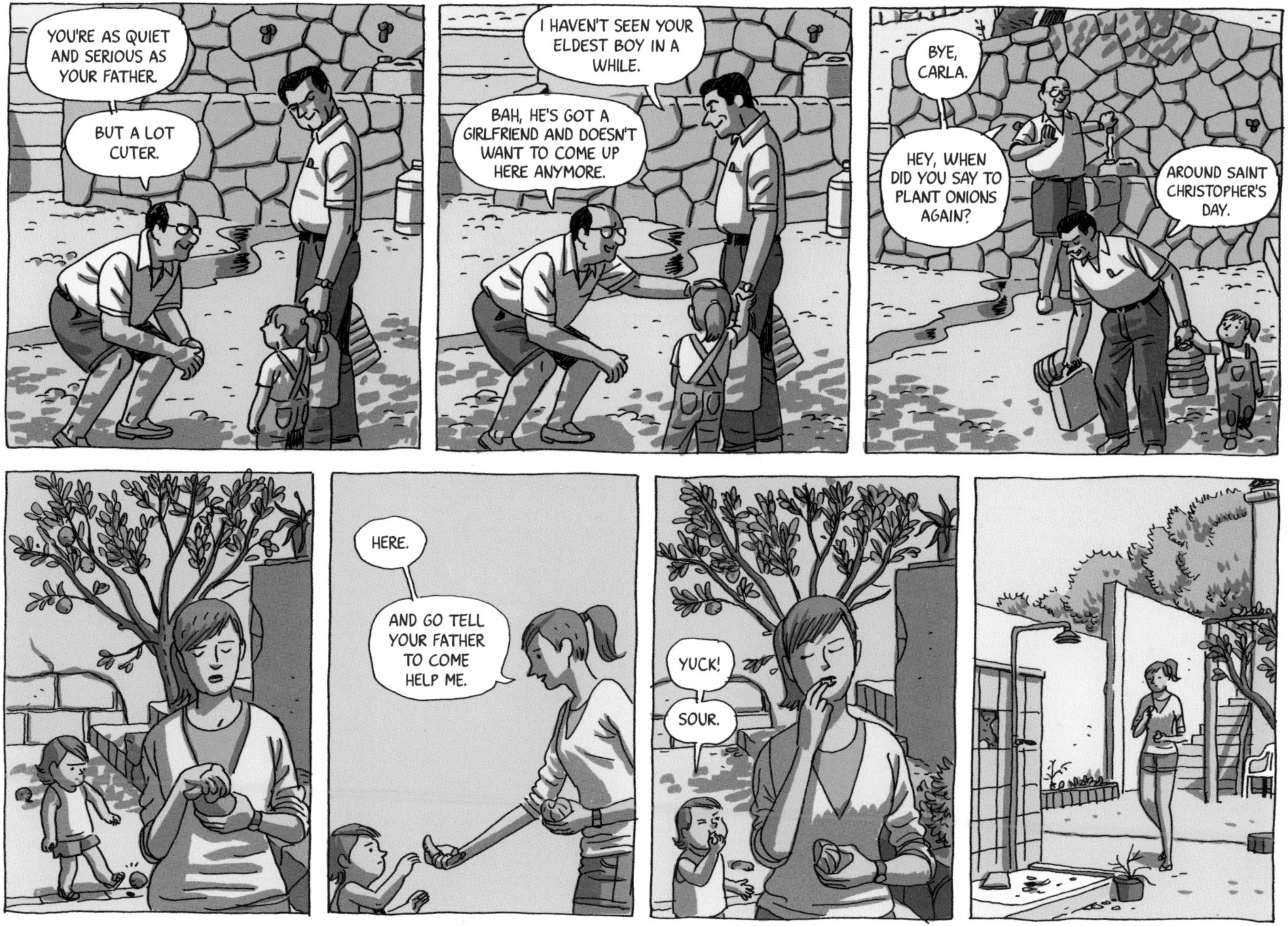
YOU'RE AS QUIET AND SERIOUS AS YOUR FATHER.
BUT A LOT CUTER.
I HAVEN'T SEEN YOUR ELDEST BOY IN A WHILE.
BAH, HE'S GOT A GIRLFRIEND AND DOESN'T WANT TO COME UP HERE ANYMORE.
BYE, CARLA.
HEY, WHEN DID YOU SAY TO PLANT ONIONS AGAIN?
AROUND SAINT CHRISTOPHER'S DAY.
HERE.
AND GO TELL YOUR FATHER TO COME HELP ME.
YUCK!
SOUR.

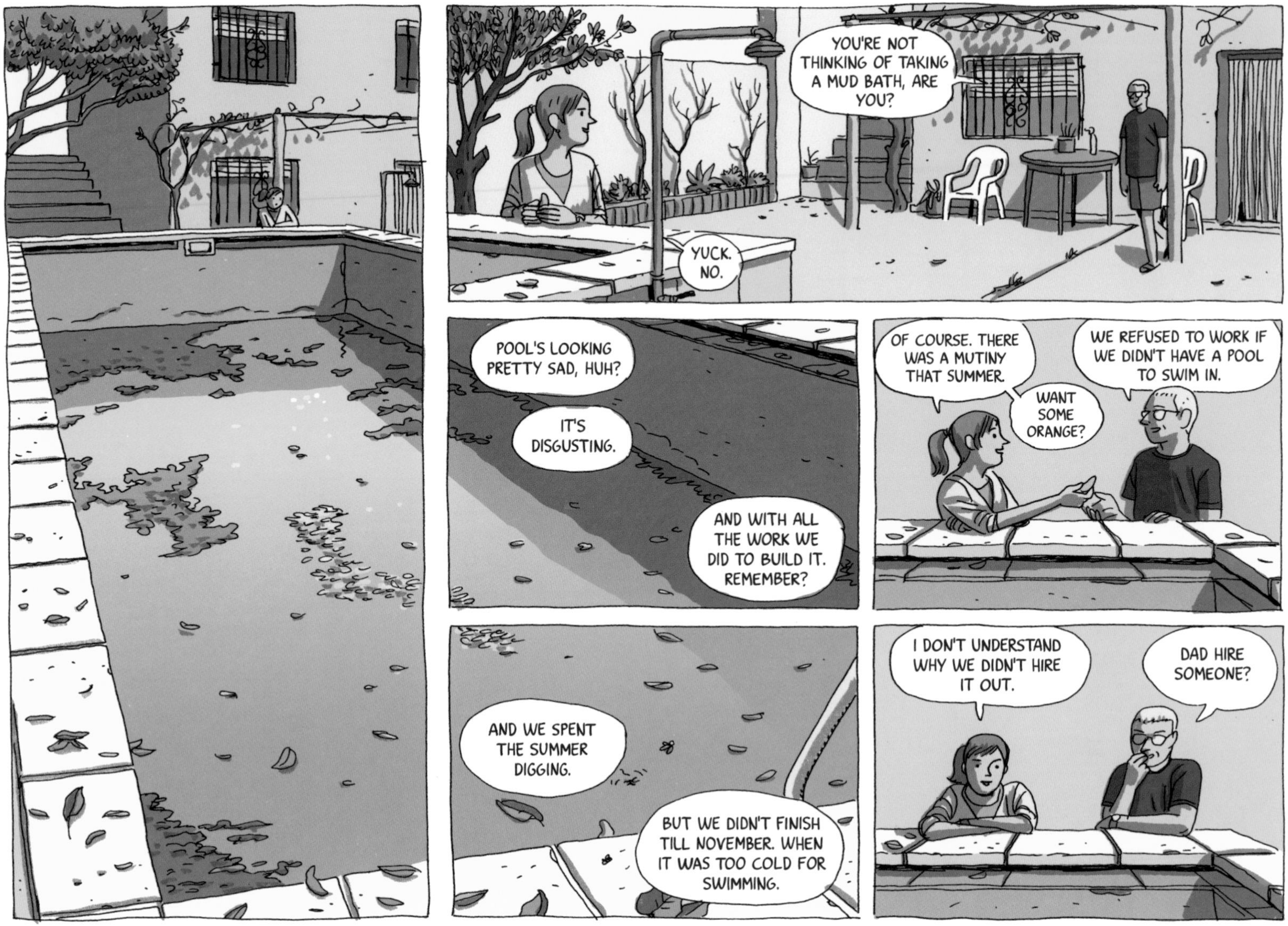
YOU'RE NOT THINKING OF TAKING A MUD BATH, ARE YOU?
YUCK. NO.
POOL'S LOOKING PRETTY SAD, HUH?
IT'S DISGUSTING.
AND WITH ALL THE WORK WE DID TO BUILD IT. REMEMBER?
OF COURSE. THERE WAS A MUTINY THAT SUMMER.
WANT SOME ORANGE?
WE REFUSED TO WORK IF WE DIDN'T HAVE A POOL TO SWIM IN.
AND WE SPENT THE SUMMER DIGGING.
BUT WE DIDN'T FINISH TILL NOVEMBER. WHEN IT WAS TOO COLD FOR SWIMMING.
I DON'T UNDERSTAND WHY WE DIDN'T HIRE IT OUT.
DAD HIRE SOMEONE?

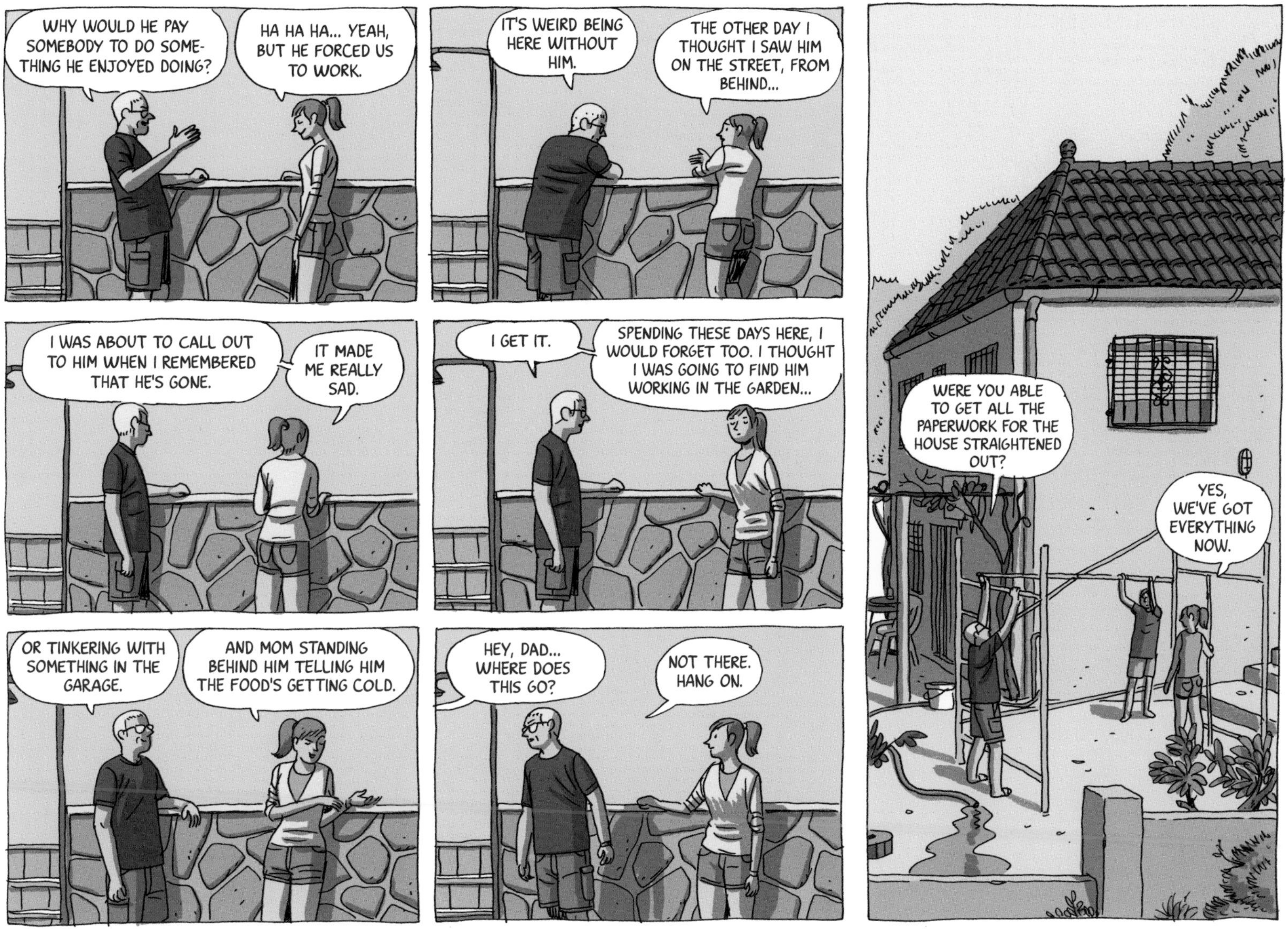
WHY WOULD HE PAY SOMEBODY TO DO SOME-THING HE ENJOYED DOING?
HA HA HA... YEAH, BUT HE FORCED US TO WORK.
IT'S WEIRD BEING HERE WITHOUT HIM.
THE OTHER DAY I THOUGHT I SAW HIM ON THE STREET, FROM BEHIND...
I WAS ABOUT TO CALL OUT TO HIM WHEN I REMEMBERED THAT HE'S GONE.
IT MADE ME REALLY SAD.
I GET IT.
SPENDING THESE DAYS HERE, I WOULD FORGET TOO. I THOUGHT I WAS GOING TO FIND HIM WORKING IN THE GARDEN...
OR TINKERING WITH SOMETHING IN THE GARAGE.
AND MOM STANDING BEHIND HIM TELLING HIM THE FOOD'S GETTING COLD.
HEY, DAD... WHERE DOES THIS GO?
NOT THERE. HANG ON.
WERE YOU ABLE TO GET ALL THE PAPERWORK FOR THE HOUSE STRAIGHTENED OUT?
YES, WE'VE GOT EVERYTHING NOW.

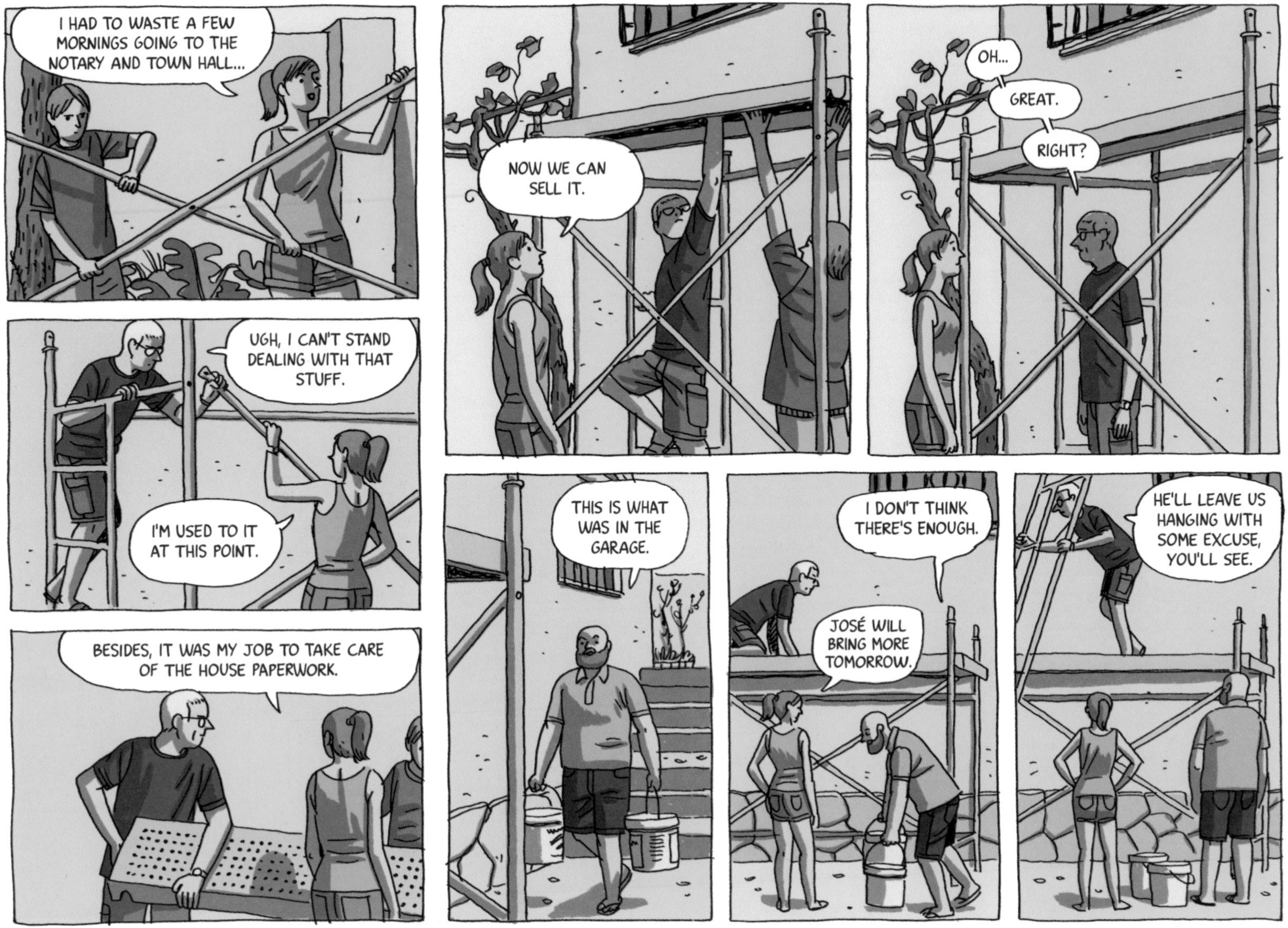
I HAD TO WASTE A FEW MORNINGS GOING TO THE NOTARY AND TOWN HALL...
UGH, I CAN'T STAND DEALING WITH THAT STUFF.
I'M USED TO IT AT THIS POINT.
BESIDES, IT WAS MY JOB TO TAKE CARE OF THE HOUSE PAPERWORK.
NOW WE CAN SELL IT.
OH...
GREAT.
RIGHT?
THIS IS WHAT WAS IN THE GARAGE.
I DON'T THINK THERE'S ENOUGH.
JOSÉ WILL BRING MORE TOMORROW.
HE'LL LEAVE US HANGING WITH SOME EXCUSE, YOU'LL SEE.

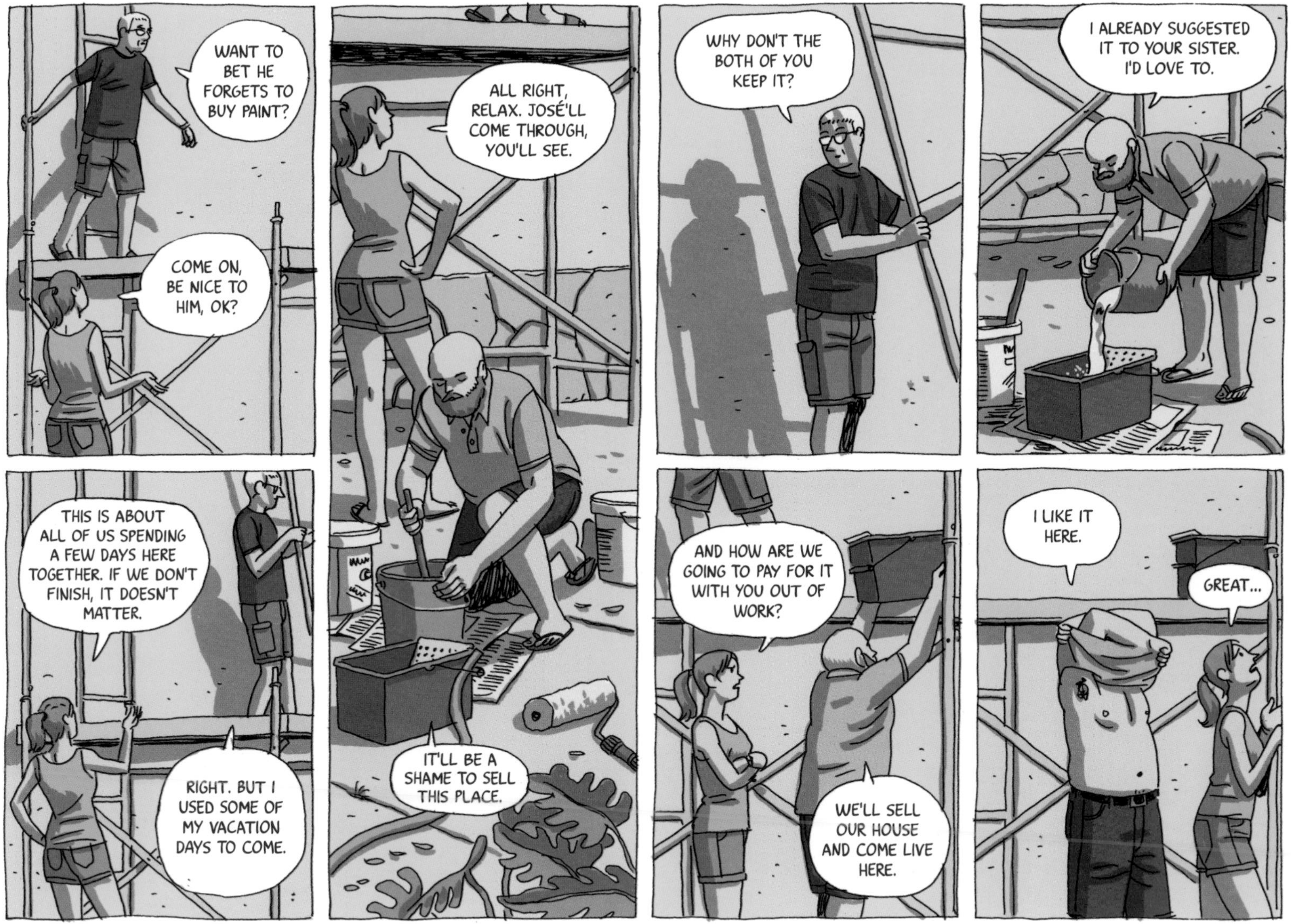
WANT TO BET HE FORGETS TO BUY PAINT?
COME ON, BE NICE TO HIM, OK?
THIS IS ABOUT ALL OF US SPENDING A FEW DAYS HERE TOGETHER. IF WE DON'T FINISH, IT DOESN'T MATTER.
RIGHT. BUT I USED SOME OF MY VACATION DAYS TO COME.
ALL RIGHT, RELAX. JOSÉ'LL COME THROUGH, YOU'LL SEE.
IT'LL BE A SHAME TO SELL THIS PLACE.
WHY DON'T THE BOTH OF YOU KEEP IT?
I ALREADY SUGGESTED IT TO YOUR SISTER. I'D LOVE TO.
AND HOW ARE WE GOING TO PAY FOR IT WITH YOU OUT OF WORK?
WE'LL SELL OUR HOUSE AND COME LIVE HERE.
I LIKE IT HERE.
GREAT...

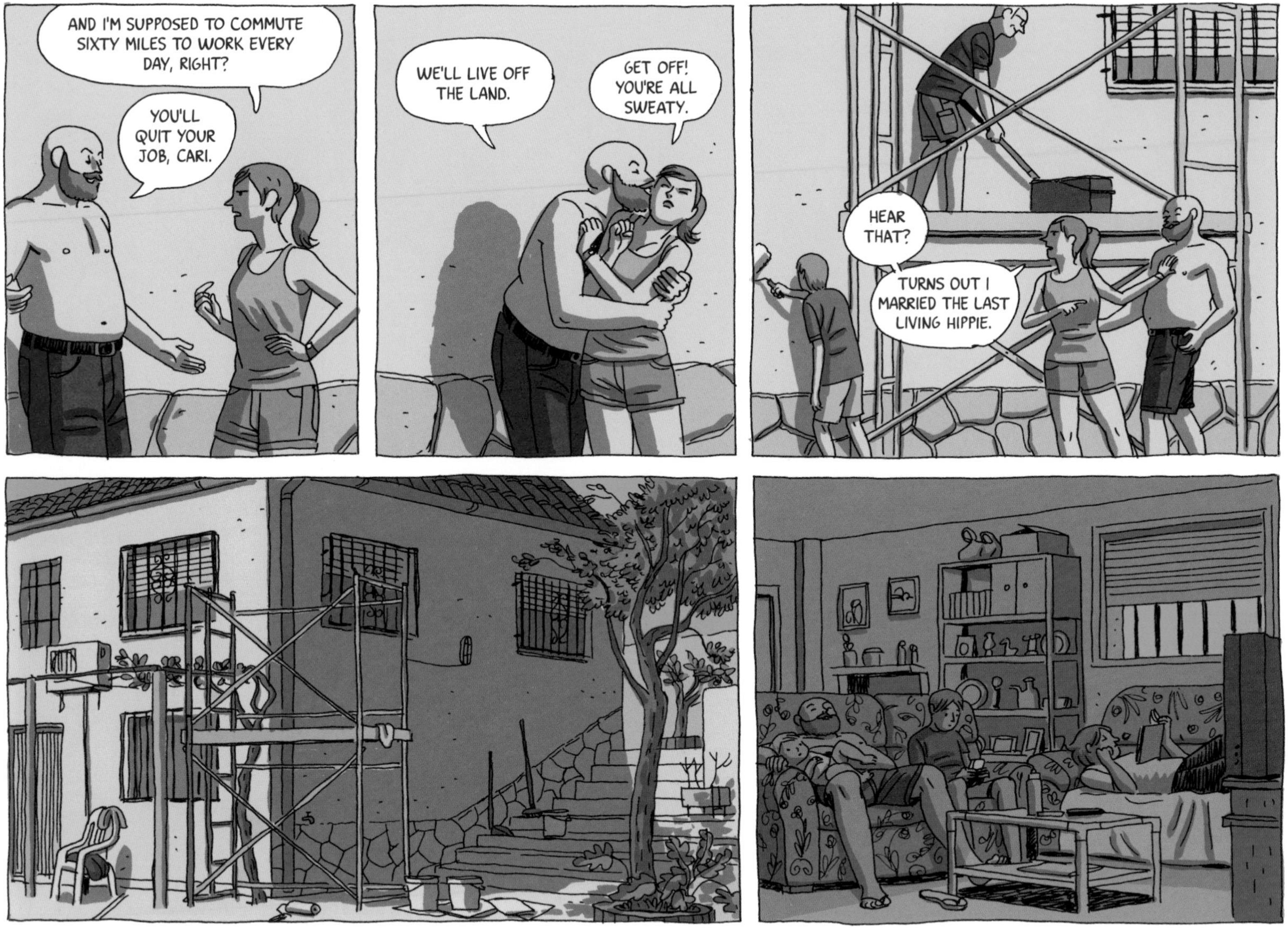
AND I'M SUPPOSED TO COMMUTE SIXTY MILES TO WORK EVERY DAY, RIGHT?
YOU'LL QUIT YOUR JOB, CARI.
WE'LL LIVE OFF THE LAND.
GET OFF! YOU'RE ALL SWEATY.
HEAR THAT?
TURNS OUT I MARRIED THE LAST LIVING HIPPIE.

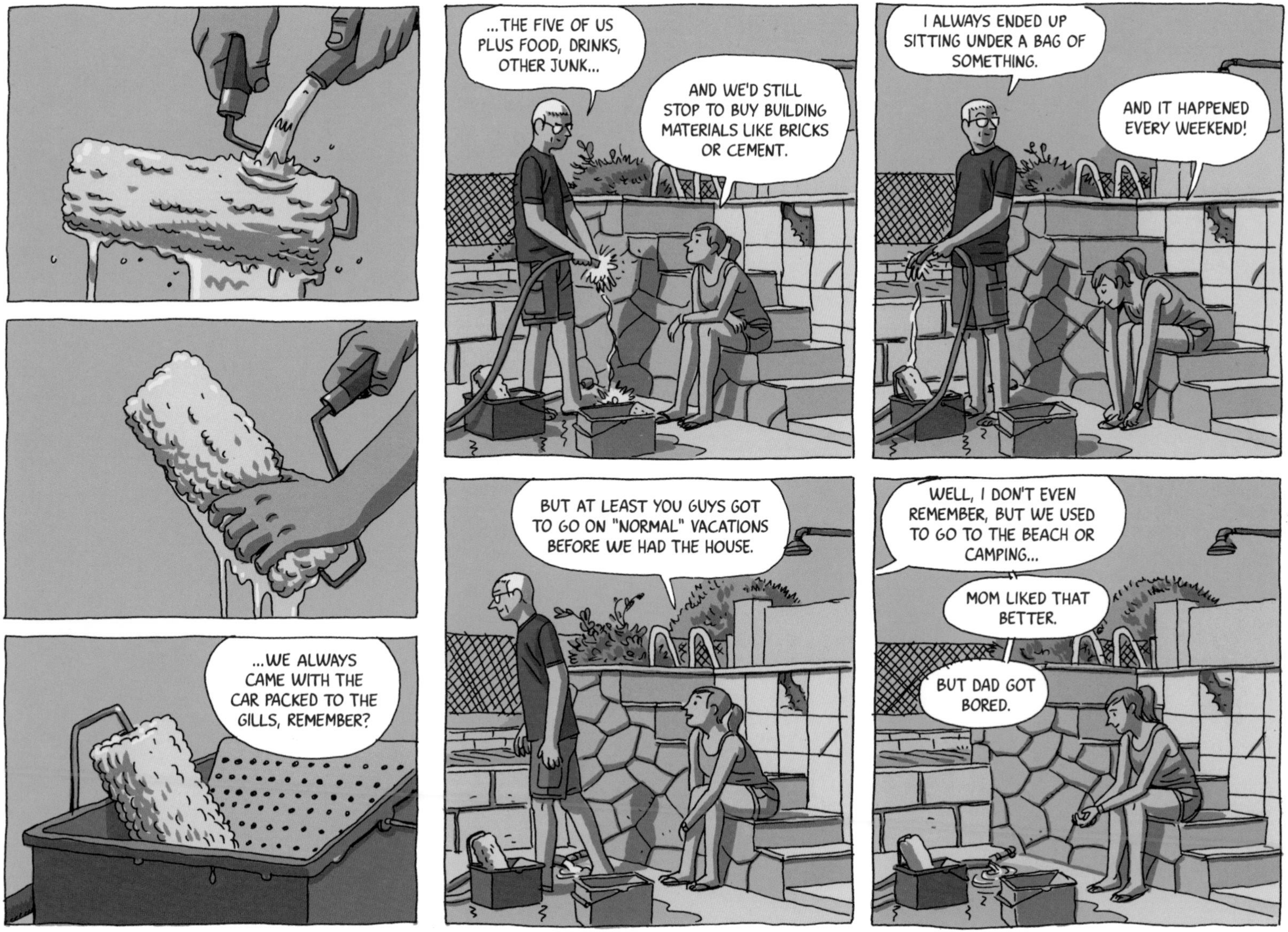
...WE ALWAYS CAME WITH THE CAR PACKED TO THE GILLS, REMEMBER?
...THE FIVE OF US PLUS FOOD, DRINKS, OTHER JUNK...
AND WE'D STILL STOP TO BUY BUILDING MATERIALS LIKE BRICKS OR CEMENT.
I ALWAYS ENDED UP SITTING UNDER A BAG OF SOMETHING.
AND IT HAPPENED EVERY WEEKEND!
BUT AT LEAST YOU GUYS GOT TO GO ON "NORMAL" VACATIONS BEFORE WE HAD THE HOUSE.
WELL, I DON'T EVEN REMEMBER, BUT WE USED TO GO TO THE BEACH OR CAMPING...
MOM LIKED THAT BETTER.
BUT DAD GOT BORED.

VICENTE...

DO YOU THINK DAD SUFFERED IN THOSE LAST FEW MONTHS?

I DON'T KNOW.

I'D LIKE TO THINK HE DIDN'T.

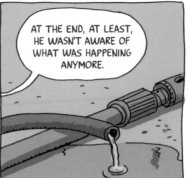

AT THE END, AT LEAST, HE WASN'T AWARE OF WHAT WAS HAPPENING ANYMORE.

DID WE DO EVERYTHING POSSIBLE?

I MEAN, DO YOU THINK WE COULD HAVE PROLONGED HIS LIFE?

THERE WASN'T ANY-THING ELSE WE COULD DO. THE OPERATION SAVED HIS LIFE, BUT THERE WAS NO FIX.

THE DOCTORS SAID IT WAS JUST A MATTER OF TIME.

BUT MAYBE WE COULD HAVE TALKED TO OTHER DOCTORS...

OTHER TREATMENTS THAT WOULD HAVE GIVEN HIM EVEN JUST A FEW MORE YEARS.

DAD WAS REALLY SICK, HE WAS OLD... THERE WAS NOTHING WE COULD DO.

I WOULD HAVE LIKED FOR HIM TO BE ABLE TO ENJOY HIS GRANDDAUGHTER.

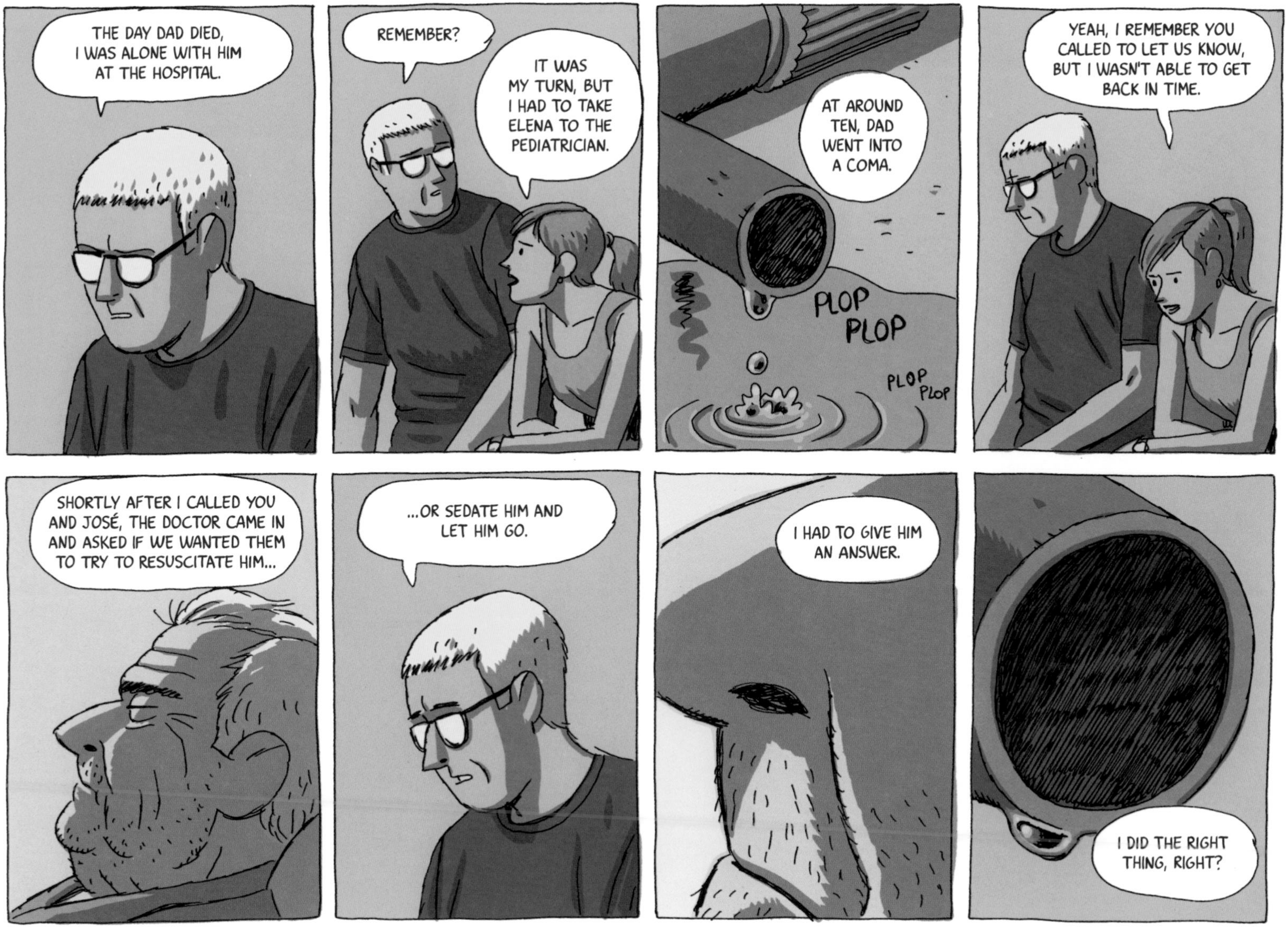
THE DAY DAD DIED, I WAS ALONE WITH HIM AT THE HOSPITAL.
REMEMBER?
IT WAS MY TURN, BUT I HAD TO TAKE ELENA TO THE PEDIATRICIAN.
AT AROUND TEN, DAD WENT INTO A COMA.
PLOP PLOP
PLOP PLOP
YEAH, I REMEMBER YOU CALLED TO LET US KNOW, BUT I WASN'T ABLE TO GET BACK IN TIME.
SHORTLY AFTER I CALLED YOU AND JOSÉ, THE DOCTOR CAME IN AND ASKED IF WE WANTED THEM TO TRY TO RESUSCITATE HIM...
...OR SEDATE HIM AND LET HIM GO.
I HAD TO GIVE HIM AN ANSWER.
I DID THE RIGHT THING, RIGHT?

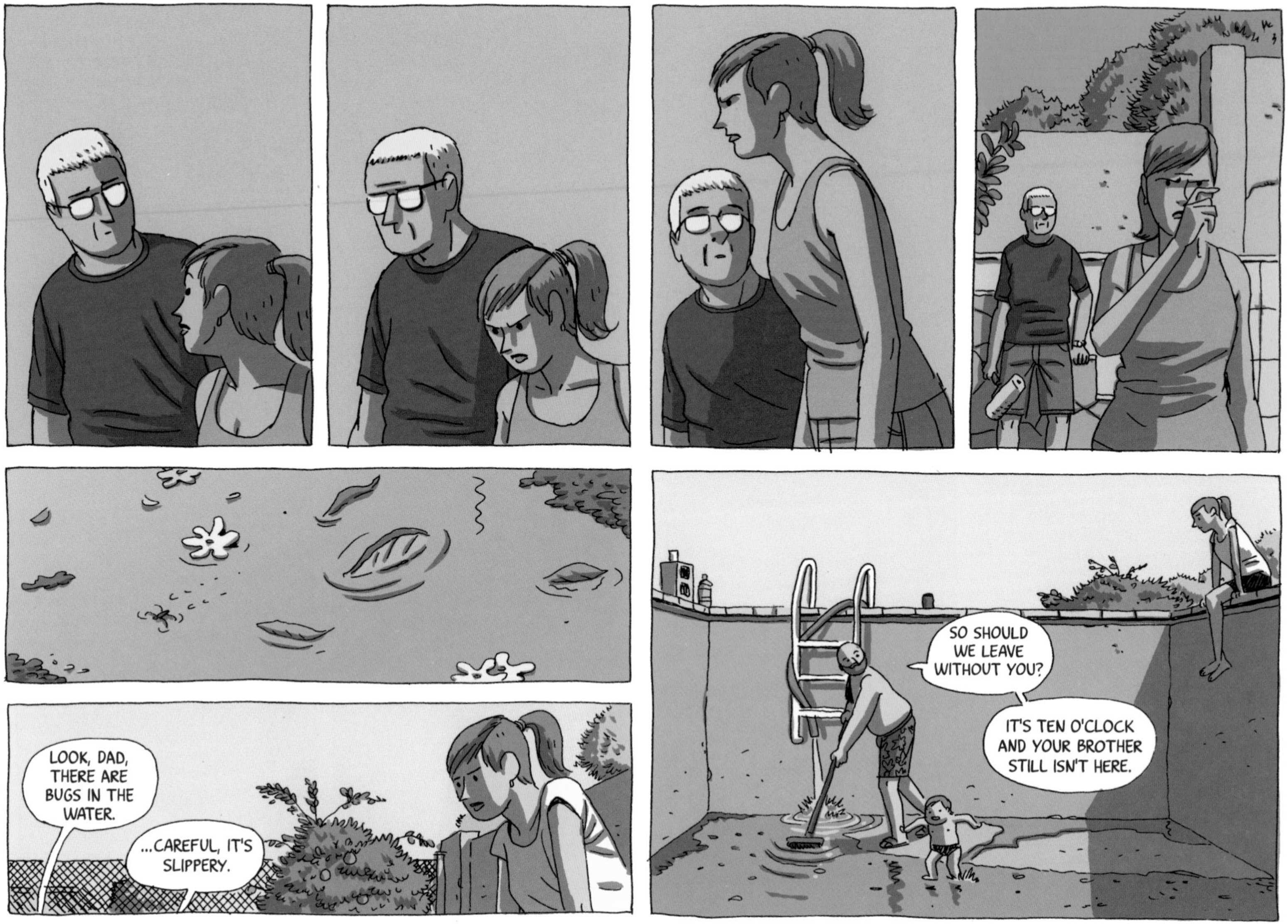
LOOK, DAD, THERE ARE BUGS IN THE WATER.
...CAREFUL, IT'S SLIPPERY.
SO SHOULD WE LEAVE WITHOUT YOU?
IT'S TEN O'CLOCK AND YOUR BROTHER STILL ISN'T HERE.

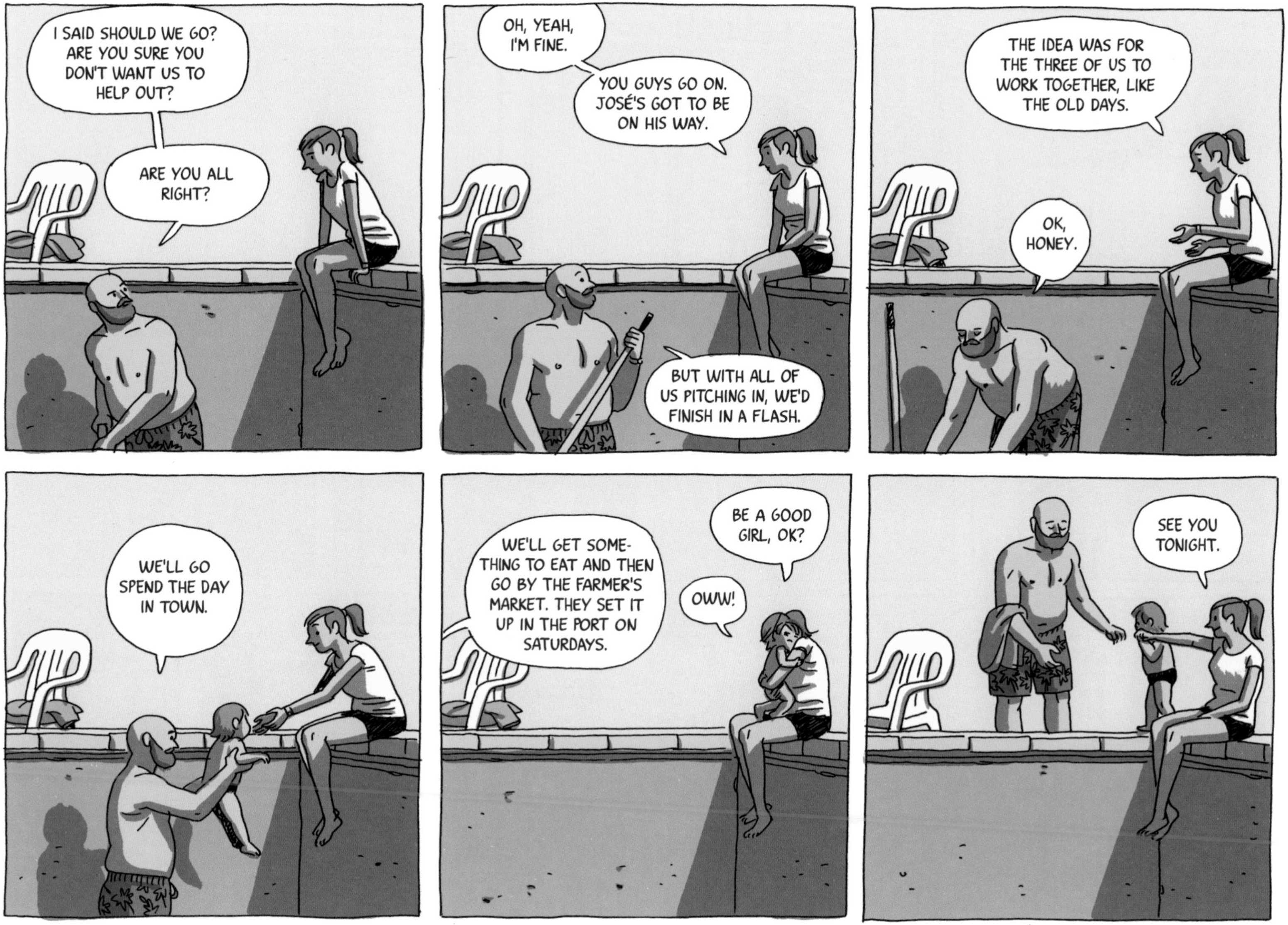
I SAID SHOULD WE GO? ARE YOU SURE YOU DON'T WANT US TO HELP OUT?
ARE YOU ALL RIGHT?
OH, YEAH, I'M FINE.
YOU GUYS GO ON. JOSÉ'S GOT TO BE ON HIS WAY.
BUT WITH ALL OF US PITCHING IN, WE'D FINISH IN A FLASH.
THE IDEA WAS FOR THE THREE OF US TO WORK TOGETHER, LIKE THE OLD DAYS.
OK, HONEY.
WE'LL GO SPEND THE DAY IN TOWN.
WE'LL GET SOME-THING TO EAT AND THEN GO BY THE FARMER'S MARKET. THEY SET IT UP IN THE PORT ON SATURDAYS.
BE A GOOD GIRL, OK?
OWW!
SEE YOU TONIGHT.

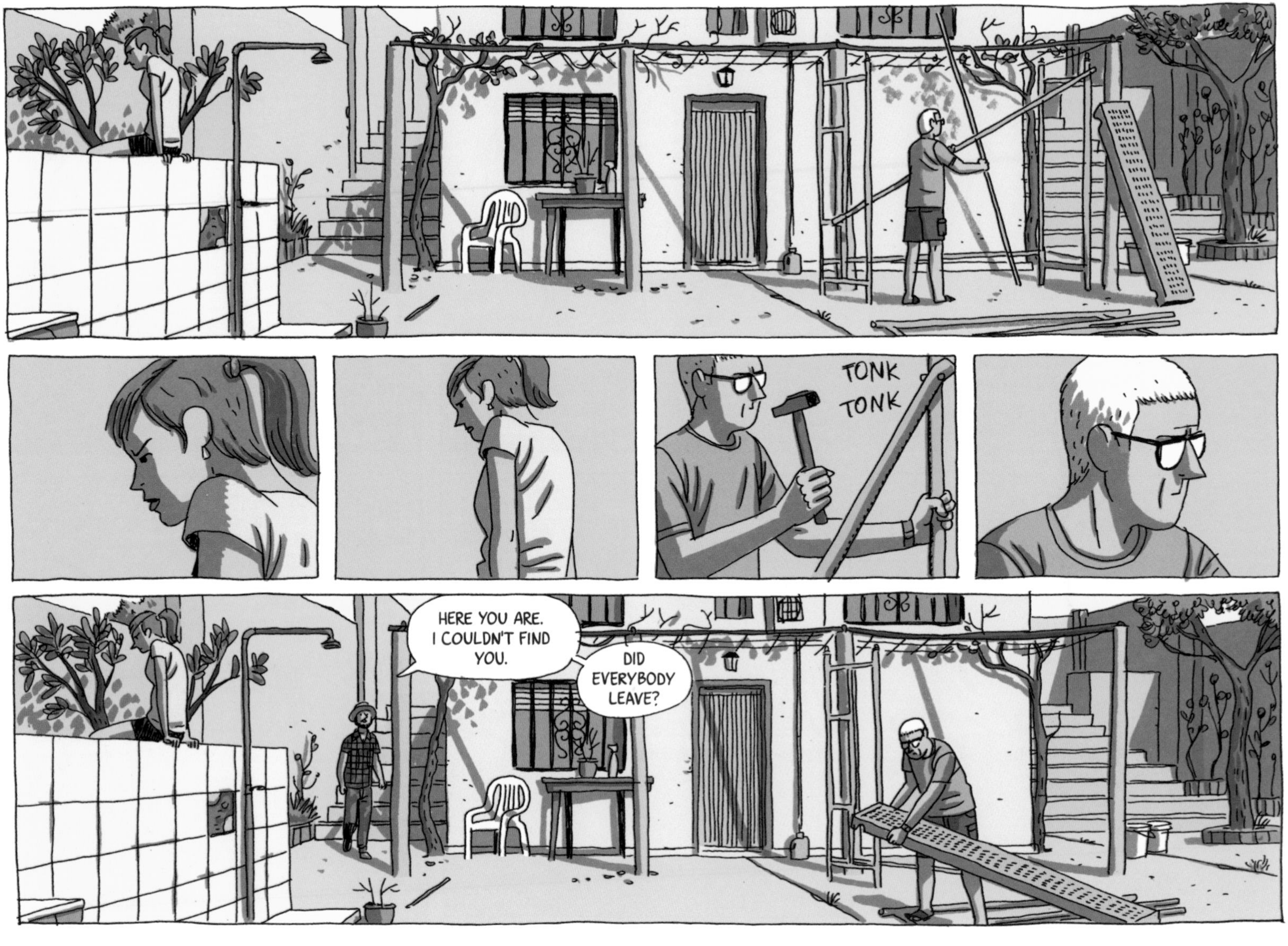
TONK
TONK
HERE YOU ARE. I COULDN'T FIND YOU.
DID EVERYBODY LEAVE?

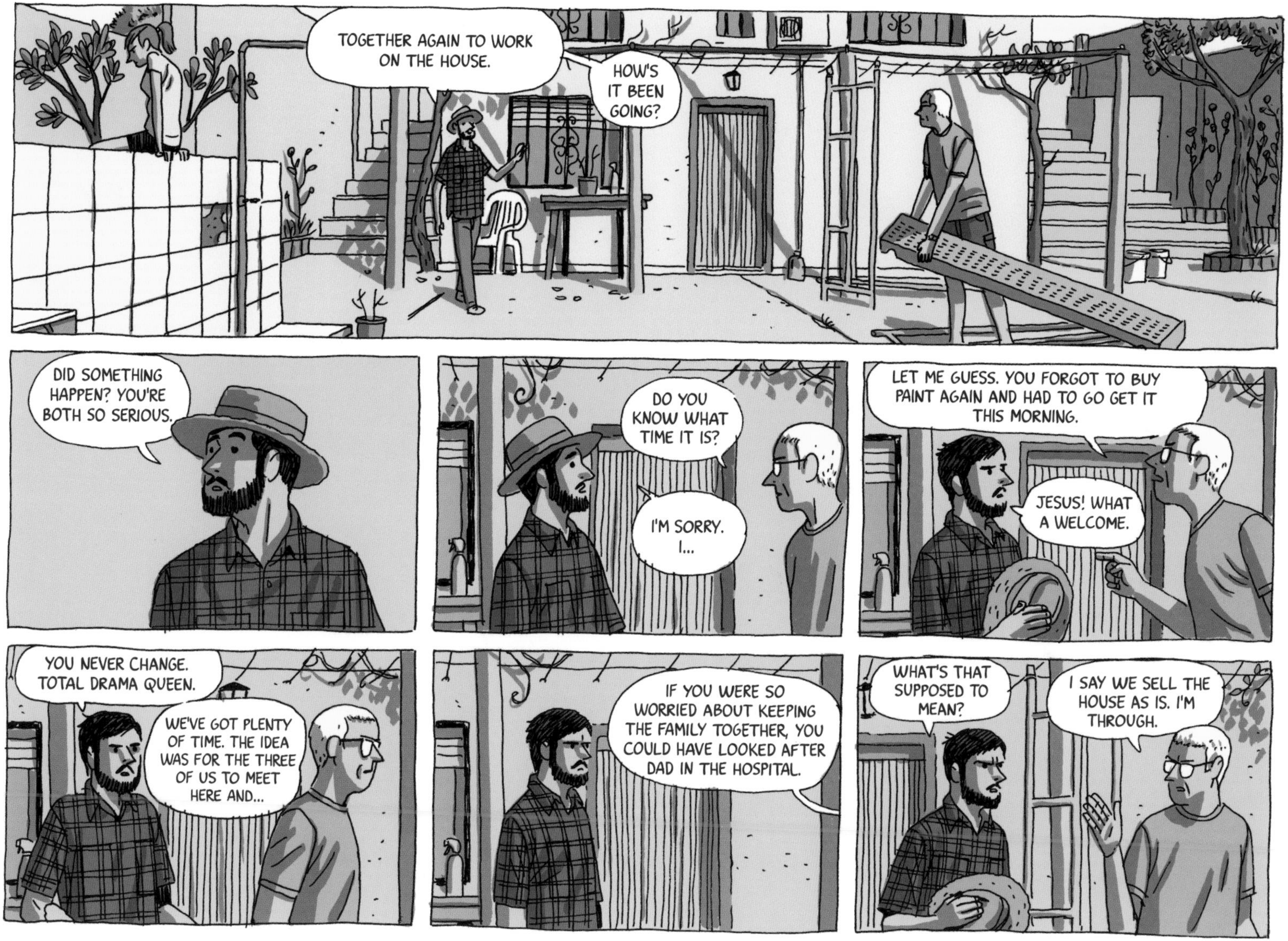
TOGETHER AGAIN TO WORK ON THE HOUSE.
HOW'S IT BEEN GOING?
DID SOMETHING HAPPEN? YOU'RE BOTH SO SERIOUS.
DO YOU KNOW WHAT TIME IT IS?
I'M SORRY. I...
LET ME GUESS. YOU FORGOT TO BUY PAINT AGAIN AND HAD TO GO GET IT THIS MORNING.
JESUS! WHAT A WELCOME.
YOU NEVER CHANGE. TOTAL DRAMA QUEEN.
WE'VE GOT PLENTY OF TIME. THE IDEA WAS FOR THE THREE OF US TO MEET HERE AND...
IF YOU WERE SO WORRIED ABOUT KEEPING THE FAMILY TOGETHER, YOU COULD HAVE LOOKED AFTER DAD IN THE HOSPITAL.
WHAT'S THAT SUPPOSED TO MEAN?
I SAY WE SELL THE HOUSE AS IS. I'M THROUGH.

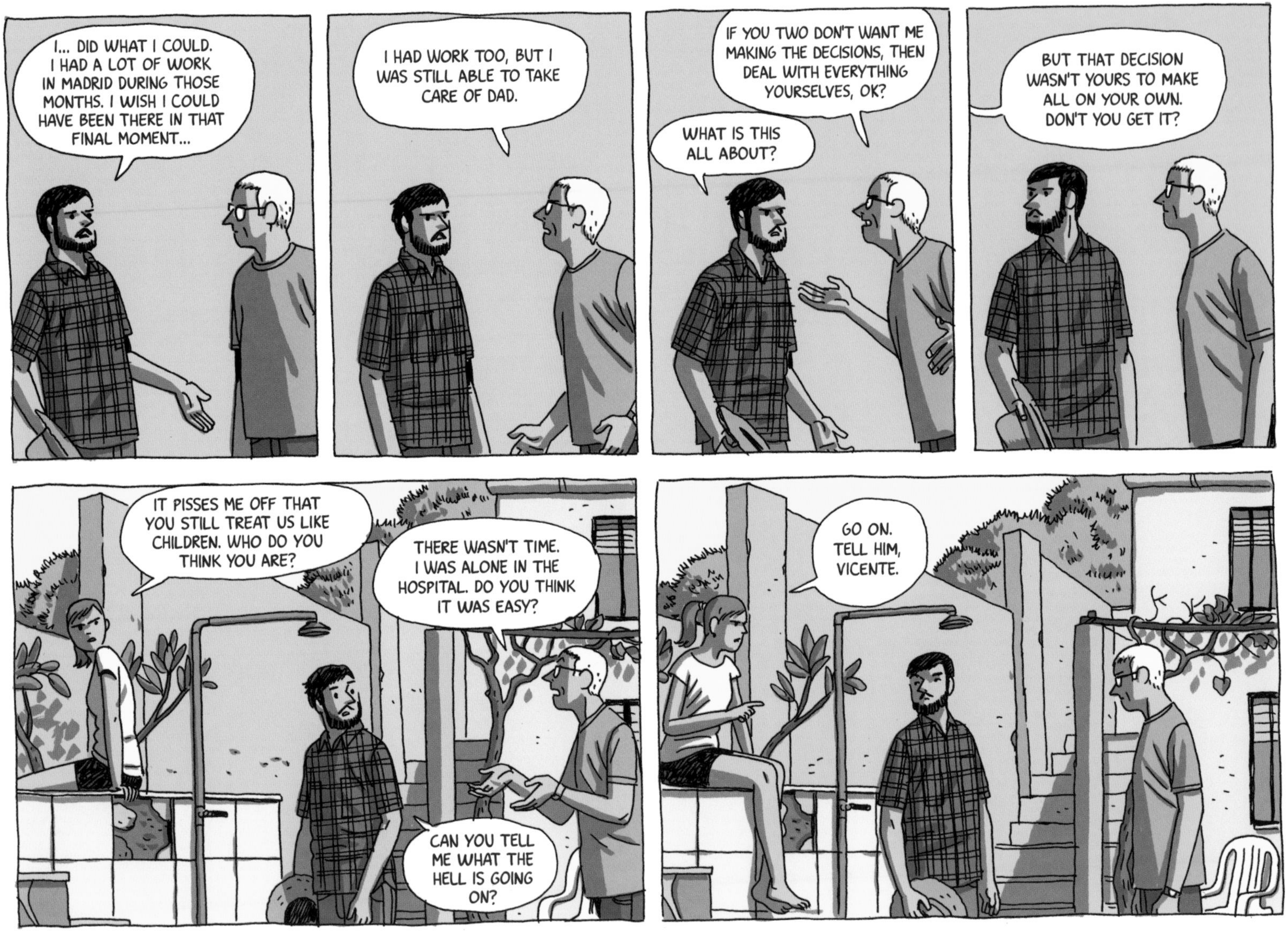
I... DID WHAT I COULD. I HAD A LOT OF WORK IN MADRID DURING THOSE MONTHS. I WISH I COULD HAVE BEEN THERE IN THAT FINAL MOMENT...
I HAD WORK TOO, BUT I WAS STILL ABLE TO TAKE CARE OF DAD.
IF YOU TWO DON'T WANT ME MAKING THE DECISIONS, THEN DEAL WITH EVERYTHING YOURSELVES, OK?
WHAT IS THIS ALL ABOUT?
BUT THAT DECISION WASN'T YOURS TO MAKE ALL ON YOUR OWN. DON'T YOU GET IT?
IT PISSES ME OFF THAT YOU STILL TREAT US LIKE CHILDREN. WHO DO YOU THINK YOU ARE?
THERE WASN'T TIME. I WAS ALONE IN THE HOSPITAL. DO YOU THINK IT WAS EASY?
CAN YOU TELL ME WHAT THE HELL IS GOING ON?
GO ON. TELL HIM, VICENTE.

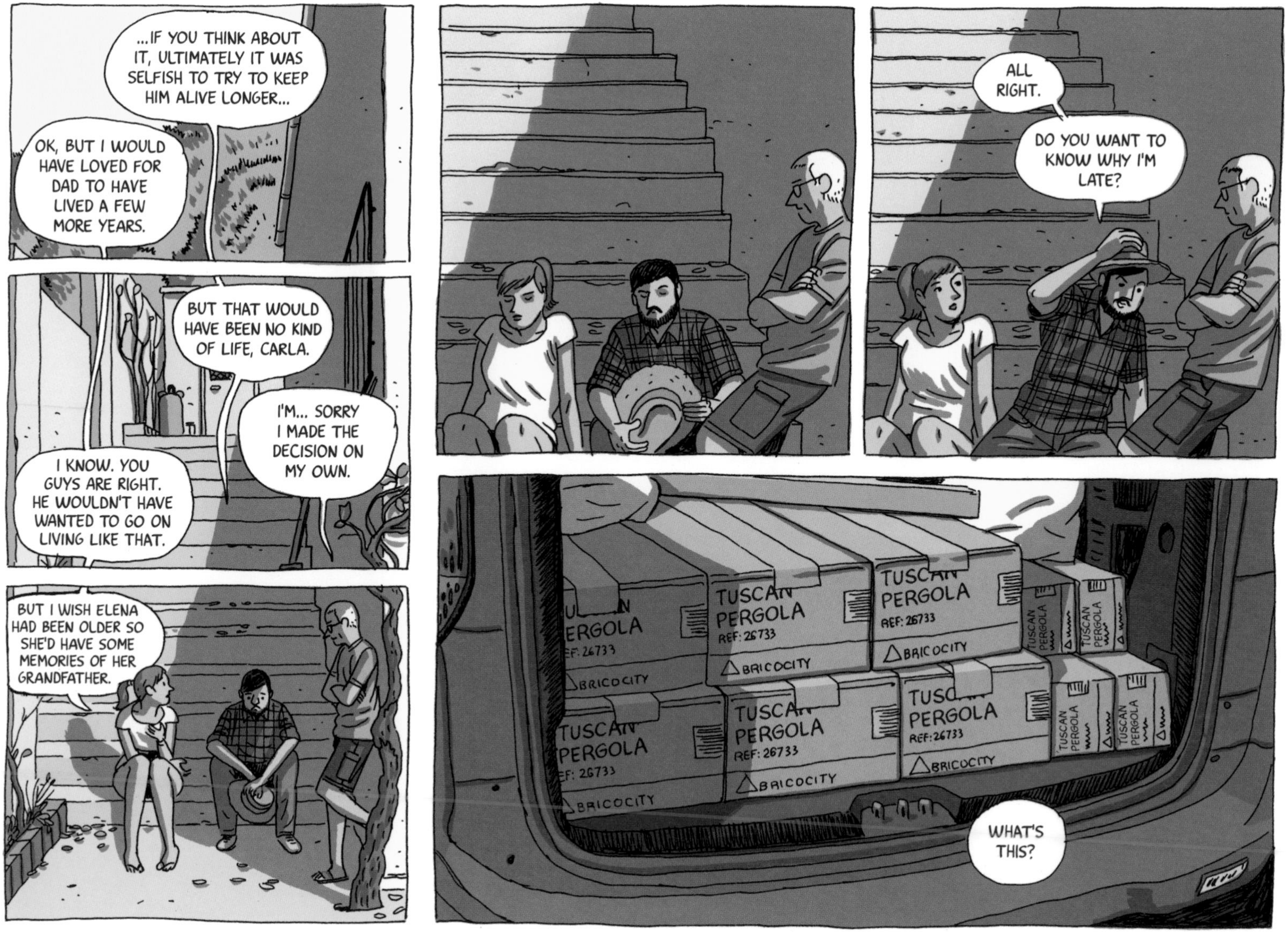
...IF YOU THINK ABOUT IT, ULTIMATELY IT WAS SELFISH TO TRY TO KEEP HIM ALIVE LONGER...
OK, BUT I WOULD HAVE LOVED FOR DAD TO HAVE LIVED A FEW MORE YEARS.
BUT THAT WOULD HAVE BEEN NO KIND OF LIFE, CARLA.
I KNOW. YOU GUYS ARE RIGHT. HE WOULDN'T HAVE WANTED TO GO ON LIVING LIKE THAT.
I'M... SORRY I MADE THE DECISION ON MY OWN.
BUT I WISH ELENA HAD BEEN OLDER SO SHE'D HAVE SOME MEMORIES OF HER GRANDFATHER.
ALL RIGHT.
DO YOU WANT TO KNOW WHY I'M LATE?
TUSCAN PERGOLA
REF: 26733
BRICOCITY
WHAT'S THIS?

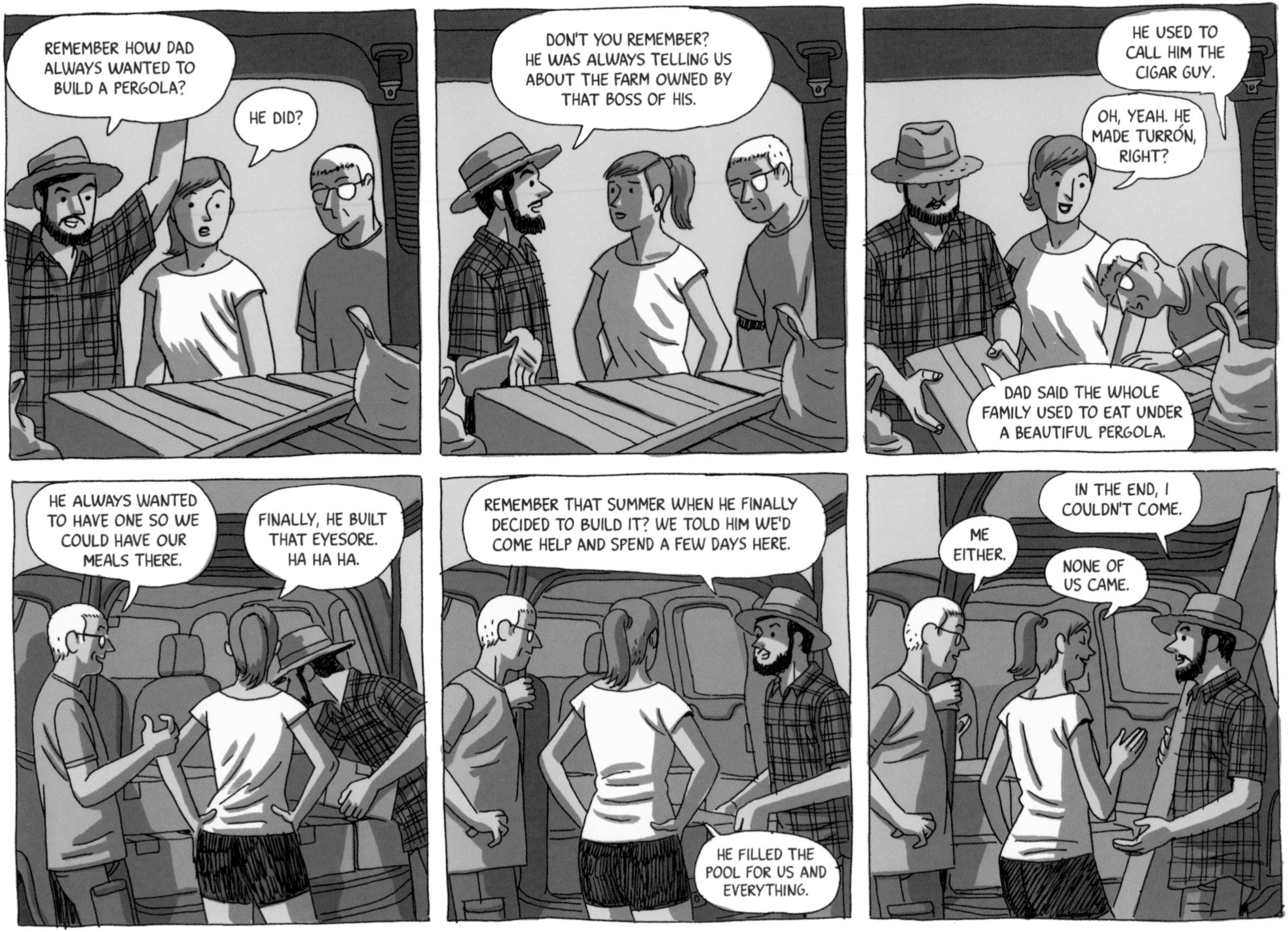
REMEMBER HOW DAD ALWAYS WANTED TO BUILD A PERGOLA?
HE DID?
DON'T YOU REMEMBER? HE WAS ALWAYS TELLING US ABOUT THE FARM OWNED BY THAT BOSS OF HIS.
HE USED TO CALL HIM THE CIGAR GUY.
OH, YEAH. HE MADE TURRÓN, RIGHT?
DAD SAID THE WHOLE FAMILY USED TO EAT UNDER A BEAUTIFUL PERGOLA.
HE ALWAYS WANTED TO HAVE ONE SO WE COULD HAVE OUR MEALS THERE.
FINALLY, HE BUILT THAT EYESORE. HA HA HA.
REMEMBER THAT SUMMER WHEN HE FINALLY DECIDED TO BUILD IT? WE TOLD HIM WE'D COME HELP AND SPEND A FEW DAYS HERE.
HE FILLED THE POOL FOR US AND EVERYTHING.
IN THE END, I COULDN'T COME.
ME EITHER.
NONE OF US CAME.

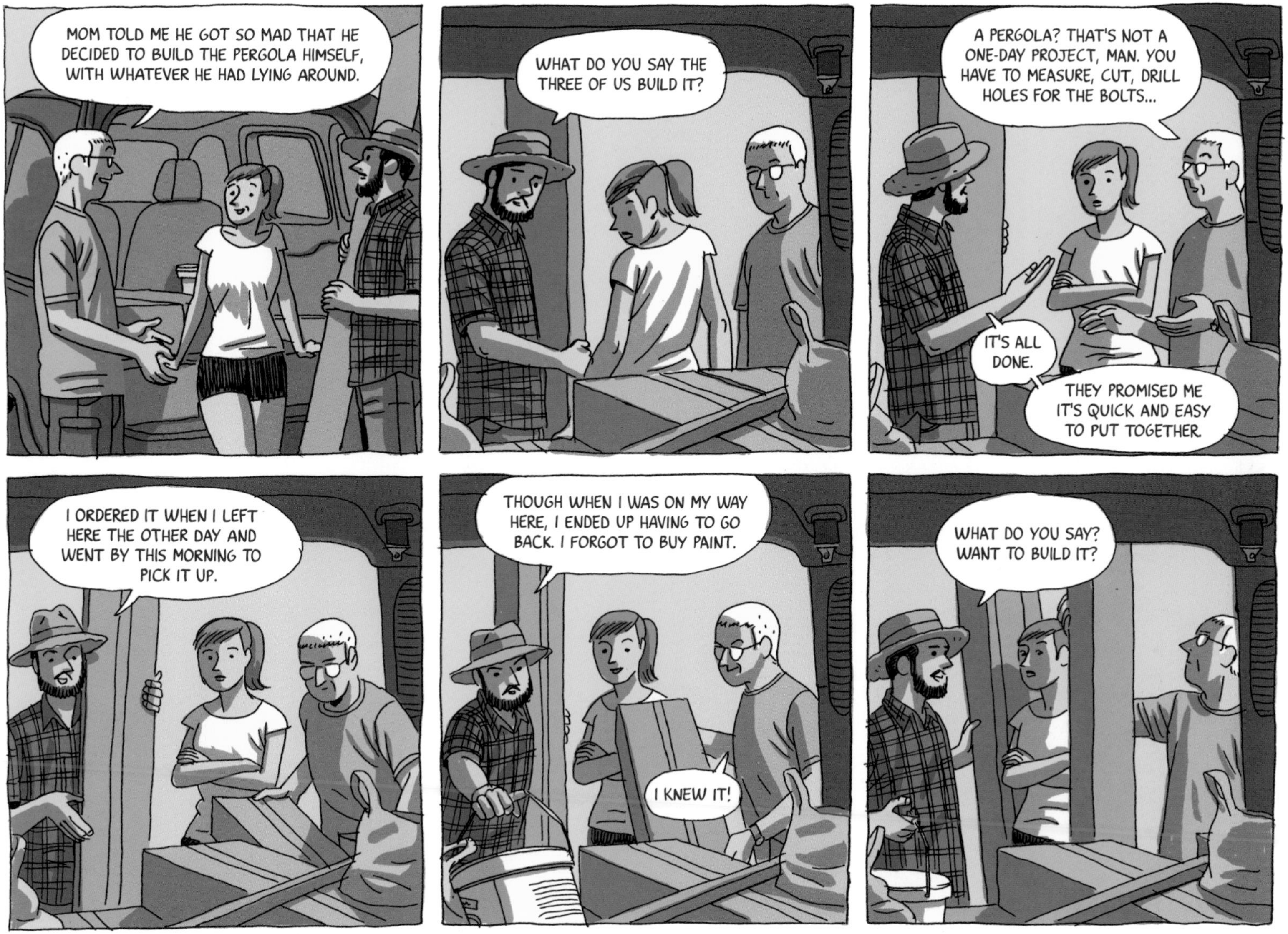
MOM TOLD ME HE GOT SO MAD THAT HE DECIDED TO BUILD THE PERGOLA HIMSELF, WITH WHATEVER HE HAD LYING AROUND.
WHAT DO YOU SAY THE THREE OF US BUILD IT?
A PERGOLA? THAT'S NOT A ONE-DAY PROJECT, MAN. YOU HAVE TO MEASURE, CUT, DRILL HOLES FOR THE BOLTS...
IT'S ALL DONE.
THEY PROMISED ME IT'S QUICK AND EASY TO PUT TOGETHER.
I ORDERED IT WHEN I LEFT HERE THE OTHER DAY AND WENT BY THIS MORNING TO PICK IT UP.
THOUGH WHEN I WAS ON MY WAY HERE, I ENDED UP HAVING TO GO BACK. I FORGOT TO BUY PAINT.
I KNEW IT!
WHAT DO YOU SAY? WANT TO BUILD IT?

BUT... WHY?

I MEAN... WE'RE GOING TO SELL THE HOUSE.

WHY NOT?

HE WOULD HAVE LIKED IT.

WE OWE HIM.

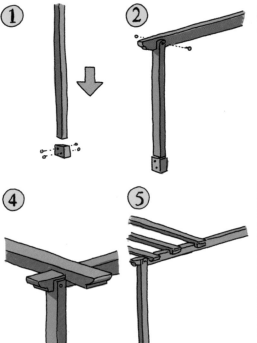

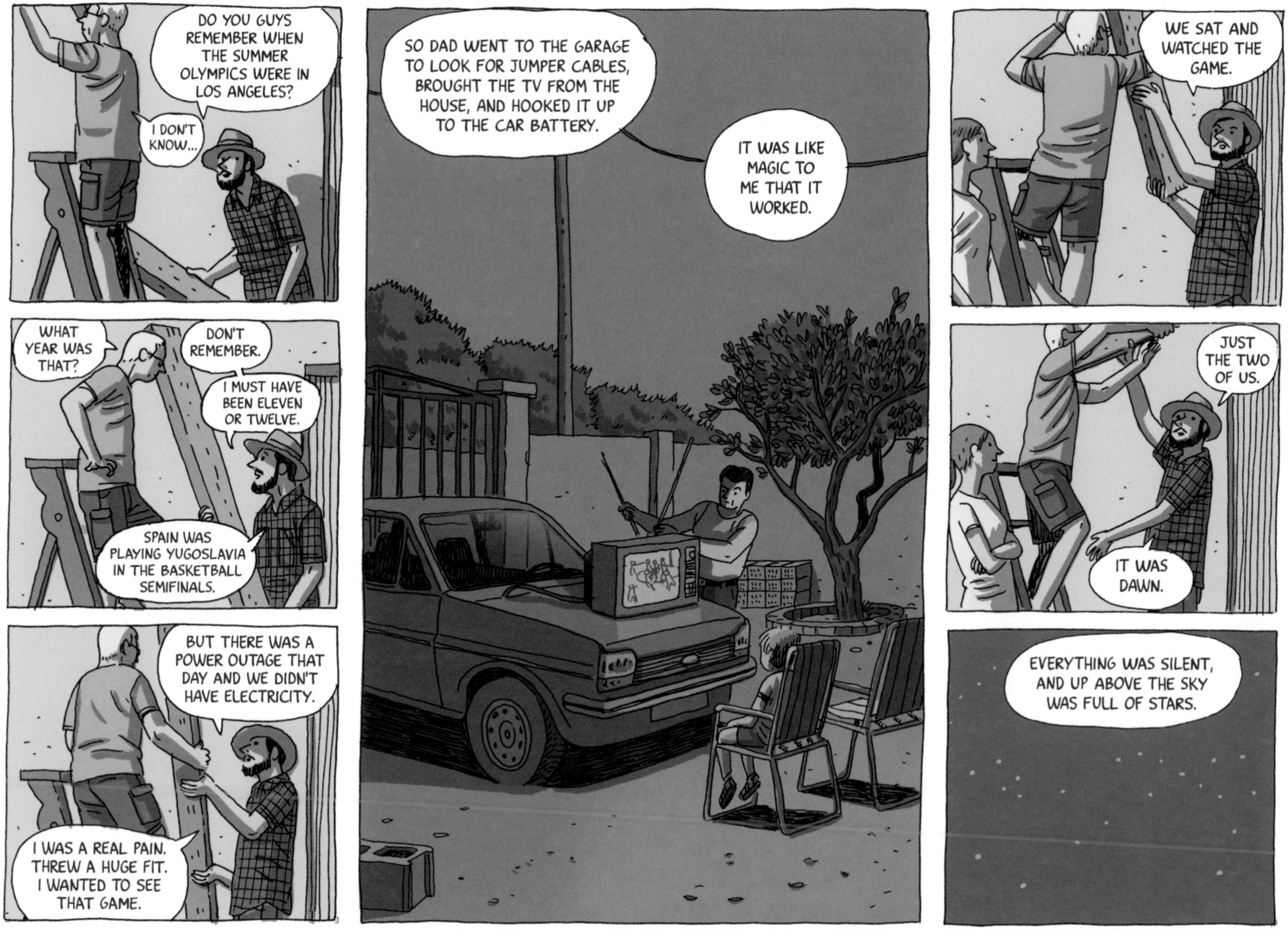
DO YOU GUYS REMEMBER WHEN THE SUMMER OLYMPICS WERE IN LOS ANGELES?
I DON'T KNOW...
WHAT YEAR WAS THAT?
DON'T REMEMBER.
I MUST HAVE BEEN ELEVEN OR TWELVE.
SPAIN WAS PLAYING YUGOSLAVIA IN THE BASKETBALL SEMIFINALS.
BUT THERE WAS A POWER OUTAGE THAT DAY AND WE DIDN'T HAVE ELECTRICITY.
I WAS A REAL PAIN. THREW A HUGE FIT. I WANTED TO SEE THAT GAME.
SO DAD WENT TO THE GARAGE TO LOOK FOR JUMPER CABLES, BROUGHT THE TV FROM THE HOUSE, AND HOOKED IT UP TO THE CAR BATTERY.
IT WAS LIKE MAGIC TO ME THAT IT WORKED.
WE SAT AND WATCHED THE GAME.
JUST THE TWO OF US.
IT WAS DAWN.
EVERYTHING WAS SILENT, AND UP ABOVE THE SKY WAS FULL OF STARS.

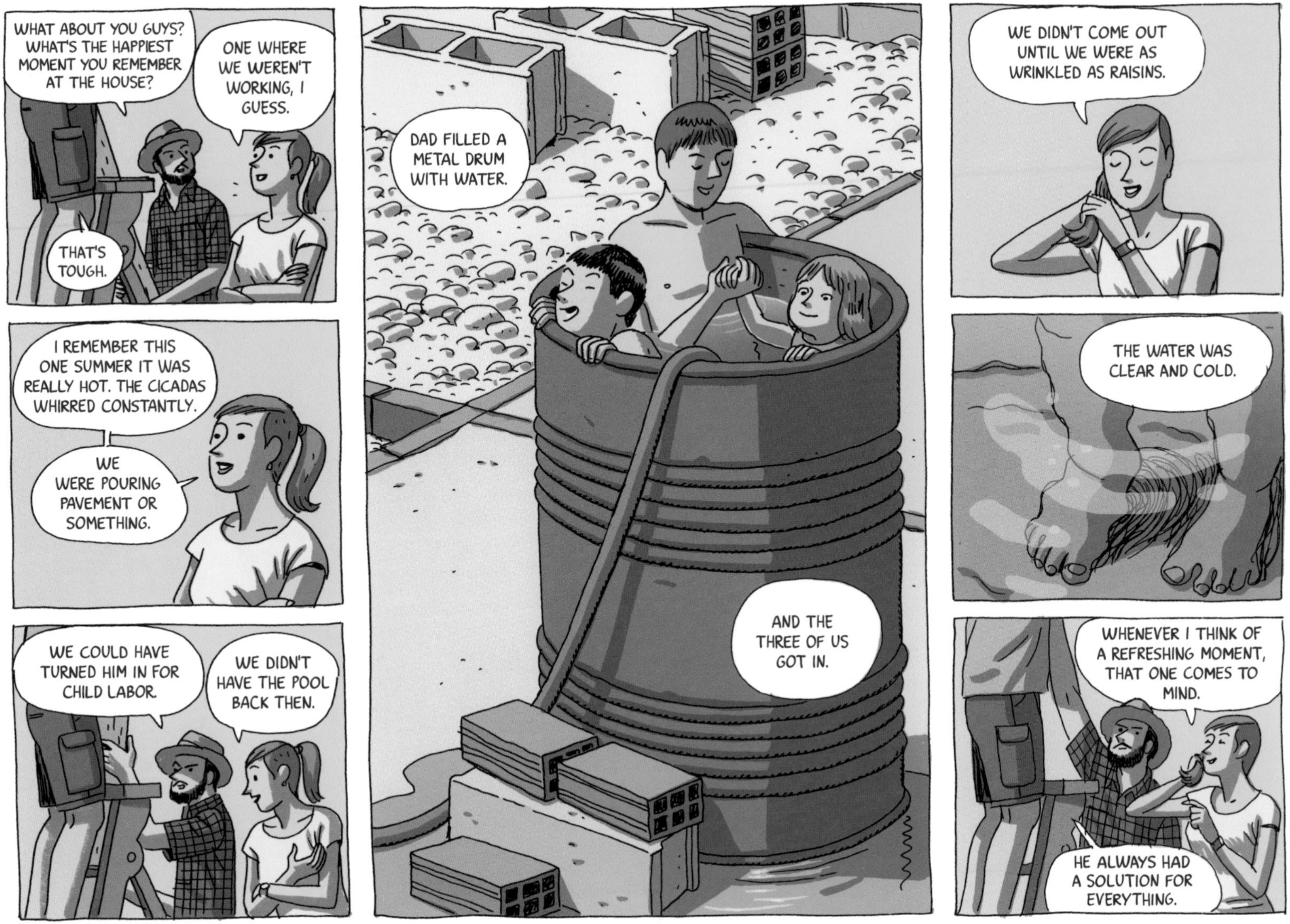
WHAT ABOUT YOU GUYS? WHAT'S THE HAPPIEST MOMENT YOU REMEMBER AT THE HOUSE?
ONE WHERE WE WEREN'T WORKING, I GUESS.
THAT'S TOUGH.
I REMEMBER THIS ONE SUMMER IT WAS REALLY HOT. THE CICADAS WHIRRED CONSTANTLY.
WE WERE POURING PAVEMENT OR SOMETHING.
WE COULD HAVE TURNED HIM IN FOR CHILD LABOR.
WE DIDN'T HAVE THE POOL BACK THEN.
DAD FILLED A METAL DRUM WITH WATER.
AND THE THREE OF US GOT IN.
WE DIDN'T COME OUT UNTIL WE WERE AS WRINKLED AS RAISINS.
THE WATER WAS CLEAR AND COLD.
WHENEVER I THINK OF A REFRESHING MOMENT, THAT ONE COMES TO MIND.
HE ALWAYS HAD A SOLUTION FOR EVERYTHING.

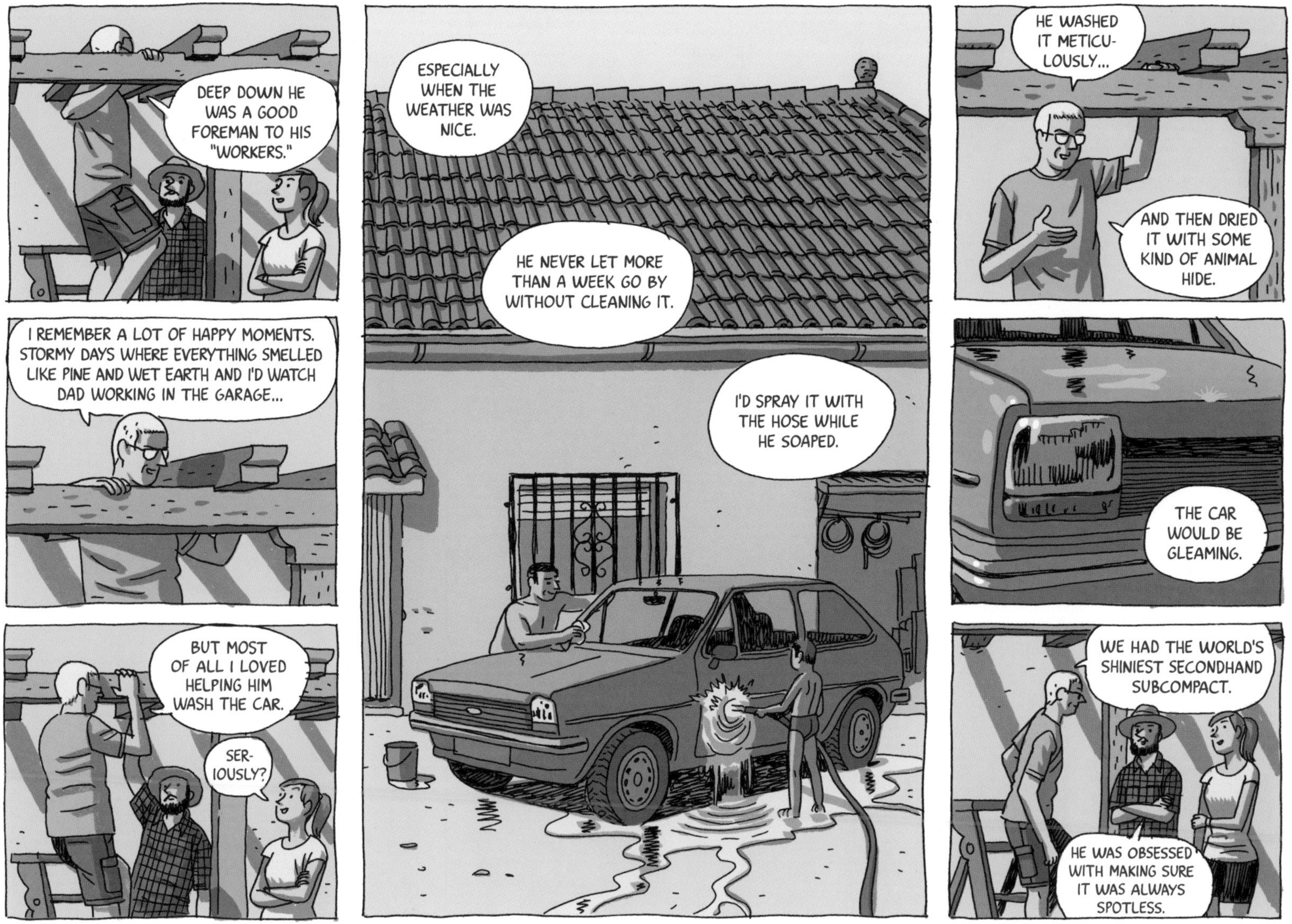
DEEP DOWN HE WAS A GOOD FOREMAN TO HIS "WORKERS."
I REMEMBER A LOT OF HAPPY MOMENTS. STORMY DAYS WHERE EVERYTHING SMELLED LIKE PINE AND WET EARTH AND I'D WATCH DAD WORKING IN THE GARAGE...
BUT MOST OF ALL I LOVED HELPING HIM WASH THE CAR.
SER-IOUSLY?
ESPECIALLY WHEN THE WEATHER WAS NICE.
HE NEVER LET MORE THAN A WEEK GO BY WITHOUT CLEANING IT.
I'D SPRAY IT WITH THE HOSE WHILE HE SOAPED.
HE WASHED IT METICU-LOUSLY...
AND THEN DRIED IT WITH SOME KIND OF ANIMAL HIDE.
THE CAR WOULD BE GLEAMING.
WE HAD THE WORLD'S SHINIEST SECONDHAND SUBCOMPACT.
HE WAS OBSESSED WITH MAKING SURE IT WAS ALWAYS SPOTLESS.

OF COURSE, HE USED TO BE A DRIVER. KEEPING IT IMMACULATE WAS AN OBLIGATION.

THAT'S WHY HE DROVE SO WELL.

IT'S TRUE, HE NEVER EVEN SCRATCHED THAT CAR.

RRRRRRRR

AND HE WAS STILL DRIVING UP TO THE DAY OF HIS SURGERY.

HE DROVE THERE ON HIS OWN, IN HIS CAR, FROM HERE TO THE HOSPITAL.

THAT WAS THE LAST TIME HE DROVE.

AND NOT A SCRAPE. JUST LIKE ME, HA HA HA!

LATER I'LL SHOW YOU GUYS THE DENT CRISTÓBAL PUT IN THE CAR.

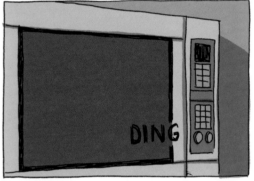

DING

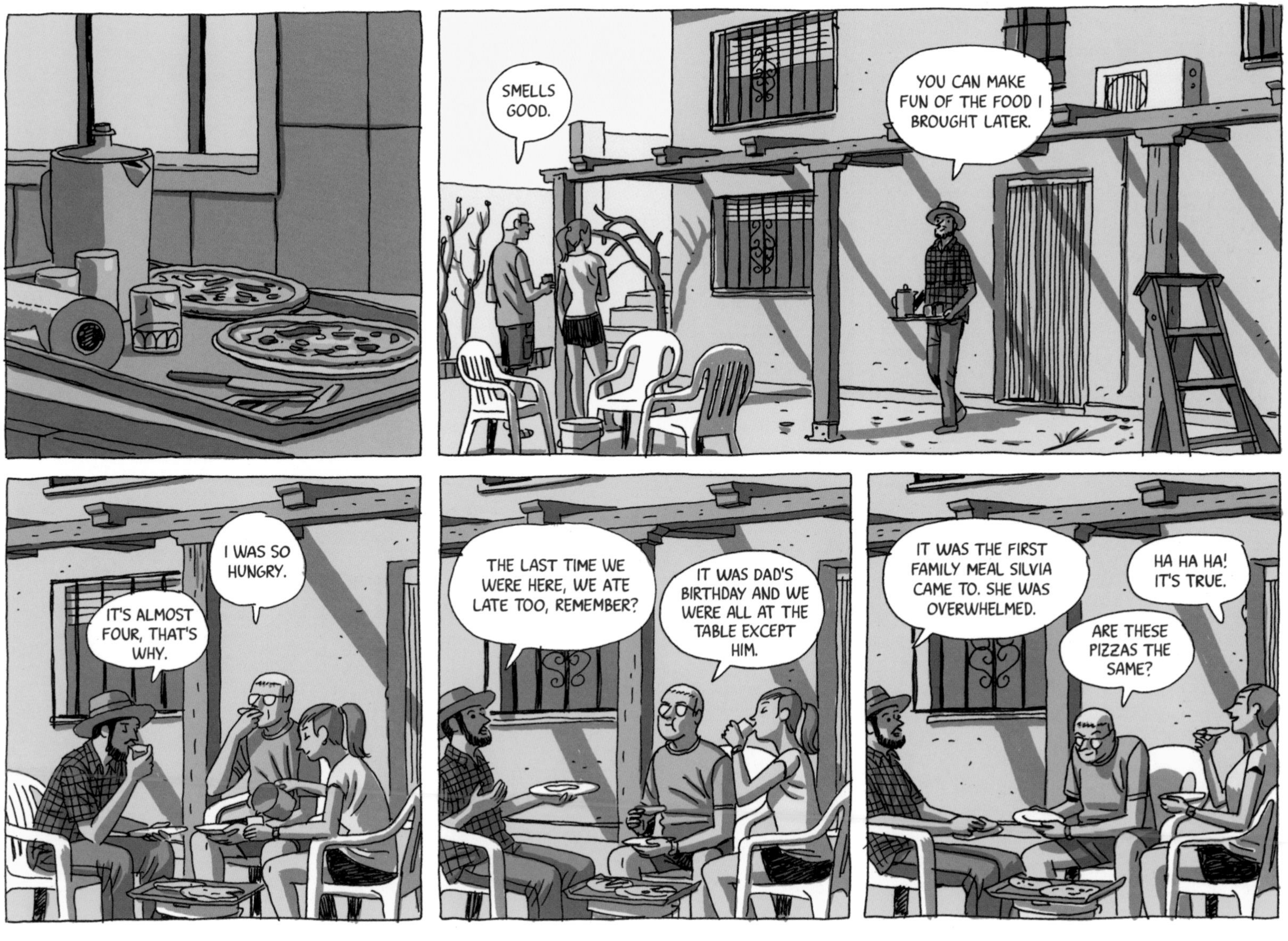
SMELLS GOOD.
YOU CAN MAKE FUN OF THE FOOD I BROUGHT LATER.
I WAS SO HUNGRY.
IT'S ALMOST FOUR, THAT'S WHY.
THE LAST TIME WE WERE HERE, WE ATE LATE TOO, REMEMBER?
IT WAS DAD'S BIRTHDAY AND WE WERE ALL AT THE TABLE EXCEPT HIM.
IT WAS THE FIRST FAMILY MEAL SILVIA CAME TO. SHE WAS OVERWHELMED.
HA HA HA! IT'S TRUE.
ARE THESE PIZZAS THE SAME?

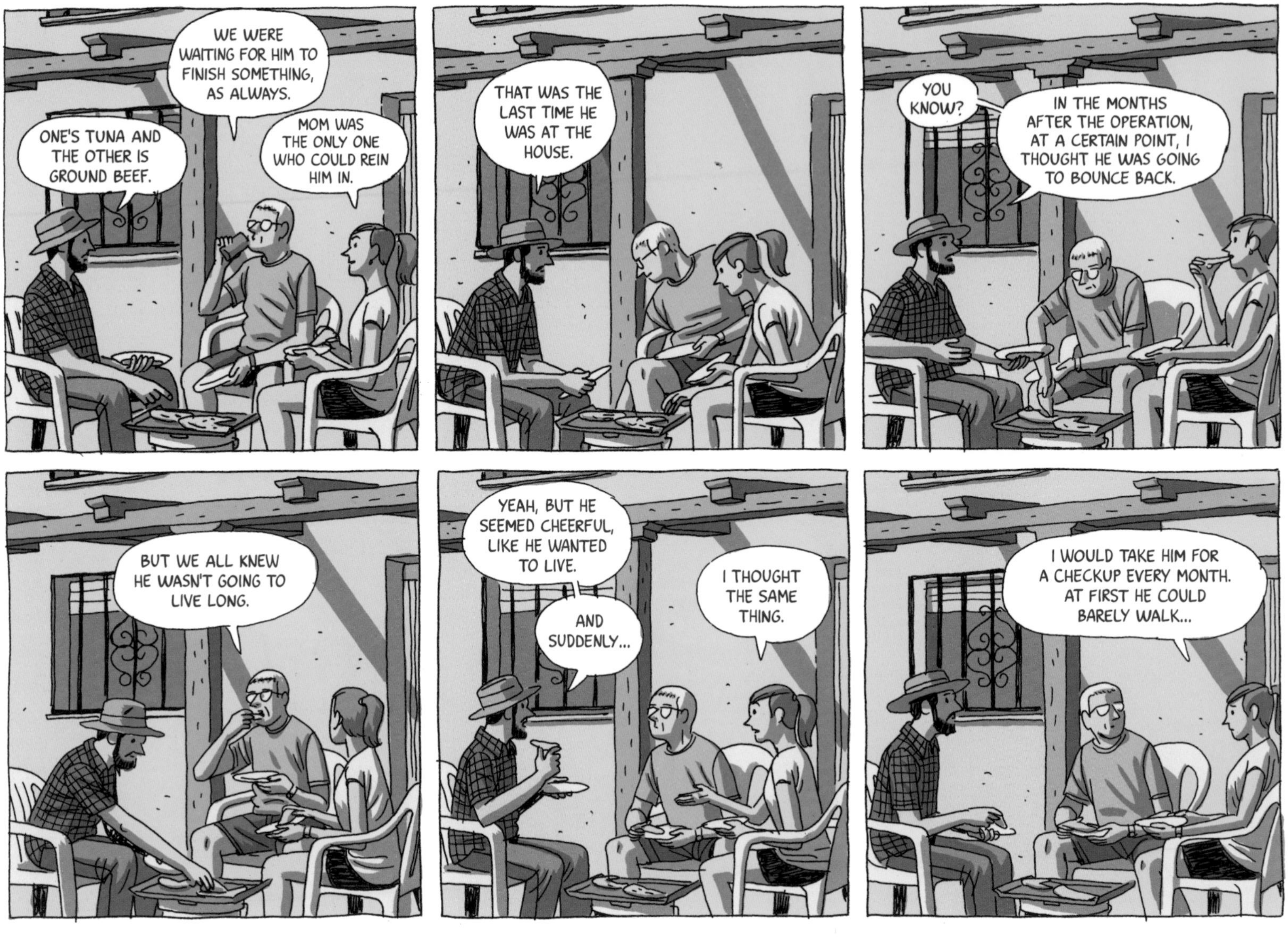
WE WERE WAITING FOR HIM TO FINISH SOMETHING, AS ALWAYS.
ONE'S TUNA AND THE OTHER IS GROUND BEEF.
MOM WAS THE ONLY ONE WHO COULD REIN HIM IN.
THAT WAS THE LAST TIME HE WAS AT THE HOUSE.
YOU KNOW?
IN THE MONTHS AFTER THE OPERATION, AT A CERTAIN POINT, I THOUGHT HE WAS GOING TO BOUNCE BACK.
BUT WE ALL KNEW HE WASN'T GOING TO LIVE LONG.
YEAH, BUT HE SEEMED CHEERFUL, LIKE HE WANTED TO LIVE.
AND SUDDENLY...
I THOUGHT THE SAME THING.
I WOULD TAKE HIM FOR A CHECKUP EVERY MONTH. AT FIRST HE COULD BARELY WALK...

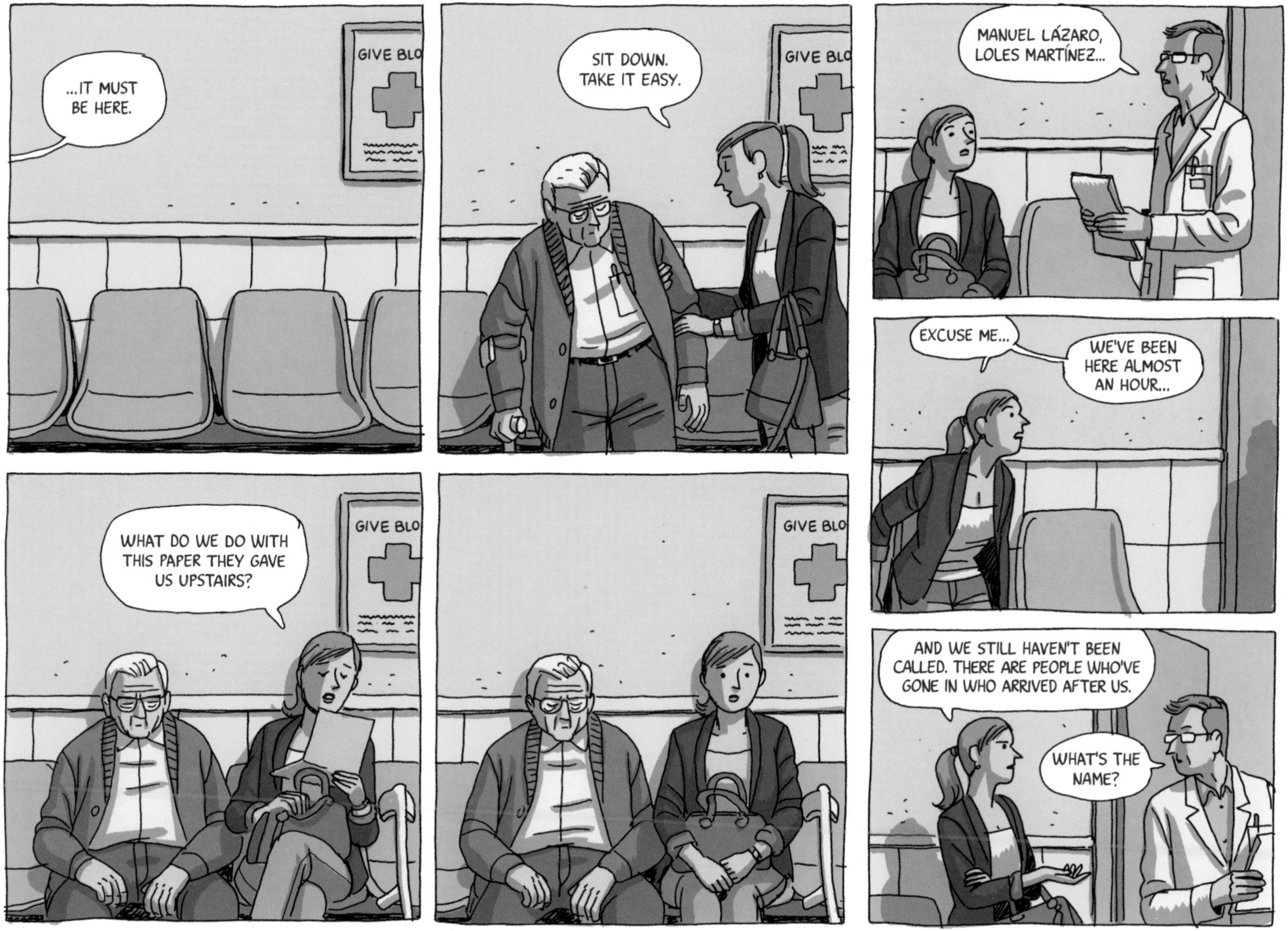
...IT MUST BE HERE.
GIVE BLO
SIT DOWN. TAKE IT EASY.
GIVE BLO
MANUEL LÁZARO, LOLES MARTÍNEZ...
EXCUSE ME...
WE'VE BEEN HERE ALMOST AN HOUR...
WHAT DO WE DO WITH THIS PAPER THEY GAVE US UPSTAIRS?
GIVE BLO
GIVE BLO
AND WE STILL HAVEN'T BEEN CALLED. THERE ARE PEOPLE WHO'VE GONE IN WHO ARRIVED AFTER US.
WHAT'S THE NAME?

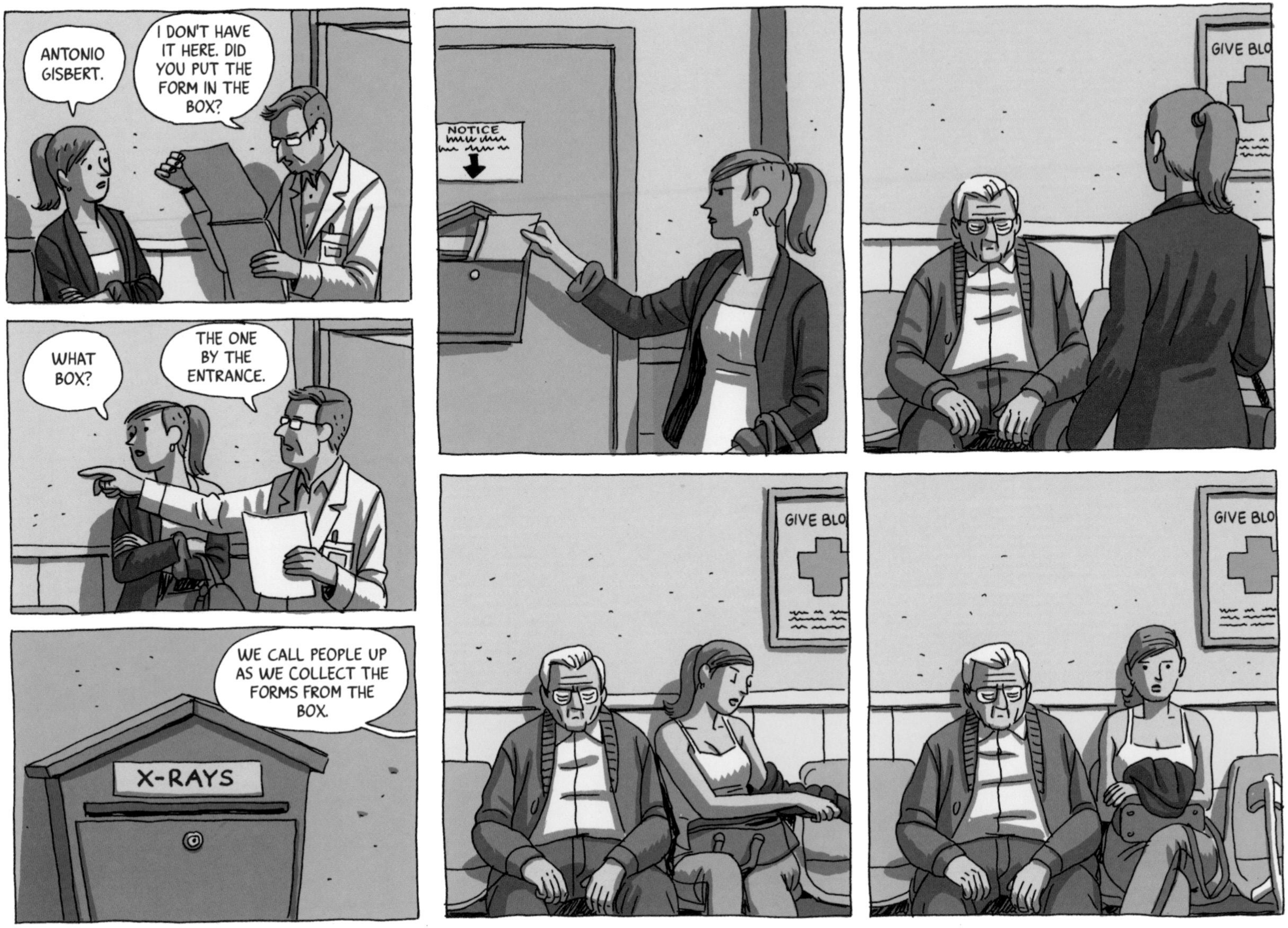
ANTONIO GISBERT.
I DON'T HAVE IT HERE. DID YOU PUT THE FORM IN THE BOX?
WHAT BOX?
THE ONE BY THE ENTRANCE.
X-RAYS
WE CALL PEOPLE UP AS WE COLLECT THE FORMS FROM THE BOX.
NOTICE
GIVE BLO
GIVE BLO
GIVE BLO

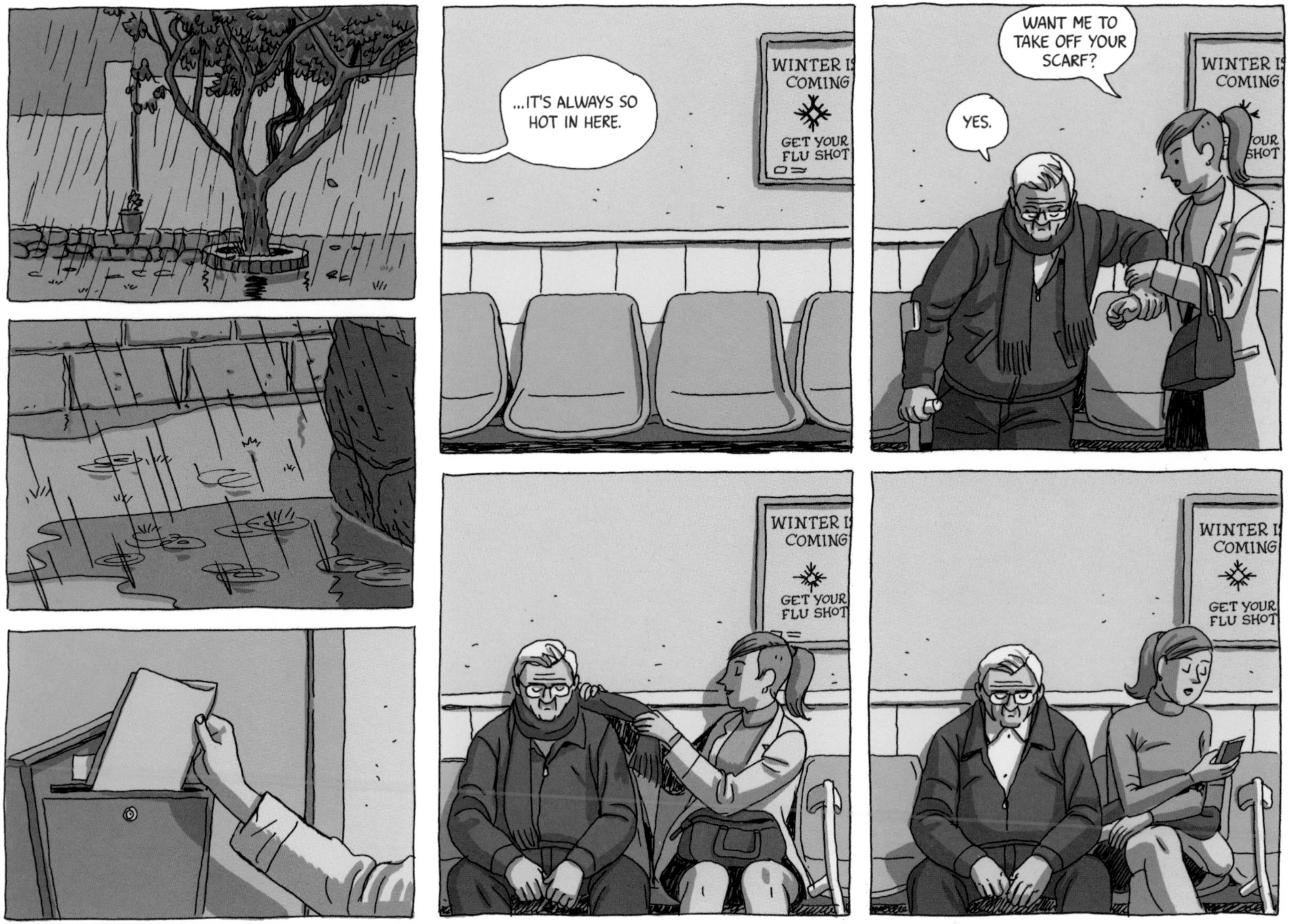
WINTER IS COMING
GET YOUR FLU SHOT
...IT'S ALWAYS SO HOT IN HERE.
WANT ME TO TAKE OFF YOUR SCARF?
YES.

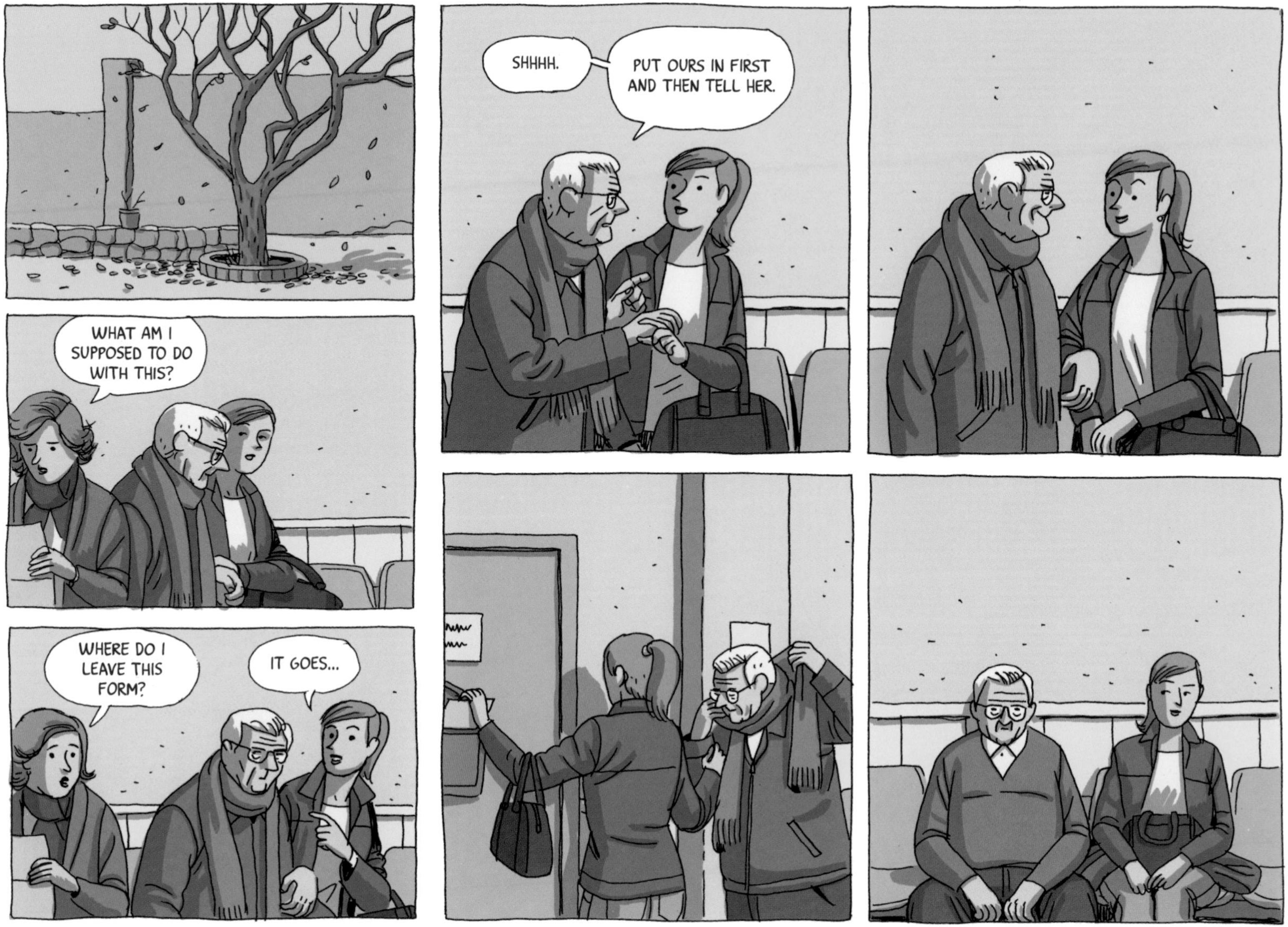
WHAT AM I SUPPOSED TO DO WITH THIS?
WHERE DO I LEAVE THIS FORM?
IT GOES...
SHHHH.
PUT OURS IN FIRST AND THEN TELL HER.

Spring is coming.
and so are allergies

NEXT WEEK IT'LL BE APRIL ALREADY.

Spring
and so

YEAH, I CAN'T WAIT FOR THE WEATHER TO GET NICE SO WE CAN GO OUTSIDE WITH ELENA.

Spring
and so

I NEED TO PLANT THE POTATOES AND CUCUMBERS SOON.

Spring
and so

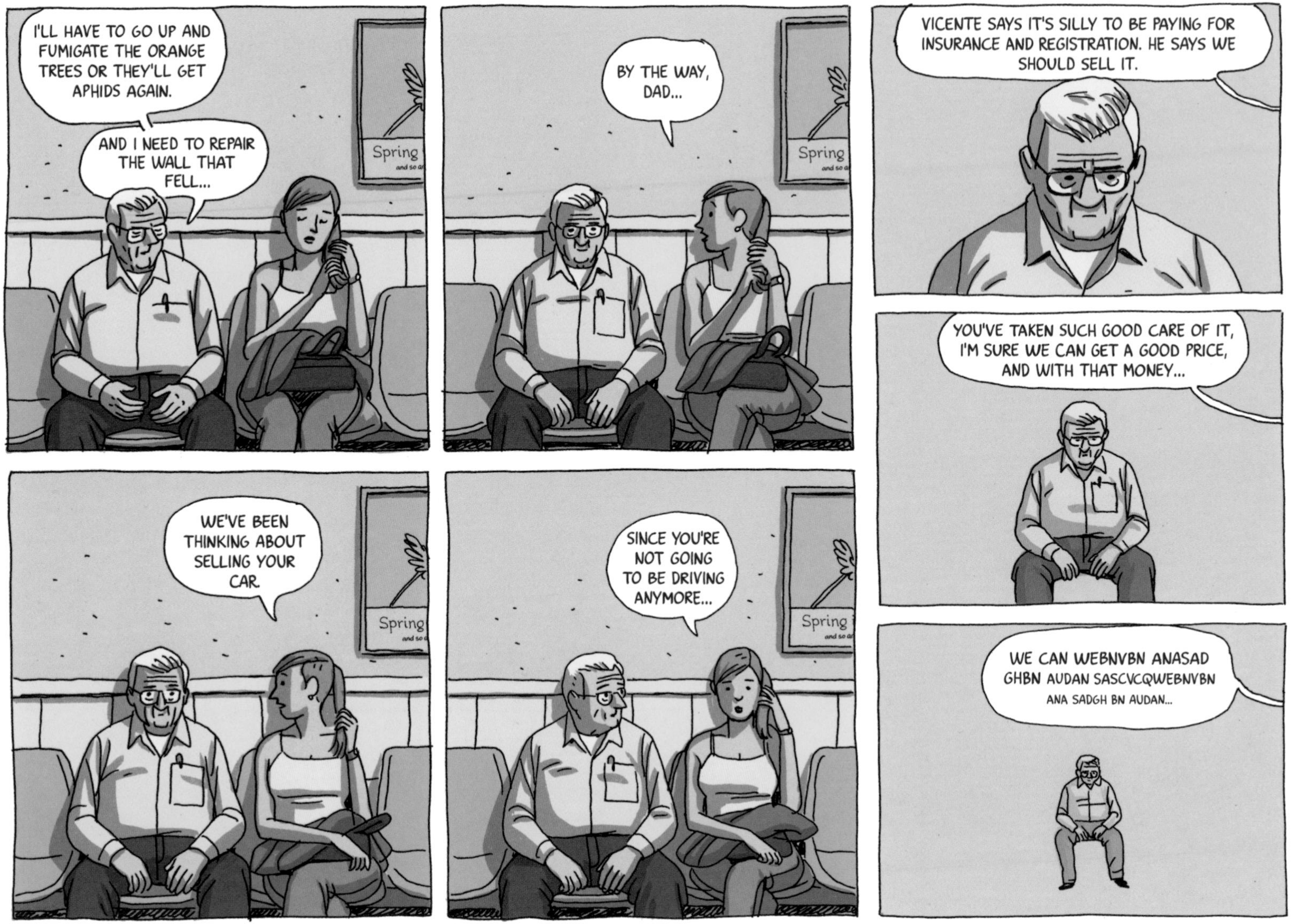
I'LL HAVE TO GO UP AND FUMIGATE THE ORANGE TREES OR THEY'LL GET APHIDS AGAIN.
AND I NEED TO REPAIR THE WALL THAT FELL...
BY THE WAY, DAD...
VICENTE SAYS IT'S SILLY TO BE PAYING FOR INSURANCE AND REGISTRATION. HE SAYS WE SHOULD SELL IT.
WE'VE BEEN THINKING ABOUT SELLING YOUR CAR.
SINCE YOU'RE NOT GOING TO BE DRIVING ANYMORE...
YOU'VE TAKEN SUCH GOOD CARE OF IT, I'M SURE WE CAN GET A GOOD PRICE, AND WITH THAT MONEY...
WE CAN WEBNVBN ANASAD GHBN AUDAN SASCVCQWEBNVBN ANA SADGH BN AUDAN...

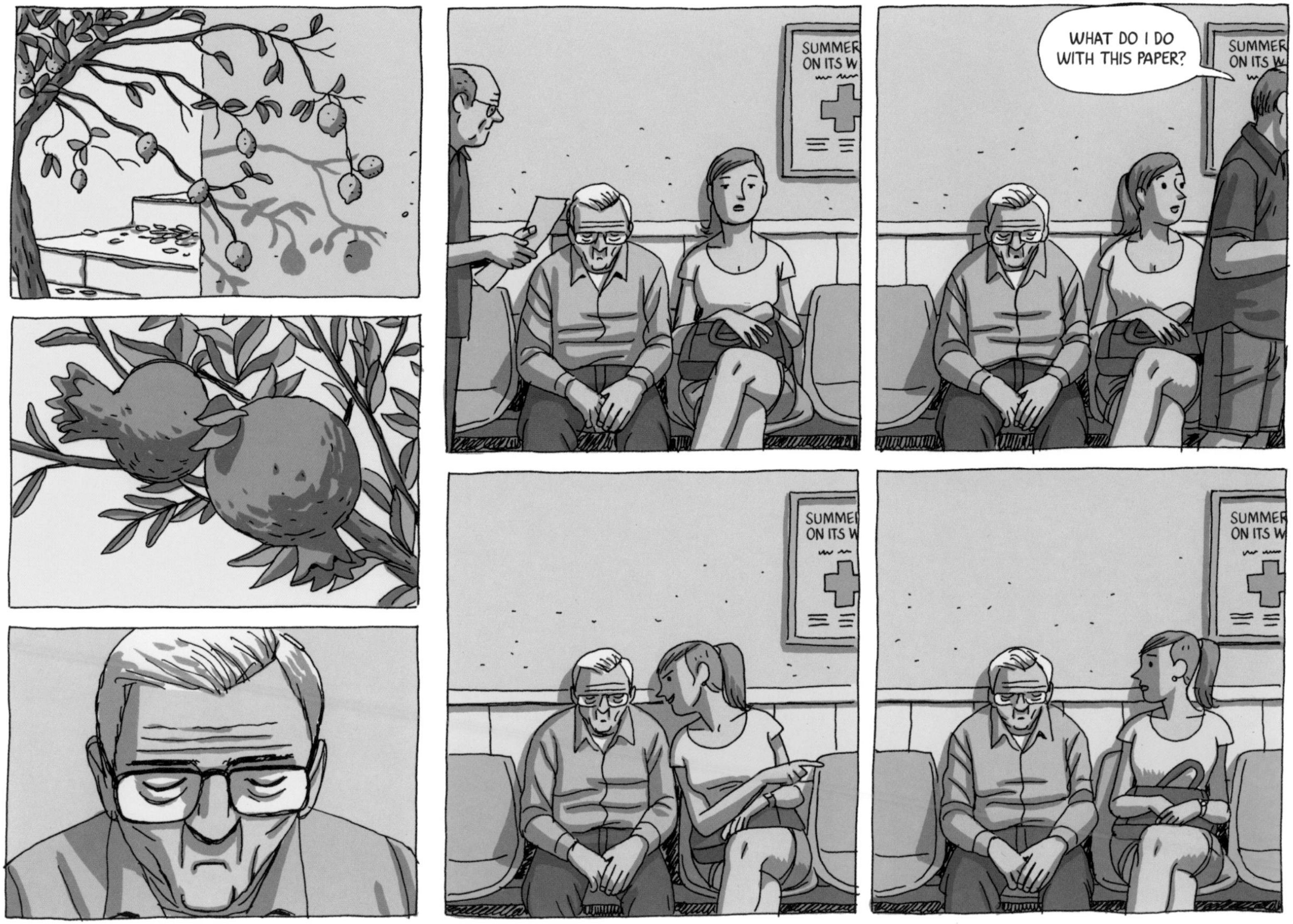
SUMMER
ON ITS W
WHAT DO I DO
WITH THIS PAPER?
SUMMER
ON ITS W
SUMMER
ON ITS W
SUMMER
ON ITS W

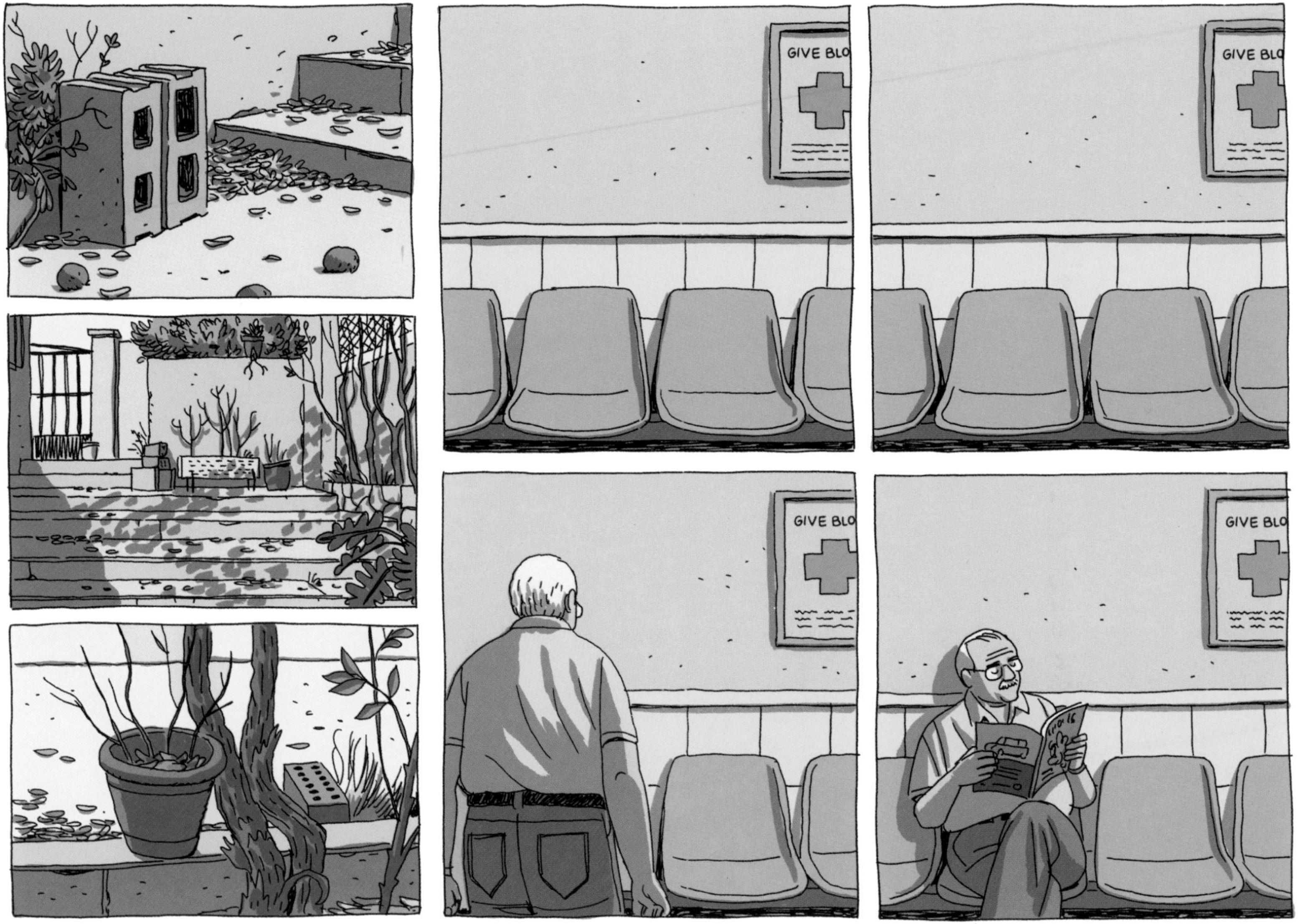
GIVE BLO
GIVE BLO
GIVE BLO
GIVE BLO

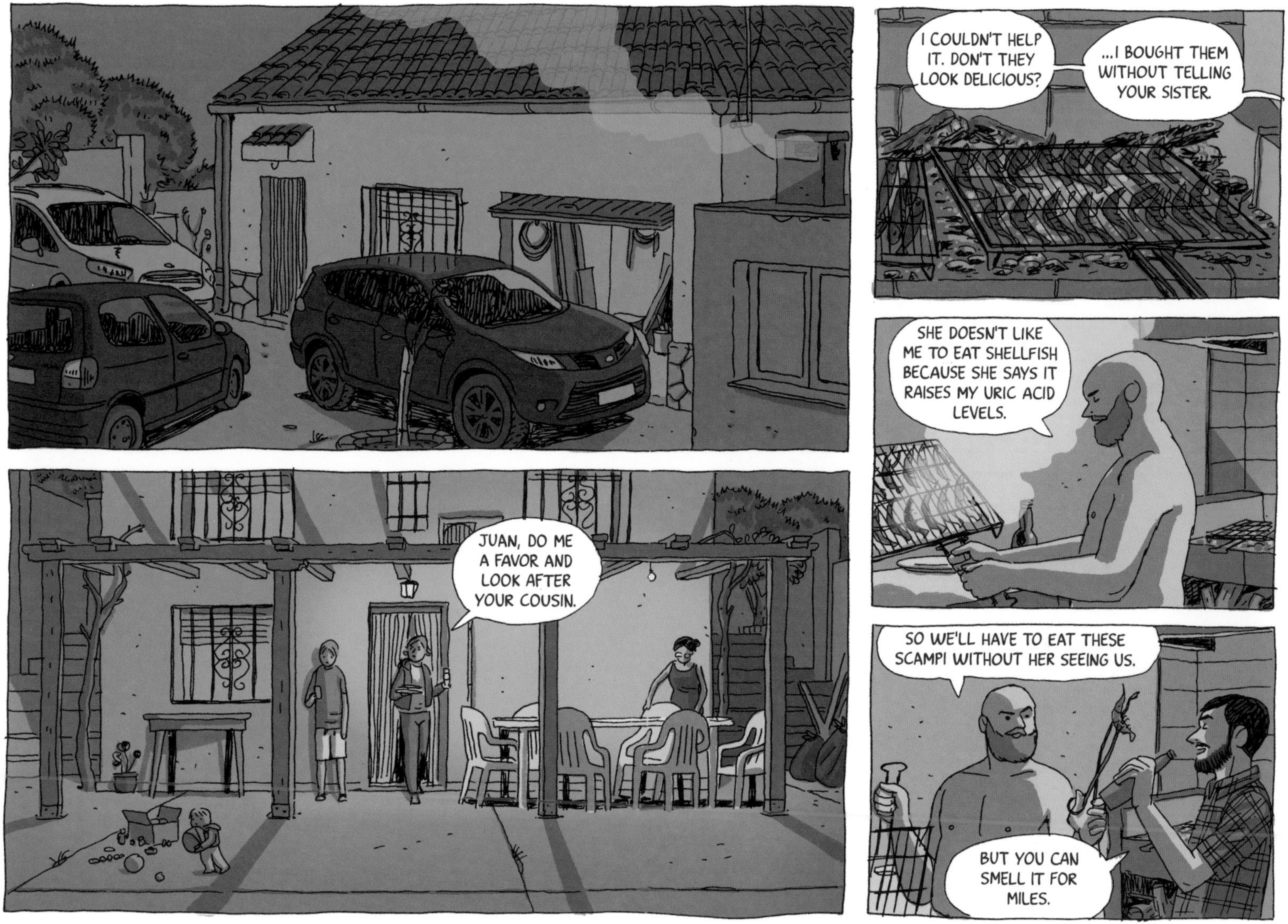
JUAN, DO ME A FAVOR AND LOOK AFTER YOUR COUSIN.
I COULDN'T HELP IT. DON'T THEY LOOK DELICIOUS?
...I BOUGHT THEM WITHOUT TELLING YOUR SISTER.
SHE DOESN'T LIKE ME TO EAT SHELLFISH BECAUSE SHE SAYS IT RAISES MY URIC ACID LEVELS.
SO WE'LL HAVE TO EAT THESE SCAMPI WITHOUT HER SEEING US.
BUT YOU CAN SMELL IT FOR MILES.

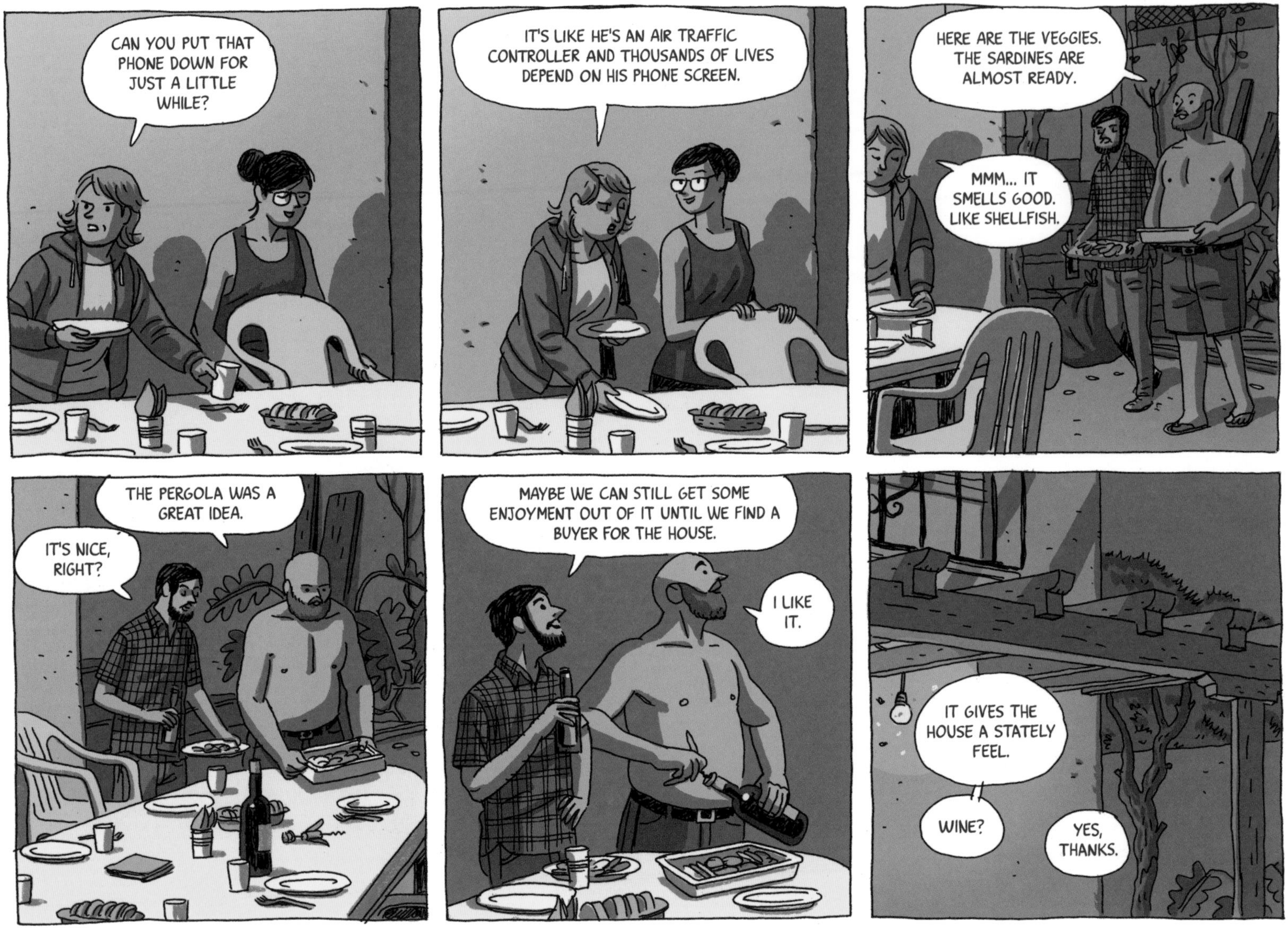
CAN YOU PUT THAT PHONE DOWN FOR JUST A LITTLE WHILE?
IT'S LIKE HE'S AN AIR TRAFFIC CONTROLLER AND THOUSANDS OF LIVES DEPEND ON HIS PHONE SCREEN.
HERE ARE THE VEGGIES. THE SARDINES ARE ALMOST READY.
MMM... IT SMELLS GOOD. LIKE SHELLFISH.
THE PERGOLA WAS A GREAT IDEA.
IT'S NICE, RIGHT?
MAYBE WE CAN STILL GET SOME ENJOYMENT OUT OF IT UNTIL WE FIND A BUYER FOR THE HOUSE.
I LIKE IT.
IT GIVES THE HOUSE A STATELY FEEL.
WINE?
YES, THANKS.

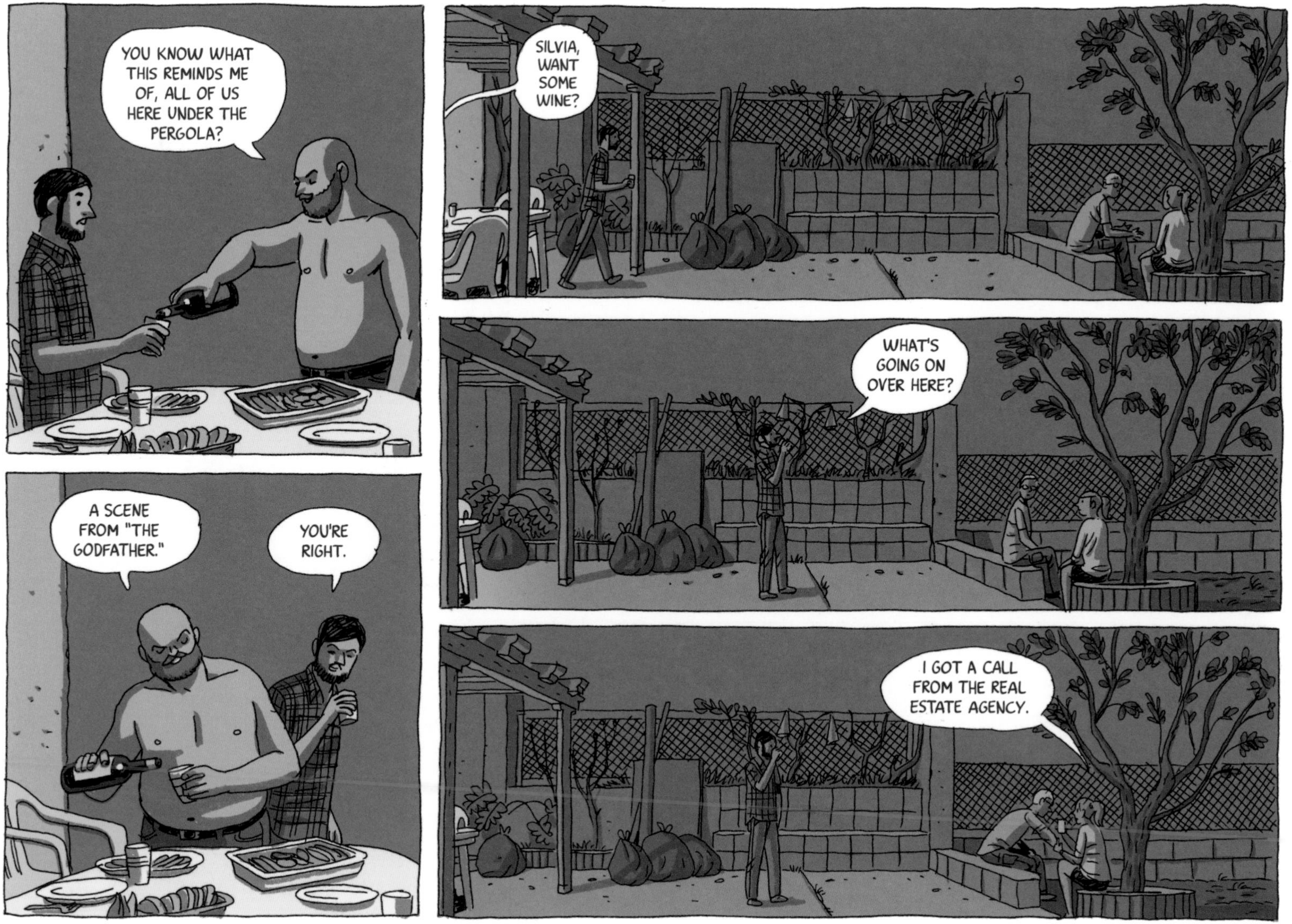
YOU KNOW WHAT THIS REMINDS ME OF, ALL OF US HERE UNDER THE PERGOLA?
A SCENE FROM "THE GODFATHER."
YOU'RE RIGHT.
SILVIA, WANT SOME WINE?
WHAT'S GOING ON OVER HERE?
I GOT A CALL FROM THE REAL ESTATE AGENCY.

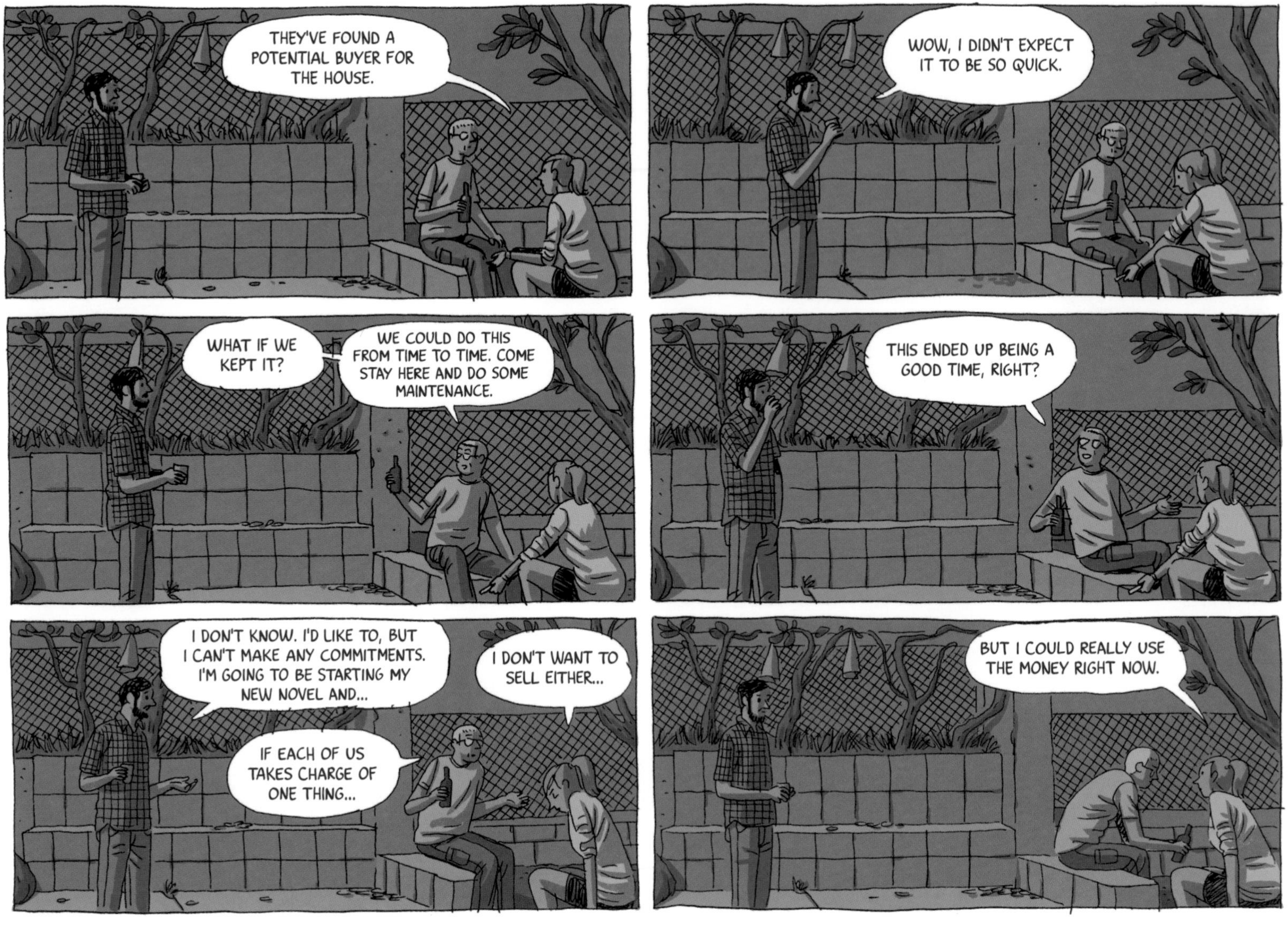
THEY'VE FOUND A POTENTIAL BUYER FOR THE HOUSE.
WOW, I DIDN'T EXPECT IT TO BE SO QUICK.
WHAT IF WE KEPT IT?
WE COULD DO THIS FROM TIME TO TIME. COME STAY HERE AND DO SOME MAINTENANCE.
THIS ENDED UP BEING A GOOD TIME, RIGHT?
I DON'T KNOW. I'D LIKE TO, BUT I CAN'T MAKE ANY COMMITMENTS. I'M GOING TO BE STARTING MY NEW NOVEL AND...
I DON'T WANT TO SELL EITHER...
IF EACH OF US TAKES CHARGE OF ONE THING...
BUT I COULD REALLY USE THE MONEY RIGHT NOW.

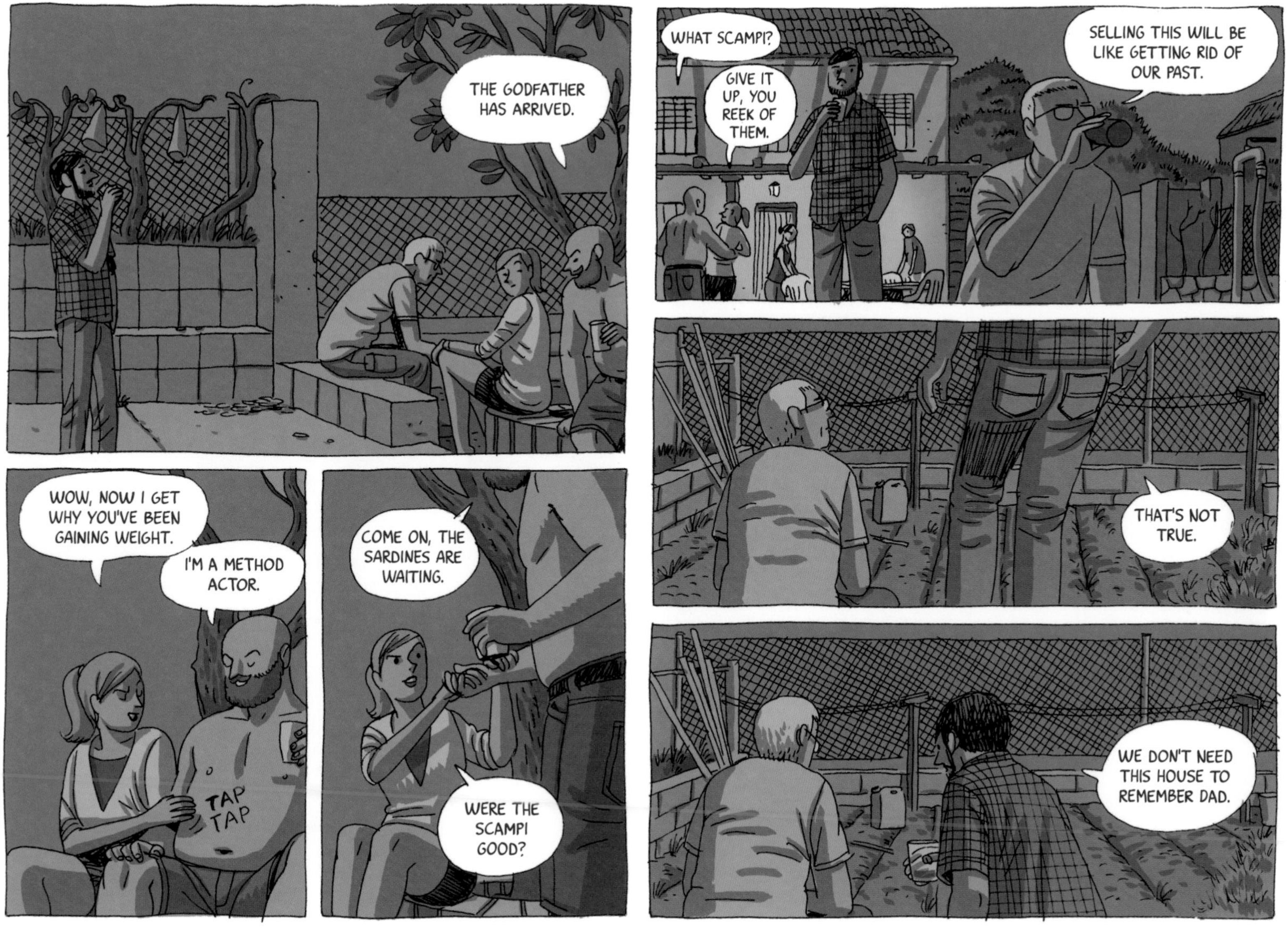
THE GODFATHER HAS ARRIVED.
WOW, NOW I GET WHY YOU'VE BEEN GAINING WEIGHT.
I'M A METHOD ACTOR.
TAP TAP
COME ON, THE SARDINES ARE WAITING.
WERE THE SCAMPI GOOD?
WHAT SCAMPI?
GIVE IT UP, YOU REEK OF THEM.
SELLING THIS WILL BE LIKE GETTING RID OF OUR PAST.
THAT'S NOT TRUE.
WE DON'T NEED THIS HOUSE TO REMEMBER DAD.

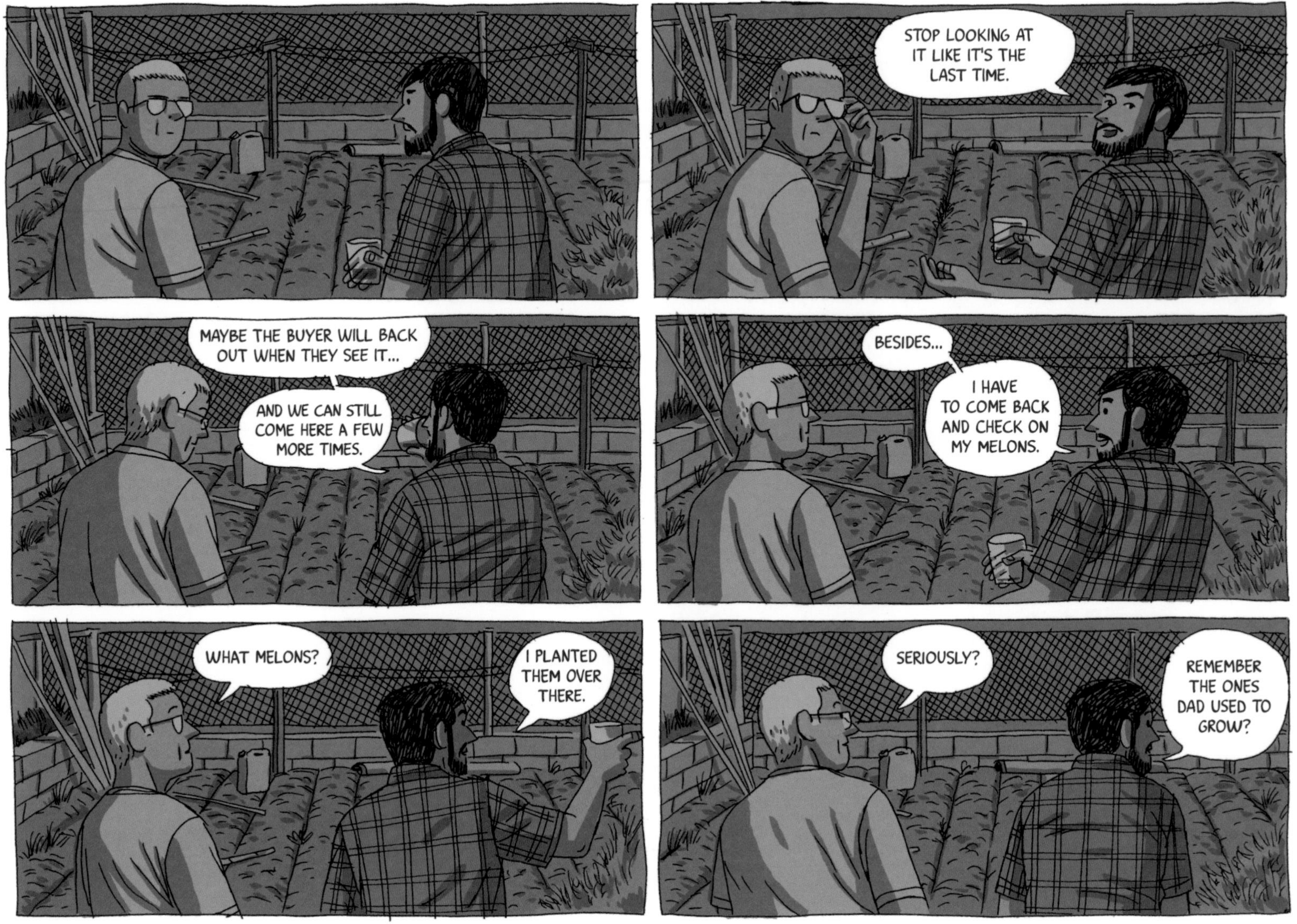
STOP LOOKING AT IT LIKE IT'S THE LAST TIME.
MAYBE THE BUYER WILL BACK OUT WHEN THEY SEE IT...
AND WE CAN STILL COME HERE A FEW MORE TIMES.
BESIDES...
I HAVE TO COME BACK AND CHECK ON MY MELONS.
WHAT MELONS?
I PLANTED THEM OVER THERE.
SERIOUSLY?
REMEMBER THE ONES DAD USED TO GROW?

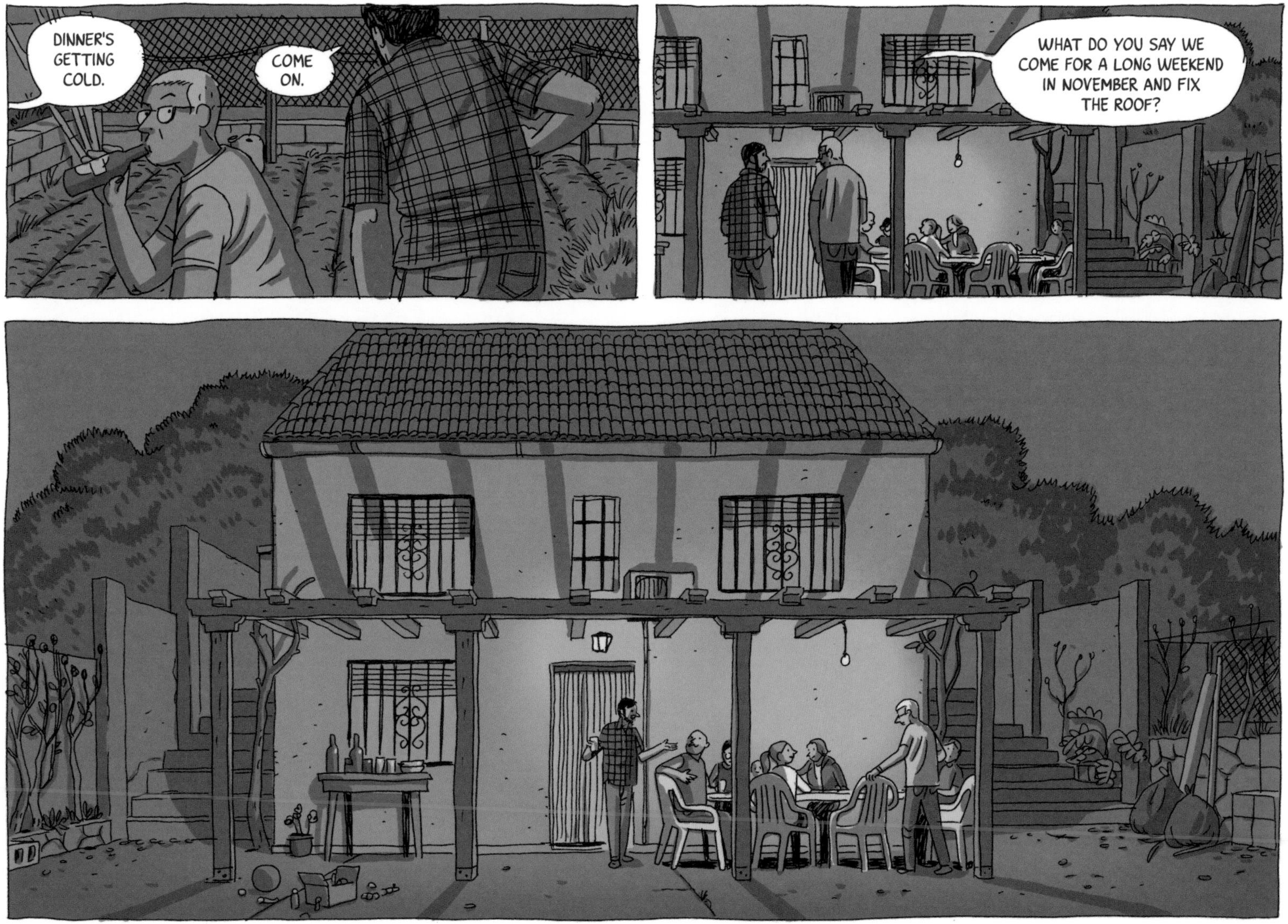
DINNER'S GETTING COLD.
COME ON.
WHAT DO YOU SAY WE COME FOR A LONG WEEKEND IN NOVEMBER AND FIX THE ROOF?

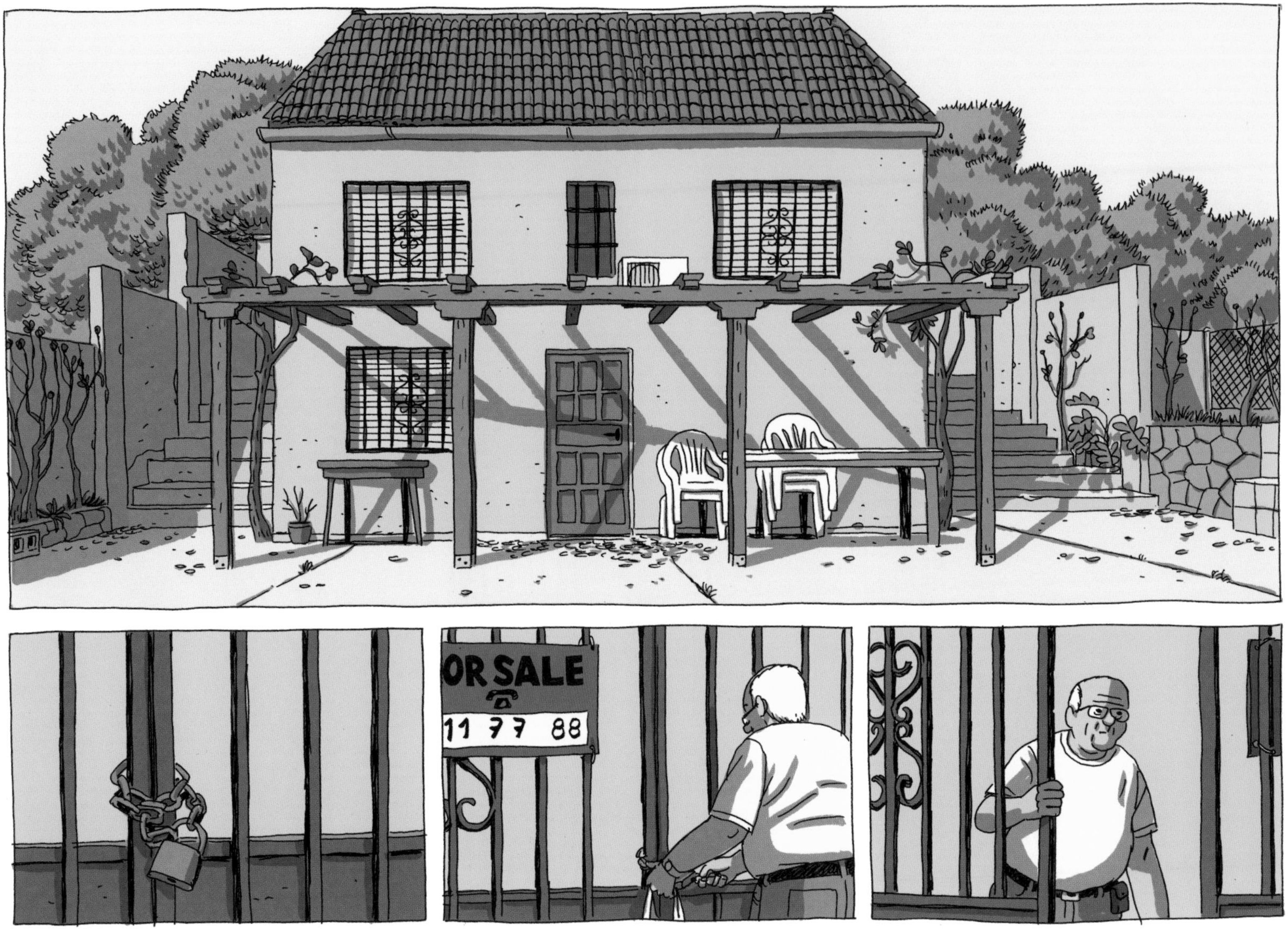
OR SALE
11 77 88

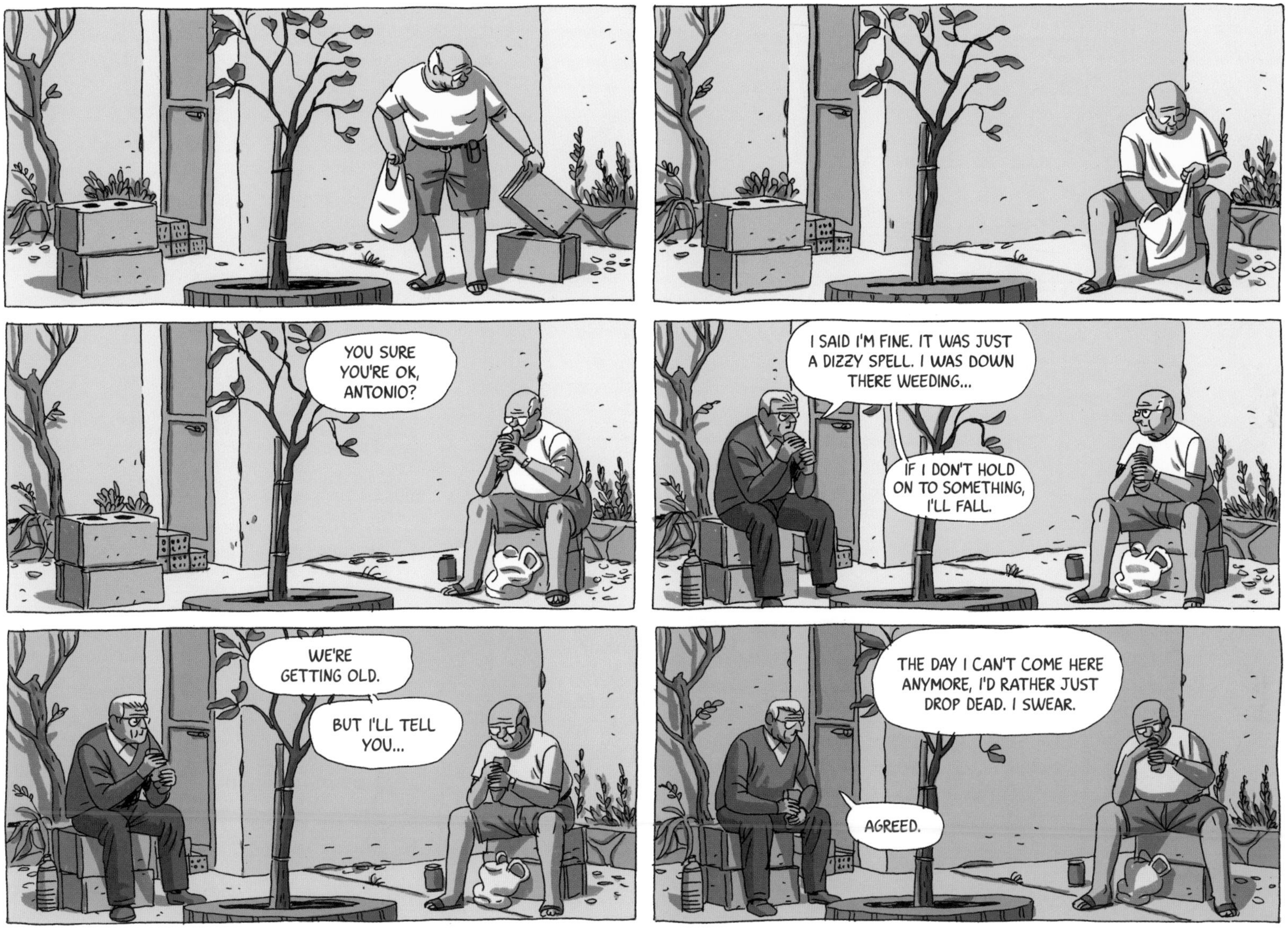
YOU SURE YOU'RE OK, ANTONIO?
I SAID I'M FINE. IT WAS JUST A DIZZY SPELL. I WAS DOWN THERE WEEDING...
IF I DON'T HOLD ON TO SOMETHING, I'LL FALL.
WE'RE GETTING OLD.
BUT I'LL TELL YOU...
THE DAY I CAN'T COME HERE ANYMORE, I'D RATHER JUST DROP DEAD. I SWEAR.
AGREED.

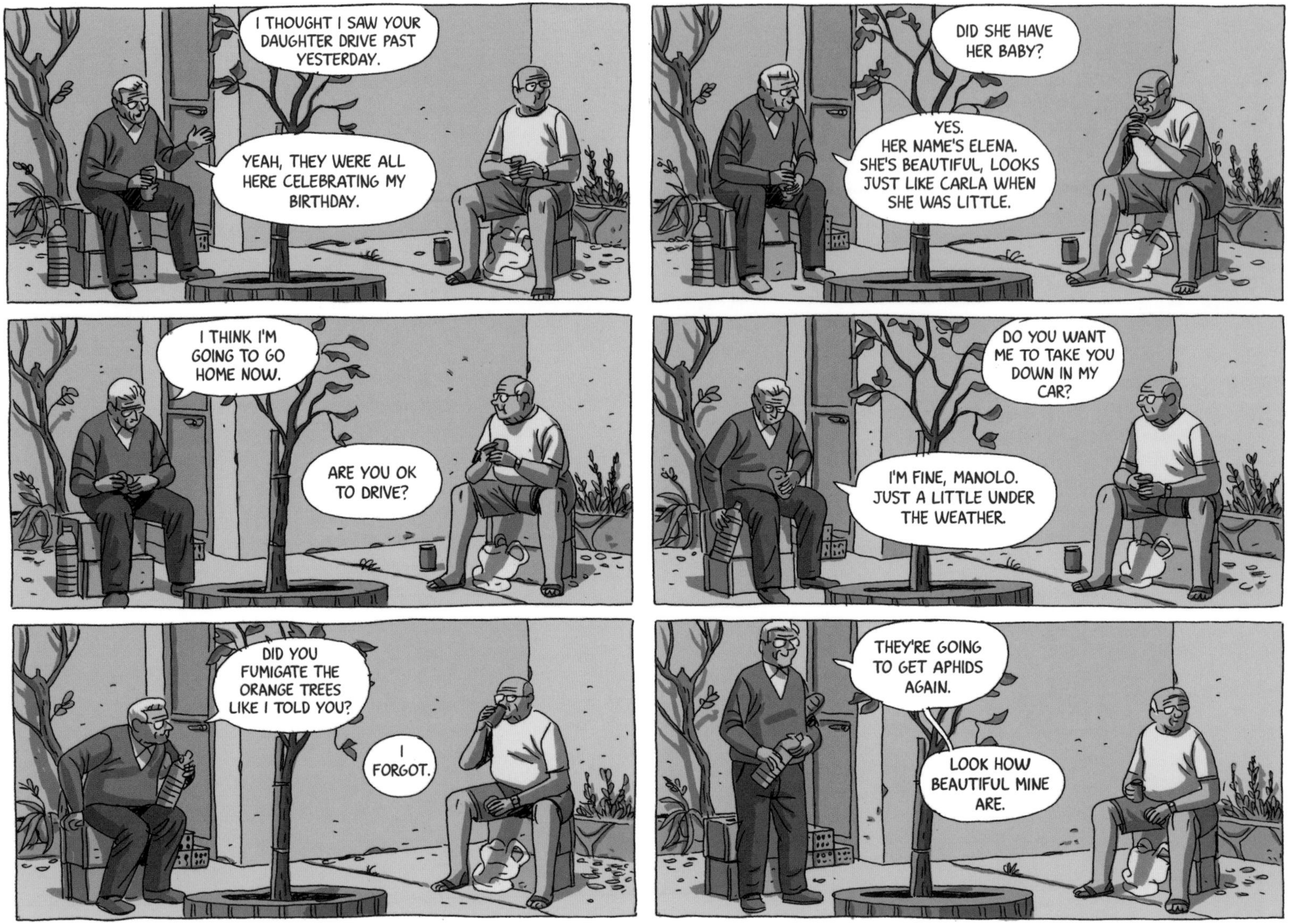
I THOUGHT I SAW YOUR DAUGHTER DRIVE PAST YESTERDAY.
YEAH, THEY WERE ALL HERE CELEBRATING MY BIRTHDAY.
DID SHE HAVE HER BABY?
YES. HER NAME'S ELENA. SHE'S BEAUTIFUL, LOOKS JUST LIKE CARLA WHEN SHE WAS LITTLE.
I THINK I'M GOING TO GO HOME NOW.
ARE YOU OK TO DRIVE?
DO YOU WANT ME TO TAKE YOU DOWN IN MY CAR?
I'M FINE, MANOLO. JUST A LITTLE UNDER THE WEATHER.
DID YOU FUMIGATE THE ORANGE TREES LIKE I TOLD YOU?
I FORGOT.
THEY'RE GOING TO GET APHIDS AGAIN.
LOOK HOW BEAUTIFUL MINE ARE.

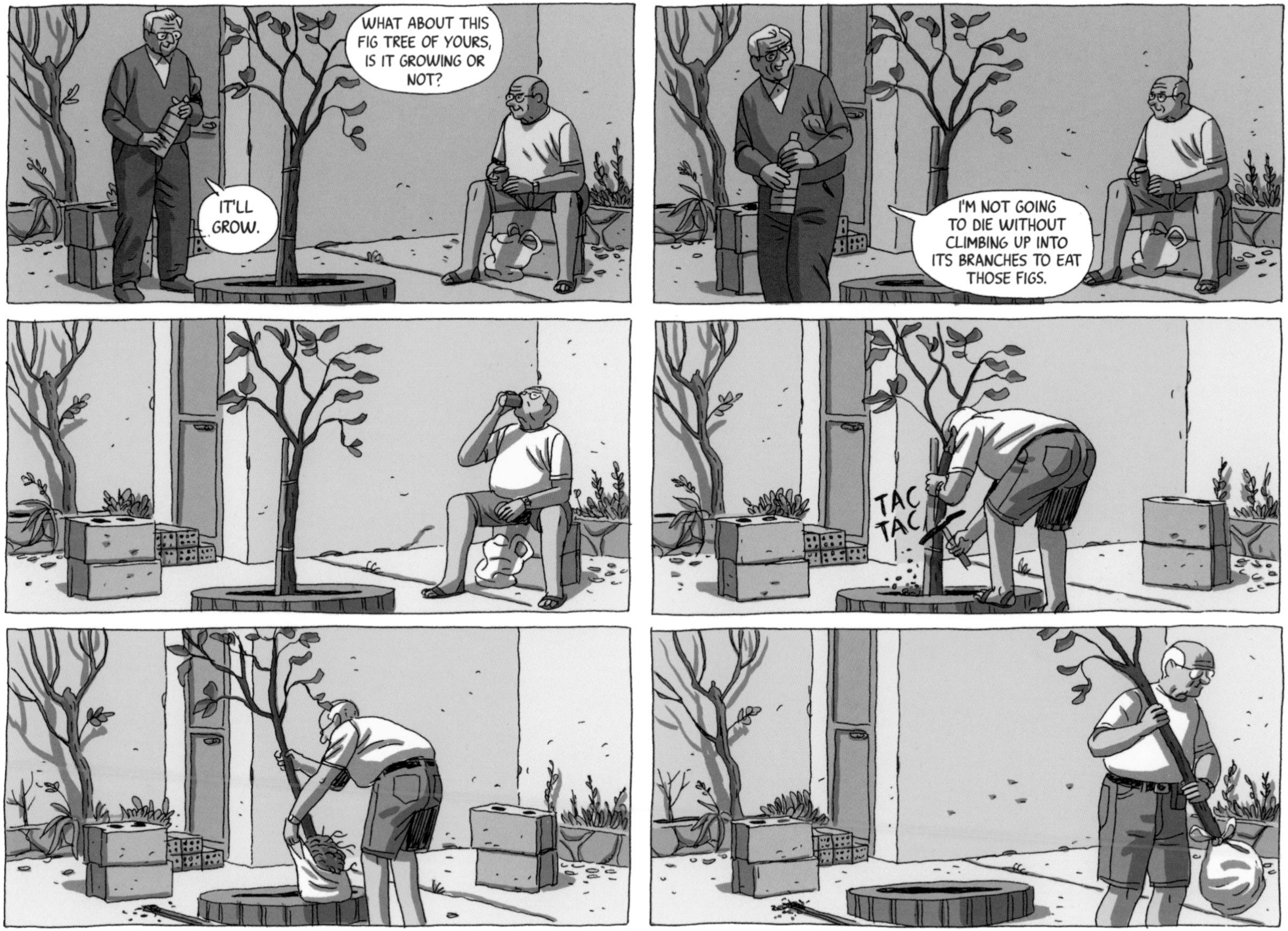
WHAT ABOUT THIS FIG TREE OF YOURS, IS IT GROWING OR NOT?
IT'LL GROW.
I'M NOT GOING TO DIE WITHOUT CLIMBING UP INTO ITS BRANCHES TO EAT THOSE FIGS.
TAC TAC

Paco Roca (Valencia, Spain, 1969) is a comic book author and illustrator. He started out working in advertising and ended up establishing an illustration studio in his native city. He soon started to interweave the projects that earned him a living by creating stories in comic book form. He has published two previous books with Fantagraphics: 2016's Eisner Award-nominated *Wrinkles* (for which he won Spain's National Comic Award in 2008, prizes for best script and best work at the 2008 Barcelona International Comic Fair, and a Goya Award for best script in 2012 for the movie adaptation directed by Ignacio Ferreras, which was also awarded the trophy for best animated movie), and *Twists of Fate* in 2018 (which won the Zona Cómic prize and a prize for best Spanish work at the 2014 Barcelona International Comic Fair).

Translator: Andrea Rosenberg
Editor: RJ Casey
Supervising Editor: Gary Groth
Designer: Keeli McCarthy
Production: Paul Baresh and Eric Reynolds
Editorial Assistance: Christina Hwang
Promotion: Jacq Cohen
Associate Publisher: Eric Reynolds
Publisher: Gary Groth

Fantagraphics Books, Inc.
7563 Lake City Way NE
Seattle, WA 98115
www.fantagraphics.com

First Printing: 2019
ISBN 978-1-68396-263-2
Library of Congress Control Number: 2019933653
Printed in China